DEADLY PORTFOLIO

A KILLING IN HEDGE FUNDS

— *John J. Hohn*

Outskirts Press, Inc.
Denver, Colorado

Deadly Portfolio
A Killing in Hedge Funds
All Rights Reserved.
Copyright © 2010 John J. Hohn
v4.0

Cover Photo © 2010 JupiterImages Corporation. All rights reserved - used with permission.

Outskirts Press, Inc.
http://www.outskirtspress.com

ISBN PB: 978-1-4327-5875-2
ISBN HB: 978-1-4327-5972-8

Outskirts Press and the "OP" logo are trademarks belonging to Outskirts Press, Inc.

PRINTED IN THE UNITED STATES OF AMERICA

Dedication

To my wife Melinda, the love of my life, who has enabled so much for me over all the years we have been together.

To my children—James, Joseph, Eric, Gregory, Rachel and Matthew—with gratitude for their friendship and love.

Acknowledgements

Many friends contributed to this work. My best friend, Joseph P. Frisina, slashed into the 165,000 word first draft and with unerring instinct for the story line helped me pare the volume down to manageable size. Ernestine Godfrey copy edited the first rewrite and made several helpful suggestions which I incorporated into final version. My dear friend Betty Grigg, one of my first readers, also made numerous suggestions that proved to be very helpful.

I am indebted Terrence D. Bogard, MD for his help in directing my research into the toxicology issues that are key to the plot. Jerry Wesson, retired law enforcement, helped me tremendously with the legal and police issues. I also want to thank the Ashe County Sheriff's office for their help with forgery cases and the division of responsibility between local and county law enforcement. I am indebted to my son James M. Hohn for his help with the EMS procedures and to my brother James C. Hohn for sharing his knowledge of boats with me.

Finally, I want to recognize my former colleagues Forrest Childers, Elizabeth Vernon and Marcia Turnage whose friendship and support made the three years leading up to my retirement the best of my entire career.

Chapter 1

"Morrie come in yet?" Matthew Wirth called out from his office.

"Yeah, I'm here." Morrie Clay slid his six-foot-four frame out from behind his desk, stroked his thinning black hair, and stepped next door into Matthew's office. "I came by earlier but you were on the phone."

"Have a seat. That was Mac McAllister," Matthew said. Sixty-eight and trim, Matthew looked the part of a senior partner with a full head of gray hair, strong chin, and thoughtful green eyes. "He's moving his account."

"My God. No! Why? What'd he say?"

"His wife, Rene. Remember the meeting last April?"

"Yeah. But move the accounts? It doesn't add up. The meeting was all Rene . . . they always are. That account's done well, Matt . . . really well."

"She's been pressuring Mac to make this move for months, even before we met."

"Realigning those accounts was good estate planning. It needed to be done. She knows that . . . doesn't she?"

"This has nothing to do with what they do or don't need. She's hot about her money in her accounts, and Mac's had enough. He's giving in to her."

"It's an $18 million account. It'll be tough to replace."

"I know. I wanted you to have it when I retire. I'm sorry. Doesn't look like that's going to happen."

"How'd you leave it with him?"

"He only called to give us heads-up. The transfer request will come in after the first of the month. But we're not to let on that we know anything. Rene didn't want him to call early like this thinking we'd put up an argument."

"We can't . . . we can't let this happen. He's been with you for . . . what . . . 15 years. We can't let this slide."

Matthew had turned his chair and looked out the window at the bright Carolina morning. "No, Morrie, Mac's not gonna welcome any overtures to reconsider. They'll be at the lake for the party this weekend, and I want them to be comfortable."

Morrie stood up. "Maybe at year end . . . maybe next year . . . but I can't see letting this go now . . . not without a fight."

"There'll be no fight!" Matthew said turning back to find Morrie glaring at him. "Mac doesn't go back on his decisions and he didn't make this one lightly. The barrel's gone over the falls. It's a dead issue."

Morrie wheeled and strode out of the office.

Matthew considered going after his partner but checked himself. Morrie usually took things in stride, almost never lost his composure. Asking him to accept the loss of their most prestigious account without a fight might be expecting too much. One lost account didn't portend an exodus. Morrie would inherit all the clients that Matthew had acquired over nearly two decades in business. Come year end, Matthew would be out of the practice. Morrie would have the operation to himself. He'd make the best of it.

The two men had a history. They had worked together years earlier at Southern Central Bank and Trust. Matthew, disgusted with the political infighting, left the bank first, and over the intervening decade, lost track of Clay. Reunited when Morrie joined Stuart, Tompkins and Earl, the largest financial advisory firm in Charles City, North Carolina, the two men renewed their friendship, and as soon as Morrie completed his training, they became partners.

With his retirement a scant three years away, Matthew began breaking off with his clients and cutting back his schedule; first to three days a week, then to two, and finally in this their third year together, three days every other week. Morrie had taken over the day-to-day management of their accounts. With the liabilities in a partnership assumed jointly, Morrie promised that Matthew's retirement would work out as they planned.

"I'd better get this out of the way," Matthew finally said under his breath, picked up the phone, and pressed the intercom button for the partnership's associates.

"Cheryl, would you and Louise please step in for a minute?"

The partnership between Matthew and Morrie set the tone for their team. Cheryl, married with a daughter entering college in the fall, had worked with Matthew for more than ten years. Clients praised her work. Louise was added to the team staff several months after Matthew and Morrie began working together. She managed their schedules, booked appointments, prepared proposals and reviews, and a performed a host of other duties that gave the partnership an edge in service.

Both women appeared at the door. "It's bad news, isn't it?" Cheryl said.

"Why would you think that?" Matthew asked.

"From the way Morrie left," Cheryl said.

"He left . . . the office?"

"Yeah. Didn't say a word. Just bolted out the back. Looked really upset. I've no idea where he's going," Cheryl replied.

"There's nothing on his calendar," Louise said.

"Well, it is bad news. He may be upset, but you know Morrie, steady ol' Morrie. He'll be fine. It's the McAllisters."

"Oh, God," Cheryl said. "That woman's at it again?"

"Yes. But this is the last time. They're moving their accounts."

"I knew it. I just knew it," Cheryl said. "That was so off-the-wall . . . the way she came in here after your last meeting and wanted to work with Louise and me. 'I want us to be good friends. Now, I want you to call me Rene,'" Cheryl said mimicking Rene McAllister. "God, we didn't know what to do. Neither one of us is licensed."

"She makes me think of an ostrich."

"Louise," Cheryl gushed, "that's too funny."

"I mean it. So tall. Intense. I never know what she's going to do next. They're not moving the accounts because of either one of us are they?" Louise asked.

"No. Nothing like that. Rene McAllister simply doesn't trust her husband . . . or Morrie and me, for that matter. We got on her bad side when we tried move some assets around to implement their estate plan. Everything came out even. She had as much under her name and he did under his, but she became convinced that we're in cahoots with Mac and trying to take her money away. Mac's given up, saying to hell with it. She wants everything with a different firm . . . one she thinks she can trust . . . and he's not going to stand in her way."

"So she won out after all?" Cheryl said. "That doesn't make any sense."

"There's no point in picking her reasoning apart. We're losing the accounts. OK? I want the transfer to go as smoothly as possible."

"Of course," Cheryl said. "Seems unfair, though . . . especially to Morrie. To you too . . . after all you've done."

"I know. Let me know when Morrie comes back. I may have underestimated how he'd take this. And, one thing more . . . we . . . none of us . . . are supposed to know that this is happening just yet. So, if Rene McAllister . . . or Mac . . . calls about anything, don't let on that you know anything. Understand? Mac just wanted us to alert us in case Southern Central jumped the gun with the transfer request."

Announcing the McAllisters' decision to his staff focused Matthew's feelings. As he turned back to his work, the finality of it struck him. He remembered the day, sixteen years earlier, when McAllister agreed to an appointment. Matthew tried to conceal his excitement over the size of the account when McAllister handed over a printout of his holdings and asked for an analysis and recommendations. The account was larger by several times than any Matthew had ever opened.

Word had quickly spread throughout the office that Matthew had signed the McAllister account. Veteran advisors, who had ignored Matthew from his first day on the job, drifted past his cubicle, and with affected nonchalance, asked about his good fortune, worked their way around to inquiring how large the account was, whether it represented all of McAllister's holdings, and what he, a rookie, had done to persuade McAllister to put the money with him.

Matthew broke off his reverie and buzzed Cheryl on the intercom. "Did Morrie say when he'd be back?"

"No. He didn't. I was busy filing and looked up to see him charging out the back door. He had his brief case with him."

"Was there anything else troubling him that you know?"

"We're all caught up. Louise is ready to start the second quarter reviews as soon as the June month-end run is completed. I can't think of a thing."

"I'll want to see the June statements for McAllister as soon as they're available."

"We can get them on-line probably by July sixth. Monday."

"Thanks." Matthew replaced the handset. In six months, he would not be bothered with concerns like the one that came up on this day. Morrie could handle them all by himself. For now, however, Matthew had no way of knowing what was behind Morrie's sudden departure from the office.

He said nothing to anyone in leaving the office. He had pulled Rene McAllister's account into view on his monitor screen. The over night totals, if anything, were worse. The $749,000 that he had invested in the hedge fund listed at less than $483,000. On this Wednesday, the second of July, Morrie knew that the predicted downturn in the market would be the tide going out, draining away the profits that had been covering the wreckage at the bottom of Rene's account. The fund would loom as a huge loss lodged in the mound of debt that he incurred in making the unauthorized purchase. For months he had hoped it would recover. He had bet his career that it would.

The totals rattled in his thoughts as he headed north on the interstate to the lake. At random moments he became aware that he was hardly paying any attention to traffic. The best place to think things through was at the lake. No phones. No interruptions. Everything at the office could wait until tomorrow. He needed to cover a lot of ground before the holiday weekend got underway.

He pulled his Mercedes off of the interstate and onto the blacktop road that led through Heron Lake Township, a small resort community servicing the residents of nearby Lake Heron. Rene McAllister was always difficult. Distrustful of his recommendations, she insisted on doing things that he could not support and threatened frequently to complain to her husband when he refused to implement her suggestions. "Clueless," he muttered, "so goddamn clueless."

Morrie dreaded meetings with her. She was not as knowledgeable as she pretended, often presenting complete fabrications as researched support for her own opinions. She interrupted him with questions or comments that were unrelated to what he was trying to explain. Confronting her was out of the question. After a time, Morrie allowed his preparations to become casual. If he could not hold her to an agenda, why prepare one? Discussion meandered from topic to topic with him responding as best he could and always with the reassurance, though without providing any detail, that her accounts were performing very well. She seemed indifferent to anything he said, showing so little concern that he realized that he could say nearly anything and it would not be questioned.

The blacktop road around the lake, Lakeside Drive, was shaded and barely wide enough for vehicles to pass. The homes on the lakefront maintained high hedges for privacy at the roadside. As Morrie pulled onto the wide concrete apron at the back of his home, he was surprised to see his wife's Lexus LX SUV inside the open garage.

"Hey," he shouted entering the laundry room.

"What are you doing home?" his wife called out. He heard her coming to meet him. "You feeling OK?"

He hugged her and kissed her on the forehead. "Nothin' going on at the office," Morrie explained. "I needed to be out here where it's quiet so I could think."

"Want some coffee. It's fairly fresh." She turned toward the coffee maker that sat on the granite countertop at one side of the room.

"Yeah. OK." Morrie pulled out a chair from the breakfast table and peered out the window into their backyard.

"Things slowed down with the long weekend coming up?" Monica asked crossing to him with a steaming mug.

"It always does."

"So why push it. You've been so busy . . . working so hard."

"It's worth it . . . all of it, even when things don't always work out."

"Something fall through for you guys?"

"Mac McAllister's moving his accounts."

"McAllister. I know that's huge." Monica offered the coffee to him, setting it down on the table when he refused to look up at her. She sat down opposite him. Something was not right. This was not her Morrie. She reached out and touched his forearms. If she had any complaints about her husband of nineteen years, it was that he seldom showed any emotion. "Tell me about it? Just looking at you . . . I can tell something's wrong."

"Remember how elated I was last December when I made this huge commission on a hedge fund deal? It put us over top for the year. Qualified us for a bonus that meant more than $84,000 between the two of us . . . Matthew and me. Remember? Matthew was thrilled. He took us out to dinner with Shirley and him?"

"I remember. I was so proud . . ."

"Well, you shouldn't have been. The big sale was in Rene McAllister's account. I put $749,000 in a hedge fund for her. Nobody knows it. Not her. Not Mac. Not even Matt. I didn't get Rene's consent to buy it. I'm not allowed to do that. I always need to get the client's approval. Now, they're going to find out everything when the accounts are audited for the transfer, and it's going to be my ass. I've gotta figure out how I'm going to get out of it. I can't just fucking tell them I made a three-quarter-million dollar trade without her approval." Morrie slammed his chair back and stood up. The chair crashed against the kitchen wall and bounced back onto all four legs, banging on the tile floor. He looked down at the table, reached for his coffee mug and then withdrew his hand, and paced to the center of the room.

Monica studied him. Morrie had never been handsome, nice looking perhaps, but not one the girls in the sorority considered a catch. He looked terrible now. His eyebrows were pinched, brow furrowed, and lips stretched across his teeth. "Sit down, Morrie, please. I feel like you're hovering over me, and it makes me uneasy."

"Ah shit!" Morrie returned to the table and sat down.

"Couldn't you sell it before anyone finds out?"

"No. There's no market for it. I bought the damn thing with borrowed money . . . on margin. I borrowed $609,000 using the $4,000,000 in assets in her account as collateral. McAllisters don't know that either. And the fund lost money. Lots of money. I thought I'd hold it a couple of years, get out with a profit and nobody'd be the wiser. But it crashed . . . just fucking tanked. It's down forty-five percent. The only way to repay the margin loan is to sell other securities . . . and I'm sorry . . . no matter how ignorant Rene McAllister is, she'd notice there were suddenly a lot of sales in her account . . . that dozens of stocks were missing. I can get a couple of buys or sales past her in any given month. But a wholesale sellout . . . never." Morrie looked up at his wife. She was listening. But he could tell that she had not grasped the significance of all that he had said. It would mean the end of their lifestyle, the cars, the lake home, the home in town, private school for the boys. He searched her brown eyes.

"OK, what's to stop you from getting money somewhere and putting it into the account?" Monica asked.

"I'd never get away with it. Besides, even if I had the money, which I don't . . . I'm talking about $600,000 or more . . . I . . . we don't have the time. The weekend. That's it. If I had a couple of years . . . yeah, then. But now I can't. Matthew won't keep me once he hears about it. Our compliance people will lynch me . . . and maybe worse . . . ." His voice trailed off.

"I never asked Rene. I wasn't sure. I set up the papers and never did anything. Just left them on my desk," Morrie began again. "Then Cheryl happened to notice them and called to tell me we needed to get the paperwork in by the close of business that day, or it'd be too late. We had to get the money in that day, or we'd be out, and she asked me what to do, I told her to sign Rene's name and send the papers in."

"Can she do that? Sign for a client?" Monica asked.

"No. It was supposed to be just a stop-gap measure to beat the deadline."

"That's legal?"

"No. But it's done. I figured I'd get Rene into the office the following week. She'd sign papers then, and we'd submit them as replacements to the copies Cheryl signed. But the next week was really busy . . . year-end on top of us. About Thursday, Cheryl reminded me, and I promised to get Rene in the next day for certain. Well . . . guess what? McAllisters had left town for the British Virgin Islands . . . or some goddamn place. We hear that, and the very next day the commissions from the previous week hit. Ol' Matthew is so excited. He sees that fat commission. He knows we made bonus.

He comes into my office happier than anything and congratulates me. I just kinda froze. I never thought McAllisters would move the account. . . ." Morrie looked up. "All I needed was more time."

"Just ask for more time then. Get them to delay it. Delay the move."

"Not for as long as I need. I need months to work this out. I don't know how to do it yet."

"You'll come up with something," Monica said getting up and walking around the table to her husband. She wanted to stroke the back of his neck, but something kept her from reaching out.

Morrie raised his head. "Maybe." He slid his chair away from the table and stood up. "You here all day?"

"No. I was about to go into Charles City. I've errands to run, and agreed to meet my friends for lunch. Andrew Sherman and Jason said they were going into town, and they took Michael to the country club. They'll be back for dinner. Do you want me to stay? It's nothing I can't do some other day."

"No. Go. That's fine. But you can't breathe a word of this to anyone. I'm going down to the dock. I know I need to tell Matthew. I have to decide how and when to do it." Morrie crossed the kitchen. "With this party coming up, maybe we can put things off 'til next week."

Morrie felt out of place in his business suit as he crossed his lush lawn to the long dock on the beach. The dock bridged the water like a spatula with a long handle resting on the shore as on the rim to a bowl. He loosened his tie and took off his suit jacket as he reached the steps to it. A breeze was blowing in from the bay. The sunlight flickered off the ripples and the wake from the occasional passing boat. He walked the length of the dock to the broad sunbathing area at the end. The lake bottom fell away quickly to a depth deep enough for diving at the end of the dock. He sat down on the built-in wooden bench, noticing that his sons had once again failed to put away the water skis.

He needed a strategy to give him some control over the McAllister accounts. An excuse. He knew his business. Far better than most. He looked into the water in the shadow of the dock. Small sunfish and an occasional perch hovered there, hiding from predators. His sons, when they were younger, would drop a line down among them and pull it away from the smaller fish in hopes a larger one would be attracted to their bait. They spent hours at it.

He loved his children. He loved Monica. He had been true to his own career plans, rejected the corporate ladder for the chance to succeed in the brokerage business. He wanted to be one of the most successful in the profession—not just locally, but nationally. There had to be a way out of this jam. Others were slipping things past their clients and the compliance department. They bent the rules routinely and got away it, and he wasn't going to be tagged the first time he stepped out of line. Something would happen—a charmed event. A fateful reversal in the way things were going. He'd make a case with Matthew for delaying the transfer and present it tonight when his senior partner returned home."

Chapter 2

Monica nosed her Lexus through the hedge flanking their driveway and onto the blacktop road that led to town. Morrie never came home from work unless it was to relax and to be with her and the boys. Today he was upset. The situation couldn't be as bad as he made out. He always worked things out. Even in the years at Southern Central Bank and Trust, when the politics were running hot, he kept his cool and found his own way. Many begrudged him his promotions and his position, but he did not make enemies. The political intrigues became just so much history when he joined Stuart, Tompkins and Earl.

She remembered the day that he came home and announced that he was thinking about changing jobs. She thought nothing of it at first. Thought he was just running his usual list of annoyances and his mood would pass. She knew something more serious was afoot when he asked her to sit down with him. He wanted to change. Leave the certain salary at the bank for an entry level position with a brokerage firm. She was not sure how to react. They were doing well enough. Sure, they could use more income. Who couldn't? But Morrie wanted to change. She needed to listen. He would not entertain anything that would threaten their goals. Not Morrie.

Starting out, after all, had not been easy. Both wanted to succeed in their careers. She wanted to run her own health spa, perhaps start a regional chain, so that she could use her physical education and science major in a field that was an abiding interest to her. Morrie's maneuverings at the bank, however, made it obvious that his career would eclipse hers. It didn't matter. They were getting what they wanted.

She accepted a supporting role and decided to stay at home. When her first son was born, the decision to abandon a business career became easier to accept. When she found she wanted to become pregnant again, she scrapped what remained of her career plans. They would provide the best for their sons. For her, that meant all of the things that she had missed. Growing up in a small town in central North Carolina had given her enough exposure to Greensboro and Winston-Salem society to know that her family was not part of it. Her father, a dentist, was a popular man but far from wealthy. She envied the girls who drove their own late model cars, attended the private schools, and always seemed in the know. The boys who attended those schools appeared more poised and knowledgeable. She yearned to move up in the world, to the larger homes, better automobiles, vacations abroad—all the things that an father disdained as pretentious.

If she was to achieve her goals, she needed to capitalize on her assets. Among them she counted better than average looks, considerable athletic talent, a quick mind, and a determined spirit. "Beware the woman who knows her own mind," was the only quote from her father that she grew to respect over time. Her mother never expressed an opinion of her own, gave in to the wishes of others, and with the years, was overtaken by resentment. She became chronically depressed. Monica grew ashamed of her and resentful of her father. She counted the days to high school graduation knowing then that she could get away.

Morrie may have been passive like her mother, but he knew his own mind, and given time, he would express his views on any subject. Unlike her father, Morrie was ambitious—willing to work hard to achieve the goals that he set for himself. He was going to be wealthy, to be recognized. She loved his drive and grew to love him. Morrie, the intellectual with the reluctant smile, who could hardly dance a step, the guy capable of unflinching loyalty and awkward affection was going to be her man. Their marriage may have fallen a bit short of what she had hoped. She may not have loved him as much as she felt capable, but he was steady, a good father to her sons, and she felt their future was secure with him. He never forgot anniversaries, birthdays, or the kids. He loved her, loved spending time with her, loved making love to her, loved watching her come into view and loved watching her walk away. Their clashes over the years had been only the chaffing of her more aggressive nature against his cautious approach to life and others. Charles City and Pelican Bay on Heron Lake were perfect for everything they longed to make their own. They were getting there.

"I'm sorry I'm late," she said walking up to the table around which her friends were already seated. "One of those days. I got off to a late start and been behind all day."

"It's OK. Susan just got here herself, and it gave us time to talk about you," Marcia Matthews replied. "You look bushed! Anything wrong?"

"No. I guess I'm still flushed from working out . . . tearing a shirt to get here on time."

The group met frequently for lunch, although Monica and Joyce Sherman were neighbors at the lake and saw one another often during the week. Susan and Marcia were friends of long standing. They had homes on the fairways of the exclusive Sterling Creek Country Club, home of the annual Carolina Coastal Open.

"So, so, so. What's new? I know that you weren't talking about me because I am dull and uninteresting," Monica said.

"We were just discussing the Wirth Fourth-of-July party. We're all going again this year, at least for the cocktails and bar-be-que. Jay's hosting two foursomes at our club. I think that Morrie is playing in one of them," Susan Miller said.

"Yeah," Joyce said, "I don't think that there'll be any takers for water skiing or jet skis this year. Leave that to the kids."

"I thought that Matthew didn't want kids," Marcia said.

"Well, not kids . . . *kids*," Joyce replied. "Young people. You know, who still are proud to show up in public in a bathing suit. No cellulite! Ha! I can tell when I'm being ogled and when I'm just being looked at. Last couple of years, I've just been looked at. But you, Monica, you look like a college girl. How do you do it?"

"Keeping up with two teenage boys is all," Monica said. "And I love my tennis and working out."

"Well, you look great. We hate you for it. By the way, speaking of your boys, your Michael. What a sweetheart! I was coming out of Belk's the other day loaded down with packages, and he spotted me from half way across the parking lot and came running up to give me a hand. What a charmer! The girls'll be all over him in a couple of years."

"The girls can wait. I don't want him growing up too fast. He's my joy."

"How's Morrie?"

"God, that man and his job! It's all he thinks about. Came home early today worked up about something . . . oh-oh, I'm not supposed to say anything. But I was glad to get away. Suddenly, everything's a crisis. He didn't used to be that way. Now that he and Matthew are working in partnership, he's reacting to things differently."

"He's a lucky guy," Susan said. "Jay said that we're leaving our accounts with Morrie when Matthew retires and that he'll have the best clientele in the city. You guys have done so well. We're all proud of you."

"I know . . . and don't think I'm not grateful. We both are. Matthew's been so good to him . . . and Shirley is as sweet as she can be. We'll be at the party. We're co-hosting as we did last year."

"Shouldn't we order?" Joyce asked, picking up her menu.

"I suppose Mac and Rene will be there for most of the day," Monica said. "She looks just awful lately. I walked up on her at Lowe's the other day and hardly recognized her. She's so pale, and her hair . . . my God . . . looks like she cuts it herself."

"Poor Mac," Marcia said. "He let her start that little business, that gift shop, just to keep her happy. Have you been in there? I didn't see anything I liked."

"Skinner Thorpe is helping her," Susan said. "Ha, some help. I'm sorry, I just can't stand that woman."

"I avoid her. I'd like to say she's a typical Yankee, but she grew up in Greensboro. She cultivated that pushy bitch style all on her own," Joyce said. "Let's order. I can't sit here all day and talk."

"I'm home!" Monica called. She put her packages on the table where she had left her husband a few hours earlier and glanced at the clock. Four-thirty. A filet on the grill would get Morrie's mind off of things. She saw his feet at the end the chaise lounge on the front porch. "Hey! I said 'I'm home,'" she shouted. His feet moved. At least he wasn't asleep. She walked through the house to the porch.

"I'm sorry. I didn't hear you."

"Did you talk to Matthew?"

"No, he's not home yet."

A bottle of Dewers was on the floor at the end of the chaise. "Oh, yeah," Morrie said, "Jason came back after lunch and dressed to go to his job. Mike called and asked if he could be late. He's at the club. One of his buddies wanted to play another round and his folks would give him a ride home. I said it was OK."

"How late is late?"

"Not till after supper. He'll grab a burger at the club."

"So you just decided you'd drink away the afternoon?"

"I've only had a couple. I've been thinking this thing through. I needed to relax."

"Morrie, this is so unlike you. Are you going to talk to Matthew? That seemed awfully damn important earlier."

"He'll be home for supper, and I'm going over after . . . to his place."

"Meanwhile, you thought you'd get drunk so that everything would go well, right?" Monica said, surprised at her own anger.

"Oh, come off it. I just wanted to ease off a little. I'll take a nap after supper. I'll be fine."

"I thought I'd ask you to grill a couple of filets, but I don't know . . ."

"That's fine. I'd be glad to . . ."

"No. Forget it. We have plenty of leftovers. Take a nap and we'll eat. I don't want you upset with this thing hanging over us."

"It's no trouble."

"We'll save the steaks for some other night. We'll eat in about an hour. You should change. You can't see Matthew in your suit . . . not after you said you weren't feeling well? I'll call you when supper's ready." Monica wanted to change also, but Morrie headed for the bedroom and she decided to let him have as much time as he needed. She picked up the bottle of scotch and the empty glass and returned to the kitchen.

"A gal jock." The thought awakened Morrie. Why that? He hadn't thought about Monica like that since leaving Wake Forest.

He'd been dreaming. About college. About seeing Monica on campus. Her assertiveness captivated him right from the start. Not strident like some of the women with New Jersey license plates on their BMW's. Her confidence was charismatic. Some guys almost feared her, a gal jock—too much to take on. But he wanted a strong partner to help with his plans for a family and the future.

"Hey! Get up! Supper's ready," Monica called.

"Be right there." Morrie shuffled to the closet where he pulled on shorts and a golf shirt and slipped into a pair of sandals.

"You feeling better?" Monica asked as he walked into the kitchen.

"Well, yeah. I don't look forward to talking with Matt, but I gotta do it. A team in Atlanta ran afoul of something a couple of years ago, and they held both responsible. Both guys got fired. One guy didn't know anything about the violations. Anything. I hate to think I've gotten Matthew into trouble . . . not after all he has done for me."

"I saw Matthew's Buick pass on the road. He's home. You told him you were coming over later, didn't you?"

"No. I didn't. I'm not sure how to say what I want. I need him to convince Mac not to move the accounts. At least, get Mac to delay the move so I have more time to consider alternatives. Postpone until the end of the year. Maybe keep a couple of accounts long enough for me to dispose of Rene's hedge fund."

Monica slid her Teflon spatula under a steaming portion of curried chicken and rice casserole onto his plate. "Help yourself to some Brussels sprouts. You going to call Matthew right after dinner?"

"Maybe I'll just wander over there."

"They may have plans . . . or guests."

"All right, damn it, I'll call right now." Clay pushed back in his chair and stomped to the wall phone near the dinning room door.

"Matt, I want to talk through the McAllister thing . . . like you said. Would tonight be OK . . . About 7:30? . . . Great. . . See you then. . . Your deck? . . Great." Morrie returned to the table. "Now, can we eat?"

After eating, Morrie sat down on the porch to wait for his appointed time to see Matthew. The yard between the beach and the porch had fallen into deep shade. A breeze induced a slight roll to the lake, and the sun, lower on the horizon, struck the upper branches of the trees, gilding them with a coppery brilliance and then skipped half way across the bay where the waves winked into the retreating light. Lights from neighboring homes began to glow in the shadows and the neighborhood was quiet except for the desultory robins greeting the onset of a dusk scented with bar-be-que lighter fluid and hickory smoke— an evening that fulfilled everything that Morrie had ever wanted when he came at the end of the day. He peered back though the house to the kitchen.

"Hon?" he called. "I'm going over to Matthew's. I don't know how long I'll be."

"OK. Don't worry about the time. I'll wait up."

Lights were on in the Sherman home on the lot between his home and Wirth's. Tom and Joyce Sherman befriended Monica and him from the beginning. The couples met when Monica and he began visiting the construction sight for their home. Crossing in front of the Sherman home, Morrie spotted Matthew reclining in a chaise on his deck. He waved and his partner waived back. "Nice evening."

"Beautiful!" Matthew responded. "I'd get up but I've been looking forward to this since two o'clock this afternoon. Some Shiraz's open on the table, and glasses too . . . I think. Help yourself."

"I'll pass. I had a couple before dinner. You seem relaxed."

"Yes, I am, and I want you to make lots of money the rest of the year so that I can do more of this. God, I love doing nothing at all. Haven't done enough of it all my life. Had jobs since I was 12 years old. I'm done now. Ah . . . before you sit down, can you fill my glass." Matthew took a quick final swallow and held it out to Morrie.

"Glad to. Shirley inside?"

"No. She got a call from our daughter all excited about something and wanted her mother to come over."

Morrie could see that Matthew had downed more than one glass of wine. He was more languid than usual, a little louder, more expansive. Morrie pulled a wrought iron chair away from the table, turned it to face Matthew, checked the cushions to make certain neither was damp, and sat down.

"Who called this meeting anyway?" Matthew asked. "If you're still bothered by this McAllister thing, we can talk it out some more . . . but honestly, Morrie . . . I don't think it's going to do much more than help you deal with your feelings about it."

"It's bothered me all day. There's got to be a way to keep these accounts. We should fight for it. I think you gave in too easily. You acted like it was a done deal. No point."

"It *is* a done deal. But I can understand that you'd want to know why I reacted as I did. Trust me on this. I know McAllister. He won't want to listen to any appeals to reconsider. He showed us the courtesy in letting us know, and I accept that as final. I won't be party to any effort to get him to change his mind."

"Would you mind if I did on my own then?"

"Yes . . . damn it . . . I'd mind. I assured Mac that we'd let events move ahead without any interference on our part. I don't want you . . . or anyone else . . . going against that. We keep our promises. That's what our practice is all about. Two years from now, none of this will mean a damn thing. It'll be over and forgotten."

"Maybe I'll take you up on that glass of wine," Morrie said. Matthew smiled and turned his head to one side as if to indicate he did not want to discuss the subject any more. Morrie poured a glass of wine and strolled to the edge of the deck. The lake was nearly dark. In the distance, he heard children playing and remembered what the early dark had held for him when he was a boy on a summer evening. Every minute in the yard at the edge of the light felt as though he was stealing time, time alone, away from his parents, away from a call to come in and get ready for bed, and he remembered rejoicing in the cool and the shadows, the excitement of pushing further into the night than he ever dared before. A cabin cruiser glided past the front of the Wirth dock. Its running lights bounced off of the rippled surface of the lake; its exhaust popped and sputtered when water slapped at the stern.

He turned back to Matthew. "Seems like all the wrong reasons for losing an account. Suppose we had one more meeting. Suppose we had an attorney, even her attorney, sit in on it and a CPA, maybe our own estate planning specialist. I mean . . . what good does it do to let Rene McAllister continue in the wrong. She wins this, but she loses in the long run. You and I have always made an effort to keep people from making mistakes that could cost them financially. Don't we have a responsibility here?"

"Whoa, boy. Taking the moral high ground, huh?" Matthew straddled the chaise and raised himself so he could look at Morrie. "What makes you think that Rene McAllister believes for one minute that the money in her name is truly hers? She's smarter than that. She's nuts, but she's smart. She doesn't want to be set straight. That's not her agenda. All she wants is to keep ol' Mac off balance . . . keep raising just enough hell so he's willing to do damn near anything to calm her down . . . to keep the peace. Look at how she behaved in our last meeting. Called Mac a liar to his face. Monica'd never do that to you . . . nor Shirley to me. Pushing this thing is sticking your hand into a basket vipers."

"I can't see letting an account go for all of the wrong reasons."

"Reason's got nothing to do with it? A shaky marriage does. A neurotic female who's never lived up to her own expectations of herself. No court in the land could arbitrate the differences that have taken root in that marriage and get it back on solid ground."

"So, we're the victims in this . . . of a husband who is afraid to fight with his wife . . . a wife whose view is driven by paranoia."

"We're not victims. We've had a profitable account on the books for almost fifteen years. Our turn is up. It would've been nice if we could've kept it, but it was very good while it lasted. Lighten up, Morrie. This isn't like you. Is there something here that's a concern for you and you haven't told me?"

"No. Nothing. Just me. I don't like seeing this account go out the door. There're some I'd love to see go. I'd hold the door for them. But not this one. I just thought I'd sound you out on it one more time. How much time did you say we had on this?"

"Mac wanted the June month-end with us, and the transfer would take place once everything was wrapped up for the second quarter."

"If we could get him to leave just one account with us until the end of the year, one with at least $1,000,000 in assets, then we wouldn't be docked on the client retention bonus. Would he listen to that?"

"I don't know. Maybe. It'd have to be one of his accounts though. Not one of Rene's."

"The one I had in mind is Rene's. What if we came up with some technical reason for delaying it until year end?"

"That wouldn't be the truth. This is just not going to go down with you is it?"

"We're giving up probably $15,000 apiece in the client retention bonus with all this moving out. As long as we hold on to $1,000,000, it wouldn't be counted as a lost affluent client."

"We'll replace before the year is out, replace it and then some."

"It's still a loss. It still means $15,000 . . . conservatively," Morrie said.

"The commission schedule doesn't dictate my decisions."

"Well, don't get me wrong, but if he's a friend," Morrie said, "and you appealed on that basis, why is it a compromise of your integrity?"

"'Compromise my integrity.' Come on, Morrie, that's bullshit."

"I didn't mean to sound sarcastic. I'm just looking for some middle ground here."

"I'll think about it." Matthew said. "This'll all look different in a day or two. You'll see. You going into the office in the morning?"

"Yeah. I need to make up for the time I lost today, not that there's much going on this close to the holiday. You going in?"

Morrie heard the resignation in his own voice. If McAllister were to leave one account, it would not help if it was not the one with the hedge fund in it.

"No. It'd be a waste of gas. Shirley has a honey-do list as long as my arm because of the party."

"How'd it go?" Monica asked when Morrie stepped on to the deck.

"God! I didn't see you there."

"So?"

"He was a little around the bend with his wine. We talked about asking McAllister to cancel the transfer. You out here for a smoke?" He could smell the rich scent in the darkness.

"Just a couple of hits," she replied. "No lectures, please. I was just trying to ease back, and this stuff helps."

"I know our friends are pretty casual about it, but I don't like it. Everybody's convinced tobacco causes cancer, but nobody ever says anything about pot . . . grown who knows where with who knows what pesticides and herbicides on it."

"Drop it. OK? A couple of hits now and then aren't going to hurt anyone that much. It keeps my migraines at bay. The boys aren't home yet. What's the harm? Besides, you changed the subject. What'd you mean you didn't tell him anything?"

"It'd be better if he were sober . . . in the morning. Turns out that McAllister wasn't supposed to tell Matthew until after the party. He only called because he was afraid Southern Central might jump the gun and contact us before he did. So, we're not to let on that we know until after the party."

"Mac and Rene are going to be at the party? After this?"

"Yeah. Crazy, isn't it? Rene wants to carry on as though nothing has changed," Morrie said.

"The bitch. Do you know that she has a place in her shop dedicated to accessories that are supposed to memorialize dead pets? She wants customers to bring in pictures of their pets. Then she uses them to help create something for display that she says helps with the grieving process. This from the woman put her own family dog to sleep without telling her husband. Mac came home one night and wondered where the dog was."

"I don't give a shit about anything Rene does. We just need to go ahead as if nothing has changed. I'm going down to the dock . . . just for a few minutes."

Monica watched her husband's tall silhouette disappear into the darkness. Then she reached for the pipe and the matches.

Chapter 3

"Who was on the phone?" Tom Sherman shouted. "What the hell time is it anyway?" He rolled over in bed and looked at the clock. 9:40 AM. It was Thursday at the lake, July 3. Because of the holiday weekend, boaters and jet skiers had already taken over. He heard them churning up the water, banging across one another's wakes, engines roaring as the props and the exhaust cleared the water and became suspended momentarily in the open air. "A peaceful goddamn place isn't it?" he muttered. "Just what everyone needs, a nice quiet place at the lake to recover from a hard day at work."

"That was Shirley Wirth. I'm sorry. Did it wake you?" his wife called.

"Yeah. I want the goddman bedroom phone turned off the nights I came home late."

"I'm sorry. I thought I did. It's time to get up anyway. Why don't you come on down? I can fix you a nice breakfast. There's fresh coffee. We can sit on the deck."

"Yeah, right, and listen to all those morons running around on jet skis." He threw back the covers, swung his legs over the side of the bed, and sat up. He had the day off. He wanted to relax. A little golf on TV, maybe. A good wine later. He retrieved a Carolina blue tee shirt from the neatly folded stack that Joyce placed in the bureau drawer. The bathroom mirror showed that his coarse sandy brown hair was wildly disheveled. "Shit," he muttered realizing that the only way he could get control over it was to shampoo, and a shampoo meant a shower, and he did not want to take the time for a shower. He pulled on a pair of hospital surgery scrub pants and cinched the draw string tight, sucking in his stomach for a second glance into the mirror. At 51, the size of his waist nearly equaled his age. His face was heavier; his ruddy cheeks puffy from sleep. He found a baseball cap with a *Sterling Creek* insignia and pulled it down over his forehead by the bill. The aroma of fresh coffee reached him.

"Why the hell would Shirley Wirth call. She lives right next door?" he asked entering the kitchen.

"About tomorrow. I guess it was just easier for her." Joyce finished pouring a mug of coffee for him. She nodded in the direction of the deck. "Go on out and get comfortable. I'm bringing it to you with some fresh orange juice. How do you want your eggs?"

"What about tomorrow?"

"She was wondering . . . that is, Matthew and she were wondering whether our boys could drive the boats tomorrow for the water skiers at their shindig."

"What'd you tell her?" Sherman sat down at a glass topped table on a black wrought iron chair that scraped across the raw wood of the deck as he pulled in behind him.

"I said I couldn't speak for them. I said I'd mention it to you."

"Why? Because I *can* speak for them?"

"No, Tom, just whether it was a good idea . . . whether we should let them ask the boys." Joyce set a mug of coffee and a tall glass of orange juice on the table in front of him. It was bright, cool morning. The noise from the lake was more intrusive than usual. Dew was still on the grass in the shade in the yard. Hummingbirds buzzed the feeder that she had set up for them at the edge of the deck.

"They can decide for themselves," Tom finally said.

"She said they'd pay them . . . for their time."

"My kids don't need money." Tom took a long drink of orange juice. He winced as the cold liquid hit his stomach and set the tumbler down on the glass table as if he were rapping out a pronouncement.

"They didn't want to ask it as a favor."

"Why not? We're neighbors, aren't we?"

"Oh, Tom, please don't tell me it's going to be one of those mornings. I was so looking forward to having you home for the weekend, having some time and a little fun together. I can't help what Matt and Shirley want. All I did was answer the phone."

"I wouldn't ask Jamie to back a car out of the garage. Andrew might be interested though. Do you know if he has any other plans?"

"I don't. He hasn't said anything about this weekend. You know how kids are. How do you want your eggs?"

"And Jamie?"

"Still in bed. He usually sleeps this late. I didn't hear him come in last night."

"Just as well. I'll mention it to Andrew."

"Good. Now . . . how do you want your eggs?"

"Lightly basted. Maybe that older Clay kid could help. They usually use their boat anyway."

"Well, see what Andrew thinks, and I'll call Shirley once I know."

"My eggs?" Sherman asked.

"I'm sorry."

"I could use a refill once you get things started." He held up his coffee mug and smiled.

Joyce snatched the empty cup from his hand and walked back into the house. She turned the gas on under the skillet, walked to the refrigerator, and took two eggs out of the egg holder. The massive stainless steel appliance roared to life as if it had been violated, the compressor fan pushing hot air over her feet and across the floor.

"OK, sit up," she said sliding the screen door to the deck open with her foot. "This is a new brand of Canadian bacon. I hope you like it." He grunted and then both turned as they heard the sliding screen door open once again. It was Tom's twenty-one year old son, Jamie.

"Not too early for you is it?" Sherman asked.

"Naw, not bad." Jamie stretched and yawned. His dark brown hair was matted to one side from sleep, his brown eyes were bloodshot and slit with fatigue. He struck Sherman as thoroughly dissipated in his faded, torn blue jean cutoffs and soiled *Hardrock* tee shirt. "You mind if I have some coffee and rustle some eggs myself?" Jamie asked of nobody in particular.

"My God, is that you?" Sherman asked. "Do you realize how offensive it is when you don't shower?"

"After breakfast," Jamie responded turning to Joyce as if he expected an answer from her.

"No," Joyce said. "It's easier for me to do it than to clean up after you."

"Whoa! You're not sitting at this table," Sherman said noticing his son reaching for a chair. "No, sir. Take a shower now, God damn it, or move well down wind from me. How can you stand it?"

"Humans can get used to anything." Jamie slouched back toward the end of the deck near the lakefront.

"Yeah, well, I don't care to get used to anything when I know immediately I don't like it. Go shower! And shave! And put on some decent looking clothes. You've got a closet full."

"Ah, shit."

"I'll have breakfast ready for you when you come down," Joyce said.

"Don't bother. I'm outa here."

"It's no trouble," Joyce said.

"Forget it."

"Don't take that tone with her. You're her guest here. You treat her with respect or find somewhere else to live." Sherman took a big bite of toast and looked up at his son.

Jamie turned and yanked open the screen door, and disappeared into the dark of the house. A moment later, Joyce and Sherman heard his car start, back out of the driveway, and accelerate off, tires squealing in protest.

"Please, don't start," Joyce said. "I didn't want the day to start this way. I never want any day to start this way. You're out-of-sorts. He's just aching to get your goat. I've promised myself I could tough it out until he moves out, so let's just let it go at that."

"Surly shit," Sherman said with half a mouth full of toast. "Learned at the foot of a Jedi master," referring to his first wife with whom all the children sided when the couple split up. He chased his half-chewed toast with a slug of orange juice.

"Please, just leave it alone. I know you can't throw him out. I also know that I can hardly stand another day with him here, especially when you're away. He doesn't respect me. His room stinks. If I didn't send the cleaning lady in there to pick up his clothes and make sure they get washed, the house would smell to high heaven in a week. Some days I think we should move back into town and let him live out here until he's ready to leave. Then I won't need to deal with him everyday."

"I'll talk to him."

"No. You won't. You'll yell at him, and he'll think I put you up to it. You'll leave and then, if anything, matters will get worse."

"I sure as hell can't hang around here and referee things between the two of you. How am I supposed to do that? Any suggestions?"

"There, you see, I can't even talk about it. It'd mean so much to me if you realized how difficult it is. When he goes out a night, I wish sometimes he'd never come back. I know you want him to turn into something some day. But right now, waiting for him to get a clue about what he is going to do with his life, is all I can take." Joyce pushed back on her chair and stood up. "I need to make sure the guest rooms are ready. Maybe your stinky son will stay away so we don't need to be embarrassed by him."

On a quieter day, Sherman would have enjoyed taking out the sailboat, inviting Joyce to come along, but with the jet skis and speed boats plowing up the lake, it would be too hazardous. He was reluctant to go back into the house. Joyce was angry. She had a right to be. His willingness to understand was overridden by his own frustration with his son. Jamie was the oldest child from his first marriage which ended in a bitter divorce. Life downstream from his divorce had been chaotic. He regretted his affairs, regretted that he was not more forthright and simply asked her his wife for a divorce before fueling her fissionable anger with his infidelity.

His affairs came to light one day when Sears called and asked his wife where she wanted the new washer and dryer delivered. He had ordered them for an apartment that he used for his trysts, an arrangement about which his wife knew nothing until that fateful call was placed. "Of all the fucking, goddman rotten luck," he bellowed upon hearing what had happened. And while the incident turned into a matter of rueful humor, it was the pivotal event that launched their acrimonious divorce.

He stood up and stretched. "Shit," he said realizing that he had done a lot toward sabotaging his day off with his inability to get on top of his mood. He heard a jet ski throttle back and looked up to see his younger son, Andrew, pulling his craft up to ramp near their dock. "Hey, sport!" he yelled. Andrew looked up and waved. "Up and at it, are you?" Sherman watched his son secure the jet ski.

"Too busy out there today. No fun. I knew it would be crowded because of the Fourth tomorrow, so I got out early, but it got busy real quick. Really bad," the youth said jogging up to the deck.

"So, how've you been?"

"Great, Dad. Your day off?"

"Today, tomorrow, Saturday and Sunday, but there's the party next door tomorrow . . . so that's the picture."

"OK." Andrew, well tanned from his hours in the sun, had filled out over the summer. At six-feet-two, he looked like an athlete in peak condition, an impression his closely cropped sun-bleached hair and ready smile reinforced. He extended his fist. His father responded and the two touched knuckles. "You doin' much today? I mean . . . think we could get in a round of golf?"

"Probably won't get a tee time this late. But I'll call and see. You gotta give me some strokes, though."

"Great."

"I need clean up and change." Sherman noticed the dishes on the table from his breakfast and picked them up. Joyce was not in the kitchen so he put his dishes in the sink and went upstairs. Joyce was in the kitchen when he returned.

"I just called for a tee time for Andrew and me," Sherman said.

"I knew you were calling. Andrew told me." He noted the tone of resignation in her reply. "He's in the garage getting his clubs. He said that you'd probably have lunch at the club if they worked you in."

"We got paired with another foursome who had a couple cancel. We really need to get going."

Andrew was staring down into the Porsche Boxter when he entered the garage. "You want to take it?" Sherman asked.

"God, Dad. What's this all over it . . . that awful smell?"

Sherman recognized the odor immediately as sulfuric acid. The top was down on the car, and he saw as he walked up that the interior of the vehicle—the leather seats, the dash, the door panels, the carpet—had been splashed with the acid, turning the fabric and leather into a foul-smelling mush. Acid had also spilled on the finish of the exterior and had eaten through the paint. "Jesus Christ!"

"What is it, Dad?"

"Sulfuric acid! Some son-of-a-bitch doused my car with sulfuric acid. I don't believe this. Joyce! Get out here! Was the garage door open when you came in?" he demanded of Andrew.

"Just now?"

"Yes, just now, God damn it."

"Yes."

"How about earlier this morning?"

"I wasn't out here earlier this morning."

"When you came in last night?"

"Yeah . . . I think it was?"

"Where'd you park your truck?"

"Out by the basketball hoop, where I always do, but . . . yes . . . the garage door was open"

Joyce appeared at the door to the garage. "What on earth? People can hear you." She stopped a couple of steps inside the garage.

"Have you been out here this morning?" Sherman asked.

"Here? In the garage? No. Why would I be?"

"Smell anything?"

"Yes. Rotten eggs . . . or someone's been very, very sick."

"Sulfuric acid."

"What?"

"Some son-of-a-bitch poured sulfuric acid all over my Boxter. Did you see anyone, at any time this morning . . . or hear anyone . . . out here?"

"No, Tom. No. Not at all."

"Think about it!"

"I am thinking about it. The only person who has been out here was Jamie. You knew that. He left when we were on the deck together."

"Naw, shit, this is even beyond him. God damn it! I've only had the car two weeks. Why would anyone do this?"

"*Fatal Attraction!*" Joyce exclaimed.

"What?" Sherman roared.

"*Fatal Attraction.* The movie. Where the woman douses the guy's car with acid because he stop paying attention to her."

"My God, Joyce . . . that's got nothing to do with anything," Sherman said looking at his wife in disbelief.

"Was the garage door open all night?" Joyce asked quickly to turn back her husband's disdain. Tom did not get it. Maybe the late nights were not because of work.

"Yes. One was. Who the hell would think there'd be any trouble way out here. I didn't close it when I came in because the door opener might wake you." Sherman looked more closely at the driver side bucket seat. "The shit's been there for several hours anyway. It had to have been done sometime last night."

"What'd ya gonna do, Dad?" Andrew asked.

"Hell, the damage's done. There's no neutralizing it now. Not that you could anyway. I'm calling the police."

"So, no round today, I guess," Andrew said.

"Yeah, get in the Lexus. We'll take it. I'll call the cops on our way. Joyce, you let the police know what happened. Tell them I'll be back in about five hours, OK?"

"Don't you think you should stay? Talk to them yourself? I don't know what to say."

"You know as much as I do. You heard everything we said. Besides, they probably won't get anybody out here until we get back."

"But, Tom . . . ." She stopped. She turned away. "Whatever you say. Not my car. Not my house. Not my children."

"Let's go," Sherman said to his son. "I'm not giving up my day, too."

Joyce suddenly felt detached from all that was going on around her, as she felt when she was on duty as a nurse. All that mattered was that she execute on her assigned tasks and keep her feelings from interfering. As it turned out, Tom was right. The police said that they could not get an officer out to the house before late afternoon.

Sherman, through years of professional discipline, was able to put aside the troubling events of the day and enjoy his round of golf with his son. Upon returning home, they found a police cruiser in the driveway and a black sedan with state plates parked beside of it.

A Heron Lake policeman was seated in the living room in one of two matched fireside chairs. Sherman knew the officer from seeing him in the village. He did not recognize a second man in plain clothes who was seated and talking with Joyce. The man did not respond to his entrance as promptly as his associate, and Sherman felt a tinge of annoyance at his indifference. The man was older, perhaps in his late fifties, a full head of gray hair, and when he stood up, Sherman noticed that he was slender, tanned, and somewhat shorter than Sherman himself, perhaps about five-feet-ten-inches tall.

"Dr. Sherman," the man said. "This is Officer Ray Fletcher and I'm Detective James Raker with the Melville County Sheriff's office. We were just visiting with your wife about your Porsche."

"They needed both of you?" Sherman asked.

Raker chuckled. "It's a jurisdictional question out here as to whether it is a county or a village matter. We're inside the extended village limits of Lake Heron Township, and that's why Officer Fletcher is here. He's on the Heron Lake Township force. I'm the liaison officer for the Melville County Sheriff assigned to Heron Lake Township. On matters like this, we often work together."

"I see." Sherman took a seat on the couch beside Joyce. "Have you seen the car?"

"Just a quick look. Your wife said you believe it happened last night, after you got home. The garage door was open all night?"

"Right," Sherman responded. "We didn't notice it until this morning when we were getting ready to . . ."

"Do you have any idea as to why somebody would do this?"

"No.

"But you're sure it was done last night."

"Yes. I was at my office, meeting with my partners. I didn't get home until about 12:15. I didn't notice anything then."

"Did you drive the car yesterday?"

"No. I drove my Lexus."

"Did you look at the damaged car upon your return?"

"No. The garage door behind it was closed. It was parked where it is now, in the space farthest from the door."

"Is there anybody you know who holds a grudge or would have a motive for doing this?"

"Nobody!"

"You're sure?"

"Yes."

"So," Raker said, "we should believe that somebody, bent on vandalism, with sulfuric acid . . . a choice that certainly indicates forethought . . . picked out your Porsche Boxter at random, even though it could not be seen from the road because the garage door behind it was closed, entered the premises, and defaced the vehicle. You and I have discussed this, Mrs. Sherman, but has anything come to mind during the course of my conversation with your husband?"

Joyce shook her head.

"Let's take a closer look at the vehicle then," Raker said. "Can we get the lab out here?" he asked Officer Fletcher.

"Yes, sir, they're on their way."

A police van had pulled into the driveway. Two officers consulted briefly with Raker and Fletcher and taped off the area around the Porsche.

"This may take a while," Raker said. "Officer Fletcher and I are through for now, but we may need to talk to you once the lab boys get done. When they are finished, Doctor, call your insurance company, unless the lab people tell you otherwise. I'm sorry about this. That's a beautiful car and a terrible thing to have happen."

He extended his hand to Sherman who at first did not notice the gesture, and upon realizing he was to reciprocate, quickly grabbed Raker's hand and shook it.

"Man, I'm glad that Sherman's older son, Jamie, wasn't involved," Fletcher said as he and Raker made their way to their vehicles. "He's under investigation. He's a known dealer around the lake. SBI's watching him and hope to find out who his suppliers are. The Deputy Chief warned me before I left that we shouldn't say anything that'd tip them off that we had their son under surveillance. The perp might be someone the older son knows, somebody trying to send him a message . . . something territorial. I want to question the neighbors to see if they heard or saw anything last night. How about you?"

"Nothing for now. I'll call in what's happened. Our guys have the lab, so I'll let you know what they report. Let me know if you turn anything up."

"Great." Fletcher looked at the homes of either side of the Sherman. "Boy, some people really have it rough, don't they. Look at these barns."

Raker nodded, and as he was getting into his car, he noticed Joyce Sherman walking back into the Sherman house—an attractive brunette, very polite with an engaging smile, yet something was missing for her amidst all the comforts of their home. Sherman, Raker noticed, ambled back into the garage to observe the lab technicians at work. The doctor turned suddenly and walked back toward the house. Even at distance Raker could read the doctor's lips.

"Fuck!" The doctor yanked open the door to his home.

Chapter 4

"Looks like you had a little help finishing off the wine last night. Party doesn't start until tomorrow, you know," Shirley said as she entered from the deck with an empty bottle of Shiraz in one hand and two wine glasses in the other. She gave Matthew, who was still in his pajamas, a peck on the cheek as she passed him on her way to the kitchen sink. He was seated at the breakfast table, taking a few moments as he did each morning, to enjoy coffee, and as he always teased, the sight of his wife. Her flowing red hair had been overtaken by gray, but she looked as much the Irish lass as ever, fair skin, freckles, and hazel eyes.

"Morrie spent about an hour with me. The McAllister thing troubles him more than I thought. He wants me to ask Mac to leave the accounts with us . . . or at least a couple. You hate losing a large account. Always. But it's never the end of the world."

"Why'd anybody want Rene McAllister for a client? Here she's pulling the business away from you and coming to our party anyway. And she'll act as if she's one of our good friends the whole day."

"I can go along with it. Mac's spent a lot of money with me over the past fifteen years. We're not to let on that we know."

"I know," Shirley sighed. Why'd you think Morrie's so wrought up?"

"Surprised me." Matthew slid his chair back from the table and walked over to the coffee-maker for a refill. "I knew it would be tough but I thought he'd take it in stride. He cares more about money than I ever did. Whenever you lose an account, you ask yourself what you did wrong . . . where you failed. You want to go back and explain. It stays with you for days . . . weeks afterwards. But all Morrie's been thinking about is the money . . . the commission schedule . . . the bonus considerations.

"For months I wanted him to take on some of my smaller accounts . . . schedule meetings or call them . . . but nothing happens. I run into a someone and hear that Morrie hasn't been in touch and I'm embarrassed."

"Morrie likes the big shots," Shirley said, "the money boys, but you . . . ha! . . . you've always let the little people matter. Sometimes too much."

"I can work with anybody, but the money guys are different. They may listen to your advice and take it sometimes. You think things are going really well, that you've won their confidence, until you get pulled aside in the clubhouse before being introduced to one of their friends and told that the introduction to new guy in the foursome is a friend—not a business thing. Translated that means 'don't call on this guy or he'll think I referred you.'" Matthew pushed his chair back. "I need to get dressed."

"You all set for the party?" Shirley asked.

"Oh, screw the party!" He heard Shirley laugh as he made his way toward the bedroom. If pushed, Matthew would acknowledge that the party was not as much fun as it had been years earlier. He and Shirley were parents then, not grandparents, and an all-night party did not require a two day recovery period. They were not even all-night parties any more. The crowd was older. Morrie and his wife Monica were among the youngest and with them came younger guests. The congeniality Matthew enjoyed seeing had wilted. Matthew's friends were put off by the politeness of the younger guests. Clay's friends, by contrast, acted as if bridled by chaperones, restrained for any attempt at spontaneity or revelry. It would be the same this year. But this year would be the last that Shirley and he would host.

The parking lot had less than half the usual number of cars in it when Morrie pulled into his reserved space. Weekends during the summer started on Friday at noon, but with the Fourth-of-July falling on Friday, Thursday would be a half day as the markets closed at noon. He greeted Cheryl and Louise and headed straight for his office. Signing on to his computer, he pulled up the McAllister accounts. The hedge fund had lost more ground. It would take $609,000 to retire the margin loan. Too much.

He pressed the intercom button on his phone. "Louise, do you have the number for Brule Mountain Funds?"

"Gimme a sec. Yes. Here it is. 617-555-5947. Ted Robinette's on extension 2942."

Robinette answered on the first ring. "Ted, Morrie Clay at Stuart, Tompkins and Earl. I only half expected to catch you in today."

"I was practically out the door, Morrie. What can I do for you?"

"I'm in a bind, Ted. I've got a position in one of your hedge funds that I need to get redeemed."

"Can't do it. Not until the open period in December."

"You don't understand. I need to have it done as soon as possible. A client of ours is moving an account, and he wants it sold before the account transfers. I want an exception on this, Ted. Matthew and I have done a lot of business with you guys over the past few years. We'd appreciate an accommodation."

"I wish I could, Morrie. I really do. But it wouldn't be legal. The prospectus for the fund prohibits it."

"Can I sell my client's shares to some other client? As a private placement?"

"It takes an exception up and down the line. I've never seen one go through."

"You're sure?" Morrie asked.

"Absolutely. Get your client to leave it with you until December and redeem it then. We appreciate all that you and Matthew have done with us, but our hands are tied on something like this. OK? Not to change the subject, but have you and Matthew received our invitation to the regional meeting in Atlanta yet? We have box seats for the game between the Falcons and the Panthers. It ought to be a great game."

"No . . . I mean . . . I haven't seen the invitation. I don't think I'll be available. Thanks. Matthew might take you up on it." Morrie hung up and in a sudden burst of anger pounded the top if his desk with his fist. "Damn."

"Something wrong?" Cheryl called from her desk.

"No. Nothing. Sorry."

"Sounded like a big 'nothing' to me. If anything worse comes along let me know in advance will you?"

"Yeah. Yeah." Morrie spun around in his chair and looked out the window. Getting the fund out of Rene's account would be a big first step. With it gone, he could apply the sale proceeds to the margin loan and come up with a strategy for paying off any remaining balance. From his corner office, he could see a bright, sunny weekend was getting underway.

Morrie learned, throughout his life, that he could ignore certain problems and ultimately a solution would work out. He was penniless in graduate school. He made ends meet with partial payments on charge accounts and credit cards. He attacked his first job gunning for a big raise as soon as possible. He shoved his concerns about his debts out of mind and focused on his work.

The McAllister situation could not be pushed aside. He needed to cut his losses, get straight with Matthew, and find a way to enlist his partner's help. Matthew had no way of knowing what was coming. He'd be shocked. Matthew never broke the rules. If anything, the senior partner steered clear of situations that would draw his compassion into conflict with his insistence on the truth and ethical standards. Maybe compassion would win out this time. Matthew might break off the partnership, but better that than an SEC investigation or going into arbitration. Morrie could find a way to continue as an advisor with the firm.

He shuddered at the thought of starting over with a different firm. The days spent telephoning former associates and friends, asking for appointments and a chance to sign them up as clients had been grueling. Once he exhausted the list of people he could call by first name, he moved on to people who were mere acquaintances, persons who might or might not recognize his name and remember him. When that list ran out, he focused on the largest employers in Melville County. Securing a copy of the company directory and opening it at random, he called everyone with the title of vice president or higher. Most terminated the call as soon as he introduced himself.

If he secured an appointment, following up afterwards, if anything, was worse. A prospect might express interest but not agree to open an account during a first meeting. It fell to Morrie to continue to call on a regular basis. The first and second calls were usually well received. The congeniality faded after the second call. Removing a prospect from file meant Morrie flushed all of the time that he had invested. To forge ahead, however, risked straining the relationship—sometimes to the breaking point. Secretaries eventually intervened, politely reeled off excuses for their bosses, making neither encouraging nor discouraging comments to help him with an agenda for the next call.

Morrie's wealth was logged in his book of business. With it, his success was assured. The addition of Matthew's clients would make Morrie one of the top producers in his company. If he lost Matthew's book because of the McAllister situation, he would go back to operating on his own—a solo producer. As a worst case outcome, he would return to banking, perhaps as an account manager for a trust company, where he could use his investment management experience to secure a good salary and title. But he would never again ask himself to start prospecting from square one. Anything but that.

The phone rang. Cheryl answered.

"It's Monica," Cheryl called.

"Just wanted to see if you're doing OK," Monica said. "We didn't talk last night when you came back, and you left so early we didn't get a chance this morning."

"It's a little hard to talk here."

"Did you really mean what you said? I mean . . . about losing your partnership with Matthew . . . maybe even your job."

"I said, 'it's hard to talk about it here. Didn't you hear me? And yes . . . I meant every word. We've never faced anything like this before."

"That'd mean the house or the lake place, Morrie. We can't support two mortgages if you lose this job. It'll be hard enough if you lose the partnership."

"You think I haven't thought about that?"

"No, honey, no. It's just taken time to sink in. I started to worry, and felt like I needed to talk to you . . . ."

"We'll talk when I get home. I'll be early. Nothing's going on here. I decided not to tell Matt anything last night. Better to wait until after the party. Two more days. We can get along until then."

"I'll see you when you get home, then. Do you want lunch here?"

"I'll grab something on the way back. If I can't make it by three, I'll call."

He and Monica had a special ritual for the end of the week. She had a bottle of champagne waiting the evening he returned after making his largest sale ever, a sale that put him into recognition club for the first time. He grinned recalling. Everything was going to come true. He was recovering for the time that he had lost leaving the bank. This would be much better. More independence. No politics. Just hard work. The payoffs were just beginning.

"Penny for your thoughts," Cheryl said from the doorway.

"Wow. You caught me way out there somewhere," Morrie said looking up. "What is it?"

"It's so slow. Would you mind if Louise and I left at lunch for the day? We could put the phone on voice mail."

"No. That's fine. Let the calls come through to me. I'll cover for you."

"You don't need to do that. It makes me feel guilty asking."

"That's OK. It's quiet. The market closes at noon. Go. Have a good weekend."

"Thanks. We can get away a little earlier for the beach. It's going to crowded . . . the freeway . . . I mean . . . leaving town."

"Yeah. A head start'll be good. Ah, Cheryl," Morrie asked. "Remember when we put Rene McAllister into the hedge fund last December? Did she ever come in and sign the agreement?"

"No. She didn't come in. You said you'd arrange for it . . . go to the house to see her. I never gave it another thought. She did sign, didn't she?"

"Yeah, well, I think. Probably have everything in my office file. Just too lazy to look. You never noticed it in their file?"

"Never looked. If you have a signed copy, we need to replace the file copy . . . the one I signed. I don't like doing that . . . ever."

"I'm sure I have it somewhere, and if not, we can still get it. We'd need to back date it, but we can set things right. Forget it. I'll work it out."

"Yeah, jeez, what a start to a long weekend. Thanks for letting us go early. Have a good weekend yourself. I hope the party's a success."

Client associates, the titles held by Louise and Cheryl, were lectured never to sign anything on behalf of a client or an advisor. In practice, however, the rule would occasionally be broken and steps taken after the fact to set the records straight. Delays and bottlenecks in the flow of the paperwork could mean delayed commission payments, missed opportunities in the market and missed tax breaks for a client. Documents that were slipped through usually were less formidable—acceptance of privacy statements, acknowledgement that a prospectus had been received, proxy rights waived, confirmation of trade notices waived, and the like—were almost never checked and never created a problem that could not be easily rectified. A minor correction in the original—whether dividends were to reinvest or not, inclusion of the client's full middle name or some other minor change—and a new agreement could be submitted with instructions to replace whatever placed in file earlier.

Morrie did not want Cheryl to fear for her job. He did not want to fear for his. He would find a way. It could all wait until after the party at the lake.

Chapter 5

The Fourth-of-July dawned, a Friday set to burst forth with sunlight and good times. Matthew pulled on his knee length swimming trunks and bright orange tee shirt, slid into his flip flops, and headed for the dock. The sky was a bright blue, rich with expectations. The sun, barely up on the horizon, cast long shadows across the lawn. In the shade, the last of the night was encapsulated in baubles of dew, and his toes grew cold and wet as he padded toward the beach. The sun would eventually find every droplet and each would glisten brightly before vanishing into the rising heat of the day. In the distance an outboard whined out onto the mirror surface that shimmered with the first intimate minutes of the day.

Matthew was open to whatever the day promised. He was a grateful man. No wishes or plans. Just acceptance of the light and the hour. Far from wealthy—most of his clients had heftier balance sheets than he—his life was more comfortable than he had ever dared to dream. He remembered when he could not pay the bills at the end of the month. Remembered filling out *Pell* grant applications for his children when they were in college. His regrets that he could not help them more.

"What if," Shirley had asked when he announced that he wanted-ed to change jobs and go to work for Stuart, Tompkins and Earl, "I lose my job because my division at Universal American is sold off. And then this doesn't work for you. You'd be in your fifties. Not an easy age to find a new job."

"I'll make a go of it," Matthew replied, concealing his own misgivings. He had tried sales jobs earlier in his career that did not work out. This was different. If all it required was hard work, he'd prevail.

The caterers had set the bar-be-que in place, the additional chairs and tables, the portable bar. He glanced back to see if anything had been overlooked, and then as if impatient with himself, turned back into the sun and looked out over the lake. The years would pass. There'd be fewer surprises. The end of events was imbedded in the opening minutes no matter what the occasion—Fourth-of-July, Christmas, vacation, travel. The same'd be true this weekend. Soon, Shirley and he would be cleaning up after the caterers. The flywheel of the year would have flashed by, igniting the laughter, the reminiscences, the fun and the teasing, and the slower, more deliberate pace would settle back into their lives.

Their children were now parents; he and Shirley, grandparents. Two of Matthew's four children lived in Charles City and were frequent guests at the lake. Lorraine, their oldest, had married Jeff Turner, a successful attorney. Jake, Matthew's first son, married his high school sweetheart and ran a successful insurance agency. Both couples were raising families. Lorraine and Jeff had three children; two sons and a daughter. Jake and Nancy had two sons. The grandchildren ranged in age from 8 to 17, and all loved visiting the lake and water skiing.

His grandchildren faced a world very different from the one he knew as a boy. They needed to mature more quickly. Television, DVD's, iPods, cell phones, text messaging, drugs, video games, were all at work culling one child after another away from the home and parents and into a world where the young lived apart, revered alien influences, and spoke a different language. Technology was the Trojan horse of the generation, entering the home as entertainment, as a gift, and children mastered and cherished it to such an extent that most of their interaction with one another was no longer face-to-face but device-to-device.

He thought about his granddaughter's skimpy bathing suits, low cut jeans, and skirts so short that the act of sitting had to be practiced as if it were part of a gymnast's routine. Perhaps retirement wasn't going to be peaceful after all. Perhaps he would simply be promoted to different responsibilities with limited resources and less clout.

He heard footsteps behind him on the dock. Shirley was walking toward him, her cotton dress flowing along with each step.

"It's been so long since I joined you on one of your early reveries," she said as she approached. A breeze had come up. The water rippled as if eager to break up the light and move the hour toward mid-day. Gulls swooped in the wind over head, calling as they cleaved through the air. "I hope you don't mind company."

"I welcome it." The wind caught her hair and pulled it back as she walked. Her fair skin glowed in the sunlight. Most of her freckles had faded with the years, but the few that remained danced as if in response to the shimmering surface of the lake. She slid under his outstretched arm and put her arm around his waist, hugging him gently and dropping her head against his shoulder. "We've a big day ahead," he finally said.

"Looking forward to it?" she asked.

"Oh, yes. But not like I once did."

"How's that?"

"Hard to say. The day's always been special to me, from the time my brother and I were kids in Iowa and had our own stash of fire works to shoot off . . . and now . . . now that we're here together . . . after all these years. It is a cumulative thing. A summing up. But there's less and less that's new each year. Tomorrow, I'll be out here. The big party'll be over. Friends will have left. Some we won't see for another year. Some, maybe, never again. And our life will go on."

"That's bad?"

"Oh, no. I love our life. The pace and the tempo of it. The rituals we've built into every week . . . every day. We're lucky."

"I know. We have a good life. I'm grateful."

"I find myself sort of detaching, in spite of myself. I see others . . . younger people like Morrie and Monica . . . or our children with their families . . . see them struggling with the problems we faced. The problems may have a different face on them now, but they were the same that all of us took on. What we lacked in wisdom we made up for with stamina."

"So you've been thinking about our grandchildren?"

"Of course. I don't know what my own role is with regard to them. I never had grandparents. I don't know from my experience what is valuable to children and what, God help me, is just sermonizing. Last night, as I was dropping off to sleep, I remembered how my father tried to talk to me, when I was young and thought I had all the resources in the world at my command . . . including unlimited time. I saw him as a tired old man preaching about things that had no more relevance to me than knickers and spats. I don't want to impose my views on my children . . . or grandchildren. But I want what I've learned from my life to be valuable to them. I want to be more than just a loving old Grampa who doesn't understand the world any more."

"Why are you thinking that way? Our children adore you. It may seem that they are not listening to you . . . but is probably because they want you to see and hear what they have found out . . . what they have achieved."

"Yeah. Well. I want to know that I'm needed . . . it's my nature."

"Whoever would have thought?" She hugged him again. "Think back. What things made you feel closest to your father. Things that convince you now, years later, that he cared for you and loved you. I'll bet the list gets pretty long before you get to anything that he tried to tell you."

"We flew a kite together one Wednesday on his afternoon off. Just the two of us. Out in the country in a meadow. The kite we bought at the dime store wouldn't fly, and he got us back into the car, drove us to the lumber yard, bought two dowel sticks, and we went home and made a new kite out of newspaper. 'I can damn well make a kite that will fly,' he said. We mixed our own paste from flour and water. It was wonderful. We went back out to the field, and it flew so high that all the string spooled off into the sky. I can see it so clearly to this day." Matthew turned to Shirley. "How come you know all these things, and I am so little help to myself?"

"You're just one damn lucky guy, that's all."

"I am that."

A wake from a boat rolled steadily toward the dock and slapped against the swimming ladder and the pilings. His own Boston Whaler raised up at the bow as the swells passed along its keel and then sloshed back down into the water as the waves heaved up the stern of the craft.

"You know I value your perspective on everything," Shirley said. "You see me as clearly as I see you. And I know I have my blind spots. Give yourself a little more credit. You're not troubled are you . . . about things?"

"No. Not really. Retirement, maybe. A little. I'm all through in less than six months. That's it. No more income . . . just social security for the rest of our lives. We need to live on what we've saved. Like pushing off from the dock. We'll need to get by with what's in the boat because our stores will not be replenished along the way."

"But you've been so positive."

"I know. And we've accumulated a lot. More than I ever dreamed. I just don't ever want to see the days when I had to count pennies . . . when I couldn't afford to fix the handle on the refrigerator door. Remember? We opened it with a screwdriver. You went to a Laundromat because we couldn't afford to fix the washer. I don't want to run out of resources when I'm the least capable of doing anything about it."

"I think you're getting way ahead of events," Shirley reached up to stroke the back of his head. "Let's go back up to the house now and let matters take their own course for a couple of days. These things get solved sometimes without any interference from us. You know, the Christian Science school of retirement financial planning."

He laughed. Shirley was better than he in letting events reveal more practical solutions to the challenges of the day. "You are the most assertive man I have ever met," she often reminded him. "Can't you hold back a little? Moving too quickly sometimes makes matters worse than if you left them alone." He hugged her, and putting his hand on her shoulder, turned her toward the shore.

"I should've had the boat tuned up. I hope it holds up for everyone." They walked slowly up the dock toward the shore. Matthew could feel the cotton in Shirley's dress catch the heat, almost as if it had been freshly pressed.

"Oh look, there's Mitch," Shirley said suddenly. "Yoo-hoo," she shouted to their friend who was standing on their deck. The people staying with them were perennial guests, as comfortable as in their own home. Nestled into the same bedrooms every year, they minimized hosting duties by helping themselves to whatever they could find in the kitchen and the liquor cabinet.

Mitch and Jeanette Krueger had arrived after dark the previous evening. Tired from their drive from Washington, DC, they visited only briefly with their hosts before retiring. "Yoo-hoo yourself," Mitch shouted back. "What are you two love birds doing out this early in the morning?"

"Early?" Matthew responded. "Hell, it's almost seven-thirty. You said you wanted to sleep late."

"Too damn quiet. There's so much traffic noise in our Georgetown apartment, it blocks out my own thoughts so I can sleep. Good morning, darlin'," Mitch greeted Shirley as she climbed up to the deck.

"Good morning, darlin'," Matthew mimicked and stepped forward as if to kiss Mitch. Mitch stepped back laughing.

"Jeanette must've loved the quiet," Mitch said. "She was dead away when I left the room."

"You're early for brunch. Did you get any breakfast?" Shirley asked.

"In the kitchen. The coffee was on. I had a bagel. That's all I need for now."

"Good, because you and I are headed for the Country Club. You won't break 100 if you get into the *Bloody Marys* too early. I'm going up to change. Let's be on our way by 8:15. OK?"

"Fine by me," Mitch said. "I'm ready when you are."

The rest of the day rolled by as if it had been choreographed. The caterers arrived. Brunch was served until nearly noon as guests continued to arrive, eat, and change into recreational clothing, whether for tennis, golf, or water sports. Andrew Sherman and Jason Clay showed up at their appointed hour as ski boat pilots for anyone who cared to go for a turn. The crowd attending were either Matthew and Shirley peers, in their mid-fifties and older, or they were contemporaries of Monica and Morrie Clay, in their late thirties and forties who still had families at home and were in mid-career professionally. All were clients of the Clay-Wirth group. The older group settled for golf and tennis at the country club, while a few of the men took a turn at water skiing. Those who tried, blubbery and pale, hair matted dark and dripping from their pink chests and legs, lunged back on board after taking a turn, and gasped for air under a barrage of jibes about their performance. Wet and rumpled, upon regaining footing, each dove for the beer cooler and joined others on board in goading the next victim into the water—anything to deflect attention away from the recognition that they were—everyone of them—becoming old men.

"I haven't done this since last year," was one excuse. "I'm not in shape," was another—a conclusion everyone on board had reached without benefit of a testimonial.

"That's the last goddman time I'm ever going to do that. I shouldn't have tried it this year."

"This boat's too slow to pull a man my size. I kept sinking down into the water, couldn't keep the tips up. It needs to go faster so you'd plane . . . you know . . . hydroplane . . . and it'd been easier on my back. Jesus!"

The younger group scheduled either tennis or golf and departed early to take advantage of the court and tee times. The older women frequently paired with a younger partner for matched doubles at tennis or made up their own golf foursomes.

Tennis players and golfers, upon returning to the Wirth residence in mid-afternoon, changed into beach wear, downed a beer, a gin-and-tonic, or a *Bloody Mary*, and headed for dockside where the jet skis were moored. A competitive auction for the next turn finally resulted in a time limit per turn. The limit, predictably, was ignored by participants who stretched their rides for a longer period of time depending upon how much beer they had consumed before taking over the controls. Some of the women joined in. (Monica Clay having the best figure and greatest legs of the group—a consensus). The competition would last until the cocktail hour, an arbitrary milepost in day, as the bar had been open since noon.

The water skiers were spent. The jet skis were returned to their berth hoists and raised out of the water for the night. The aroma of roasting pork and beef bar-be-que mingled with the scent of hickory smoke and drifted through the long shadows on lawn setting appetites on edge. For nearly an hour, the house fell quiet. Everyone had retired to their bedrooms to change into evening wear. Most napped to recapture good drinking form. Some, intoxicated or exhausted, proved difficult to revive, exasperating their spouses.

"Morrie," Monica prodded, "Morrie, get up! Get dressed! We're going to be late. Our own guests finished in the bathroom. They'll be leaving without us. Get up!"

"Aw, God. What a fucking charade. How do you do it? We're standing at the edge of disaster, and you carry on as if nothing's wrong."

"There's no other choice. Forget it for now. Come on. Please, Morrie, these are your clients and our guests. You can't lie around feeling sorry for yourself. Get dressed."

Morrie had pulled off his swimming trunks upon entering the bedroom an hour earlier, flopped face first on the bed, and dropped immediately to sleep. He sat up now and suddenly became aware of his nakedness. "Shit," he muttered, picked up his wet trunks, and waddled into the bathroom. Sleep had not sobered him.

"I'm not going to shower," he yelled through the closed door. "I need to dry my hair though." He looked into the mirror above the basins and ran his hand through his damp, tangled hair.

"Good. We don't have time."

"What?"

"Good. I said, good!"

"Good what?"

"Good you aren't taking a shower."

"Oh. OK!" Morrie opened the cabinet door below the basin, retrieved the hair dryer, groped for the plug on the end of the cord, and jabbed it into an outlet. The dryer roared instantly to life, startling Morrie. Monica, as usual, had not turned it off with the switch on the handle when she had last used it. He fumbled with one hand for a hair brush, and finally locating one, was relieved to see that it was actually his. Still nude, he raised the roaring dryer to his head and jammed the brush into his matted hair.

"Fuck," he thought looking at himself, tall and gangly, chest somewhat sunken, shoulders rounded, belly sagging, a roll just above his penis. There was no boy left in the man. No sir. He was looking at a beaten up, defeated middle-aged guy. Truth will out, and it was coming out on him. Coming out too damn soon. Maybe as soon as tomorrow. Maybe tonight. No, not tonight.

Tonight, do as Monica does. Pretend nothing is wrong. Nothing is wrong. Just like the years before when everything was OK. Just a year ago. Just one short year ago. He turned off the dryer. His hair was as dry as it was going to be. Stop thinking about things. Go to the party. Face Matthew and McAllister and his wife. He shook his head. He could do that. He could do that because he had no other choice.

"Are you done in there?" Monica shouted.

"Yes. Yes, I'm done." Still naked, he walked back into the bedroom. He looked at Monica. "You look so beautiful," he said. "You've always looked like the prettiest woman to me . . . always."

"OK. OK. You look beautiful too, but put on some clothes. Come on." She led him by the arm to his dresser, picked up a pair of freshly folded boxers and handed them to him. "Here. Now, please, hurry. I want to help Shirley as a co-hostess."

Morrie toppled forward attempting to pull on his shorts and grabbed the dresser to catch himself. "You go ahead, then. I'll be right behind you." he said.

"No. We're going together. Sit on the bed. What do you want to wear . . . those new linen shorts with the madras shirt . . . nice and cool? Your Birkenstocks?"

"My Docksiders."

"Too homely. Feet look white as milk in them."

"Birkenstocks don't hide feet any better."

"OK. Just, please, hurry."

Monica looked Morrie over one more time before leading him out of the bedroom. When she reached up to smooth several strands into place, Morrie decided that she was trying to kiss him, and he leaned forward puckering his lips.

"You're impossible," Monica said.

Outside, the late afternoon breeze washed over him, and Morrie felt better. A mockingbird at the far end of the deck waxed into song, a virtuoso improvisation that followed them across the front of the Sherman house toward the crowd mingling in the cloud of laughter on the deck of the Wirth home.

Chapter 6

The cocktail hour, like most, was a loosely organized affair. Couples appeared at the deck of the Wirth home, were greeted, shook hands with those they had not met earlier in the day, chided and were chided in return about their exploits on the golf course, tennis courts, or on the water, melted into the mix of company already present, ordered drinks, and drifted from one conversation to another, occasionally stopping to graze the spread of *hors d'oeuvres*. The aroma of beef and pork roasting at the bar-be-que whetted the most reluctant appetite. Few joined the festivities completely sober. Many napped only long enough to give their digestive systems enough time to process the afternoon intake and establish the confidence that they could partake of more without getting into trouble. Laughter drowned out the music Matthew piped out to the deck. A crescendo of jumbled conversation swamped neighboring yards and rolled across the lake.

Women wore soft colorful summer evening dresses. Men had changed into short sleeve shirts, unbuttoned to the chest, and pleated, belted walking shorts, their bare feet stuffed into loafers. With the area softly lighted, several recesses of the deck and yard became nearly dark as the evening progressed, creating the illusion of privacy in what otherwise was an auction for listeners and attention. Matthew reveled in the hubbub.

"I'd love to run out of gin, just once," he said. "Come on . . . drink up."

"If you guys don't finish the shrimp and the mushroom caps, I'm giving everyone a doggy bag when you leave."

"I've seen you at the bar only once all night. You can't nurse that all evening."

Matthew spent a few minutes with each guest and moved on. Shirley was also circulating, a gracious foil to her husband. "Ignore him. He carded a birdie today. He'll be insufferable for the next several days."

Morrie and Monica drifted from couple to couple as well, occasionally introducing people to one another, but for the most part, content to get a conversation started in a group and then move on to other guests.

"You going to continue this tradition once he retires?" a guest asked Morrie.

"I guess. I hadn't thought it about it. Yes. Sure I am," then glancing at Monica, "*we* will. At our place though," Morrie said nodding toward their home two doors down.

From one clutch of guests to the next, conversations buzzed about the vandalism to Tom Sherman's Boxter. "Who do you think did it, Tom?" one guest asked.

"No idea. Whoever it was, they were very careful. No prints turned up that didn't belong to anyone other than our family."

"Maybe one of them did it," a listener said. "Just kidding."

"I wouldn't rule it out," Joyce said under her breath.

"What was that?" another in the circle asked.

"Nothing," Joyce said smiling. "We have an adult delinquent in the house, but I don't think he'd be capable of this. It'd require too much effort." She raised her gin-and-tonic to her lips. Sherman downed the last of his drink, grabbed Joyce's upper arm, and began pulling her toward the edge of the crowd.

"Perhaps," he whispered, "we can leave our domestic troubles at home. Do you mind? Have you had too much to drink? You need to eat something. You need something in your stomach right away."

"Let go of me." Joyce pulled away. "I'm fine."

"This is no place . . ."

"I know. It's no place to talk about *your* son. Don't lecture me." Others around them stopped talking and began looking at them. "I'm sorry. I just . . . I just get so frustrated."

"Let's get something to eat. Some shrimp, or wings."

"Tom, please, you're patronizing me. You eat if you want. I see Monica. I'm going to visit with her." Joyce raised her hand to get Monica's attention and weaved her way through the crowd toward her neighbor.

"Matthew, you need to stop running everything for people," Shirley cooed sidling up to her husband. "Your party is huge a success. You don't need to be shepherding every conversation. People'll have more fun."

"I'm not *shepherding* anything."

"You are! And you have been all evening long, dispatching this couple to the bar, someone else to the *hors d'oeuvres*, steering people around the deck . . ."

"I always do those things."

"I know, dear. And I wish like fury I'd said something years ago."

"So I'm not the Fezzywig of whom you are so fond after all."

"Just back off a little. Everyone'll enjoy you much more if you do."

"OK," Matthew said, but as he turned to go, Mac McAllister emerged from the crowd.

"Shirl! Shirl. I have somebody I want you to meet," McAllister called.

Shirley turned to see McAllister leading a young, dark haired woman toward her and noticed immediately how attractive she was—slim, tanned, silken shoulders and arms, dark eyes, an engaging smile. She had to be at least fifteen years younger than Mac.

"Shirley . . . Matthew . . . may I present Ms. Denise Becker," McAllister said. "Your hostess, my dear, the esteemed Mrs. Shirley Wirth, the queen of Pelican Bay society."

"Welcome, Denise," Shirley beamed and extended her hand.

"Shirley, I've heard so much about you and your husband from Mac. I'm delighted to meet you. I didn't want to believe Mac that it would be OK for me to drop in on your party uninvited like this, but he insisted."

"As he should have," Shirley said. "Mac's a charter guest. Almost a co-host. You couldn't be more welcome. Have you met Matthew, my husband?"

"Yes, we met at the country club just the other day. Good to see you again," Matthew said and extended his hand, grasped Denise's just long enough to feel how soft her palm was and then glanced up to see McAllister grinning broadly at him.

"Denise moved to Charles City in February," McAllister said, "to take the position of president of the domestic products division of Southern World Textiles. We met when she accepted a position on the Arts Council board."

"So you're finding your way around our city?" Shirley asked.

"Oh, yes. I lived in Chicago most of my life and have always

heard about southern hospitality, but never experienced it first hand
. . . other than a few business trips," Denise smiled. "It's been so
easy to get to know people."

"Not like Chicago then?" Matthew asked.

"Well, comparisons are odious," Denise laughed. "Let's just say
. . . different. Chicagoans have their own special charm," she said
smiling and reached out to touch Matthew's arm.

"Let me add to my wife's welcome. We're glad you're here and
have a chance to meet our friends. Have we missed meeting your
husband?" Matthew asked.

"No. Well . . . I mean . . . yes. You have missed meeting him."

"That's because he isn't here," McAllister laughed.

Denise reached out and touched McAllister on the arm to acknowledge her amusement but also, as Matthew preferred to think,
to silence him. "The move here hasn't worked out as well for him as
it has for me. We've separated, and he's negotiating with his company to return to his old position in Chicago."

"I'm sorry," Shirley said. "Is it going to work out for you . . .
either of you?"

"I'm afraid not. We've been married eleven years, but no children,
and . . .well . . . it's just another one of those things. Irreconcilable
differences. That's the phrase isn't it?"

"So I've heard," Matthew said.

"Come on, we have others to meet. You can share your life
history with Shirl some other time," McAllister said. "Let's have
some fun." He tugged Denise's bare upper arm and headed toward
another group of guests.

"Nice meeting you," Denise said turning back and smiling at
Shirley.

"You, too, Denise." Shirley waved. "Now . . . what was that all about?" she asked Matthew.

"Damned if I know."

"You and I both know that Mac and Rene have been having trouble for years. What's Mac up to?"

"Another one of Mac's things."

"Mac's things?"

"Well, he has . . . ah . . . infatuations from time to time." Matthew cleared his throat. "I don't think anything ever comes of them. He likes to flirt."

"He's not having an affair with her?" Shirley asked.

"It's not his style. He likes to flirt. Some guys call it 'snake handling.'"

"Must make Rene furious. If I ever caught you *flirting!* My God, this is public enough."

"I'd think being so out in the open would dispel any rumors. Don't people usually try to keep affairs secret?"

"He's flaunting her!"

"Eye of the beholder." Matthew shrugged.

"He stops just short of pawing her, and I don't see her discouraging him. With Rene right here! The man's a boor!"

"He's used to having his own way, and he's not above doing something to provoke Rene. He's probably settling some score with her that we don't know anything about."

"You don't approve of the way he carries on, do you?"

"Not my place. Do I approve? No. Am I offended? Maybe . . . a little, mostly because he takes my silence as approval . . . or perhaps admiration. He's grandiose enough to think that every man in the room would rather be in his shoes when he has a beautiful young woman on his arm."

"And that doesn't bother you?"

"My opinion doesn't matter. I won't see him much of him now that he's moving his account. I was the one who initiated all along, and guess what," Matthew laughed, "I always picked up the tab. Now, let's drop it. We should be getting the dinner underway."

The warm yellow light of the setting sun flooded the corridors between the lakeside homes. The shadows from the shrubbery and trees deepened, and the darkened water of the lake glittered with reflected light from the eastern sky that was still aglow as the day faded.

"Everybody! Listen please!" Matthew shouted. "Find a place for your drinks. My chef advises that all is ready. So please . . . grab a plate and get in line. You know the routine." Few were willing to break off their conversations as abruptly as he wished. Matthew called, "OK, everyone," several times to no effect, and then he walked over the a group close to the serving tables and steered them toward the serving line. Others lined up slowly, most conversations continuing unabated as plates were heaped with steaming beef and pork smothered in sauce, corn-on-the-cob dripping with butter, po-tato salad, three-bean-salad, hot pork-and-beans, cold slaw, chips, salsa, biscuits, and wedges of melon. Male guests loaded their plates as if they resented the distraction; and women, equally distracted, picked judiciously among the offerings.

"God, Matthew, are you sure you have enough here?" one guest quipped.

"If not, we'll send out for more."

"I'll never find room. It all looks so good." The line inched down the long table and attracted stragglers until all the guests broke free of the queue and returned with their loaded plates to the tables where their drinks awaited.

"We have wine," Matthew called out, "if you're tired of your drinks, just set them aside. The caterer's people will be coming around with the wine." The rumble of conversation ebbed as guests began to eat.

The lake remained choppy with wakes from the pleasure boats, and although the temperature had dropped several degrees from the afternoon high, skiers were still skimming across the water, jumping wakes, throwing up silvery curtains as they made deep slalom turns in the water. Rooster tails from the scores of jet skis charging in and out of the mix shot up like pearls tossed into the evening light.

Mac McAllister, after making the rounds with Denise Becker, had trouble finding his wife. He finally spotted Rene emerging from the house with her friend Skinner Thorpe. "Hold my place," McAllister said to Denise and walked over to Rene and Skinner.

"I'm holding a place in line for you," he said. "Skinner, care to join us?"

"Us? Meaning whom exactly?" Skinner asked.

"Rene and me."

"The two of you?"

"Yes. And Denise Becker. She's holding our place in line."

"You've invited her?" Rene asked.

"I want the two of you to get to know one another. She's new in town. I want her to become better acquainted with everyone."

"Mission accomplished, I'd say," Skinner said smiling at Rene.

"You go ahead," Rene said. "I'm not hungry. Skinner and I'll pick our way through later." Rene said.

"OK." McAllister could see that Rene was drunk. She was probably angry that he had spent so much time with Denise. He knew that they would fight later, perhaps just before bed, but if not then, in the morning, hung over and full of loathing for one another, and he rehearsed his come-backs quietly to himself, amused with what he envisioned as his master stroke, "But you told me to go ahead and eat with her. You said that's what you wanted." He turned and walked back to Denise. Her dark hair shone softly in the dusky light. She glided, he thought. Her legs tapered as if they bore no weight at all. Her dress hugged her butt, firm like a girl's, and he wanted to slide his hand slowly down the small of her back, past her waist to the top of her ass. Her husband had to be a fool for leaving her. The job could not have been the only trouble between them. She was probably a pistol in bed with demands that he couldn't deliver. The thought of her stepping out of her dress, letting it drop to her ankles and then sliding her half-slip over her thighs excited him. He smiled as he approached knowing she knew nothing of his thoughts.

Chapter 7

The fireworks display, sponsored by Heron Lake Township, became more spectacular every year. Launched from a barge in the middle of the lake, the rockets and aerial display bombs lit the dark sky so brilliantly at times that the entire lake and the shoreline were illuminated. For the Wirth party, the half-hour pyrotechnics became a turning point of the evening, calling all guests and their hosts back together to share the spectacle. Couples took their seats in the chairs on the dock. Some sat on the benches in the Wirth 26-foot Boston Whaler and the Sherman speed boat that were tethered dockside. Others, content to remain on shore, sat on the lawn or folding chairs. The show provided a second-wind to the festivities, giving those who had any distance to drive home a chance to sober up.

Matthew, anticipating the end of the show, returned to the deck to make certain coffee and other refreshments were ready. "Fresh coffee," he shouted as the first returned. The crowd would be reduced by more than half. Only those who lived within walking distance or were house guests of others nearby would linger. Shirley positioned herself near the driveway to bid good-bye to everyone making their way to the cars.

The guests who remained settled into chairs on the deck. The evening had cooled. The bar was self-service, the caterer taking advantage of the fireworks display to clean up and depart. Several of men queued up to refresh their own drinks and their partner's. Conversations became less in earnest.

The younger guests converged around Morrie and Monica Clay. Morrie turned up the volume on the stereo so the couples could dance and soon several were shagging to beach music that was popular when they were in college. As the sound of their fun increased in the cooler evening air, older members of the party drifted into the spacious Wirth home for the relative quiet it afforded.

"It's a damn good thing that we're all neighbors," Tom Sherman said laughing into his drink. "I'd hate like hell to be lying in my bed listening to this racket." The lake was still. Lights from the opposite shore reflected in the glassy surface. A few running lights were wending across the inky dark—late revelers on pontoon boats or cruisers taking advantage of the calm. Smoke from the fireworks display drifted slowly toward the beach and with it, the acrid odor of cordite.

"I think I'll ask them to play some slower stuff?" Tom Sherman finally said. "I never could shag . . . or whatever the hell it's called. You don't have time for that kind of thing in med school."

"There's plenty of other stuff in the CD rack," Matthew said.

Taking Joyce by the hand, Tom walked out onto the deck. "What'd ya say we try a little slow dancing for a change," he shouted. Moments later, the strains of *Strangers in the Night* floated across the deck. Frank Sinatra's honeyed baritone seemed more romantic to Sherman than he had ever heard before, and he was pleased that the younger couples appeared to enjoy the slower tempo. Mac glided by and winked at him. Tom noticed he was holding Denise Becker very close, his hand in the small of her back. After all the trouble the last couple of days—the vandalism to his car, the police, and Jamie—Tom was glad to be holding Joyce, feeling her close, and letting his feelings drift off with the music into the night.

Skinner Thorpe could tell that Rene McAllister was in trouble the moment she saw her friend stumble into the kitchen. Rene braced herself against the counter and then lurched toward the back door. Her eyes met Skinner's. "Oh, God," Rene said holding back the tears. "Oh God, Skinner. This is so horrible. So fucking awful!"

Skinner stepped up and caught Rene. "Everything will look better in the morning, dearie. You know it will," she said in her whiskey hoarse voice, realizing she was feeling more anger than compassion for her drunken friend. "You need to go home now, dear. Can I help you go home?"

"I jus' need some air. I'm jus' going outside to get some air. I'll be all right."

"You're sure?"

"Yes, I'm sure. Don't make a scene, God damn it! Jus' let me be." Skinner released her, and Rene drew a deep breath, stepped a little too deliberately toward the back door, and slumped out into the night. The damp night air folded in around her, and with it, the quiet. So quiet. All of a sudden. So cool. So very cool. "I'll jus' follow those little lights," she said looking down the narrow concrete walk that threaded through the backyards of the neighborhood. She laughed remembering that they were the same lights over which the homeowners had argued one summer.

"I'll jus' follow the little lights to my own house," she muttered once more. That silly Sherman woman thought they'd attract prowlers. "Right. Fucking prowlers always like to see their way. Ha! Prowlers! Shit!" She stumbled. "Gotta get hold of myself." She had lost her sense of direction. She looked about. "Now that's the

Wirth place," she said, and turning, "and that's Sherman's God-awful place. So the path's got to be back there." She lost her balance and tumbled forward, and catching herself with her hands, ended up kneeling on the grass. "Fuck. Can I be that goddman drunk? I should go down to the dock. I could get some air there. Out on the water. It's quiet. Cooler. I can find that."

Rene got to her feet slowly, steadied herself until she got her bearings, then staggering, made her way between the houses until she reached the lawn in front of the Sherman home. The Sherman dock lay another thirty yards in the shadows ahead of her. Exertion drew fresh air into her lungs. Her head cleared somewhat. She could see the steps to the dock and heard water lapping on the beach. "So different now," she whispered. Away from everybody. So damn tiresome. Mac jus' loves it. Loves the parties. And the lovely Denise. Poor Denise! Making a perfect ass out of herself letting Mac show her around like that.

"Summer's half over," she had heard Mac whisper to Denise. Why the whisper? What did he mean by that? Summer's half over. Summer's half over. Meant something. Half? Half of what? Summer? Too late in the evening for small talk. That meant something to Denise. The party? The party was half over? They're going to meet afterwards? Of course. Mac and Denise are gonna meet. It was in his voice. There's no point in saying 'Summer's half over' when he said it. No point at all. Mac's clever. The asshole. 'Half over.' What time was it then? She turned back to the light to look at her watch. 11:46.

At the edge of the grass, Rene stopped and looked at the steps that she had to negotiate to get up on to the dock. "Easy," she said under her breath and placed one foot on the first step to the dock, took a breath, and pulled herself up onto the structure. "Better watch my step," she said. "Ha! In more ways than one!" She laughed and lurched forward, struggling to maintain her balance, down the length of the dock. The night was clear. No moon. Across the bay, she could make out the lights on the docks almost a mile away. Late fireworks were still being launched from the opposite shore. "This is what everyone wants," she said opening up her arms as if to present the lake and all the homes around it to the stars. "Ha! Just as much a hell here as anywhere. Only it costs more." She looked down at the inky water.

During the years leading up to Mac's retirement, Rene tried to plan how they would spend the their time once he quit work. Mac never took much interest in her ideas. They went to Europe, not once but several times. They made trips to South America, the Caribbean; she even suggested a tour of the Orient. Mac never objected to any of the excursions but he was never enthusiastic. When they returned home, he went back to the routines he adopted shortly after retiring from Maplethorp Corporation. He played golf three times a week and hung out in the clubhouse with his pals. He had board meetings to attend. Telephone calls were coming into the house at all hours. His daily life spun along with its own momentum. If she fit in along the way, he was gracious and generous. If she chose to remain on the sidelines, he was equally understanding. Never a complaint. Never a fight. Life with Mac grew to be monotonous and bland. Disappointment cascaded through her like ice.

"Rene? Rene, is that you?" A woman's voice called out from behind her.

"Yes? Who is it?" Rene heard footsteps approaching on the wooden dock. A figure was silhouetted against the faint light spilling out on to the lawn of the Sherman home.

"Monica. Monica Clay. Are you all right? I saw you fall."

"Yes. Yes, I'm fine. Please, don' bother. You shouldn't trouble yourself. Don' take yourself away from the party for my sake. Go back. I won't be long."

"I want to talk to you, please, Rene. It's important."

"In the morning! I'm only sober enough to know I don' wan' to talk to anybody."

"No, please. It's so hard to find the privacy." Monica came to a stop an arms length away from Rene.

"I jus' wan' to be alone."

"It's about Morrie and Matthew."

"I don' care. I'm tired of caring about other people."

"Morrie said you're going to move your account to another advisory firm. Is that true?"

"I don' think Mac's said anything like that to either Morrie . . . or Matthew."

"No. No. Morrie said you didn't like working with him, and since Matthew was going to retire, you wanted to move the business. Please, I'm imploring you to give Morrie a chance. I don't know why you would think of him as less than absolutely trustworthy and competent, but I assure you he is good . . . very, very good at what he does. Matthew would never have kept him on if he wasn't."

"It's none of your business. It's our money . . . Mac's and mine. You shouldn't be talking to me about this. It doesn't concern you."

"But it does, Rene. More than you know. We've worked so hard . . . Morrie and I . . . to fit in and be a part of things. Morrie's dedicated himself to making things better for me and the children. He doesn't deserve this."

"Our account can' be the only one Matthew and Morrie handle. It can' be that important. You weren't supposed to know. I don' want to talk about it."

"I know you don't. And it's humiliating for me to come to you like this. Look at me . . . I'm begging you. Please, Rene, surely there's something I can say . . . or promise . . . that'll help you change your mind. Isn't there anything . . . "

"No. There's nothing. I don' trust the whispering and laughing behind my back. Matthew's weaseled his way into Mac's confidence, and your husband is jus' riding on his coattails. They wan' to throw my money around like so much garbage to be picked up and hauled off. I know what's mine. Your husband and Matthew shouldn't have tried to interfere with things. They should jus' butt out."

"Won't you at least consider waiting until the end of the year. It'd make such a big difference. This'll crush Morrie's chances for a bonus. Another six months. Is that asking too much?"

"This is not . . . not my problem.. Now, if you won' leave, I'm going." Rene lunged forward and tried to step around Monica. Monica reached out to grab her arm, but Rene recoiled from her grasp and tripped. "Oh!" Rene's breath left her as she pitched sideways into the black water.

Monica knew the depth of the water. Rene was in over her head. Inebriated and weighed down by her dress, Rene would not be able to swim to shore. Her only hope was to swim back within reach of the dock. Monica looked around frantically for a life jacket or float cushion. The Sherman speed boat had been tied up to the Wirth dock. Nobody had brought it back from the afternoon activities. Jamie's fishing boat was not there. She turned to run back to the Wirth home recognizing that if she called out her cries would not be heard over the music playing on the deck. She took off at a run but stopped abruptly when she spotted an oar lying to one side of the dock.

She grabbed the oar and rushed back to Rene who had gone under. "Oh, my God. Oh my God," Monica yelled. Minutes seemed to pass before Rene, head and shoulders, broke back to the surface thrashing wildly, gasping for air. Monica held the oar out to Rene, but once extended, Monica did not have the leverage to support it, and it fell, striking Rene sharply on the head above one eye. Rene sank back under the surface. "Grab hold!" Monica cried. She could not to run back to the Wirth home for help now. There wasn't time. Rene was going under for a second time. Monica would only have one more chance to rescue her. She thought of jumping into the water herself, but Rene thrashed so violently when she broke the surface that Monica was afraid that Rene would pull her down as well.

"Drunken bitch," Monica cursed under her breath straining again to extend the oar to where she expected Rene to emerge. The dim swirling of her Rene's dress was all that Monica could see in the dark water. That expensive dress! That heartless, selfish woman! "I'm watching her drown. There's nothing I can do. I can't get to the house and back here in time." Her thoughts raced.

Rene surged to the surface again. Monica swung the oar to her and Rene hit it with one arm as she struggled to swim, and then pushed it away. Fighting the oar, Rene floundered and went under for a third time. Unwieldy as it was, the oar was Monica's only hope. She probed to the depth of a foot or more hoping to find Rene. Something bumped against the oar. Rene! Monica pushed down on the oar hoping that Rene would grab hold.

"Grab on! Grab on!" Monica yelled. Rene had not taken hold. The water calmed. She felt Rene again. The oar stopped hard against Rene's body. Monica nudged the oar, just enough to keep Rene from returning to the surface, and Rene sank away. Probing several times more, Monica felt nothing. Rene was not going to surface again. Monica looked around.

Nobody in sight. Not a sound of anyone near. Rene's accident had saved her, had saved Morrie, had saved everything. Nothing would change. She would wait a few more minutes. Wipe the oar of finger prints! Then run to the Wirth home and deliver the alarm. She pulled the oar out of the water, wiped it with a handkerchief and laid it down where she had found it. There'd be questions. What had she done to save Rene? Why didn't she come for help sooner? Questions pummeled her thoughts like a hail stones. It'd be better to leave things as they were. Just leave. Make certain nobody saw her and go back to the party as if nothing had happened.

The sound of an approaching outboard pierced the silence. In the distance, dim red and green running lights were heading directly for her. "Jamie!" she thought, "coming in from fishing." She dashed off the dock and sprinted to her home next door. Once there, she turned and watched Jamie tie up at the dock. He packed his gear under the seat of the boat and stepped onto the dock. He noticed nothing amiss. Just Jamie, returning from his usual excursion out onto the lake to fish. He stopped briefly as if he was considering joining the party on the Wirth deck. Monica held her breath. Then he turned and continued on his way to the Sherman house. The screen door slammed as he entered the porch.

When Monica reentered the Wirth home by the kitchen door, she found Mac McAllister and Skinner Thorpe eye-ball-to-eye-ball in an argument.

"All I asked was 'Have you seen Rene?' for Chrissake," Mac roared.

Skinner, always delighted with the anger of others but especially when she was the cause, snapped back, "And all I said was 'she left here over half-an-hour ago to get some air, and I don't know where she went.'"

"You don't think she'd try to walk home from here? This dark. It's nearly three-quarters-a-mile."

"Mac. She said she was going to get some air. My impression was she'd come back to the house here."

"Was she drunk?"

"Plastered. Could barely stand."

"And you let her go out. Jesus, Skinner, you're some kind of friend."

"You're concerned? How utterly intriguing. I didn't see much of that throughout the day." Skinner paused. "I offered to go with her. She didn't want me to. She insisted."

Mac turned suddenly and confronted Monica as she was trying to slip by the pair and into the dining area to join others. "You been outside?" he demanded.

"Yes."

"Did you see Rene?"

"Yes. Briefly."

"Where was she? How long ago?"

"In front . . . of the Sherman house. Maybe a half-an-hour ago. I saw her in the yard between the two houses. She fell. I went out to see if she was OK."

"And?"

"She was just terribly, terribly drunk and told me that she wanted to be left alone." Monica could see that Mac believed her. Her pulse raced. She wanted to take a deep breath, but she steadied herself. "She hasn't come back yet?" Monica asked nonchalantly turning to Skinner.

"No, God damn it, and it's time to head for home," McAllister said. "I'm going to check upstairs. She might have gone up there and passed out." Skinner returned Monica's gaze and shrugged her shoulders.

"Where have you been?" Morrie asked when Monica found him. "I've been looking all over for you."

"Just outside for a minute. I went back to the house to check on a few things. How much longer do you think we need to stay? I'm tired."

"Let's see our guests off, and call it a night."

McAllister returned from checking the bedrooms, walked out onto the deck, and announced that Rene was missing and asked for everyone to help search for her. "She's probably outside of the house here somewhere. If everyone would take a couple of minutes and look around with me, I'd sure appreciate it."

Several couples broke off to join in the search, and walking directly from the deck into the yard, strolled down to the lake shore to look for the missing woman.

When the search of the immediate neighborhood produced nothing, Joyce went to see if Rene had gone next door to the their house since earlier in the afternoon she had made their bathrooms available to the guests at the party. She entered the kitchen and found Jamie making a sandwich from an array of food and condiments that he had taken from the refrigerator.

"Please pick up after yourself," she said, choosing neither to stop nor look at him.

"You guys down at the dock?" Jamie asked through a mouth full of potato chips.

"No."

"Thought I saw somebody down there as I was pulling in."

"How long ago was that?"

"I don't know. A while ago. I went upstairs but couldn't sleep so I came back down because I was hungry."

"Could you tell who it was?"

"No. Probably a woman though. It was dark. She was walking away . . . running actually. I lost sight of her."

"People from the party have been wandering around all over the place all evening. There's no telling." Joyce stopped briefly and turned reluctantly to Jamie who was remedying a case of the munchies. "And, don't forget the floor. Look. Your chips are on the floor. And a pickle."

"No problem."

Joyce spun around to continue her search, but finding only Jamie in the house, returned to the Wirth home and announced that Rene was not next door.

"What's wrong?" Tom asked as she rejoined him.

"It's so depressing. We were having such a nice time. I mean . . . . I actually thought that we're getting away from things for a while . . . for one evening!" Tears welled up in her eyes. "Is that too much to ask . . . one evening?" He reached out for her. She pulled back.

"What's depressing? What?"

"Jamie's at the house. Making a mess in the kitchen."

"I'll make sure he cleans up."

"Will you? Will you, please?"

Tom nodded. "Of course."

"Good. I'm going home now. And you promise that when I walk back into my kitchen in the morning it will be as spotless as it was when I left this afternoon. You promise."

"I promise."

"Say 'good-night' to Matthew and Shirley for us."

The search for Rene was eventually abandoned. Most considered her disappearance was a simple miscommunication between her and her husband. Phil and Noreen Osgood, houseguests of the Sherman's, excused themselves and retired. The Clays' guests, Gerald and Judy Albright, had also departed. McAllister had made his good-byes with Denise earlier, saw her to her car, and waved as her Porsche eased onto Lakeside Drive. When he gave up the search, the few remaining at the party who knew about Rene's disappearance met in the kitchen.

"Suppose she decided to walk home?" Mac asked. "Nobody's at the house. I tried calling, but if she passed out, she wouldn't answer the phone."

"Somebody could have given her a ride . . . somebody who left earlier," Skinner said. "Nobody would've come back to tell us they'd picked her up."

"Well, if she's out in one of these yards, I give up. We looked everywhere," Matthew said.

"I should be at our house if she shows up there. Hell, she may already be there now," McAllister said.

"Yes. Go," Matthew replied. "If she shows up here, we'll call. Chances are everything's OK, and we'll laugh about this in the morning."

"Goodnight from Joyce and me." Sherman extended his hand to Matthew. "Thanks. We had a great time." He hugged Shirley, nodded to McAllister and Skinner, and walked out the back door.

"Good, I'm going, too," McAllister said. He looked at Skinner one more time but did not detect any disproval. Morrie and Monica turned, as if on cue, to follow Mac out of the house.

"Call us if you need us," Morrie tossed back at Matthew and Shirley. "Thanks for everything."

"Yes, thanks," Skinner said. "Shirley, please call me once this gets straightened out. Mac and I had words earlier, and I'm not sure that he would. Ha!" she forced a laugh, "Rene won't want to acknowledge she caused so much concern. She'll be sleeping it off until noon or later. Bye-bye."

"And so to bed," Matthew said holding out an arm to his wife. Shirley moved in close and put her arm around his waist.

"My, my, so literate. I lose track. Is it Fezzywig or Samuel Pepys who offers to accompany me to my boudoir?"

"Neither, my dear," Matthew replied in a poor imitation of W. C. Fields. "Rather, the love of your life." Then more seriously, "Thank you for all that you did." She smiled and hugged him.

"Not at all," she whispered. "Not at all."

Chapter 8

Monica grabbed her Morrie's hand once they were out into the night. She was afraid that she could not hide her agitated state from anyone. In the morning, perhaps someone would recall how flushed she looked, how furtively her eyes moved from one person to the next, and how she appeared to force herself to be calm. Now that it was just Morrie and she, she could relax. Morrie shuffled along beside her. "Glad that's over?" she asked.

"What a farce."

"I think we carried it off pretty well, myself."

"To what end? My God, this was a charade." He stopped and yawned. "You know, there were actually times when I forgot everything and enjoyed myself . . . as if nothing was wrong. Soon as I caught myself, the feeling went away. I've put everything I've worked for . . . everything we've built together . . . in jeopardy."

"Don't talk about it. OK!" Monica startled him by pulling him around and reaching up to touch his cheek. "You're tired. This isn't over. I'm not giving up. Something will happen." She bit her lip. In the morning, Rene's body would drift up somewhere. Rene was not coming back to take anything away from them.

"Come on, ol' thing," she said. They entered the house. All was quiet. Their guests had preceded them by at least an half an hour.

To her dismay, Morrie dropped fully clothed onto their bed before she turned down the covers. "Come on, Morrie, it's my bed too. Get undressed. You smell like a soggy cigar."

Morrie pulled himself up. She turned back the covers as he fumbled with the buttons on his shirt, managed to remove it, dropped his walking shorts to the floor, kicked off his Docksiders, and collapsed back onto the sheets face first, pulling a pillow under his head as an after thought. He was asleep. She walked to the bath, disrobed and pulled on her floor-length summer nightie. She would not be able sleep. The alcohol or the hits off the joint at the party no longer had any effect.

The air was cool in the bedroom. She walked to the window that faced the lake and swung it open to hear the waves on the beach, a favorite sound, always calming, full of the memories of the peaceful times, times with the children, with Morrie, by herself alone on the grass in the shade enjoying the breeze as if it were a gift, every sound around her as if it were a personal, intimate symphony refusing to seek resolution. Pressure mounted in her eyes, a heat, and tears rose to quench it. She sobbed unexpectedly, convulsively, and found that she did not want to stop. She wanted empty herself of a thick sadness, of the contempt she held for herself. She saw Rene's summer dress swirling like a ghost in the water. She could feel the desperation of the drowning woman's struggle. Remorse erupted with each muffled sob, and as it drained from her, she felt hot self-loathing funnel into her breast, flooding the vacancy her sobs created. There was nothing she could do. Now, she knew, she must see everything through.

"Rene? Rene?! Rene! God damn it!" Mac yelled entering the house. "Probably passed out," he thought deciding to search the rooms. "Why the hell you'd go off like that and not tell me you were leaving? Jesus. Everyone was looking for you." Not finding her in the her bedroom, he searched the first floor and then moved up to the second level realizing with each step that she would not have bothered to make the climb. After checking all three bedrooms, he rumbled back down to the ground level.

"One of her goddman tantrums." He dropped into an over-stuffed chair in the great room. "I should wait up for her," he yawned. His head fell back against the cool leather cushion. He had been drunk, sobered up, and then, drinking again, reached the familiar state in which disabling intoxication seemed achievable only if he downed huge quantities of alcohol quickly. He nursed his drinks along for hours, enjoying himself, delaying the onset of both sleep or a hangover. A bone-deep fatigue was taking over at this hour, however, and the events of the earlier evening felt like the remote past.

"If she's walking, she'd be here by now," he thought and decided to go out in the lakeside yard and look for any evidence that she had returned. What if she had begun to walk home but did not make it all the way? How would she have come? The beach or the path along the road? Probably the path along the road, the one illuminated by low voltage garden lights.

He trudged down the path looking from one side and the other, checking any place at which Rene might stop—a swing, a gazebo, lawn chairs. He retraced better than half the distance to the Wirth home before deciding to turn back but walk along the shore of the lake in the event Rene had decided on it as a route.

It was darker nearer the beach. The homes were quiet, although several had left a lamp lighted near a door or over a deck. The pale glow spilled on to the grass and faded into the shadows nearer the lake shore. A long, long time had passed since he and Rene enjoyed sharing a home. Their marriage stagnated into an embittered competition. She wanted something that was beyond him to give. He tired of trying. Feeling the years weighing on her, Rene decided that she had not had the impact that she wanted in her life, had not succeeded in a way that others would acknowledge. Her yearning and ambition attracted new friends and alienated old ones. She sopped up attention. Reveled in it. But there was steady turnover among her acquaintances. Their friendships with Rene were mini versions of his marriage to her. Adore or be gone. Agree or go. No dialogue. No negotiation. And while she pretended not to notice, the women at the club began avoiding her. Invitations at different seasons of the year were not as forthcoming, and more and more, those he and Rene issued were declined. They finally stopped entertaining altogether except for family or the occasional friends who visited from out of town.

Years earlier, when they met, she had just completed her MBA, and nine years younger than he, she was eager to get established in a career at Maplethorp Corporation. He noticed her immediately. Tall, with a striking figure, energetic in her conversations, she impressed him as trying a little too hard. It did not take much effort to get to know her.

He was married at the time with two children, but he and his wife had reached a plateau where soccer games took precedent over dining out. Discussions about school progress reports superseded celebrating unexpected promotions. He began traveling more. Homecomings became a recitation of a list of things that required his attention. Disciplining the children was usually at the top. Rene changed all of that.

Rene reintroduced him to intrigue. She had emerged from an unfortunate early marriage with custody of two children, a responsibility that did not deter her from taking advantage of her employer's program to pay her tuition for night classes in graduate school. When she joined the marketing department at Maplethorp, she had been single for several years, turning heads in every department until her reputation for being unavailable preceded her and eligible males were content to ogle from a distance.

McAllister, himself, only wanted an affair, all the precautions about dipping into the company inkwell notwithstanding. He surprised himself. He fell in love, or at least it felt like love, and found the risks he was taking to be exhilarating. Rene stood up to him. She wanted things of him. Expectations about how he was to treat her. As he complied, her aloof façade was carefully dismantled—stowed but not discarded—and she seemed to become the fulfillment of everything that he ever wanted in a woman.

His wife was not to know. But it became less and less a concern as he and Rene grew more confident of one another's affection. They became careless, and upon returning from a business trip late one Friday evening, Mac's wife confronted him. He decided to come clean and admit that he was involved. He was surprised that she was upset, surprised to find that she was enjoying their life together, that she still loved him. To assuage her tears, he promised that he would see a marriage counselor with her while reassuring Rene that he was doing so only to let his wife down easy. After several sessions, the counselor conceded that the two were not making progress and asked whether they wanted to continue their work on a reconciliation or simply negotiate an agreement to separate and divorce.

Mac had tired of the pretense. He wanted Rene. He wanted a fresh start, to get it right this time, and not let the mundane overwhelm the romantic. He bullied his wife into submission. "Look," he said one night, "we can go on spending money on this shrink if you want, but every dollar we spend is one less that I can afford for child support or alimony or whatever else your attorney thinks you deserve after letting our marriage fall apart from dry rot. The price of dragging this out is my generosity. I hope that's clear."

She agreed to a divorce. The price in many ways was much higher than Mac anticipated. The children sided with her. Her attorneys established that she lacked the credentials to become re-employed at a level that would enable her to maintain the life style she enjoyed while married to him. The price tag was huge. He decided it was worth it. His career had taken off. He could afford the alimony for however long it lasted. His failed marriage was re-corded as sunken cost. The kids would be out of college eventually and on their own.

With the divorce behind them, Mac and Rene moved openly in Charles City society. They enjoyed being the couple of the season and the thinly veiled curiosity friends had about their relationship. North Carolina required a one year waiting period before a divorce became final, but it proved a formality. Mac was not looking back. His son and his daughter were cool toward him and very concerned about their mother. Her children, his stepchildren, never spoke to him if they could avoid it. They would all get over it. She was not going to pay for Melville County Country Day tuition. She was not going to buy a car for them. Pay for the gas. The insurance. He was. She was not going to make certain that they had their choice of the best colleges. He would. Everything would come back to him in time.

Mac realized that he was no longer looking for Rene in the dark of the neighborhood yards. As the light of his deck came into view, he rubbed his eyes and took a deep breath. Nothing serious could have happened to her. She was just off by herself somewhere or with friends who did not have the presence of mind to call or were misled by some story she told them. She was probably pissed. He was too tired to enjoy recalling how he had tormented her with Denise. There would be other parties. Other opportunities. He smiled remembering how Denise felt as they were dancing. Her supple back. She seemed to enjoy his company, but as usual, no hint of seduction, no flirtation, no innuendo. She was smooth. They were approaching the fragile time when one or the other would need to declare the attraction with the risk that it would not be reciprocated. "One hell of a tease," he conceded as he mounted the steps to the deck at the house.

Inside, he looked at the clock. 1:40 AM. "Shit," he said and realized he could not go to bed without knowing where Rene was. He dropped down on the couch in the great room. She would be sure to see him when she returned. Within a few minutes, he was sound asleep.

Chapter 9

"Matthew. Matthew!" The urgency in Shirley's voice pulled Matthew out of his chair. She was on the lakeshore near the Sherman dock, beckoning to him. The sun was shining brightly on the water behind her. "Come quick! Come here!"

He tossed down his paper, hurried down the steps and across the lawn. As he approached, he saw the reason for her alarm. A woman's body lay in the shallows, face down, her sodden dress wrapped around her. "It's . . . it's Rene," Shirley said. Matthew broke into a trot. He lost his footing momentarily in the soft sand but plunged into the water and bent down to pick up the body of Rene McAllister.

"Help me!"

Shirley waded in and together they pulled Rene up on to the beach.

"Oh God," Matthew said trying to catch his breath.

"We should get help," Shirley exclaimed.

"Yes. Call 911. Then bring a blanket or something and come right back."

Shirley hurried back to the house. A few minutes later she returned with a large blue blanket, and the two spread it over the body. They heard a siren in the distance. An EMS truck arrived first. They heard the doors slamming behind Matthew's house. The vehicle had parked in their driveway.

"Hey! Down here!" Matthew shouted, concerned when nobody appeared. Two uniformed men carrying a resuscitator emerged from behind the Wirth home and trotted to the beach. In the distance the siren of yet another vehicle was heading their way.

"This is where you found her?" one attendant asked, and the other pulled back the blanket.

"She was in the water. We pulled her out," Matthew replied.

"Did you see her swimming or hear her call for help?" the man asked as he watched his partner lean over the body and then look up and shake his head.

"No. I saw her lying in the water out a little ways," Shirley replied.

"Do you know who she is?" the same man asked.

"Yes," Matthew replied. "She's Rene McAllister. She was a guest at our house yesterday and disappeared as the party was ending. We hoped that she'd gone home."

"What time was that?"

"About 11:30 or so," Matthew replied. The siren from the second vehicle drew closer and died away as it too turned into the Wirth driveway.

"You know her next of kin then," the man said.

"Yes."

"Have you contacted them?"

"Not yet," Matthew replied. The attendant crouched near the body pulled the blanket over the dead woman's face. "Should we do that now?" Matthew asked.

"Yes. Now stand back. The police are here, and the area is going to be cordoned off until they get done. Jess," he said, addressing his partner, "we may as well get a body bag and the gurney." A man in uniform and another in plain clothes appeared at the side of the house. Matthew recognized Detective James Raker and Officer Fletcher from their last visit when the two investigated the vandalism to Tom Sherman's car.

"Where are you going?" Raker asked as they met half way between the beach and the house.

"To call the woman's husband," Shirley replied.

"Can I ask you to please remain at the house until we have a chance to talk to you, and please, do not call anyone other than the husband, otherwise we'll have people all over the place." Matthew nodded.

A crowd began to gather in response to the sirens. Joyce Sherman emerged next door onto the deck to her home.

"Please keep back, people," Officer Fletcher ordered. "We're going to have more personnel coming in here. Make room for them. Thank you." More sirens could be heard in the distance.

"Hello." McAllister said, his voice weak and raspy on the other end of the line.

"Mac, this is Matthew. Mac . . . ah . . . we have something to tell you. It's about Rene, Mac. Ah . . . do you have anyone there with you now?"

"No. Why? Did she finally show up?"

"She's dead, Mac. She drowned sometime last night. Shirley found her body this morning down by the Sherman dock."

"Dead? You're sure it's her?"

"It's her, Mac. No mistake. Do you want me to come get you."

"At your place?"

"Yes. Well . . . no, actually . . . down next to Sherman's dock.

The police and EMS people are here right now. Do you want me to come get you?"

"Oh . . . no! My God . . . no. I'm OK. I'll be right there."

"Come to our house first."

"Right. Your house. I will."

Matthew heard McAllister pull up and went out to meet him. "Do you want to come into the house?" he asked.

"No. I want to see Rene."

"She's dead, Mac. There's nothing to see. Nothing you'd want to see."

"No. I want to see her."

"You need to prepare yourself. She's . . . she's all covered with sand and wet and . . . well . . . she looks pretty bad." McAllister peered over Matthew's shoulder to catch a glimpse of what was going on at the lakeshore. "Come on then. I'll go with you."

The police cordoned off the area of the beach where Rene's body was found with yellow and black ribbon. The crowd continued to collect and gawk at the EMS and police. Matthew and McAllister pushed their way through the people toward the beach. Matthew was surprised at the size of the area that the police isolated. The ribbon stretched from the Sherman dock, up into the yard to a folding chair, and then at an angle to a tree on the lot line between the Sherman and the Clay property. Officer Fletcher was walking the length of the Sherman dock with the roll of ribbon closing the area at the end of the dock so that the water immediately in front of the body would be in the restricted zone. Detective Raker looked up as Matthew and McAllister approached.

"You need to respect that barrier," Raker called out.

"That's my wife."

Raker rose to his feet immediately and walked over to confront McAllister. "You're McAllister?" he asked.

"Yes. Alan McAllister. Can I see her?"

"At the moment, no, sir. I'm sorry. We need to make certain we can move her without disturbing the scene . . . so it will not be compromised. It won't take long," Raker explained. "I'm sorry. Your wife's been dead for several hours, apparently from drowning. Why don't you and your friend go back to the house. When we're through here, we'll let you know. You can view your wife's body before we take it to the medical examiner."

McAllister strained to see Rene's body which lay more than 50 feet away in the sand. "This is an accident, isn't it? Why the police?"

"Just routine," Raker replied. "Please, the quicker we can get on with it, the better. I'll want to talk to you in a few minutes." Matthew put his hand on McAllister's shoulder and nudged him to turn. Mac conceded reluctantly, and the two men trudged back to the deck where Shirley was standing. She had been joined by Joyce Sherman. "Have you had breakfast or anything?" Matthew asked.

"No. I'm not hungry."

"Well, come sit down. A cup of coffee, maybe?"

"Fine."

"I'm so sorry," Joyce whispered as he stepped onto the deck. "I'm so very sorry." McAllister walked over to a chair and sat down. Moments later, Shirley reappeared on the deck with two steaming cups of coffee. The four sat silently for several minutes.

"So she wasn't breathing or anything . . . when you found her?" McAllister asked.

"No," Matthew replied.

"How did you find her?"

"I found her, Mac," Shirley said. "I was up early taking a walk along the shore. At first, I didn't know what I was seeing. She was lying face down in the water just a few feet out where it's shallow. I thought it was a sail or something from a boat . . . something from all the traffic on the lake yesterday . . . but as I drew closer, I recognized Rene's dress," Shirley words were becoming more difficult. Tears welled up in her eyes. "My heart just stopped. But I had to see . . . and I walked right up to the water's edge. Then . . . then I knew, and I called for Matthew right away."

"We dragged her up on the beach," Matthew said. "I could see that she was dead, Mac. Her lips were blue. She wasn't breathing. He skin was all pasty . . . like it had been under water for a long time. We called 911 . . . and then I called you."

"My God, who would've thought?" McAllister groaned. "I mean . . . I thought she'd gone off somewhere. That I'd find her at home . . . or near the house. I went out looking for her, but I never thought anything like this would. . ." His voice trailed off.

"Everybody did everything they could to find her last night," Joyce said. "We looked everywhere."

McAllister waved off her remarks. "I just can't bring myself to believe it. I know that's her down there . . . but somehow . . . I don't know . . . I just can't quite get around it. What's the matter with me?" he said looking up at Matthew.

"You need time is all," Matthew responded. "More time."

"You know . . . we didn't get along well these last few years . . . but I never would've wished this on her. She was pretty drunk last night, wasn't she?" Matthew, Shirley and Joyce looked at one another, surprised by Mac's apparent indifference to what was happening.

"Very," Matthew replied softly.

"I wonder if she suffered," McAllister said.

From the deck the activities of the police and EMS team could be seen over the heads of the onlookers. Matthew noticed that the two EMS attendants had eased Rene's body into a black body bag, zipped it shut, and lifted it onto a gurney.

"I've always heard drowning is a very peaceful death," Joyce offered.

"Not one I'd choose," McAllister growled. "What's going on down there?" he asked and stood up to see for himself. Detective Raker was holding the black and yellow ribbon high above his head so that the EMS attendants could roll the gurney underneath it. They headed for the ambulance, pushing their way through the crowd toward the deck. When they reached the house, Raker had them stop, came up on the deck, walked over to McAllister, and asked him quietly if he still wanted to see the body.

"Yes," McAllister said and followed Raker off of the deck to the gurney.

"God," McAllister moaned. Sand still covered much of her face, and her hair remained plastered to her forehead. "God, it hardly looks like her." He looked again. It was she. Rene. His wife. Dead.

He could not look at her any more. He stepped back and nodded to Detective Raker who, in turn, nodded to the EMS attendants. One of them stepped forward and pulled the zipper up the front of the bag, closing it over Rene's face. McAllister felt Matthew's hand on his shoulder.

"Come on, ol' man," Matthew said. "Let's go sit down." Back on the deck, they heard the ambulance doors slamming closed and the vehicle's engine fire up. As they heard it accelerate down the street, they—Mac most of all—felt themselves surrendering Rene out of their care. A finality overtook them. McAllister drew a deep breath and slumped back into this chair.

Moments later, Detective Raker appeared at the foot of the deck. Matthew looked up and was relieved to see that most who had come out to investigate had left the yard. The police were still occupied at the scene. "I know this is not a good time," Raker said. "There never really is a good time, but I need to ask all of you a few questions. May I come up?" He looked at Matthew. Matthew, in turn, looked to McAllister. Their eyes met and McAllister waived off the question.

"I'm going to need a list of all your guests from last night. We'll talk to the neighbors, as a matter of routine. I'd like to start with you who are here now, but I need to proceed one at a time. Is there some place that would be private?"

"Of course," Matthew replied. "Right here, if that's OK. We can go back into the house."

"I need to know who each of you is. Can I start with you, mam?" Raker asked Joyce.

"I'm Joyce Sherman . . . a neighbor. That's our house right over there." She pointed. "It's our dock that you've roped off . . . where the body was found."

"You discovered it?"

"No. I came over when all the commotion started."

"I discovered it," Shirley said.

"Yes, I'm sorry. You told me that earlier. You are?"

"Shirley Wirth."

"Right, and this man is your husband," Raker said nodding in the direction of Matthew.

"Yes."

Raker continued to establish the identity of everyone on the deck including Mitchell and Jeanette Krueger and Felix and Nickie Kraft, the overnight guests in the Wirth home who had also joined the group.

The sirens awakened Monica who had fallen asleep in her chair by the open window. She shivered realizing why they were coming and hurried to the back of the house to see an EMS ambulance pull into the Wirth driveway. She ran back into the bedroom. Morrie was sound asleep where he dropped hours earlier. "Good," she thought and raced into the walk-in closet to change into shorts and a cotton blouse. She checked her hair as she passed the mirror on her way out of the room and walked slowly out onto the deck. From her vantage point, she could see Shirley and Matthew at the water's edge by the Sherman dock. She drew a sharp breath. On the sand in front of them was Rene's body. She pulled back instinctively and watched as the EMS attendants trotted to the beach. Her neighbors spotted her on the deck when they passed to join the crowd of onlookers. She smiled and waved.

"What the hell is going on?" Morrie asked minutes later from the doorway to the deck. He had pulled a bathrobe over his boxers. Bloodshot eyes, disheveled hair, he reminded Monica ruefully of the times that she had teased him in the morning about his appearance.

"I don't know. They found something down there on the beach . . . a body . . . I think. They took it away, and now they're just looking things over."

"A body? Whose body?"

"A woman's I think. It looked like a woman's when they put it in the bag." Monica heard the quavering in her voice.

"You didn't find out. My God, it is less than 300 feet from here."

"I just felt funny about it. So many people went down there when they heard the sirens . . . standing around gawking. I didn't want to be part of it."

"Rene McAllister!" he said so loudly that Monica jumped. "I'm going down there." He took a couple of steps, and then realizing that he needed to dress, turned back. "Shit!" he said and dashed back into the house.

"You coming?" he asked Monica when he returned. She shook her head. She was glad that he was gone, if only for a few minutes. She strained to see the day ahead. Nothing. Wait and see. The worst was over. There'd be questions. She'd have answers. Be ready. As simple as possible. As close to real events as possible. Unembellished. Truthful but with omissions.

"Where were you at the time Mrs. McAllister left the party?" "Had you observed her condition?" "Why were you absent at that time?"

"It's Rene!" Morrie announced as he thundered back up onto the deck. "She drowned last night. An accident. They think she was drunk and fell into the lake."

The crowd was slowly dispersing. The police continued to mill around in the area. One officer paced the length of the Sherman dock, looking into the water on both sides of the pier. He stopped and crouched down several times and eventually came to the oar where Monica dropped it. Her heart stopped. Was anything on the oar that would place her at the scene? The officer hailed another man who was obviously in charge. He nodded to the man on the dock.

"Yeah, God," Morrie said sitting down, "I didn't like the woman at all, but this doesn't make anything easier."

"What?"

"Telling Matthew about her account."

"Will you still have to do that? I mean . . . this is sad . . . but with Rene out of the way, won't they cancel moving accounts? Mac likes Matthew . . . doesn't he?"

"Her assets could stay with us, yeah, but they'll be moved into a marital by-pass trust. With her alive, at least I stood a chance of getting her signature on a new limited partnership agreement for the hedge fund and replace the one Cheryl signed. That's not possible now."

"But if Mac leaves the account with you, you will be OK, won't you?"

"No. The trust people will find hedge fund and they won't want to hold it. It's an unregulated investment. Too risky. They'll find the margin loan. They won't take an account with its assets pledged as collateral. I'll need an explanation for the signature if anyone questions it. I'm in as much trouble now as I ever was."

"Really? . . . Morrie. Really? I can't believe that. I just can't."

"Rene's death buys us a little more time . . . a week or two. Her assets'll be frozen. The attorneys'll take over and work everything out. Nothing's changed. I need to think it through again." He shook his head.

"Her death solves nothing . . . for us?"

"No! Why do you keep asking? I said 'No,' and that's the answer. Jesus!"

"Don't get angry."

"I thought about killing her myself a couple of days ago, but I knew then that it wouldn't make any difference. Not that I would, of course. It just passed my mind. Where are you going?" he asked as Monica jumped up and ran back into the house.

"I don't know. I need to be alone."

"How about breakfast? Any coffee?"

"Fix it yourself!"

Chapter 10

Monica was in the bedroom before her thoughts caught up with her. Rene's death was supposed to solve everything. She walked over to her reading chair and collapsed into it. The night before, she could cry. She saw Rene's head erupting out of the dark water, rivulets glistening on her face in the faint light. She saw Rene gasping for breath, arms flailing and crashing against the oar. Heard herself shouting "Grab hold! Grab hold!" and felt the woman bumping against the oar right up to the instant when she realized that she didn't want to save Rene. She wanted her to drown. An impulse had fired within her. She eased the oar into Rene's chest until the swirling of Rene's party dress, barely visible in the black water, sank from sight. Alone in the dark, a surge of relief had rushed through her until the night brushed against her cheek and called her back to herself, and she recognized where she was and what she had done—alone on the dock, shivering, holding the oar, looking into the dark water. The moment would not leave her. It whined in her thoughts like the like a distant outboard motor.

"What the hell was that all about?" Morrie tromped into the bedroom.

"What was what all about?"

"'Fix it yourself.' You sounded angry."

"I am angry."

"At me? What for?"

"No. Not at you. The situation."

Morrie walked sat down on the unmade bed. "I know," he said, "the only thing this does is buy time. A week, maybe two. It depends upon how quickly the trust company moves."

"How can you possibly sound so calm . . . so fatalistic? Why, Morrie? Why would you do this? We didn't need the money. This . . . this was all so unnecessary. So utterly pointless. How much did you make off of this? No. Don't turn away. How much, God damn it?"

"You think I haven't felt all of that? Asked myself the same questions." He stood up and started pacing back and forth. "I thought if I hit a home run, McAllister would be pleased. He'd leave the accounts with me once Matthew retired. People were making a killing in hedge funds up until the end of the year. God, I'd give anything to go back and undo this. Anything."

"I've tried to stay optimistic, Morrie, but if this turns out as you said it could, I don't know how I can forgive you. I can't even see what tomorrow looks like. We're middle aged, Morrie. Not college kids. We had it made! On top of the heap . . . nothing but good times ahead of us. What were you thinking?"

Monica was surprised at her own anger. She looked at Morrie. Balding. Bent. His face lined and beginning to droop, especially around the eyes, his flaccid body lacked the vitality it had once, a vitality that made up for the lack of physical attraction she felt. The man had romanced her, made love to her, planned a future with her, and fathered her children. She felt no connection with him. She looked away.

"Please," Morrie said, "just don't . . . I'm hanging on here. I can't shut off my own thoughts. Sometimes . . . I think I'm going crazy.

You're the one who's been optimistic. I've been borrowing your hope, realistic or not. I've tried to think of everything, and maybe . . . who knows . . . something will pop up that will make a difference. But this isn't helping . . . getting angry with each other. It won't help anything." He walked to the closet and searched for a shirt.

"Morrie, I think somebody's at the door. I'm not dressed. You have to get it." Morrie emerged from the closet buttoning a short sleeve shirt and stuffing it into his cargo shorts. He nodded and walked out of the room. Morrie was right. Being angry with one another was not going to help. She heard voices from the back of the house. "Who is it?"

"Officer Fletcher, the man who was here yesterday about Dr. Sherman's car. He wants to talk to us."

"I'll be right down," Monica called out. She dressed quickly and found the two men seated in the dining room.

"Officer," she said taking a breath, "we didn't expect to see you again so soon. Have they found who vandalized Dr. Sherman's car?"

"Ah . . . no, mam. It's a different matter this time. You're aware that a woman's body was discovered in the water near your neighbor's dock?"

"Yes. We saw all the commotion."

"I'm here about that. Just a few questions . . . if you don't mind." He nodded to the notebook that he had placed on the table.

"Oh, no. As I said . . . we saw all the commotion." Monica pulled a chair out and sat down. "Is there some question about her? Rene, I mean? Wasn't her death was an accident?"

"Ah . . . yes, mam. This is just routine. It may be an accident, but we need to complete an investigation just the same. You and your husband attended the Wirth party yesterday. Is that correct?"

"Yes. We were co-hosts. It's for our husbands' clients. We hold one every year . . . have now for several years." Monica sighed and ran her fingers through her hair.

"Yes, mam. We know that. Did you see the deceased at the party?"

"Yes. Several times . . . during the course of the day."

"How would you describe her . . . her appearance . . . her behavior?"

"Well . . . I don't know Rene McAllister very well. She's kind of eccentric, I guess. She never looks like she takes very good care of herself. She's always sort of rumpled and pale."

"Did you talk to her?"

"Yes. Briefly. Just once."

"And when was that?"

"I was dancing with my husband, and I noticed her walking outside, and I saw her fall. I went out see if she was OK."

"What time would you say that was?"

"Time? Time . . . late. Quite late. About midnight."

"You spoke to her when you went out to see her?"

"Yes. I wanted to see if she was all right. When I caught up with her, I found that she was just terribly, terribly drunk. We didn't have much of a conversation. She insisted she was fine and only wanted some fresh air. That's what she said . . . at least. That's what I could make out."

"How long were you with her?"

"A couple of minutes. At the most. She doesn't like me very much."

"I thought you said you didn't know her."

"Well . . . we both know who the other person is. I didn't mean . . . I didn't mean to suggest that we weren't acquainted. We're just not friends. That's all. Why? Is my conversation with her that important?"

"Several others reported that Mrs. McAllister was very intoxicated. You've simply corroborated what's been reported. How about you Mr. Clay?"

"Me?" Morrie was surprised by the question as much as he was at Monica's discomfort.

"Yes. Did you talk to the deceased or see her at any time?"

"No. I mean . . . yes, I saw her. I saw her the same time that my wife did. But I didn't go talk to her. I don't remember having anything to say to her all day yesterday."

"Fine, sir. Mrs. Clay, do you think the deceased would have been intoxicated to the point she could have fallen off of the dock and then been unable to extricate herself."

"Well . . . fall . . . certainly. She was barely able to walk a straight line when I saw her. I can't say whether she would be capable of saving herself. I just don't know."

"Where did you go after you spoke to the deceased?"

"I came here . . . to our house. I wanted to see if our son had come home and check on a couple of things."

"How long were you here?"

"Fifteen minutes. At the most. Why? Is that important?"

"Mrs. Clay, you were, as far as I can tell, the last person to have seen Mrs. McAllister alive. I just wanted to know, for the record, what you did after you parted company with her. That's all. And," Fletcher said shoving back from the table, "that really is all, unless either of you have something else to add."

"No, I don't think so," Morrie said. Looking at Monica he asked, "You, honey?"

"Me? No. Just what I said."

"Thank you for your time, then. If we have further questions, someone from the Sheriff's office will get back to you. If something occurs to either of you that has any bearing on the woman's death, please give us a call. I'm leaving my card here on the table."

"Of course," Morrie said. "We want to help anyway we can. It's a terrible thing to have happen right here. So close."

When Fletcher re-entered the kitchen, he turned back and said, "That's curry I smell isn't it? I noticed it when I first came in the house."

"Yes. Oh. One of my cooking binges. I'm always trying new things. Curry tends to hang in the air, doesn't it?"

"I love curry," Fletcher said. "There's a great little place in Charles City off I-77. It's Indian. My wife loves to go there."

"Really."

"Yes, well, I'd better be going. Bye again." Monica heard the door slam as the he exited.

Detective Raker turned to Joyce Sherman and said, "Ms. Sherman, perhaps I could ask you to excuse us now. I do want to talk to you and your husband when I am done with the folks here. Will you be next door for the rest of the day?"

"You want me to leave?"

"Yes, mam. Please. I need to get individual testimonies from everyone. It's all works better if we talk to those who appeared to be most intimately involved first. I'd like to visit with you and your husband later. Is he home today?"

"So I should go back home and wait?"

"If you don't mind, please, mam."

"Ah . . . well . . . I," Joyce looked at Shirley, then Matthew, and finally McAllister, stood up, smiled, and walked off the deck. "Later, then."

Raker turned to McAllister. "You may not be up to this right now, Mr. McAllister. It could wait, but the sooner we get it out of the way, the better."

"I understand."

Raker looked up at Shirley and Matthew. "I guess I need to ask you to excuse us also."

"Not at all," Matthew said as he stood up. Shirley walked over to McAllister and placed her hand on his shoulder.

"You're welcome to stay here as long as you like, Mac," she said.

McAllister nodded. Once Shirley and Matthew were beyond hearing distance, Raker asked, "What can you tell me about all that happened here, Mr. McAllister. Take your time. I know this can be difficult."

"Ah, God, I haven't sorted it out yet. Last night . . . at the party . . . I couldn't find Rene. I wanted to go home. It'd been a long day. I figured she was off somewhere . . . with her friends . . . whatever."

"What time was this? When you first became aware she was not here with the others?"

"About midnight, I'd say. Yeah . . . midnight. I started asking around. Someone said she'd gone out the back of the house . . . maybe a half-hour or so earlier."

"So about 11:30?"

"Yeah, about then."

"Who saw her leave?"

"Skinner Thorpe."

"Skinner Thorpe. He was a guest?"

"*She*! She was a guest. She's one of Rene's better friends."

"Unusual name for a woman."

"Yeah, but it fits. If you knew her, you'd see that."

"Skinner saw her leave?"

"Yeah. In fact, we had words about it. I was pissed she let Rene walk out when she saw my wife was so drunk. She always drank too damn much at these affairs. I thought she could've gone out somewhere . . . in the area around the house and maybe passed out . . . sat down somewhere. I finally told Matthew and Shirley that I couldn't find her, and a bunch of us went out looking for her."

"How long did you search for her?"

"God, I don't know. Seemed like forever, probably about 15 . . . 20 minutes. Everyone was tired."

"Why'd you stop?"

"I thought that she might have walked home. Our place is about three-quarters-of-a-mile from here. She's very independent . . . and stubborn. So I went home to look for her. I walked back up path this way to intercept her, and I walked the shore on the way back, but I didn't find her. When I got back to the house, I decided I'd wait up for her. I fell asleep on the couch. Didn't wake up until the Matthew called this morning." Mac's voice trailed off. "Nobody thought anything was seriously amiss," Mac volunteered suddenly. We thought she was asleep somewhere in the neighborhood, maybe at someone else's place. It was a party . . . you know . . . anything can happen."

"Had your wife ever done anything like this before?"

"What? Wander off?" McAllister leaned forward in his deck chair and shook his head. "No. She was an unpredictable woman. That she's suddenly gone didn't alarm me. I was annoyed, but not alarmed. She's walked out on me in public places to make a big show. But she never went off so that I could not find her right away."

"I need to ask, if you don't mind," Raker said looking up from his notes, "how would you describe your relationship?"

"Oh, shit," McAllister sighed and slumped back. "I don't know. Pretty bad, I guess. Pretty bad." He nodded slightly. His eyes dropped.

"I'm sorry. My wife died of colon cancer just seven weeks ago, Mr. McAllister. I know this can't be easy for you, but can you be a little more specific?"

Mac drew a deep breath. "Maybe it's the sort of thing couples our age just need to go through. We weren't interested in one another any more. No romance left. Just a couple of tired older people . . . tired of each other . . . tired of what we were living through each day."

"Any recent quarrels or arguments? Anything anyone else is likely to report?"

"Hell, you're likely to hear anything. We didn't hide that we weren't getting along, but we didn't hang our wash out in public either. Rene was probably pissed at me yesterday because I didn't spend any time with her. I had a young guest I was introducing around, a woman, and I spent most of my time with her . . . nothing romantic . . . someone I met who moved to town recently, and I wanted others to get to know her . . . so I made it a point to get her introduced to everyone."

"Her name?"

"Denise Becker."

"Was she here when the deceased disappeared?"

"No. I walked her to her car and saw her off. After she left, I decided to go home. That's when I started looking for my wife."

"Well, thanks, Mr. McAllister. I don't want to hold you up any longer. If I can be of help in any way, please call. Here's my card." McAllister reached up slowly for the detective's card. "You've got a rough few weeks ahead of you."

McAllister shook the detective's hand. "I know. Thank you."

Raker's interviews with Matthew and Shirley produced nothing more than corroborating testimony to what McAllister had already told him. The guests in the house also had nothing to add. He excused himself, thanking everyone, and exited the back door to the cruiser where he and Officer Fletcher had parked it. Not finding Fletcher there, he decided to visit the Shermans next door. He jotted Fletcher a quick note, posted it on the steering wheel and walked across the bright concrete drive to the Sherman home.

The mid-day sun beat down on the driveway. A breeze from the lake funneled between the two homes and brushed his trousers. It was unusual for him to be in the same neighborhood, talking to the same people about two different crimes in less than a week. He was going through the motions, being thorough, as he had learned from years of police work. He did not care about Dr. Sherman's sports car. He'd been in neighborhoods like Pelican Bay on Lake Heron many times. Wealthy neighborhoods. Neighborhoods of privilege, power, and sumptuous comfort. Edina. Lake Minnetonka. Grosse Point. After a while, they all looked alike. They felt the same. Huge homes, extravagantly furnished. Expensive automobiles, one for every driver in the family with the children driving better cars than he would ever own.

He had cultivated a clinically professional manner in dealing with the wealthy. They acknowledged his authority and, perhaps, respected his experience, but they also considered him a public servant and expected him to keep his place. The lines were not clearly drawn. They became evident only after they had been crossed, and he had crossed them frequently enough to develop a sixth sense about what he could do and say and what he could not.

He stepped into the shade of the Sherman home and rang the doorbell. It chimed deep inside the house.

"Mrs. Sherman. Can we take a few minutes to go over the events of this morning?"

"Certainly. Please, detective, come in. My husband is here. You . . . you asked earlier, if he would be, and . . . well . . . he is. In the living room."

The home opened up into a large living area at the center of the house. Light streamed in through louvered skylights on either side of the vaulted ceiling. A stairway on one side lead up to a balcony that ran along three sides of the room. Sherman was standing when his wife ushered Raker into the room.

"Detective," Sherman acknowledged.

"Dr. Sherman." Raker accepted Sherman's direction to an modern easy chair opposite a large couch. He waited for Joyce to be seated on the couch.

"I don't suppose there're any developments on the vandalism to my car?"

"We're working on it. The department is. I've been here since taking the call this morning. I'm afraid I can't update you on any recent developments. I'd like to go over the events of this morning and last night, if you don't mind."

"No. Fine. We understand."

Raker asked the Shermans the same questions in the same order as he had asked everyone. "If I understand both of you, then, you did see Mrs. McAllister several times during the day, and you both noticed that she became more intoxicated as the day wore on. Is that about it?"

"Yes," Sherman said. Joyce nodded.

"Is there anything else you would add?"

"No," Sherman said.

"Tom, there's Jamie," Joyce said.

"Jamie?" Raker asked.

"Jamie's my son," Sherman said. "He was near the dock last night where Mrs. McAllister drown. He was out on the lake fishing and came in after midnight. He told my wife that he saw someone at the dock as he was pulling up to it."

"Where is he now?"

"He went into Charles City early this morning. I don't think he knew anything like this happened when he left."

"But he was on the lake last night and returned around the time the McAllister woman turned up missing."

"Yes. That's what he told me," Joyce replied.

"Is that his boat that's tied up on your dock?"

"Yes, that's his," Sherman replied.

"His boat is cordoned off as part of the investigation site. When he returns, please tell him that he can't move it or enter it until the Sheriff's department takes down the tape. Since he reported seeing someone near the scene, we'll need to talk to him. The fishing tackle box and cooler in the boat— they're his, right?"

"Yes," Sherman replied.

"We need his permission to open them."

"What possible connection can that have with the drowning?" Sherman asked.

"Probably none. But we need his permission to open and look through them. This will all be over as soon as we get the Medical Examiner's report."

"When will that be?"

"By this time tomorrow. No one can cross the barrier until then. Please have your son call us when he returns. One more thing . . . any reason why the deceased would be on your dock last night?"

"No," Sherman replied. "I can't think of any."

"We don't . . . I mean . . . nobody makes an issue out of who uses whose dock," Joyce said. "It's that kind of a neighborhood. Nobody cares."

"Well, that covers everything." Raker stood up. "Thank you. If you think of anything else, please let me know. You have my card. I'll get back to you about the car as soon as we hear anything."

Chapter 11

"What d'ya think?" Raker asked Officer Fletcher as he got back into the cruiser. "Any point in keeping the scene under custody?"

"An accident. She was drunk, fell into the lake, and drowned. We'll get findings from the M. E."

"You didn't pick up anything from the neighbors?"

"No. This guy Clay and his wife were really uncomfortable. Not him so much, but she was . . . I don't know . . . skittish. Good looking gal. I'll say that for her. He works with Wirth. McAllister and his wife are clients of theirs. Mrs. Clay said she talked to the victim about the time of the drowning. Said the victim was too drunk to carry on a conversation."

"But she was uncomfortable?"

"Yeah. Well, people react to things differently. She didn't know the victim that well. I don't ascribe anything to it."

"I wouldn't either. We still have some people to contact. We can finish the guest list at the office over the next couple of days. The medical examiner will take a day or two anyway. We've got one more to talk to who was not on the guest list."

"Who?" Fletcher asked.

"Doc Sherman's kid, Jamie."

"Whoa! Now he's trouble. He's under surveillance by the SBI. The kid deals out here on the lake. SBI's been on him for weeks now, hoping he'll lead them to people in Charles City . . . to his suppliers. They're ass-deep in building a case. I warned the CSI guys working the scene about the kid. There's a cooler and a tackle box in the boat in the search area. They'll be looking to search both, and they need the kid's permission."

"I told his parents about it," Raker said. "The man's no kid, by the way, he's twenty-one, and we need to get permission directly from Jamie. Dr. Sherman was putting a call into him as I was leaving the house. He should be here shortly."

"Then I'd better get down to there and make sure those the CSI guys know the score."

"You calling it quits after that?" Raker asked.

"Yeah."

"If they find anything that relates to his dealing, they'd better just let it ride until we check things out with the SBI. I didn't know the SBI was involved. I hope I didn't trip up talking to the parents."

"Yeah, but we're not gonna talk to the kid without getting the all clear first. And we have good reasons for talking to him. They can't ignore that. SBI thinks the acid job on the doctor's Porsche has something to do with the kid, by the way. We're supposed to keep checking it out, but if we run into anything that involves the kid, same deal, clear it with them first. Soon as we get back we need to tell them we're going to talk to the kid about the drowning and getting into his stuff."

Shortly after Officer Fletcher departed, Monica Clay heard someone at back door. The chimes had barely died away when she heard pounding as well. "I'm coming," she yelled. It was Jamie Sherman.

"Let me in, Mrs. Clay. Please!" The Jamie forced his way into the foyer.

"What is it? What's wrong?"

"Close the door! Please! Close it."

"Fine. Fine. It's closed. You're a fright. What's wrong?"

"You have to keep this for me. For a couple of days. Out of sight somewhere." Jamie produced a large plastic bag from under his shirt. "Find a place. The freezer. Someplace! Someplace like that."

"Jamie . . . settle down. You're not making sense. Now . . . catch your breath . . . sit down . . . and tell me what you want."

"OK. OK." Jamie pulled a chair out from the kitchen table and dropped into it. "Look. You've been one of my best customers from the first. I just met a police car on the way here, and there's another one parked by my house. I don't know what's going on. Whatever it is, I can't go home. Not with this bundle. Hold it for me. OK? Just for a couple of hours."

"That's a lot, Jamie. If I got caught . . ."

"You won't. Nobody'd suspect you. All I need is to walk in over there, and they'd have me with the goods. I can't chance it. I can come back here later this afternoon and pick it up and take it down to my boat. That's not too much to ask is it?"

"You can't get at your boat."

"What d'ya mean? It's right there, tied up at the dock where I left it last night. It is, isn't it?"

"Shirley Wirth found Mrs. McAllister's body down by your dock this morning. She drowned last night . . . sometime around midnight. The police are investigating and cordoned off your boat because it's in the area. That's what all this about."

"Oh God . . . great."

"Great?"

"Yeah. Oh, wow! I know how bad that sounds, but I thought it had something to do with me. Phew! Boy. What a relief." Jamie shook his head. "So why are the cops all over the place? It was an accident, right?"

"They need to ask all the questions. They need to be thorough. The whole area's been cordoned off until they determine the cause of death."

"That couldn't take too long. A couple of days, right? Look, Mrs. Clay, I don't have anywhere else to turn. My dad called. I'm expected at the house, and I told him I'd be right there. I gotta show. I can't drive around until the cop leaves. He may be waiting for me. My dad's mad at me. Please. I don't need the hassle right now."

"I can't take the risk. If they came in and found it, they'd accuse me or my husband of being dealers."

"No! They won't! You guys . . . you're too straight. They'd need a reason to come in here. They don't have one?"

"Not to look around, they don't. But an officer left not fifteen minutes ago. It might've been his car you passed."

"What'd he want?"

"He wanted to know whether I had seen Mrs. McAllister . . . spoken to her . . . around the time she drowned. Whether I thought it was an accident."

"What'd you tell him?"

"I told him the last I saw of her she was walking toward the water in the direction of the Sherman . . . your family's . . . dock."

"Wow! Shit! Right. Our dock. She drowned near our dock. Why? Do they think I was there . . . at the dock?"

"I don't know. Maybe somebody said something. It doesn't matter. Your boat is in the cordoned off area. It's part of the investigation."

"Did the guy who was here . . . the cop . . . ask you about my boat?" Jamie ran his business from this boat. "Dockside Delivery," he would jest. "Pot to your dock," was another one of his slogans.

"No. But it's cordoned off. They'll probably ask you where you were around the time that she drowned."

"So nothing's changed then? I can't walk into the house or get to my boat with this stuff. Please . . . please . . . you gotta help me? I'll make it worth your while. Here," Jamie reached into a front pocket of his cutoffs and pulled out a self-sealing clear plastic bag, bags that he used to break up his stash into smaller quantities for his customers.

"I don't know," Monica said.

"There!" Jamie opened the larger bag, and carefully marshaled a portion of its contents into the smaller bag. He sealed the smaller bag and tossed it onto the table in front of Monica. "That's more than you usually get. My compliments. What'd I charge you a bag? A hundred-sixty-five . . . a hundred-seventy-five bucks? What say I put another bag with that one, and you keep my stash until this all blows over? I know I can trust you, Mrs. Clay. I know I can."

Monica dropped her eyes and then looked up at the ceiling. She always prided herself in staying step ahead of others.

Jamie jumped up suddenly. "My God, you know what? I just realized. I did see someone there. Seriously. I wasn't that high. Someone was on our dock when I was coming in off the lake. It was . . . it was a woman, Mrs. Clay, wearing a dress, and she ran away . . . toward . . . toward this house . . . toward your place."

Monica froze. Jamie was staring wide-eyed at her. "Was it you, Mrs. Clay? Is that who I saw?"

"No. I wasn't down by the dock. I talked to Mrs. McAllister up near the house."

"But the person . . . the woman ran this way. I know that . . . I know that for sure."

"I can't help what you saw, Jamie. I wasn't there."

"Whoever it was, she made a beeline out of there. Ha!" Jamie shouted, startling Monica, "suppose I tell them . . . the cops . . . that. Suppose I tell them I saw someone running this way, some athletic-looking younger woman? Suppose I tell them that I thought it was you?"

Monica's thoughts raced. She did not want the police coming back, questioning the veracity of her initial statements. She glared at Jamie.

"You wouldn't! The woman drowned! It was an accident. Even if I was there, it doesn't mean anything."

"You say it was an accident. Fine. So where's the harm in my telling the cops then? If you were there, you would have told them by now. Right?" Jamie smiled at her. "Tell you what, you keep this stuff for me, and I won't say a single word . . . not a single syllable . . . and I'll throw in the second bag I promised. Or could you use some meth? I'm moving meth now too. I need to know. I'm overdue at the house."

Monica reached across the table and grabbed the small plastic bag with one hand and held out the other to indicate she would also take the large bag.

"Great! Mrs. Clay. I won't forget this. Sorry I had to be rough on you. You understand. I had no choice."

"If you say anything at all, you will not see any of this again." She held up the large bag. "The police will find it, my friend, and they'll find it in a way that would make it unmistakably yours. I've got some leverage here too."

"No. No. No. Mrs. Clay. You don't get it. This is between friends. We're friends. Right? You're doing me a favor. And I'll keep my word. Believe me, I'm not saying anything. Mrs. Clay. Please. And . . . and don't forget, the meth. I can get it. Deal?" Jamie extended his hand.

"Hadn't you better go now?"

"Yes. Yes. Thanks, Mrs. Clay. I won't forget this. I promise." He took one step toward the door and stopped. "Oh shit. I can't go over there with my own bag. Here!" Jamie reached into his back pocket and produced another smaller bag of marijuana and tossed it on the table. "That's my personal stuff. Keep it separate from the rest." Before she could respond, he bounded for the back door. The combination screen buckled with the force of his charge and then closed slowly behind him.

Monica snatched the third bag from the table and walked over to the stainless steel side-by-side refrigerator-freezer, opened the freezer door, and buried the parcels at the back of the lowest shelf. Her heart was pounding as if she were in the middle of a hard workout.

"What the hell was that all about?" Morrie shouted from another room.

"Nothing. Just the kid from next door."

"It didn't sound like it from here."

Morrie was drawing nearer. Monica took a deep breath. "Well, it was. Take my word for it," she shouted back and then realized he was already in the doorway to the kitchen. She lowered her voice. "He . . . he didn't know about the drowning, that's all. He was nervous about the police being at his house and stopped here first to find out what was going on."

"What'd he think? That they're after him?"

"Yes. I guess. Oh God. I don't know."

"You don't know? You just finished talking to him for ten minutes."

"Oh fuck you, Morrie." Monica pulled a chair out from the table and sat back down. "What does it matter what that piss-ant kid thinks anyway? This isn't murder. This is an accident . . . a simple accident involving a drunken, vicious, old bitch . . . and the police are turning it into a federal case. God, how long is this going to go on?"

"You know why he's nervous. He's a small-time dealer afraid he'll get caught. You don't think anybody is suspicious about what happened, do you? I mean . . . ." Morrie stopped talking when he saw his wife turn to him. Her face was flushed. Tears pooled up in her eyes and toppled down her cheeks. Monica never cried. She looked as tired as he had ever seen her.

"Oh, Morrie. Oh, God. You don't know the half of it. I was so hopeful our problems were going away when that woman drowned. It's so deflating . . . so devastating . . . to find that nothing has changed, that we're still staring at disaster . . . that it's coming dead on for us . . . and there isn't one goddman thing we can do about it."

"So you're not mad at me any more?"

"Yes, God, I'm mad as all hell. It's all I can do to contain myself. I've never been so angry with anyone in all my life. I'm that . . . that far," Monica held up one hand to show her thumb and index finger separated by less than an inch, "from absolutely hating you. On top of that, I'm afraid. On top of that, I'm tired. But, it doesn't do anybody any good. Does it? Nothing does any good. You . . . you want to know what I'm feeling? Despair, Morrie. Pure, absolute, unadulterated, totally fucked despair. I felt hope leave me. Hope took over for what two days ago was certainty . . . when I could take so much for granted. Now it's gone . . . and I'm empty . . . and angry . . . and . . . . scared."

Every word knifed through Morrie. He'd seen Monica's volatility many times, basked in her energy when she was happy, and grateful that she could embrace disappointment and deal with it, as if by proxy for both of them. This was different. She was not speaking for both of them, not feeling for both of them. Not this time. She was withdrawing. He could not follow and comfort her with the expectation that she would be grateful for his understanding and appreciate his calm demeanor; his cooler, steadier hand. He turned and started to walk out of the kitchen.

"Don't you walk away from me now, you gutless asshole," Monica yelled. "Don't you just drift off like nothing's wrong and supper's going to be on the table as usual . . . as if everything is just fine."

He spun around in the doorway. "What do you expect from me? We've been through this. Maybe something'll break our way, but that's it. I've got to figure a way. A lot of goddamn good it will do to get all emotional. All it'll do is make matters worse . . . even worse than they are . . . . Don't you see. . . ."

"No. No. You don't see. *I said*, 'You don't know the half.' Did you hear me say that?"

"Yes, I heard you. I thought it was a figure of speech."

"I *killed* her. I killed Rene McAllister. That's the other half. Now do you understand?" Tears were running freely down Monica's cheeks. "Don't leave me alone with this."

"No. Monny . . . sweetheart. It was an accident. Everyone knows that. Why would you say that?" He sat down slowly opposite her.

"I thought I could do some good." Monica said slowly staring down at the table. "I only went down there . . . to the dock . . . so I could talk to her. She was so drunk. She could barely stand. She was just ugly. She doesn't know me. And she pushed me to get around me, but she tripped and fell into the lake. It was awful. All I could see was her dress. Then she came up, splashing and coughing. It scared me. I didn't know what to do. I couldn't reach her. The only thing I could find was an oar . . . so I picked it up and tried to reach her with it.

"It was too heavy, Morrie, and she kept drifting out farther away . . . it got harder to reach her. I knew nobody would hear me over the noise from the party. She banged against the oar two or three times, but she wouldn't grab hold. And then . . . oh God . . . it just came over me . . . why was I trying to save this woman?" Monica began to sob. "She was about to ruin my husband's career . . . and our life together? She bumped into the oar one more time, and it happened. I pushed her . . . just a little . . . so that she'd stay under. I could feel she was giving up. Like a bag of laundry . . . helpless . . . too weak. I just nudged her with the oar . . . and . . . and that was it.

"She didn't come up again. I ran back here, waited a few minutes and went back to the party as if nothing happened." Monica looked up a Morrie. He was wide-eyed.

"God, Monica, why didn't you run to the party and get help?"

"Oh God . . . oh God. . . Oh Morrie. . . have you no idea of what it's like to sit here and tell you this . . . no sense of what it's like for me." Monica took a deep breath. Of course—Morrie would want the facts. He needed facts first to understand. "It was too late! Can't you see? If she really did drown, you wouldn't need to tell Matthew anything. Mac wouldn't move the account. It would solve everything."

"But she could have been pulled out. They could've tried to revive her!"

"No! It was too late . . . I know it was too late . . . I could tell. By the time I ran back . . . got those drunks to pay attention . . . and then back down there . . . it would have been too late."

"Did anyone see you?"

"That's just it. Yes! I heard a noise on the lake . . . a boat coming my way. Running up here . . . when I got to our deck I saw it was Jamie. It was his boat. He'd come in off the lake. He could've seen me. That's what we were talking about." Monica wiped the tears from her cheeks. "He saw me. He said he saw me."

"*He* saw you. He's sure he saw you?"

"That's not the point. He can say he saw me."

"Why the hell would he do that?"

"Because he wants a favor from me. He wants me to hold his stash for a couple of days until the investigation is over. He can't go back to his house with it. The police are there now. They'd find it on him. I put it in the freezer."

"Jesus Christ. This just gets worse and worse. We can't have that stuff here. What if the boys find it? Police crawling all over the place. My God. You need to get it out of here. We could be charged with possession-with-intent-to-sell. The scrawny son-of-a-bitch. This is extortion. How long do you need to hold on to it for him?"

"Until he comes back. Maybe when the police leave and he can take it down to his boat and hide it."

"So . . . a couple of hours?"

"Hopefully. He needs it. He can't leave it here indefinitely."

"It's got to go back to him no later than tomorrow. The fucking creep."

"Yes," Monica said. "That's exactly what he is. And I can't just throw it out if he doesn't come get it right away."

"What's the longest he'd make you hold it?"

"I don't know . . . a couple of days. Until they determine cause of death. Until they decide once and for all it was an accident."

"Which it was," Morrie said.

"No, Morrie. It wasn't . . . it wasn't an accident. I *helped* her drown. I *know* that. You can't lose sight of that."

"No. Monny. No. This . . . you . . . you didn't. He can say whatever he wants but it doesn't mean you killed Rene McAllister. You're choosing to see it that way. You feel . . . you believe that you did, but the woman drowned. If you're guilty of anything, it's just running away . . . of doing nothing. That's not a crime. People pass by people in trouble all the time. They don't get arrested for it." He pulled his chair up to the table again and reached out to Monica. "Look. Look at me. You've got to stop thinking that. You're not guilty of anything. You're going to incriminate yourself just by feeling bad. Lighten up. Nobody has a thing on you. Not even Jamie. It'd be better if he didn't say anything, but even if he does, it won't amount to anything. Do you hear me?"

"Yes. But I . . . I know what I did. *I know*! I had a reason! I wanted her dead, Morrie."

"I understand, and guess what? It doesn't matter one damn bit to anyone except to you. Give it up. You're worrying over something that's never going to happen."

"You don't know that! You're no lawyer. You're just guessing. Hoping for the best."

"No. No, you're wrong, Monica. I may not be a lawyer, but common sense tells me there's nothing you've done that breaks the law. Nothing. You tried to rescue a drowning woman . . . a drunk . . . and when you failed . . . you panicked and ran away. It's that simple. You need to stop making more out of it than that."

"But I don't want the police coming back and questioning me all over again if Jamie says something."

"You just stick with your initial story. It'll be your word against his."

"Suppose what he says gets them to look into things more thoroughly. Suppose they find something else that makes me look guilty. My God, they've been down there all morning going over everything."

"OK. OK. I agree that we don't just throw the stuff back at him as if he isn't a threat. But we aren't going to hold onto it forever either. If he doesn't come back for it right away, we'll figure out what else to do."

"Awh, God, how can this be?" Monica stood up suddenly. "I know what I thought. I know what I did. This feels so . . . so unreal. Where . . . where's the way out of this? The relief?"

"Well," Morrie cleared his throat. "If you will sit back down, I'll tell you what I came up with, and I think it'll work just so long as you don't panic over what happened last night or let that punk Jamie scare you into doing something and blow everything up."

"Don't . . . don't lecture me. Don't you dare tell me how to feel when you don't even listen to me. I feel alone with this . . . all alone. If what I've heard so far is the best that you have to offer, forget it."

"Alright. I think you're making too much out of it. What I have to say can wait. I'm sorry you're so upset. I'm going to leave the room . . . now. Last time I tried that, you yelled at me. I assume it's OK now."

"Yes. Go!"

Chapter 12

"No. It's cool. I'd like you to look. I'd like to get my boat back. When can I get my boat back?" Jamie asked the CSI officer after giving him permission to search his tackle box and cooler.

"Whenever the Sheriff's office releases the scene. Until then, everyone needs to respect the cordoned off area."

"Cool. No problem. You want me to come down to the dock with you?"

"No. Thanks." The officer turned to Joyce and Dr. Sherman and said, "That's it for today then, folks. Thanks for your cooperation. I'll be down at the dock for a few minutes and that'll be it."

"I don't suppose there's any point in asking why you where in Charles City today?" Sherman asked his son once the officer was out of the house.

"You keep bugging me to get some kind of a job. There aren't many out here at the lake."

"You were looking for a job? On Saturday?"

"Yeah. Look, I'm going upstairs. I'm pretty tired."

"No. We need to have this out. You think being dressed like that is going to make the kind of impression that would make an employer to want to hire you? And that growth. Shave, for Christ's sake. You look like a bum."

"This is the way guys dress in the summer. I could've looked like a complete dork and worn a suit and a tie."

"Where'd you apply for a job?"

"Cinnabun."

"Cinnabun? What the hell is that?"

"At the mall. They're open on Saturday. They bake cinnamon buns and sell them. Great place. Smells terrific."

"They have career openings for near college graduates?"

"Yeah, well, I knew what you'd think. I don't want a *career* position. I don't want to be a suit. I hate those assholes. I just want a few bucks so I can move the hell out of here."

"A minimum wage, entry-level job is going to give that chance, is it?"

"Better than hanging here and being treated like I was thirteen fucking years old."

"You get by pretty well *hanging* here. Air conditioned house. Beer in the fridge. Laundry done for you. Not too shabby. How do you come up with your spending money? Your mother?"

"Yeah. Now-and-then. I get odd jobs. How would you know? You're never around."

"Where else did you apply?"

"Cinemax."

"Working the 'C' pages of the telephone book?"

"Very funny. You know . . . ha ha . . . that really was funny. I get thinkin' you don't have a sense of humor any more, but every now and then. Wow. There it is. A funny. A real one."

"Cut the crap. You know what I want. I want you back at Wake Forest this fall. Get your goddamn degree and then go be an usher at a mall theater if you want. You realize how much money you flushed down the toilet walking out on your degree? Any idea?"

"I knew it'd get back to this. Look. Dad. Get this. I don't want to go to Wake Forest. I don't want to get a degree. I want to be left alone. I want to make my own way. I'm tired of trying to fit everyone else's idea of who I should be . . . who I should become. I don't see anybody else doing what I want . . . the way I want to live."

"How is that? God damn it, if you'd tell me what you have in mind, maybe I'd be interested. Maybe even supportive. But the only thing I see is a bright young man, my son, going nowhere . . . doing nothing at all . . . not getting ready for the rest of his life. That's what these years are for . . . to prepare yourself."

"Prepare for what? Divorces? Fucking other people over when they're just trying to get by? I'm going upstairs. I wish I could have my goddamn boat back." Jamie stomped out of the kitchen.

Sherman walked into the large central living room hoping to find Joyce. She was not there. Of course not. She didn't want to hear them arguing. He saw her through the sliding glass doors on the chaise at the far end of deck with a book. He knew in a glance that she did not want him to join her.

In the middle of the afternoon, Alan McAllister received a call from the medical examiner's office asking what arrangements had made for his wife's body. The house was quiet. None of the service people were on duty on Saturday. Rene usually had a radio on somewhere. The stereo. Not now. Nothing but a leaden stillness. At any other time, he would have bolted, dashed off to the club, somewhere, anything to get away. Not today. Rene was dead. He was alone with nothing to do. The funeral home was taking care of all the arrangements. He had called the children and other family members.

He went to the bar in the family room and poured two fingers of Johnny Walker Black into a clean glass, gulped it, and sat down. His children expressed shock and disbelief when he spoke to them. None wept. That would come later. All said that they would make their arrangements to come home for the services and would get back to him. They would also be there for the money. It would be a few days before much could be decided with regard to his wife's estate. He needed to talk to Matthew Wirth and let him know that he no longer wanted to move the accounts.

Mac had never been asked to manage the tasks whenever a family member died. He remembered his father's final illness. Mac broke away from a business trip to the west coast to fly back to Milwaukee and see his father and found him nearly comatose in a hospital bed. The old man, eyes wide open, pupils dilated like windows to a empty room, struggled to recognize him. Mac could not tell sure whether the old man knew who was at the bedside. He waited with his brother for several days to see if their father's condition would change, and when the physician could not say how much longer he might linger, McAllister left to get back to his business pursuits.

He was in San Diego when the call came. He returned to his motel room to find the message light on. It was from Rene. His father had passed away that morning. His brother handled all of the details, and when McAllister asked if he needed any money, his brother declined. The funeral was held in the Catholic church in their Milwaukee neighborhood. A funeral mass. He remembered serving as an altar boy, the standing, kneeling, genuflecting, and memorizing the Latin which was later dropped for English. Even in English, the service was rigid and unwavering. He tried to find something in the service that would help him honor his father's life. Prayer wheels could have served. Droning on and on, the local choir struggled with the high mass for the dead. Nobody spoke of love, of fathers and sons, of how they could be together, understand one another, or fail to understand, and yearn to reconnect. How they could cherish their times together—hunting, fishing, working in the yard. Nothing was said of those moments in a boy's life that created a longing for more—more than his father could offer. They drifted apart—the father failing to understand the son's endeavors and achievements; the son tiring of trying to explain them.

He was in the office when the call came through that his mother had died. She followed his father out of life five years later. Again his brother handled everything—funeral arrangements, hospital bills, monument selection, the coffin, and again he attended the remote and meaningless ritual honoring his mother's life on earth.

He was glad that he and Rene did not take religion seriously. He would direct his minister to say some appropriate words for the sake of those attending. He would pay the man well. Death is the end. What lies beyond is anyone's guess. Nobody ever came back to tell of it. Religion was backward looking and earth bound. He had never heard anything in church that demonstrated an awareness of the enormity of the universe and the insignificant part the earth played in all of it. Religion, he decided, was a product of human hubris. Nothing more.

The moments that he might have celebrated in his life with Rene had become ossified by the indifference that they felt toward one another. His grief had seeped away over the years, a spoonful at a time, beginning when he realized he was no longer drawn to her. Her competitiveness and refusal to consider him fueled his anger. She would not honor him by listening to him.

"That all ends now," he said under his breath. "Just like that. It all ends now." He freshened his drink and wondered what to do about an evening meal. The phone rang. It was Denise.

"Mac, I just now heard. I'm so shocked. I'm so sorry. Are you OK?"

"I'm fine, I guess. I'm . . . ah . . . I'm just kind of numb. This goddamn house is so quiet . . . but I don't feel like I want to go anywhere. I feel numb."

"Is there anything I can do?"

"No. Not now. I think it would be best to confine ourselves to telephone contact for a few days. I don't know. It all feels awkward."

"Yes. I know. I feel the same way. Charles City is a very small town in some ways."

"It is. She looked just awful, Rene did."

"Don't dwell on it."

"I called the children. When you called, I thought it might be one of them."

"So they'll be coming right away. That's good. At least you'll have someone with you."

"Yeah . . . I guess. I don't get along too well with my kids, Denise. Too much water over the dam."

"When do they arrive?"

"I don't know yet. They'll call and let me know once they've made arrangements. I contacted Art Scheffield, and his sons are making all the arrangements. The funeral will be sometime in the middle of the week. I'm trusting all the pieces will fall into place."

"They will. You sound tired."

"Well, God, yes. Up late last night, too much to drink . . . and then the news this morning. Jesus, morning seems like a week ago. Sometimes, it just doesn't seem real . . . nightmarish."

"Get a drink and go to bed. Turn on the TV. You'll think some-one else is in the house with you. That's what I do."

"I've already had the drink. Drinks, I should say."

"I figured."

"Obvious, huh?"

"A little. You speak more slowly. I notice. I don't know if every-one would. I'll call you in the morning. One more drink and then to bed, OK?

"Talk to you in the morning."

Mac hung up the phone and turned on the TV. "Tragedy struck unexpectedly last night in the affluent Pelican Bay residential area. The body of Rene McAllister, wife of J. Alan McAllister, a promi-nent public figure and area businessman, was found on the beach in front of one of the luxurious summer homes. Mrs. McAllister drowned sometime between 12 o'clock midnight and 1:00 AM this morning. She, with others, had been attending a party at the home of Mr. and Mrs. Wirth Matthew. Police do not suspect foul play. They have reported the death as an accidental drowning, the first in nearly two years at the nearby lake and popular recreational site."

Chapter 13

"I appreciate you guys coming in here early on a Sunday like this, it being a long holiday weekend. Several of you put in some long hours already. But this is a high profile case, and I want it settled right away. You know Tim Moran with the SBI," the Sheriff said to the group assembled in the conference room of his office. "He's sitting in on this because of a possible overlap with a case that's important to his people."

Raker looked around the room and nodded to the members of the Sheriff's staff he knew. He did not know Moran. He had not been involved in matters that fell under the jurisdiction of the SBI.

"OK. What's the thinking on the McAllister case?"

"A drowning," a county CSI officer said. "The medical examiner's ready to turn the body over to the family pending the results of a couple of tests. The victim was bruised, but the evidence of trauma did not suggest an assault. The cause of death will read that she drowned."

"Nothing else?" the Sheriff asked.

"Nothing consequential," the officer continued. "The victim had sustained bruises on her right forearm before her death. They could have been sustained any time within six to eight hours prior to her death. The victim also had a small lesion just above the hair line above her right eye as if she may have bumped her head against something. Hard to say whether it was connected with her death. Probably not. There was also an elongated contusion on the victim's sternum, suggesting that she may have bumped into something earlier the day."

"Or in an effort to pull herself up on the dock," Raker said.

"Possible," the CSI officer responded, "but we didn't find anything that would support that. If she tried to pull herself up, her dress would have snagged somewhere on the rough timbers. We found no evidence of that."

"Water may have washed away any evidence of her bumping her head or bruising her arm," Raker replied.

"That's speculation," the Sheriff said. "Anything that would suggest this was other than an accidental drowning? Remember, to a person, the people we interviewed all reported that she was very intoxicated. She could have sustained those bruises in any number of ways if she was drunk."

"Which she was," the CSI officer said.

"So, anything else at all?" the Sheriff asked.

"How about the Sherman kid's tackle box and his cooler?" Tim Moran asked.

"Nothing," the CSI officer replied. "The cooler had water in it, probably from melted ice, mixed in with a small amount of beer, and a couple of pop top keys from beer cans. The tackle box had seventy-one dollars stashed in a plastic bag. Pretty careless leaving it out there like that. We found marijuana seeds in the bottom of the tackle box and a small amount of marijuana with it. Dust actually. Not enough to suggest anything other than that the kid may have been a casual user."

"OK," Moran said. "Listen, we're glad you didn't find any more than that. Our problem with the kid is unrelated to the drowning as far as we know at this time. He seemed to know nothing about it when CSI talked to him. Denies seeing anything, although he docked his boat sometime during the period that the victim drowned. So, please, just leave the kid alone. We have too much riding on him. Nothing more about this. OK?"

"I need to talk to him," Raker said.

"You are?" Moran replied.

"Detective James Raker, Melville County. I am assigned to Heron Lake Township as a liaison offer for the Sheriff's Department, co-ordinating on cases that involve both agencies."

"And you need to talk to Jamie Sherman."

"Yes. He told his stepmother that he saw somebody in the area of the drowning when he docked his boat. Now, as I hear from your report, he denies seeing anyone. I want to know why the reversal in his story."

"No problem," Moran replied. "Make it as casual as possible. Don't bring him into the station here or at Heron Lake. Ask your questions and get out of the way. Contact me when you are done. Understood."

"Yes, sir."

"Are we all on the same page?" Moran asked looking over the group. "Sheriff, it's in your hands."

"Thanks," the Sheriff said. "OK, you guys. That's it. No evidence of assault. Nothing to suggest anything? Anything in the area that could be considered a weapon or used as a weapon?"

"None."

"How about the oar that was on the dock?" Raker asked.

"What about it?" the CSI officer asked.

"Where's the oar now?" the Sheriff asked.

"Still out there."

"Bring it in. Print it, just to be on the safe side," the Sheriff ordered. "Hold it in evidence and release the scene. Any problems with that? OK. Thanks again for coming in. We're through."

Raker felt uneasy walking back to his office. Something was missing. A drowning? The contusions on the body meant something. They weren't the wounds of a typical assault—an assault on land. But an assault in the water would be different. An assailant has no leverage in water. Blows land with less force. And a weapon? The bruises were caused by something . . . a club, a tool, something. It could have been carried off. Still at the scene? Maybe. The oar? Possible. He'd check on it later. Still, it was probably an accident. He decided to review his notes.

The phone rang as he sat down at his desk. It was Officer Fletcher. "You sticking around for a while?"

"A little while. House is too quiet on Sunday. What'd you think about the meeting this morning?"

"Not much there to suggest anything other than what we thought yesterday . . . an accident."

"How sure are you?" Raker asked.

"As sure as I need to be. We could go poking around some more, but I think we'd be wasting our time. Something not working for you in all of this?"

"I'd like to know what's behind the Sherman kid changing his story . . . as I said in the meeting. I'd like to know more about the victim. People didn't seem to like her very much. She left the party to get some fresh air. I'm just wondering if there's more to her leaving. Why didn't anyone go with her? Too many loose ends that don't tie up for me. Do we have any more on the vandalism of the Sherman vehicle?"

"The lab report went straight to Moran and his crew. They don't want us messing around with it. They think it's related to the Sherman kid's activities," Fletcher said.

"The kid wasn't settling his debts? Something like that?" Raker ventured.

"Your guess is as good as mine. All I know is they don't want us involved. That takes the top two cases off my list. I don't have much else that's pressing."

"I think I'll go out and see this guy Wirth. Today, if he'll agree to it. Maybe he has some perspective on the victim and her husband that might clear a few things up. If the Sherman kid is around, I'll have a chance to ask my *casual* questions of him."

"Sure as hell isn't worth my time. I'm going home. I hate working Sundays. I was on duty all day yesterday. I'll catch you in the morning."

Raker pushed away from his desk and walked to an whiteboard and drew a timeline, beginning on the left side of the board with "11:00 PM." Underneath it, he wrote, "Victim Intoxicated." He placed a tick mark on the line further to the right. Above it, he wrote, "Victim Leaves Party." Further down the line, he placed another tick mark and above it wrote "12:30 AM" and below it wrote, "Search for Victim Begins." At the extreme left end of the line, yet another tick mark, labeling it "8:00 AM" and below, "Body Discovered." One look told him that there was a lot that was not in the picture. Beneath the time line at the 11:00 PM point, he wrote, "Others Out At Any Time: Mrs. Clay, Ms. Becker, McAllister, Morrie Clay, Wirth, Mrs. Wirth, and ?" He added the name of Jamie Sherman and in parenthesis after added "In from lake."

He walked back to his desk and stared at the board. An accident?

That did not explain the contusions or the lesion in the hair line. He picked up the phone to call Wirth.

Matthew, still in his pajamas, sat down with a coffee mug, opened his laptop, and began checking his email.

"Refill?" Shirley asked as she walked in the door.

"Great, sweetheart. Thanks."

"Sleep well?"

"I guess. Hope I didn't disturb you. I fell right off to sleep, but then the day caught up with me. I couldn't get back to sleep for all the stuff racing around in my head."

"You didn't disturb me." Shirley lowered herself into her favorite wingback chair. "I had problems too. I'm sick about it. Rene . . . right here in front of our places. Dr. Sherman's car. The neighborhood's not same. Feels different. Like something's crept in on us. Something . . . I don't know . . . something evil."

"I agree. The area's lost its innocence. It's probably been changing all along, and we didn't notice. Kids don't play hide-and-seek or kick-the-can after dark any more. They're running around plugged into these damned cell phones and MP-3 gadgets. . . ." Matthew's desk phone rang.

Matthew snatched the phone, listened for a few seconds and then turned back to Shirley. "It's detective Raker. He wants to talk to us some more."

"Now? On Sunday?"

"They're wrapping up the drowning incident. The Sheriff wants it closed as quickly as possible. He only needs a few minutes."

"Probably won't take 'no' for an answer will he?"

Matthew nodded. "What time this morning? . . . In about an hour?" He looked at Shirley again. She nodded. "That'll be fine."

When Raker arrived, Shirley escorted him into her husband's study. "Would you like me to stay?" she asked after the two men shook hands.

"If you don't mind," Raker replied.

"Not at all," Shirley said and sat down again in the wingback chair. Raker eased into a love seat that faced Matthew's desk.

"I appreciate your agreeing to see me on such short notice, especially on a Sunday." Raker produced a small spiral bound notebook. "I'll keep this as brief as possible. You were good friends with the deceased?"

"Friends, yes," Matthew replied. "Good friends, probably not. She and her husband were good clients of my partner and me. He'd done a lot for us in building our business. We saw them at the country club fairly regularly, but we never dined together, nor did we have them into our home except for the annual Fourth-of-July shindig. Mac and I play golf together three, maybe four, times a year. We have lunch together occasionally, all on a business rather than a personal level."

"And you, Mrs. Wirth?"

"That's about it," Shirley replied. "Rene and I were nothing more than acquaintances. Familiar and comfortable, but I don't think either of us held any special regard for the other. We weren't close . . . a neutral kind of acquaintance . . . if that makes any sense."

"It does. Who among the guests at the party would you regard as close friends of the victim."

"Hardly anyone," Matthew said.

"Skinner," Shirley corrected.

"Skinner? Yes, I've heard that name." Raker checked his notes. "Last name, Thorpe. Correct? We intend to talk to her. Anyone else?"

"Not at the party." Shirley said. "They're wealthy people. Their home is at the expensive end of the bay. They were here because they're clients . . . not friends in the strictest sense. Their real friends would move in different circles than we do."

"I agree," Matthew said.

"I got the overall impression that she wasn't well liked. Is that a fair statement?"

"She didn't make an effort at being liked," Matthew responded. "She was distant. Hard to figure out. It was awkward talking with her. Everybody found her that way. Wouldn't you say, dear?"

"Yes. She wasn't mean or vindictive. Just remote. In a world of her own. People like her are usually uncomfortable with people they think are beneath them."

"Did she have enemies?"

"Well, lots of people didn't care for her very much," Matthew said.

"Who for example?"

"I . . . I don't think I care to say."

"Please, Mr. Wirth, everything you saw will be treated with the strictest confidence. There will not be an inquest requiring testimony of anyone. I need the information for background purposes."

"I'm not at all sure that . . . well . . . it's generally well known that Mac and his wife didn't get along. Yesterday, he was ushering this young, leggy Denise Becker around, pawing her like a trophy. He couldn't have had much regard for his wife's feelings behaving the way he did."

"What about Ms. Becker. I haven't met her yet. Who is she?"

"We don't know her," Matthew replied. "Mac invited her. That's OK with us. I only saw her once . . . briefly . . . prior to yesterday."

"Yesterday was the first time for me," Shirley said.

"Anything romantic going on there?" Raker asked.

"Who knows? Be a damn fool to parade her around in front of everyone if there is. On the other hand, if there's going to be talk anyway, why trouble yourself with the niceties. Max fancies himself a ladies man. Talk doesn't bother him. Thinks it's a credit to his manhood . . . I'd guess."

"And she seemed comfortable with his attentions?" Raker asked.

"Completely. I wondered at first if she knew his wife was here. If she did, I don't have much respect for her. If she didn't, it's Mac's fault, and I don't respect him for that. But that's another thing, the rich end of the bay, they behave differently. More blasé about things."

"So have there been other women he has . . . what? . . sported around so others would notice?"

"Someone new each season. But this was really blatant. It isn't unusual to see him hanging out at the club bar . . . or the pool with some younger female . . . frequently enough to take notice. But I never saw him act like this before."

"Anyone else? You, Mrs. Wirth, anyone come to mind?"

"No. Nobody," Shirley replied.

Matthew shifted uncomfortably in his chair. "Well . . . you know how people take the fifth in a trial. This is a little like that."

"You're afraid you may implicate yourself?"

"No. It's just awkward. You see . . . I don't like . . . I *didn't* like Rene McAllister myself. She was rude, distrusting, and abrupt with my staff. And with me. I never cared to meet with her. She was suspicious. She recently created a situation that resulted in her husband requesting us to transfer all of their accounts to another investment firm. My partner, Morrie Clay, feels that same way . . . if not more strongly."

"You lost the accounts because of her?" Raker asked.

"Yes. Her thinking was cockeyed. She wouldn't listen to reason. Just one of those over-the-top things a man feels helpless against."

"McAllisters are no longer clients?"

"Technically . . . yes, they still are. The accounts have not transferred yet. Mac called Wednesday to let me know that we'd be receiving notification to transfer the accounts to Southern Central Bank and Trust after the first of the month."

"So, does her death change anything?" Raker asked.

"Well . . . yes . . . and no. Mac may still decide to move the accounts. I don't want take anything for granted. Her accounts go immediately into a revocable living trust as her will stipulates, and the trustee will govern how the money is invested and distributed from here on."

"Where is the trust?"

"With my company."

"So that part of her accounts would not transfer."

"Not immediately," Matthew replied. "Her husband is trustee, and he can fire us and turn it over to anyone he chooses."

"But the chances of retaining the accounts are somewhat improved because of her death."

"It adds another consideration to the equation for Mac . . . yes. A little."

"How much money are we talking about?" Raker asked.

"Nine-and-a half million, give or take."

"What's that worth to you and your partner?"

"Difficult to say. Our compensation system's on a sliding scale. The more business we do, the higher the commission scale. Figure about 30 basis points."

"Basis points?"

"Tenths of a percent. About $28,500 every year."

"That's all. Somehow I thought it would be more."

"That's all my partner and I get. The managers who do the trading get a cut too, perhaps up to half-a-percent. Of course, that's only on her half of the portfolio. We gross at least that much on his half. So, say, around $57,000."

"Losing an account like that is no a small matter," Raker said.

"No. You hear about accounts up in the hundreds of millions of dollars. They're out there, but the ordinary advisory group, like Morrie and me, seldom sees money like that. Our book of business is with clients who have somewhere between five-hundred thousand and two million to invest. The big city guys—people closer to Wall Street—walk off with the mega accounts, and that's fine with me."

"I appreciate your openness about it."

"Nothing to hide. Besides, you could find out very easily. Just ask Mac for his annual statement."

"Three-tenths of a percent," Raker said making the note.

"Give or take."

"Right. Give or take."

"One more thing," Raker said. "Did either of you notice that the deceased had bruises anywhere on her body while she was here? Any signs of an injury?"

Matthew looked a Shirley. "No. I didn't see anything," she said. "I wasn't around her that much, but . . . no. Nothing."

"I hardly saw her during the day," Matthew said. "Never up close. I couldn't say one way or the other."

Raker looked up and smiled. "Thanks, folks. This has been very helpful. All this is, as I said, confidential. I'd like to stroll down to the scene one more time . . . refresh my sense of things. Can I go out that door?"

Chapter 14

Jamie saw the CSI van pull into the driveway from his bedroom window. An officer got out of the vehicle and headed for the beach. "Why would they be back out so soon?" he asked under his breath. He dashed for the door.

"There's a cop headin' down to the dock," he shouted to Joyce in the kitchen as he passed. "Maybe I can get my boat back."

The officer had continued directly for the beach, stopped briefly to put on a pair of plastic gloves, and walked to the oar and picked it up. Jamie charged off the deck to intercept him.

"Hey, that's my oar. Where're you taking it?" he shouted half way across the yard.

"You'll get it back."

"I need that. I meant to put it back in my boat and forgot. I can't get by with just one oar."

"Yeah, well, I hear outboards are pretty reliable these days."

"That's not the point, man. That's my oar. It goes with my boat. You can't just walk off with it."

"It'll be booked in at the Sheriff's office When we close our investigation, you can claim it there."

"How long will that be?" Jamie asked stopping at the black and yellow tape restricting access to the area.

"Call the Sheriff and talk to him about it."

"Right. Call the Sheriff. Right. Can I get my boat back?"

"If you'll get out of my way, I can have this scene released and your boat back to you this morning. Now, step aside."

"This morning! Right. Great man." Jamie stepped back and watched the officer pull down the yellow and black tape and walk back to his van with the oar. Jamie could get back to business! Retrieve his stash from Monica Clay. Maybe better wait a day or two—just to be sure. If he moved it and the police returned for anything and find it, he'd be in deep shit. Better wait. Get out tonight. See people. Let them know what's going down. Everyone could wait another day or two. They'd do that rather than risk going into the town to make a new connection. Nobody was as easy or safe to deal with as he. Nobody'd move in on him with just a two day break in supply. Not if he got out right away and talked to everyone. If somebody needed something right away, he could get a bag to them. Monica would let him break it down at her house. She'd have to.

"What was that all about?" Monica called from her deck catching Jamie by surprise.

"Dude's from the Sheriff's office."

"What'd he want?"

"My oar."

"Your oar?"

"Yeah."

Monica walked to the edge of the deck so that she would not need to raise her voice. "Why'd he want your oar?"

"Wouldn't say. But I get it back. I check with the Sheriff's office in a week or so." Jamie sauntered over to his neighbor. "Must have something to do with the drowning. But I'll get it back."

Monica fought to remain calm. Could the oar implicate her? Had Rene touched it when she was in the water? Could any finger prints still be on it . . . even though she wiped it off? "Well . . . that's good . . . I mean . . . that you'll get it back. Why would they want it?"

"Cops. You know. Who knows why cops do anything? You saw them at my house the other night. Boy, I owe you one, Mrs. Clay."

"Didn't he . . . the officer . . . say anything at all? Didn't he question you?"

"Naw. He got up tight. Wanted me out of his way. That's all. As long as they keep snooping around, I need to leave my package with you."

Monica placed both of hands on the railing to the deck and leaned toward her visitor. "I want it out of my house. My husband is very angry about it. And don't talk about it where we can be overheard."

"That's cool. One thing, though. I'm gonna need my personal bag . . . you know the last one I gave you when I was leaving. Maybe not today. Too much going on, but . . . say, sometime later . . . tomorrow."

"I'll have it ready. I don't want the boys . . . or anyone to notice. I have some leverage here too."

"It's cool, Mrs. Clay. No problem."

Monica looked up. A man in a business suit was walking down to the dock, the crime scene. "Who's that?" she asked.

Jamie turned. "Beats me. Never saw him before." Both watched as the man strolled to the Sherman dock and looked along the beach on either side of it. "Another cop?" Jamie speculated.

"God, they're making a big deal out of this," Monica said and waved at the man. The man nodded and began walking toward them.

"Why'd you do that?" Jamie asked.

"Because it's what I'd normally do. If you want to look guilty of anything, just forget to act as you normally would."

"Hi," the man shouted still several paces distant. "Nice morning."

"Beautiful," Monica called back. The man was older, graying, perhaps just under six feet, perhaps in his early sixties. He had a relaxed stride, and as he approached, she noticed he was handsome, face tanned, with a very serious set to his jaw.

"Detective Raker, Melville County Sheriff's Department. Just out for another look at the scene."

"Yes. Terrible, terrible thing. I don't think any of us can walk by there without remembering what happened."

"You are?" Raker asked.

"Oh, yes. Monica Clay, and this is my friend . . . well my friend's son . . . from next door . . . Jamie Sherman. We were just talking about it. An officer just left . . . a moment before you got here. He took down the tape."

"Yeah, and he took the oar to my boat."

Annoyed at Jamie's interruption, Monica continued, "I was relieved to see it come down . . . the tape I mean. I guess that means something, that it's been decided that it was an accident . . . something like that."

"That's what the Sheriff's office is telling the press. Do either of you mind if I ask you a couple of questions?"

"Of course not," Monica replied.

"I'm cool."

"Mrs. Clay, I understand that you may have been the last person to see the victim alive. Is that right?"

"Well . . . I saw her . . . yes. Whether I was the last person to see her or not, I don't know. Somebody else may have. . ."

"But nobody at the party seemed to know where she was before her husband started looking for her."

"Yes. That's right. I just thought that . . . well . . . maybe somebody saw her after I did . . . somebody on their way home from the party . . . somebody who might have been passing . . . who lives down the beach."

"Those are all possibilities, and we're checking them. But, suppose you were the last, you said she was very intoxicated."

"Most people who had that much to drink wouldn't still have been on their feet. She didn't understand me, and I couldn't make any sense out of what she was saying. I told the other officer all of that."

"I know. I'm not suggesting that I doubt anything that has been said by anyone. I just like to get some information first hand. And you, you're Dr. Sherman's son, the one I didn't meet when I came out to look at your dad's Porsche. Somebody really did a number on it."

"Yeah . . . well . . . my Dad's toy. No big deal."

"An $85,000 automobile. That's a big deal to most people."

"Yeah . . . but . . . you know . . . he didn't need the car. It's like a lot of things he owns. He owns them just to own them. Helps him justify himself."

"Your brother and your dad didn't come up with a very long list of people they thought could have done it. How about you? Any ideas?"

"Well . . . hey . . . there're people around that resent that kind of shit . . . you know . . . ostentation . . . consumption for its own sake. Like scratching a car in a parking lot with a key. Privilege like that pisses some people off . . . that's all I'm saying."

"So it could be anyone?"

"Yeah, man. People resent that shit."

"And your stepmother said you reported seeing someone down at the dock at the time of the victim's disappearance, yet later you told a CSI officer that you had not seen anyone. What changed your mind?"

"I was tired, man. I'd been up all day. There was smoke drifting around from the dumb, fucking fireworks. I just don't think I could say that anybody was there. In fact, I feel pretty certain now that nobody was."

"Pretty certain."

"Completely certain, then. OK."

"We want to be 'completely certain' in matters like this."

"I am. It's cool."

"That's all I can ask. Well, nice meeting both of you. Thanks for your input. I'd better get back to town. Have a good day."

Raker he felt the eyes of both of them on his back as he walked away. The conversation yielded little, although Jamie's changing his story about seeing someone at the scene was troubling. The reference to smoke was obviously bogus. Fireworks had concluded fully two hours before the victim went missing. Even on a calm night the smoke would have cleared away. No names were coming off his whiteboard, least of all either Monica Clay or Jaime Sherman. He decided to drive back into Charles City.

"Got a minute?" Tim Moran greeted Raker as he walked into the City-County Office Building. "I think it's time we compare notes and have a look at what our guys have been working on."

Raker invited the SBI officer to his office. "As you know," Moran began, "we've been concerned that the investigation into the drowning could spill over into the case we're building against Jamie Sherman and the people he is tied into here in the city."

"I picked that up."

"We've got the drowning and the vandalism of the Sherman vehicle. It's a hell of a coincidence, but all the law enforcement traffic around the neighborhood could spook young Sherman and whoever he's working with. We can't prove a damn thing about the vandalism. We've worked with the lab guys, but nothing's turned up. I think the Sherman kid crossed up a supplier somewhere . . . or another dealer . . . and the acid trick with the car was a warning. Somebody's getting even. Sherman will get his money from his insurance company, and that'll be it unless it ties into something else somewhere along the line. We want to talk to young Sherman. We want him to help us."

Raker wanted to say that he was suspicious of Jamie also, but he checked his impulse.

"We're thinking we should go to Dr. Sherman first," Moran continued, "let him know what the stakes are for his son, and then get him to agree to a deal for the kid so that the lawyers aren't brought in right away. The sooner we go with this, the better."

"Why are you telling me this?" Raker shifted in his chair.

"I want you in on it. Both the drowning and the vandalism cases are on your desk, and we don't get tangled up in one another's footwork. Besides, Doc Sherman hasn't met me. It's going to be a shock to him, assuming he doesn't know what his kid's into. Having someone there he knows might make for a better outcome."

"He doesn't know me all that well."

"But you've met with him. What? Twice?"

"Right. Twice."

"How'd he strike you?"

"Another doctor. Gets his own way. A touch of the God complex. Knows best . . . about everything. Congenial enough."

"Good. So. The Sheriff's given the green light. He sees the cases overlap, and it's better to work together and avoid getting caught at cross purposes. Besides, the Sheriff's ready to close the case. He's calling it an accidental death. I don't think you will be spending more time on it. Any problem with that?"

"Yes," Raker replied. "Something's not right and keeps bothering me about the drowning. At least five people may have had good reasons for wanting that woman dead. And just as many had the opportunity."

"To what? To jump into the lake and hold the woman's head under until she drowned and then . . . what? . . . go back to the party. Not likely."

"Yeah. Well. The pieces don't all fit for me either. I'd feel better if they did. I want to run with it a little bit longer," Raker said.

"That's between you and the Sheriff. All I know is I want some of your time, and I don't want you or anybody else screwing up what we've got going with the Sherman kid. We've got two years in it, and if it breaks our way, we can shut down an organization in town here that controls most of the traffic."

"I can steer clear of anything that will be a concern. But I did talk to Jamie Sherman just an hour or so ago."

"Where? Out there? At the lake?"

"Yes. As I said in the meeting, I wanted to know why he admitted seeing someone at the site of the drowning and then later denied it. He said he was tired and wasn't sure that he had seen anybody."

"What do you make of that?" Moran asked.

"I trust his first statement. He volunteered that he saw someone. I don't know why he would later deny it."

"Anything else?" Moran asked.

"No. That was it. Very casual. Strictly about the drowning. I don't know enough about your case with him to say anything that would make him suspicious. You're probably better off keeping me in the dark."

"Great," Moran said, "for now, let's leave it on a need-to-know basis."

"Fine with me. What time do you want see Dr. Sherman? Sometime tomorrow?"

"Right. Tomorrow. Can you just stay on deck? I'll call and get back to you."

Chapter 15

Morrie was glad that Matthew was not going to report in at the office for the rest of the week. He was relieved, too, to get away from Monica. Sunday had passed with little else exchanged between him and his wife. Monica had retreated to the bedroom and spent most of the day there, emerging only to prepare the evening meal and to explain to the boys that she was not feeling well, an excuse they accepted readily because of her history with migraine headaches.

The office was quiet after a long holiday weekend. Clients were still away from home returning from the mountains and the beach. The month-end statements would be arriving in the mail during the week. The June statement would report year-to-date returns, and a simple doubling of the figure made it easy to project a possible annual return—a talking point with clients. In the year so far, returns were better than average. Morrie did not expect the deluge of calls that began the day statements arrived and continued unabated until the postal service had delivered the last in their system.

"So, how is everything? I thought you'd want to see the McAllister files. There're on your desk." It was Cheryl.

"Well, pretty bad." Morrie pushed back from his desk. "The

party was fine, but to find Rene McAllister's body the next morning. That. . . that was a real shock. Changed everything. Made all the partying seem inappropriate."

"It's all over the news. The TV. The paper this morning. I didn't know that they thought it was suicide."

"Suicide? Who said it was suicide?"

"The paper. Do you want to see it?"

"Yes." Cheryl reeled and disappeared into the open office. The day was getting underway. Phones began to ring. The morning *squawk box* program could be heard on the company closed TV network channel—the commentators straining to find a topic of interest after the holiday weekend. Cheryl reappeared and spread the newspaper in front of him.

"See! When asked," she began reading, "whether the death may have been a suicide, Melville County Sheriff Johnston responded, 'We have not ruled that out.'"

"That doesn't say that it *was* a suicide."

"Well, I know, but it says they haven't ruled it out either. I thought it was interesting that it would come out after the authorities have had time to investigate."

"I agree. Do you mind if I keep this?"

"It's your paper." Cheryl smiled. "How's the boss taking it?"

"Matthew? Matthew's fine. He's upset that it happened at his party. I talked to him late yesterday. He's concerned about Mac. We need to freeze all the accounts in Rene's name. The joint account . . . the checking account . . . can remain open. But everything else needs to be locked up . . . no more trading . . . nothing. Let the managers know. Let compliance know."

"Compliance has already called."

"Really! What'd they say?"

"Just what you did. Louise and I have already taken care of everything."

"Haven't heard from the trust people yet have you?"

"No. Should I call them?"

"No. Let it ride. Nothing's going to happen for a few days now. Not until after the funeral."

Cheryl returned to her desk. Morrie knew that Monica would not have seen the paper. He picked up the phone and called her.

"Have you seen today's paper?" he asked immediately.

"No. Why?"

"The Sheriff's Department hasn't ruled out suicide in Rene's death. I thought that might give you more perspective on how this looks to the rest of the world . . . might help you with what you've been going through. I told you. . ."

"Morrie," Monica interrupted, "I'm in no mood for I-told-you-so's. OK? They were out here yesterday morning looking over everything. They took the oar from the dock back with them. Do you know what that means?"

"Maybe not a damn thing. I thought calling you might help you feel better. I can see it was a mistake."

"I won't feel better until this is over . . . behind us . . . settled . . . when there're no more questions about any of it." She paused.

"One thing at a time," Morrie said finally. "Whenever something like this comes along, the picture improves."

"Good ol' methodical Morrison. You said you'd decided what you were going to do. It didn't register with me at the time. This morning I realized you never told me anything."

"This isn't exactly the best place to talk about it, is it?"

"Well, tonight then. No . . . damn it . . . close the door to your office and tell me now. I don't want to wait."

Morrie walked to the door, looked out briefly, and then closed it quietly. "OK. It's simple. It's the only shot I've got. I'm going ahead as if nothing's wrong. Rene's dead. She can't say that she didn't ask me to buy the hedge fund. She can't say that she didn't sign the partnership agreement and agree to leaving the margin agreement in place. If somebody challenges anything, I'll deal with it at the time. I didn't recognize at first what a difference having her out of the way makes. Worst case, it's my word against a dead woman's. They can criticize me for letting her do it, but given who she was and how she treated everyone, I can defend myself."

"Suppose somebody thinks Matthew did it?" Monica asked.

"So what? They can't prove that any more than they can prove that I did it."

"But the trust company. What was it you said about the trust company?"

"I said they would take issue with the hedge fund. They can't hold it. It's an unregulated security. They find it and everything will come to light. Finding it, though, doesn't mean they'll think that I made an unauthorized purchase. *I* was afraid that would be obvious to everyone. But it's not necessarily the case. It might not go that way at all."

"God, Morrie. One minute, we're ruined. The sky is falling! You're going get fired . . . going to prison. 'Rene's death doesn't do us any good.' Now, all of a sudden, maybe it's going to work out. Why'd you put me through this?"

"I over-reacted. It can still blow up any time. At least this is a strategy. A chance. A small one, but better than none at all."

"So it's better, but it's not better."

"Well . . . yeah . . . sort of. It's a chance. That's all I can say. At least it's a chance."

"How long will it take before this gets resolved? I hate this, Morrie."

"I hate it too. Look. When the funeral is over, the trust company will look at the files. We'll probably have a meeting with McAllister . . . Matthew and I . . . and we'll hope everything goes through without a hitch."

"That long," Monica said flatly and hung up the phone.

Morrie dropped the receiver back into its cradle and began rifling through the McAllister files until he came upon the limited partnership agreement required in buying shares of the hedge fund. At the bottom of the document was Rene McAllister's signature as Cheryl had signed it. He compared the forged signature to other documents in the file that had been signed by the deceased. "It's a stretch."

"Central Carolina Radiology. "We take radiology to a new level." The receptionist's telephone salutation stuck with Raker since getting into the car with Tim Moran to ride out to see Dr. Sherman. Sherman's group had also handled the radiology for Raker's wife Susan during the final months of her illness. The group used the slogan on the local public radio station, as if there were levels to radiology and Sherman's group was going to win out over the rest of the field because they had an inside track.

Tens of thousands of dollars went into the months that dragged on in an effort to save his wife's life. Yet, not once . . . not from the very beginning nor anywhere over the weeks that he watched her fade away did he get an explanation that helped him understand her chances for survival. Her referring doctor was prohibited from making hospital visits. In the hospital, a stranger took over. He alternated with a female colleague several days of each week, and then an internist, and then again somebody else. A few days after she was released to go home, the radiologist ordered him to bring her into the facility where they stood her up one more time to the X-ray, so frail she could hardly support herself, wincing when the female technician shoved her brittle gray shoulders against the cold frame of the X-ray machine and asked her to hold the posture until the X-ray was completed. This was one level of radiology—an inhuman level. His wife died five days after the final X-ray. Raker noticed the radiologist, the man he never saw, the man who delegated all patient contact to a technician trained at the local community college, got paid for the procedure.

His wife's oncologist met with him twice, but the vagaries of the chemotherapy and other regimens were never adequately explained to him. Every morning when he returned to the hospital to see her toward the end of the stay, he feared that he would find she had passed away in the night and nobody had either the courage or the decency to call him and let him know. One night, he answered the phone and found her weak voice on the line. The fire alarm had gone off in the hospital, and she was terrified that she would not be rescued and would die in the flames. He sped to the hospital, dashed in from the parking lot, but upon arriving found nothing amiss. When he reached the floor of his wife's room, he inquired about the fire alarm. "It does that all the time. Doesn't mean anything," the nurse at the station said. Yet nobody had reassured his wife it was a false alarm. Nobody had done anything at all.

Only the hospice people seemed to understand. "It's getting close to the end," one middle-aged woman said. "She has a morphine pump. It won't be long." He took her home for her final days. Rented a hospital bed for the living room so that she could watch TV and watch him prepare their simple meals in the kitchen. He sat up nights with her, helped her with her oxygen, held her hand, and tried to converse. Nothing was private any more. Her frail body. Her struggles with elimination. At first, it embarrassed her to have him help, gentle and patient as he was. But she grew accepting of his hands, his touch, and she smiled to acknowledge what little humor could be found in her helplessness. As her spirit drained away, she merely tolerated his ministrations, conceding to the inevitability of each tiresome, often painful, routine.

One night, she insisted in halting speech that someone was in the hall that led from the living room to their bedroom.

"There's nobody there, love," he reassured her. But she would not take his word. She insisted, moaning, that someone was there, someone in the hall, and she was afraid. She became so agitated that Raker put his hand on her bony shoulder and stepped away from his bedside chair. "Here, sweetheart, I'll go check for you. I'll go see if anyone is there. OK?"

She nodded with so much energy that she startled Raker. He walked into the hall and turned on the light. He glanced one more time back at her and then walked the length of the corridor, opening all the doors, peering into every room, and returned to her bedside.

"Gone now?" she moaned.

"Yes, Sweetheart. Gone now. You rest."

"Good. Thank you." She closed her eyes. He looked at her for several minutes, and when he was convinced that she was at rest, he sat back down.

"It won't be long now," the words from the hospice woman stayed in the forefront of his thoughts. He went into the office everyday for an hour or so to catch up on what was happening on the cases assigned to him, and see his partner and his friends. Everyone was supportive. On that final day, he opened the garage door, backed his Chevrolet out on the driveway, and headed once again for the City-County Building. Reaching the first intersection, he made a right turn, drove around the block, and returned home. He wanted to see her. Maybe this was not the last time, but he wanted to see her again—this morning.

The hospice lady smiled, not the least surprised to see him back, and left the room. Susan was exactly as he had left her, barely breathing, her cough nothing more than a gag. Her eyes were closed. He reached for her. Her pain was almost at an end. The false hopes. The reassessments that meant nothing. He wanted to see her at peace. She did not deserve the pain. If he had to leave her, her struggles should leave too. Now! While he was angry. They should go. Disappear like the ghost in the hallway. There would be time to grieve. Time to remember. But now, it was time for whatever held her to release her, to let her be. She had earned her peace, earned it with her steadfastness, her laughter, and her love over their years together.

"Hey, snap out of it," Moran barked. "We're almost here. You OK?"

"Yeah. I just don't like these places."

"Doctor's offices?"

"Yes."

"Well, we're were lucky to get Sherman's time," Moran said. They pulled into the parking lot to Central Carolina Radiology. A receptionist ushered them back to Sherman's office and asked them to wait. Raker noticed the disorder. Several files on the desk. Periodicals strewn across it and the credenza behind. An in-box heaped with mail. The door opened suddenly, and Sherman stepped into the room. He paused when he recognized Raker.

"My car?" he asked, raising an eyebrow, and then looking to Moran, "Are you involved in this?" Sherman nodded at Moran as if giving him permission to speak and then walked around to his desk and sat down.

"No, Dr. Sherman. We need to discuss some trouble with your son," Raker replied.

"My son?"

"Jamie," Moran clarified. "I'll get to the point. We're here to enlist your cooperation. We've been building on case on your son . . . had him under observation for several months . . . and we think that he could play a key role in helping us bring down a major organization here in Melville County."

"Ha! Really? You've got the wrong guy. I can't get him out of bed in the morning."

"Are you interested in cooperating with us . . . the local Sheriff's Office and the SBI?" Moran asked.

"Not until I know what this is about."

"I understand. We can arrest your son and charge him with possession and dealing. It may prove expensive to provide an attorney for defense."

"This is a threat then."

"No, sir," Moran said. "Just a statement of where things stand. Your son is in a strong position to help us with an ongoing investigation, and we'd like to enlist his help, with your support. We want you on our side in this."

"I still don't see how I can promise anything without knowing what this is all about."

"Doctor," Moran said, "your son has been dealing drugs for months now, out at the lake, and on campus before he dropped out. We've already talked to the Deputy District Attorney. If we arrest him and take him into custody, his ties with his associates will be severed and nothing will come of any of this. If he'll work with us, we can keep him under surveillance, allow him to live at home, and go about the day-to-day as he has been. We think he will lead us to the people we really want. Then we'll need his help if there's a trial. We believe those same people may be involved with the vandalism to your vehicle."

"Dealing drugs?" Sherman said. "You're sure? Ha! Unbelievable! How the hell . . . God damn it! That's where all the money is coming from."

"Sir," Moran said, "we're sure you didn't know about his activities."

"I can damn well guarantee you I didn't. Drugs! What kind of drugs?"

"Marijuana. That's all we know now. Other illegal substances may be available to him . . . meth, for example . . . but we have no reason to believe he is anything more than a casual user himself . . . dealing to support his own usage."

"You could arrest right now?"

"Yes. We're close to his movements and arresting him in the most incriminating circumstances would not be difficult."

"How serious would that be?" Sherman asked.

"A felony. If convicted, it would mean jail. The community's concerned about dealing to kids. Judges aren't going easy on this kind of thing. It'd be expensive to defend him."

"God damn!" Sherman slumped back in his chair and looked off to the side. All three men sat silently for several minutes. "Well, this is no decision. He's my son. I can't see him start his life with a felony conviction. The last place he needs to be is in jail . . . or us . . . my family . . . in the news over something like this. What do you want from me?"

"We're hoping we could arrange to meet with your son at your home with you sitting in and get you to help us persuade him to cooperate."

"Fine. I can get away from the office tomorrow. We can meet at our lake home at 1:00 PM."

Moran stood up immediately. "Thank you, Dr. Sherman. 1:00 PM it is. Detective Raker and I will be there. We don't want any fanfare. We will be in an unmarked car. There's no reason for anyone to question anything." Moran and Sherman shook hands. Raker followed suit, a little less enthusiastically, and the two turned and walked out of the office.

Raker dropped down into his chair when he got back to his office, took off his glasses and rubbed his eyes. Playing second-fiddle to another officer was enervating. "Goddamn depressing job," he muttered. He had hoped that, as he approached retirement, the stress of dealing with his assignments would lessen. Susan and he had chosen Heron Lake for their home and had signed on with Melville County because the liaison work, coordinating county cases with Heron Lake township, sounded like a cushy position. They were not aware of Susan's cancer when they decided to move from Minnesota. Being in the South and away from the harsh, confining winters of the upper Midwest, they could slow down, ease into retirement and pursue the many interests they shared. He had wanted away from the metropolitan area with the gang violence, the ever-present influence of the mob, the wasted humanity that was always part of the impoverished inner city.

Today, he felt too close to all that he and his wife had worked to avoid. The bustling lakeside township had its own seeds of corruption taking root. The mob was here, somewhere dealing drugs, hustling kids, chauffeuring runaways into Charles City and on to Atlanta or Miami. They appeared respectable, on the lake in million dollar cabin cruisers designed to go to sea. They were here, and perhaps worse, all the wannabes who aped them, trying to make a mark in the local criminal hierarchy but without as much cunning, discernment, or guile as their more experienced counterparts.

After Susan died, the future was of no concern. Getting from one day to the next—the loneliness and emptiness, the tormenting memories of her suffering took over. Now almost two months later, he was only beginning to experience moments when he felt like himself again. Release from his grief, however, did not mean that the fullness of life came back to him. He accepted the tedium of do-ing the things each week that life required in order to make it from one day to the next—laundry, grocery lists, cleaning house, balanc-ing the checking account. He no longer thought about retirement. Work, uncomplicated cases, the nature of things in a community away from the city, became a refuge, provided structure and a dis-traction. Now his job was asking for energy again, for curiosity and thought.

Something was letting go within him. His lethargy, the numbness left behind by his retreating grief, finally gave way. Disappointment yielded to anger. He wanted to strike back against his losses. Something was wrong at the lake, in the ghetto of mil-lionaires, the colony of self-satisfied, the smug privileged pillars of the community. One of their own was dead. He had questions. He could work on that. He could run from the emptiness and engage again with his experience, his wits, and his resentment.

Somewhere in the sketchy details on his whiteboard was the di-rection he needed. It was always there, rising out of the relationships of time, people, opportunity, motive, and method. Method was not on the board. He did not want to force anything; add the trivial in hopes it would become significant. The phone rang.

"The Sheriff wants to release the body of the McAllister woman, but said to check with you first," the officer on the line said.

"Not yet."

"Not yet?"

"That's what I said, 'Not yet'."

"A funeral home has called already. McAllister's some kind of wheel. The Sheriff wants the case closed and the body released."

"What was that in the paper about the Sheriff saying he had not ruled out suicide? Why close the case after making a dumb-ass statement like that?"

"All I know is he wants the case closed."

"Tell him, 'No!' He can over-rule me if he wants, but I can talk to the press too. Tell him that. Tell him I want to see everything that supports his comment that it could have been a suicide. Is that clear?"

"Yes, sir." The officer hung up.

The phone rang again, more loudly, Raker thought. "Raker, this is Sheriff Johnston. I want this goddamn case closed. We need the support of those people out there, and dragging things out isn't going to make any of them any happier with me or this office. Is that clear?"

"Telling the press the woman's death was a probably suicide really helped community relations then, didn't it."

"I didn't say it was a probable suicide. I said that we had not ruled out suicide."

"Now we want to close the case without verifying one way or the other. Is that right?"

"All right, God damn it, I shouldn't have said it. I wasn't expecting a question like that. I thought about printing a retraction, but that would just call more attention to it. If we close the case, we can lie back, and if anyone has a question, we can respond that we ruled it out. No point in pissing into the wind on something like this."

"I want forty-eight hours," Raker said.

"What the hell for? That's two more days."

"I'm not satisfied with what we have so far. I want forty-eight hours to resolve my own doubts."

"Can't do it. You have until tomorrow."

"That's not enough time."

"Look, SBI doesn't want you guys poking around out there. I want all of my people away from whatever business they have out there, and that's it. I'm sticking my neck out to give you another hour."

"Until noon, then, day-after-tomorrow. Wednesday? Yeah, Wednesday, at noon. Maybe sooner. I'll let you know, but we keep the case open until Wednesday noon."

"Not one fucking minute more. And stay away from that place. If you absolutely must go back out there, you get permission directly from me. I don't want the SBI calling my people amateurs and blaming us because their case fell apart. Got that?"

"I'll clear with you. Yes, sir."

"See that you do." The line fell silent.

"And fuck you too." Raker sat back down. "Now what, damn it?" He looked back at the whiteboard. A method. How did the woman die? How was she killed? A weapon. He grabbed the phone again.

"Evidence," a voice answered.

"This is detective Raker. You guys have the oar that was brought in from the McAllister drowning?"

"Yeah. We're supposed to hold it until the case is closed . . ."

"Has it been run through forensics?"

"Prints. That's all. We're just supposed to hold it. Nobody said anything more than printing it."

"I want it run through forensics as soon as possible." Forensics, although nominally responsible to the Sheriff's office, was run by the Charles City-Melville County Police Department who determined the lab's priorities.

"We can get it over there, but I can't guarantee you I can get it processed any time soon."

"You let me worry about that. Just get it over to them."

"I know things are backing up," Dr. Sherman barked into the telephone intercom. "I need another five minutes." He disconnected from the intercom, pushed for an outside line, and speed-dialed his lakeside home.

"Joyce, it's Tom. Is Jamie there?"

"No. He was earlier this morning. He's usually gone by this time."

"Is his boat is tied up at the dock?"

"Just a minute." A moment later, Joyce was back on the line. "No. It's not."

"Shit!"

"Why? What's wrong?"

"When he comes back, have him call me. Understand. He needs to call me the minute he's back in the house."

"I will, Tom. What's this all about? He'll want to know."

"Just tell him to call or there'll be hell to pay. OK?"

"Yes. Yes, of course."

"How much smoking doing you think Jamie does?"

"Smoking?"

"Yes. Pot. You know, marijuana."

"Quite a bit. Everyday, I'd guess. I smell it in his room . . . when I go in there . . . but he keeps it on his boat and smokes when he's out on the lake."

"Every time he lights up he's playing Russian roulette. His heart isn't built to take it. I didn't think that he could afford it. Where's the cash coming from?"

"Tom, I . . . don't have any idea . . . Not from me. What has this to do with me? Are you angry with me?"

"No, God damn it. He's too much for you. I know that. I just never thought he'd be guilty of selling pot around the lake. That's how he's getting his money . . . from selling dope."

"Oh. I wondered, but . . ."

"I suppose you suspected it all along."

"No! No, Tom. I just wondered . . . as you did . . . where he kept getting his money. I thought it was from his mother . . . as you said."

"Well, it's not. Damn him. You have him call me right away. OK?"

"Fine. Yes. Sure."

"Now, what are you doing tomorrow right after lunch?"

"Nothing. Why?"

"Find something to do. Go shopping. Something. I want you out of the house right after lunch for a couple of hours. Not a word to anyone about this. The police are meeting with Jamie and me at the house tomorrow around one o'clock. Don't tell him a thing. Do you understand?"

"Of course, Tom. I understand. Perfectly."

"Good. If anything comes up, call my pager. I'll see you to-night." Sherman hung up.

"I wish they'd lock him up," Joyce said under breath as she walked to the deck. Sherman could be impersonal, especially when he was at the office. She complained early in their marriage about his detached manner toward her, but he did not understand. One day, after a heated argument, during which she exhausted herself trying get him to understand how distancing his behavior was, the florist arrived with a dozen red roses and a preprinted note which read, "For My Sweetheart" and he had signed, "Tom Sherman, MD." Placing the roses in a vase on the dining room table, Joyce accepted the futility of ever confronting her husband again about her needs.

A cool breeze stuck her as she stepped out onto the deck. The day was bright. No traffic on the lake. The waves, reaching nearly the white-cap height, sloshed onto the beach in front of their home. In the back of the yard, a mockingbird was performing his reper-toire. Joyce looked to the left, toward the Wirth home, in hopes of spotting her friend, Shirley, but the house was quiet. A gust of wind whipped her brown hair across her eyes, and she ran her fingers through it to pull it back into place. Turning toward the Clay home, she was startled to see Monica Clay lounging on the deck.

"Hey!" Joyce waived.

"Hey." Monica looked up, but Joyce thought she sounded a less than congenial.

"Didn't I see you with Jamie this morning? Talking?" Monica raised up in her chaise. "Don't get up," Joyce said. "Let me come over there . . . for just a minute. I don't want to bust in on you. It's just terribly important that Jamie gets in touch with his father. Did he say where he might be going? His boat is gone."

"No. He didn't say. He seemed concerned about an officer who was here briefly, but that was the extent of our conversation," Monica replied.

"You mean the man who took the oar back with him?" Joyce asked.

"No. The detective. The man in street clothes."

"Oh. There was another officer here already? Talking to Jamie?"

"Yes. I'm sure it was about the drowning."

"The drowning. Of course. I was afraid . . . well . . . never mind. False alarm. I'm sorry. I shouldn't have disturbed you." Joyce turned to go back to her own home. Monica's manner had not been welcoming. There was a stridency about her neighbor that she did not like. Joyce was never quite sure of where she stood with Monica when her neighbor shifted into a more assertive mood.

"Why? What did you think the police would be talking to him about?" Monica called out.

"Well . . . ah . . . seems they want to talk to him again. Something about drug dealing. Tomorrow. Oh God, I'm not supposed to say anything, but it's important, so if you see him, let me know. You won't say anything, will you? I mean about the police. Just that he needs to come home and see me. Tom'd kill me if he knew I let the cat out of the bag."

"Not a word."

"Oh . . . good. I get ahead of myself sometimes. Just have him see me . . . or . . . if you see him . . . you know . . . Jamie . . . come back. Whatever."

"I will. Don't worry. I can keep a confidence."

"Thanks."

Chapter 16

"Another doctor's second wife," Monica thought watching Joyce walk away. A whiner. Joyce probably could not hold her own in the singles auction once out of college, but could spot an unhappy husband a mile away and lay easy claim, first to his bed, and as the stakes increased, to his devotion. Why did police want to talk to Jamie? His dealing? They had spoken to him three times already. Why hadn't it come up before now?

The detective in street clothes . . . something about his manner. Why he was poking around? He was hard to read. Probably didn't take anything either she or Jamie said at face value. Something else was up.

Monica's sons had left earlier in the day; Jason to summer basketball camp, and Michael to the country club for a round with his buddies. Jamie Sherman was probably out on the lake making the rounds, although he had not asked her to return his stash. He probably wouldn't until the police were finished in the neighborhood. They'd close the case soon enough if they decided Rene's death was a suicide. Jamie'd come back for his stash then. If he put off telling the police about seeing her at the dock much longer, he wouldn't be credible. He'd be reversing himself a second time. And the detective had asked him point blank.

If the police were onto Jamie's drug dealing, they could make life difficult for him. Jamie was smart. He'd accuse her in a heartbeat if he thought it would shift suspicion away from him. Finding the stash in her home would lead to charges. She'd couldn't explain why she had the dope. Her only real excuse would reveal her complicity in Rene's death. The publicity would be disastrous. Matthew would break off with Morrie. Morrie's reputation would be shot. Jamie'd lie through his teeth about everything. If the police were closing in, time was running out. Jamie had to be kept quiet.

"Your father wants you to call him right away," Joyce shouted to Jamie as he came up from the dock. Jamie glared at her as he stomped across the deck. "You will call, won't you? I promised him you would."

"Shouldn't make promises you can't keep."

"I promised I'd tell you to call."

"OK. You told me. Chill. I can't get him now. It's after 6:00."

"Then you need to wait for him. He wants to talk to you."

Jamie dashed up the stairs his own room. Joyce heard the door slam behind him. His foul mood was not staged for his stepmother's benefit. His rounds on the lake were disappointing. Customers were eager for a delivery. Their supplies were depleted over the holiday weekend, and they wanted him to replenish them as soon as possible. He made as many excuses as he could but finally began lying, telling them whatever he needed to say so that he could go on to his next stop. It was too much like work. He did not like fearing he could lose customers. He had taken risks to build up his business. Now, all the fuss over a drowning threatened to weaken his standing, create an opportunity for others to move in, guys from

Charles City who knew about his gig out on the lake, full-time operators who would shove him aside if he failed to come through for his customers.

It could be hours before his father returned. He was not going to wait around for one more person to jump him about something. He grabbed a jacket and bolted back out the door. "I'm sick of waiting around," he shouted at Joyce. "He's never been here when he says he'll be."

Joyce heard the storm door slam and watched for him to round the corner of the house and head for the dock, but he never appeared. Had he changed his mind? Decided to wait after all? She walked to the back door, opened it, but he was nowhere in sight. The back door to the Clay home was closing. Jamie had no reason to go over there. Perhaps he did not go far, would return shortly and be at home when Tom arrived. Tom'd be late again. Dinner'd be late. Another evening ruined because of Jamie.

An outboard motor started up. She walked quickly to the deck. It was Jamie. His 35 horsepower Johnson whined away from the dock. There was nothing she could do about it. Tom'd be angry when he came home.

"I told him to call, Tom. He doesn't pay any attention to anything I tell him," Joyce explained. "He was here. I told him to wait. Then he jumped in his boat and was gone."

"Did you tell him why I wanted to talk to him?"

"No. You said not to say anything to anyone. I assumed you meant him too."

"Just as well. Be good to know when he'll be back. Calling on his cell phone won't work. He sees the caller ID and won't answer. We'll just have to wait him out."

⌁✧⌁

As he pulled into the driveway, Morrie was startled to see the back door to his home swing open and Jamie Sherman dash out and run toward the beach. Morrie's anger flared as he remembered that Monica was holding Jamie's inventory. "What was that creep doing over here?" he asked Monica as soon as he stepped into the kitchen.

"He picked up his stuff."

"Great. Good riddance."

"No. He didn't take it all. A dime bag. The rest is still here."

"We can't hold it forever, Monica. I want that stuff out of . . ."

"Don't raise your voice. The boys are here. Dinner will be ready in 30 minutes. Go see Mike. He got an eagle on 17 today and is eager to tell you about it," Monica said. "He's in the family room."

Morrie took Monica's direction to mean that she did not want him in the kitchen. "An eagle, huh," Morrie called out. "What's this I hear about an eagle today?"

"Yeah, man," Mike responded. "On 17. Reached it in 2, Dad. In 2!" Morrie met his son in the dining room.

"Way to go!" Morrie held up an open hand and his son gave him a high five. "Must've been one hell of a drive."

"Yeah. You know how if you fly it to the top of the ridge on that fairway, you land on the down-slope, and it'll give you another forty yards. Well, I did. A perfect draw. It hit right on top of the ridge and rolled all the way down to the bottom of the hill. 260 yards. Awesome! I wish you could've seen it.

"I wish I could've too."

"That put me about 215 out, and you know how it doglegs to the left, but if you can catch that mound to the right of the green, it'll throw your ball forward . . . right on the green. I did it. I mean perfectly. Dad . . . God, it was so beautiful . . . arcing straight for the mound, grazing the top of it, and bouncing high to the left. It ended up . . . maybe . . . maybe twelve feet from the cup. No breaks. I drained it. It was so, so cool. Do you think you and I can play on the weekend? Maybe with Dr. Sherman and Andrew?"

"We can try. Why don't you call Andrew and ask him for Sunday. If his Dad can't make it, he can play with us."

"Great."

"You keep that up, and you'll get a golf scholarship. What was your final score?"

"Aw, a 75. I had a triple. Makes me so mad. I overcooked one out of bounds on four and then chunked a chip. Other than that, I had mostly pars."

Morrie left the family room for master bedroom. He pulled on a golf shirt, tucked it into the shorts he selected from his side of the closet, stepped into his Docksiders, and returned to the kitchen.

"I said, 'thirty minutes.' That was fifteen minutes ago. I don't appreciate being rushed," Monica snapped.

"Fine." Morrie retreated to the front of the house.

"Hi, Dad. Hey, Dad, did you know that Mike, the great eagle golfer, smokes pot?" Jason called out from the staircase.

"What?"

"Look what I found this afternoon." Jason held out his palm so that his father could see that he held a small amount of marijuana.

"Where did you get this?" Morrie asked. "What makes you think it's your brother's."

"In the kitchen this afternoon. I wanted a snack when I got home from work and found it on the counter. Some more on the floor."

"And what makes you think it is Michael's."

"Who else? You and mom don't smoke. Mom wasn't even at home."

"What?" Monica asked entering the room. "Where'd you get that?"

"In the kitchen."

"That's not Michael's. It's some I found . . . no . . . now listen. This morning, when I took out the garbage, I noticed a plastic bag in the grass by the road. I thought something had fallen out of the trash barrel, so I picked it up. I realized what it was and I didn't want to stand where anybody driving by would see me, so I brought it into the house and tried to open it. It popped out of my hands, and the stuff went all over the place. That's how you found it. I didn't get it all cleaned up.

"Somebody threw it out of a car when they thought they were going to be pulled over by the police. You hear the sirens out there every day."

Michael looked at Jason. "That still doesn't give him the right to accuse me," Michael said.

"No, it doesn't," Morrie said. "You did the right thing telling us that you found it, but you were unfair to accuse your brother."

"He was the only one. . ."

"Wrong, Jason. You had no reason to accuse him. You apologize."

"What did you do with the stuff, Mom?" Michael asked.

"I threw it away. I wrapped it up in newspaper and dropped it into a waste bin while I was in town this afternoon,."

"Jason," Morrie repeated.

"I'm sorry, Mike. I shouldn't have accused you."

"All right. Get washed up for supper," Monica said.

"That's yours, isn't it, Monica," Morrie whispered once the boys were out of ear-shot. "I knew something like would happen sooner or later. That's just one reason why I've wanted you to give it up."

"It wasn't mine. It was Jamie's. I needed to get it ready for him before the boys came home. I was in a hurry. Now, just drop it."

"Get it ready? What's to get ready?"

"Jamie's said he'd he come by for his personal bag, and I wanted it out where I could get at it easily."

"How did it get all around in the kitchen where the boys could find it?"

"Does it matter, Morrie? I was checking it for him. Now . . . drop it. The boys are coming to the table."

"What's to check?" Morrie said under his breath. Monica glared at him. The boys came into the room and took their places around the table in the breakfast room. Morrie knew that he would never get an answer to his last question. Monica had no reason for checking any of Jamie's marijuana. She wasn't telling him everything.

Raker had learned that having friends among the CSI staffers who worked in forensics always paid off. Whenever he had a case that involved the staff, he was attentive, appreciative, cited their work in his reports, to the press, and to his superiors. He was one of the outside guys who the lab people did not mind coming around and one who asked for a favor only when he needed one—a rare occurrence. He needed a favor now.

"What'd you find?" Raker asked walking into the laboratory. Raker was happy to see that Gene Phillips, an experienced technician, had been assigned to this case.

"Well," Phillips replied, "the oar, as it turned out, appears to have been wiped for finger prints. We found some partials. None we could identify though."

"Not surprising. Nobody we talked to on this case had any reason to be in the database. We can match them up later if comes to that. What else?"

"I found a strand of blonde hair on the blade of the oar. The blade is all binged-up. Small splits in the wood from being pushed into the dock or against rocks launching the boat." Phillips held up a clear plastic evidence bag that had been tagged and sealed. "Checked it against the victim's hair. It's a match. Came from the victim's head.

"That's not all. Because the end of the oar blade is so banged up, I picked out a few very small bits of wet cotton material, nothing more than sodden lint, and it checked against the victim's dress. The same material. The blade of the oar had to have been pushed into the woman's dress at some point. That's what's indicated, so I had a cast made of the blade end and had it compared by the medical examiner against the contusion on the victim's sternum."

"What'd you find?" Raker asked.

"The contusion appears to have been caused by the blade end of the oar, so we had digital photos taken and a computer model was constructed to demonstrate how well the victim's wound matched with the blade. The same points where the blade was splintered showed up in the wound. The differences were so slight that they could be attributed to the cushioning effect of the victim's dress."

"So. She had help."

"Yeah. She did. We found epithelial tissues that matched the victim's on the side of the oar blade. We think they may have come from the victim's arm where she was bruised. She must have lashed out at her attacker . . . tried to defend herself."

"Let me buy you dinner," Raker told Phillips. "I can't tell you how much I appreciate your good work on this. Hold the oar in evidence, but unless you see any reason to do otherwise, I think we can release the body to the funeral director. It'd help get the Sheriff off my back."

"Fine. We're done with the body now. I don't think we'll need anything else. The photos are complete, all here," the Phillips said holding up a computer diskette. "I'll take a rain-check on dinner. I'm expected at home. You've always done right by me, Jim. If this is a help, I couldn't be more pleased."

"You have no idea."

Phillip's report made Raker eager to pull everything together and begin narrowing down the suspects. He returned to his office and reviewed the names listed under the caption *Opportunity* on his whiteboard. "So," he said standing back, "someone followed her down to the dock." Or they were down there waiting. Or they came upon her by accident. Among the names listed, to whom would all possibilities apply? The timing was not precise. Did she drown before the guests went out looking for her? While they were looking for her? After they were looking for her? Who would have had the opportunity at any of the three times?

"Monica Clay," he whispered. She was not part of the search party, and no witnesses could attest to her whereabouts at the critical time. She easily could have put herself with the victim at any of the times listed. Who else? Jamie Sherman. Sherman said he saw somebody at the dock and then later denied it. Why? He could have arrived either before the search got underway or after it was called off. He would never admit seeing someone if he had he murdered the victim. Why else would he lie? To cover for someone else? Perhaps. But why? Any admission of seeing somebody at the dock would place himself at the scene, something he would want to avoid. He either lied initially when he reported seeing somebody, or his denial later was a lie.

If Jamie was telling the truth in reporting initially that he saw someone at the dock, he was probably not aware of the drowning. Saying he saw someone was an innocent statement of a fact. He denied it later because he learned of the drowning and did not want to become involved. Very consistent with his personality. What else? Can he identify the person he saw? "Write it down," Raker demanded of himself.

He found the marker and in an open corner of the board printed, "Jamie—saw someone—WHO?" Then he wrote, "Jamie's movements—time docked to time of denial—?" OK. Jamie would never had said anything if he knew the victim was dead. He did say something. Jamie comes off the list. Next.

Morrie Clay. He was a member of the search party. He was on his own before the search began, however, because his wife Monica left him to follow the victim out of the house. He was late returning to the party after the search was given up. Raker stepped to the board and wrote "Corroborate whereabouts during time of murder." Next.

Mac McAllister. Witnesses placed him in the house at the time victim left the party and for an extended period afterwards. He was a member of the search party. His only opportunity would have been when the search was abandoned. "Corroborate whereabouts after the search was abandoned. Next.

Raker stepped back to the board and wrote, "Persons unknown?" It was always wise to keep an open mind.

It was late. He yawned and looked at his watch. He'd call the Sheriff in the morning and report his findings. He had beaten the Sheriff 's deadline. Tomorrow, he wanted to see Mac McAllister again, Morrie and Monica Clay, and he and Moran were going to meet with Jamie Sherman. But that was for tomorrow. Now the worst part of the day lay ahead of him—returning to his vacant home.

Chapter 17

"What d'ya mean we can't close the case?" the Sheriff roared over the phone at Raker. "You calling me from your office here or out at the Heron Lake office?"

"Here . . . in my office. I'm always here on Tuesday morning."

"Well get your ass down to here to mine then. Now!"

The Sheriff's office was several doors down from Raker's. "Come on in here! What's this all about?" he yelled at Raker as soon as the detective appeared in the doorway.

Raker started reciting the details of the forensic report to the Sheriff as he crossed to a chair and sat down.

"Those bruises could have happened earlier in the day. There'd be a lot of horseplay around the water, a party and all?" the Sheriff said as Raker concluded.

"The woman was 49 years old. Not too likely she'd be frolicking around at the swimming dock. Besides, the strand of hair was found on the blade of the oar."

"Could have got there any number of different ways. I want this case closed. I don't want us poking around while the SBI boys have their case in progress, and I don't goddamn want the most influential part of our community riled up because we're making too much out of this. We haven't one thing to gain."

"We released the body yesterday."

"Good. But we've got to end it."

"You gave me until noon tomorrow . . . Wednesday. I thought I'd give you as much advance notice as possible. There's enough here to justify keeping the case open. We've been careful because of the SBI case. I went back out there only once . . . on Sunday . . . the day you ordered CSI to go out and pick up the oar. Since then, nobody's been there as far as I know."

"You people move down here from up North with all kinds of ideas about how we live and how we get by, and you don't even take the time to get to know what we're all about. Mac McAllister's a very important man . . . with important friends. You go making a murder case out of this, and you're going to turn the whole damn community upside down, and if you don't make your case stick, it'll all be for nothing."

"I'll make it stick if I'm allowed to pursue it. If not, you'll be the first to know that I don't have a case, and we can drop it."

"Nothing in the press, then. Not one goddamn word."

"Not from me."

"Nor anybody else."

"I can't help what others might say."

"Well, you own this one. You're working with Moran on the drug thing, aren't you?" the Sheriff asked.

"Yes."

"That ought to keep you occupied. I'll keep the case open, but you stay aware of everything that's at stake here. Understand?"

"Yes, sir. I understand."

"Good. So what's your next step?"

"I have three, possibly four, persons-of-interest. I want to talk with Mac McAllister to find out if anybody had trouble with his wife. His place is a half-a-mile or so from the crime scene."

"You're going fishing, then, aren't you. You've got a weak case, and you still need to stir around in things. Right?"

"I've got a case. It may not be all that weak either, but if you want me to make it stick, I'm not going to assume anything."

"Fine. Check with me when you come back. I want to be up to the minute on it at all times. Clear?"

"Perfectly," Raker answered. The Sheriff dropped his head to look over several papers that were lying on his desk. Raker considered himself dismissed. He was accustomed to dealing with superiors who were keyed to the political implications of a case. Pushing to keep one open was part of his job.

When he reached his office, Raker found that Tim Moran left a message demanding Raker return the call as soon as possible.

"You won't believe this," Moran roared. "That goddamn kid didn't come home last night. He took off in his boat right at supper time yesterday and never came back. Something must have spooked him. You didn't have any men out there, did you?"

"No. We stayed clear, as you ordered."

"Sherman's going to call us if the kid shows up. The kid sets his own schedule. He can be out all night, but it's not like him to stay out this late into the morning. The meeting with the boy and his father is off for now. If things change, I'll get back to you."

"Fine. But I'm not hanging around here. I'm going out to talk to Mac McAllister, the husband of the woman who drowned."

"What the hell for?"

"I'll go over the details with you later, but the forensics point to a possible homicide."

"No shit."

"At least we can't say it was accidental. Not any more. McAllister should know something about the victim's associates."

"OK. I can reach you then?"

"Absolutely."

"Fine." Moran hung up. Raker called the McAllister lakeside home.

"Mr. McAllister, this is Detective James Raker again. We met right after your wife's body was discovered. I'd like to drive out to see you today, preferably this morning. I have a few more questions to ask, if you don't mind."

"My God, what about?"

"Just a few details that don't quite add up, sir. It'll only take a few minutes."

"If you're going to come, you should make it as soon as possible. We've got a lot going on out here . . . the wake's this evening . . . people arriving for the funeral. Can you come right away?"

Driving to the McAllister home, passing the Wirth, Sherman, and Clay homes, Raker noticed that the residences farther down the bay shore were larger, the yards more expansive, the driveways wider and graced with more formal, sometimes formidable, entrances. As he eased his car up the brick drive to the McAllister home, the entrance came into view. On either side of the front steps, square columns rose to a height above the second level and supported an arched roof sheltering the glass façade to the home. McAllister, dressed in a golf shirt, shorts and moccasins, opened one of the massive wooden doors to greet him.

"I appreciate you seeing me on such short notice."

"Let's go to my office. We'll have privacy there." McAllister lumbered ahead of Raker, leading him through the gleaming marble foyer with it is vaulted ceiling and into the sumptuously furnished great room. "This way," McAllister said. "Stella. Get the calls will you. I have a meeting."

"Yes, sir," a feminine voice answered from an adjacent room."

"Our cleaning lady. She comes in on Tuesday. Here," Mac said letting Raker enter the room first. "Take that chair by the desk."

McAllister padded around his large mahogany desk. "Now. What's this all about?"

"Well, sir, in a case like this, when we don't have witnesses, we want to make sure that we have explored every possibility. . . ."

"Yeah, like it was a suicide. Why in Christ's name would the Sheriff declare it a possible suicide?"

"I hoped that wouldn't be upsetting to you. But, if you read carefully, the newspaper said that the Sheriff responded to a question and said that 'We haven't ruled it out.' The reporter made too much of it."

"I'd like to see a retraction in today's paper. They're so goddamn eager to print shit like that, then they ought to be just as eager to retract it."

"I agree."

"That's one of the reasons I agreed to see you. I'm hoping my children don't come home to read this crap. You understand?"

"Absolutely."

"Good. Why else are you here?"

"As I was saying, we want to be clear on the cause so that when we close the case there'll be no doubts floating around."

"Goddamn lousy choice of words."

"I'm sorry," Raker replied, rattled by McAllister's interruption. "That was unintentional. Shows how carefully a man needs to pick his words."

"Doesn't it."

"One of the benefits of interviewing several people is that they tend to corroborate one another's accounts. With no witness to what happened, the time of the drowning can only be approximated." McAllister looked tired slumping forward in his chair, yet every bit the wealthy industrialist—balding, gray hair pulled back from the temples, an inquisitive arch to his brows, heavy jowls falling away from thin lips.

"Why the uncertainty? What did the Medical Examiner find?"

"Your wife had bruises on her right forearm. Do you know how she might have sustained them?"

"No."

"Had you seen them earlier in the day . . . or the day before."

"No. I think I'd notice something like that."

"She also had a bruise on her sternum . . . her chest."

"I had no idea."

"Did she have an accident at any time? Did she report anything like that to you? A fall, perhaps? Running into something? Playing tennis?"

"No. Nothing. She doesn't play tennis. She gave that up a few years ago when they changed pros at the club."

"Can you account for these contusions?"

"No. You're not implying anything here, are you? Look, my wife and I did not get along, but I'd never strike her. Never!"

"I'm not implying anything. Focus on the day of the party, perhaps the day before. Where was she during that period of time? Who might she have been with her?"

"Ah, God, that's impossible. I can't even remember what I did during that period of time."

"Think back. Please, sir."

"You need to talk to Skinner Thorpe. She's always with Rene. They run that goddamn little shop of theirs. Maybe Skinner can put you on to something. Something that happened down there."

"Yes, sir. I know that name, and we plan to contact her. You say that Ms. Thorpe and your wife were close friends?"

"Yes. Very close. Couldn't stand the woman myself, but Rene took to her."

"How about enemies? Did your wife have any enemies?"

"Now what the hell is that supposed to mean? Yes. She had enemies, but nothing vicious. Just petty vindictive shit that goes on all the time. I knew she wasn't well-liked. I could tell that from the club. I'd show up alone, and everybody was my friend. Show up with her on my arm, and you'd have thought we had the plague."

"But, other than that, no running quarrels or feuds, that sort of thing?" Raker asked.

"Ah, God." McAllister dropped back into his chair. "I don't think so. She was always carrying on about this person or that, but it always seemed to pass. I think I'd rule that out. You suggesting someone might have caused those bruises? Assaulted her? What the hell are you driving at?"

"That's just it. We have several unanswered questions. We're eager to find out when she sustained those bruises. Whether someone noticed them the day of the party. Or . . . "

"So, one of two things, right? If those bruises were there before she fell in the lake, she had an accident, with somebody or on her own. If not, they happened when she fell into the lake or while she was trying to get out. Right?"

"Right," Raker said. "It's a detail, but we'd like it cleared up before we close the case."

"Suppose you can't?"

"We haven't reached that point yet. We have others . . ." Raker stopped himself when he felt his cell phone vibrate. He glanced quickly at the screen. It was Moran. He replaced the instrument in the holster

and looked back at McAllister. "Sorry about that. I can return it later."
When McAllister did not reply, Raker continued, "As I was saying, we
have others to talk to before reaching any conclusions. Perhaps someone else knows how she sustained the bruises. Did you . . ." Raker
stopped himself when the phone on McAllister's desk rang.

"She'll get that," McAllister said.

"Did you observe who your wife spent most of her time with
that afternoon . . . or even the morning of that day."

"Skinner Thorpe, of course. They're always together and other
than . . . " McAllister stopped as he heard a quiet knock on the door
to the study.

"What?" McAllister growled. Raker turned to see the door
open just enough to reveal an elderly, gray-haired woman peer in
at them.

"The telephone," the woman said.

"I told you to hold the calls."

"I know. But this is for Mr. Raker. I thought I'd better let you
know."

"Fine," McAllister said lunging for the telephone on his desk.
He dismissed the woman with a nod, and held the handset out to
his guest. "Let me know if it's private," McAllister said as Raker
raised the handset to his ear. It was Tim Moran.

"Raker, you're not going to believe this. They found the Sherman
kid. He's dead. His body was found in his fishing boat out on the
lake. The Lake Patrol spotted it and discovered the body when they
went to investigate."

"How long ago?"

"I just got word. Maybe 45 minutes. I need you back here at the
office. We need to notify the parents, and I want you along for that.
You know these people better than I do."

"How soon do you want me there?"

"As soon as you can make it."

"What if we meet at their home?"

"Fine."

"Yes. But when?"

"It'll take me twenty minutes to get there," Moran said. "Wait for me a couple of doors down from their place. I want to go over a few things with you first."

"OK. See you there in twenty minutes." Raker heard the line go dead and looked up at his indifferent host.

"We done here?" McAllister barked.

"I have everything," Raker replied. "But you, sir. Did anything we discuss prompt additional thoughts or questions?"

"No. None. Don't forget the retraction." McAllister stood up and began moving around his desk. Raker stood up in response.

"I'll do everything I can."

"Good. Most of my family are here. They'll probably be interested in everything that's been in the papers. I want something done as soon as possible. The Sheriff gets a lot of Republican support. Tell him I know that. I think he'll understand."

Raker was only minutes away from the Sherman home. He had hoped that the interview with McAllister would last longer, but he had covered everything. If McAllister was guilty of complicity in his wife's death, there was nothing in his demeanor to suggest it.

Realizing that he would meet Moran head on, Raker kept an eye out for the Sherman house, drove several homes farther down the road, and pulled into one of the driveways to turn around and find a place in the shade to wait. The mid-morning sun promised another hot July day. Raker thought of getting out of the car, but remembering Moran's command to stay out of sight, he lowered the windows of his sedan to let the breezes drifting over the hot asphalt filter through the vehicle. A lawn mower droned in the distance. Somewhere behind the hedge, children were at play. The setting reminded him of afternoons that he and Susan had spent on the grassy shore of Lake of the Isles in Minneapolis.

Moran's car appeared in the review mirror. Raker held out his hand so that Moran would recognize his vehicle. Moran stopped, walked up to Raker's car and climbed in the passenger side. "They can't reach the doctor," he said before he settling into the seat. "They left a message for him at his office. He's sure to call when he gets word."

"Are we going to wait?"

"No. We've got to move ahead. Mrs. Sherman is expecting us. She's not the kid's mother, you know. She's his step-mother. The real mother, Sherman's ex, lives in town, and she needs to be contacted also, but I'm going to wait to see how Dr. Sherman wants that handled. The body's on the way to the Medical Examiner. We need to find out what's behind all of this—the kid's death and the acid job on the car. The kid might've helped us but he's out of the picture now. The only people who knew we wanted to talk to him were his father and his stepmother. They've known for less than twenty-four hours. If a gang's involved, they must've picked up on our intentions somewhere . . . somehow."

"Doesn't sound very likely. Not in so little time."

"Not unless there's someone right here in this neighborhood . . . someone close to the family . . . picked it up. Get it?"

"Yes." Raker strained to contain his resentment. Moran was treating him like a rookie.

"Good. I'm going back to my car now. Follow me when I pull around. OK?"

Chapter 18

"I still haven't heard from my husband," Joyce Sherman said holding the door. "I don't know why he decided to go back to the office. He'd scheduled to take the day off. He just gave up on Jamie and needed to get away. What's this all about? Do we need to wait until he comes home?" she said ushering both men into the house. "We can sit in the living room."

"I'd prefer to wait," Moran said, "but events are moving more quickly than we anticipated when we said we wanted to meet with your stepson and Dr. Sherman. Mrs. Sherman . . . I'm sorry to tell you this, but your stepson was found dead this morning in his boat. The boat was adrift, and when the Lake Patrol boarded it to investigate, they found his body."

"My God!" Joyce said and began shaking her head. "Really! Really. Dead?"

"Yes, mam," Moran said. "His body is being taken to the Medical Examiner so we can determine the cause of death."

"My God! Oh, what will Tom say? My God. I can't believe this. He's gone. I . . . I'm sorry," Joyce said looking up suddenly. "You must think I'm a terrible person, but . . . you see . . . we didn't get along . . . Jamie and I. Oh, Tom . . . his father . . . he should've been here for this. He didn't need to go back to the office. He should've waited. Really . . . he should've waited until Jamie got . . . or you got here."

"It's always a difficult decision," Raker said. "Nobody wants word to reach a family member through inappropriate channels. It's not the easiest way find out about the loss of a loved one."

"Of course," Joyce replied. "You couldn't wait. I can see that. But what do I do now? I'm not the Jamie's mother. I can't authorize anything."

"We understand, Mrs. Sherman," Moran said. "But we do need to ask a few questions. The death is suspicious, and we need . . ."

"Suspicious?"

"Well, that may not be the right word. There's no evidence at the scene of violence or anything. We wanted to meet with him and his father today because we're concerned the young man was involved with dealing drugs . . . working with connections in Charles City. We think there may be a link to the vandalism of the doctor's car. That's why we call it suspicious."

"God. Yes. I can see that. I wondered how much longer he'd get by with what he was doing. I mean, I didn't know he was selling drugs, but I knew he was using marijuana. I could smell it. I could smell it in his room. I *found* it in his room. His father warned him again and again because he . . . that is Jamie . . . has a weakened heart condition, and marijuana could cause his heart to stop. But you couldn't tell Jamie anything."

"When was the last time you saw your stepson?" Moran asked.

"Last night, right after supper. He was supposed to wait for his father, but he bolted from the house. Came charging down the stairs, shouted something at me about not wanting to hang around, and was out the back door before I could say a word."

"Did you see where he went?" Moran asked.

"No. It was strange. I thought he'd go right down to his boat . . . like he always does, but when I didn't see him come around the side of the house . . . where the walk to the dock is . . . I went to the back door and looked for him. No sign of him. His car was still in the driveway. I wondered maybe if he could have gone next door . . . to the Clay's . . . he and Monica seem to get along. The screen door to the Sherman house was closing when I looked that way, but I didn't see anyone. So I really don't know where he went. Then, after a bit, I heard his outboard start up, and I saw him pull away from the dock."

The phone rang. "That might be Tom now. What should I say?" Joyce asked.

"Tell him what happened and that it's important for him to join us."

Joyce scurried into the kitchen to the wall phone. Both men could hear her. "Oh, Tom. I'm so glad it's you. The policemen are here . . . the men who wanted to meet with you. I know . . . I know, dear . . . but they're here now . . . I told them. No . . . Tom . . . Tom . . . Please . . . just listen. Jamie's dead. They found Jamie, and he's dead, Tom. He's dead. That's why they're here. Please. You need to come home . . . In about a half-an-hour then."

"So," Moran said as soon as Joyce sat back down, "you said Jamie left the house, and as far as you know, didn't go directly to his boat, but you did hear him start his outboard after a few minutes and head out onto the lake."

"Yes. A few minutes. I don't know. I stopped watching for him. I was glad he was gone. That sounds terrible doesn't it . . . but it's the truth."

"Was there anything unusual about the way he acted yesterday?" Moran asked.

"Oh God. Unusual? Yes. Jamie's unusual." Joyce shook her head. "But yesterday. No. He was his usual snotty, insolent self. He doesn't bother to be nice."

"He said nothing about why he was leaving?" Moran asked.

"He said he was tired of waiting for his father. He said that his father was never on time. And then, as I said, he bolted for the door."

"This has been very helpful, Mrs. Sherman. While we wait for Dr. Sherman, would it be all right with you if we looked through your stepson's personal effects and searched his room?" Moran asked.

"Well, I suppose. I mean, is it OK for me to give you permission. Isn't this the place in the movies where," Joyce laughed, "they always ask to see a search warrant. I don't know."

"It's OK for you to allow us, Mrs. Sherman. This is your home. We can't search any of it without your permission. You can refuse and wait until your husband gets home, and we can ask him. I just thought, since we had to wait, we could use the time more productively," Moran said.

"Well . . . maybe Tom . . . but then . . . I don't know . . . why would he refuse to let you? I mean . . . so you find something incriminating. Jamie's dead, isn't he? Oh . . . all right."

Moran and Raker were in Jamie's bedroom when Tom Sherman arrived. They found ample evidence of Jamie's drug habits but little that would suggest he was a gang member or a dealer. The room was littered with magazines, CD's, candy wrappers, and clothing. The bed was unmade. Both were relieved to be called back down to the main floor.

Dr. Sherman, breathing heavily, paced the living room. The strut that most took for arrogance was gone.

"Where's my son?" he demanded.

"His body's on the way to the Medical Examiner. May be there by now." Moran answered scrambling down the stairs and crossing to the doctor. Raker followed, happy to concede the lead in the proceedings to his associate. "We've a lot to go over with your, sir, if you feel up to it," Moran said.

"If *I* feel *up to it*. Yes. I want to know what's being done. How did you find him? Was he dead when you found him? Who found him?"

"The Lake Patrol found him about two hours ago. His boat was adrift in the main body of the lake. He failed to respond when they hailed him, so they drew along side and boarded. He was dead when they found him. An ambulance was sent to the public access area, which is where they towed the boat with the body. That's as much as we know right now."

"Had he sustained any injuries?"

"There were no signs of violence. He may have had an accident of some kind because one foot was banged up, like he had stubbed his toe badly on something. But other than that, no wounds of any kind," Moran replied.

"How long had he been dead?"

"That's being determined. The body had cooled enough to suggest that he had been dead at least three or four hours."

"What else?"

"A two ounce bag of marijuana was found in the bottom of the boat with a pot pipe. Nothing else of consequence. The boat is being processed by our crime scene investigation people right now."

"What are your concerns now?" Sherman asked and nodded to Moran and Raker to be seated as he sat down next to Joyce on the couch.

"We want to know your son's movements prior to his death," Moran said. "We got some details from your wife, who was the last to see him alive as far as we know. Did you have any contact with him yesterday?"

"No. I tried, but couldn't reach him. Joyce told him I wanted to meet with him when I got home, but he ran off before I got here."

"What time did you get home?"

"About Eight o'clock."

"And, Mrs. Sherman, you didn't tell your stepson why his father wanted to meet with him."

"No. Tom didn't want me to, so I said nothing except that he was to wait."

"Dr. Sherman. Had you noticed anything unusual about your son's behavior in the last few days?" Moran asked.

"Ah, God. He's been impossible for almost a year now. Sullen, insolent, rebellious. I couldn't get him to do anything. I wanted him to go back to school in the fall, get his degree, but it's been a clash that's gone on all summer long."

"Nothing unusual then?" Moran asked.

"No. Nothing unusual. Same exasperating stuff."

"We didn't find anything of interest in his bedroom," Moran said. "I don't think there's much more we can do here for the moment. The fishing boat will be in custody until the crime scene people are through with it. Do you have any questions of us?"

"No," Sherman said. "I'll want to know the Medical Examiner's findings as soon as they are available. We need to make funeral arrangements."

"Will you be contacting the boy's natural mother?" Raker asked.

"Yes. Of course. Right away," Sherman replied.

"You'll excuse us then," Moran said standing up.

"I'll show you out," Joyce said and followed the two men to the back door and watch them step out onto the concrete driveway that was shimmering with heat.

"Tom! Tom!" Joyce called upon returning.

"In here!" Tom answered from his study, a seldom-used room off of the living area. The door was slightly ajar. As she entered, she saw her husband seated in a chair at the side of his desk. The desk, littered with reprints of medical articles, household bills, brokerage statements, and unanswered correspondence, spoke to her of futility. Sherman did not look up when she entered. Slumped in his chair, chin on his chest, he stared at the oriental rug beneath his feet.

"I don't . . . don't know what to say, Tom," Joyce said. "I know this must be terrible for you. I can't imagine . . . ."

"No. You can't. I never thought after all of this . . . this struggling . . . and effort and . . . God damn it . . . worry and money . . . . I wanted to do the right thing. The right thing for my kids. Not this. Never anything like this." Sherman's eyes filled with anguish. "I never understood what drove the kid. He had a right to be angry. About his mother and me. About all the disruption in his life. The embarrassment of the rumors around the divorce. The goddamn quarreling. But to turn his own life upside down . . . to be so contrary. Everything he's done the last six months has been self-defeating. Systematically, unrelentingly killing off his life . . . ruining his chances. I'll never understand." He dropped his head again.

"I wish there was something I could do to console you. I know you've tried. I know how important it was to give your children a good home . . . a happy home . . . and how much you wanted to make up for all that had gone wrong. Please, please don't make it harder on yourself by blaming yourself."

"I need to call his mother."

"Fine. Well, I don't need to be party to that." Joyce turned to leave the room. As she reached the threshold, she looked back, "I am here for you, Tom. I want to help. Please. Don't make this worse by blaming yourself. Andrew and Ellie are not the least like Jamie. Remember them."

"Yeah, well, Jamie was a good kid too until the last year or so."

"Jamie was 21 years old. He was responsible for his own decisions. Not you."

"Joyce, this is all over now. No need to harp on the same old tune."

"I didn't mean it that way. I know that I haven't been . . . well . . . much help. I've wanted to do more. I'll keep trying. I promise. It's what I want. Just tell me."

"Fine," Sherman said without looking at her. "I want some time alone now."

Chapter 19

Raker was relieved to part company with Moran after their visit with the Shermans. He'd acknowledge that SBI personnel received better training than county or city officers. They worked more involved and important cases, cases that took months—sometimes years—to prosecute. In his short tenure with the Melville County Sheriff's office, he had seen several cases botched by failures to coordinate and exploit the experience of other non-SBI officers. He began jotting down his notes from the interview, when the back door of Sherman home opened suddenly. Joyce Sherman started to run across the driveway.

"Mrs. Sherman. Mrs. Sherman, please," Raker opened the door to his vehicle and called out. She stopped. "Oh . . . Yes. . . Detective. I thought you'd gone . . . I . . . I want to see my friends." She looked distressed.

"I'm sorry, Mrs. Sherman," Raker said stepping toward her. "There's just one thing that I need to clarified . . . if you don't mind."

"No. No," Joyce sniffled and brushed the hair from her eyes. "What is it?"

"You said that you thought Jamie might have gone next door . . . to the Clay's . . . when he left the house last night. Did I get that correctly?"

"Yes. I said that. I don't know that he did, though. I didn't actually see him go there. I just saw the storm door closing and thought maybe someone let Jamie in."

"But you'd have seen someone going out."

"Yes. Of course."

"Would the timing between when you saw the door closing and Jamie leaving the house be about right for him to have traveled the distance between the two houses?"

"Yes. About that. I kept expecting him to come around the side of the house so I was pretty conscious of the how much time he took. He should have come into view in a few seconds and he didn't. That's why I went to look."

"Fine. Thank you, Mrs. Sherman. Again, my condolences to you and your husband."

"Thank you." Joyce turned and scurried to the back door of the Wirth home.

Raker got back into his car. Why would Jamie go to the Clay home before getting into his boat? He had seen someone at the scene of the drowning. But who? Raker needed to know. "Someone we know," he said under his breath. Someone he, or one of the other officers, had already interviewed. Of all the names he had considered, Morrie Clay and his wife were unaccounted for at the time of the drowning. They were gone from the party the longest. Both had motive, and aside from Wirth, were the only ones would benefit from Rene McAllister's death. He looked at his watch. Two-forty-three. He opened his mobile phone and called Tim Moran.

"I'm still out here at the lake. You got away so fast that I didn't have a chance to clear a few things with you. I've got people out here I want to talk to. With the Sherman kid out of the way, maybe everything has changed as far as you're concerned, but I wanted to check with you to be sure. I'm still working on the drowning victim."

"I thought the Sheriff was closing the case."

"Nope. Not yet."

"This damn thing is blowing right out from under us with the kid dying the way he did. We've lost a chance at an informant with no leads to the acid job on the car. We're looking at more than two years of work getting flushed."

"It's too early for M.E.'s report is to be in on the kid."

"Yeah. I just took a call and it looks like an overdose. They're thinking his heart stopped because the pot triggered it," Moran growled. "Maybe something from the boat or the kid's body'll give us direction. CSI's still working on it."

"I want see the Clays, Sherman's neighbors. Any problem?"

"Fine. But steer clear of the Shermans. We don't know what we're dealing with just yet. Is this anything I should be in on?"

"Strictly about the drowning."

"OK. But I want in on anything involving the Shermans. On either case . . . yours or mine. OK?"

"No problem."

As Moran hung up, Raker depressed quick dial number for Gene Phillips at CSI.

"You working on the Sherman kid case?" Raker asked.

"Raker? Yeah. Why? What's up?"

"What do they have you doing?"

"The usual. There's not much here. The M.E. has the body, but there're no signs of a fatal injury or indication that he was poisoned. As far as the boat goes and the kid's personal effects . . . nothing. Only his dime bag."

"Did you test it?"

"Yeah. It's the same stuff that's on the street right now. Pretty fresh actually, almost too moist . . . as if it had been dampened or something."

"Anything else in it?" Raker asked.

"No."

"Check it real close, will you, for any foreign substances."

"Anything I find will need to be written up in the case file, and this is an SBI case, not county."

"I don't give a shit. I just want to know. You won't get in trouble for spending too much time on it, will you?"

"No. Just thought you ought to know that whatever I do will get reported. If questions come up, I need you to back me up as the officer who requested the work."

"No problem. I'll see Moran in the morning anyway. How soon do you think you can get to it?"

"This time tomorrow."

"Here, dear, you sit here while I get Matthew. He's out on the deck," Shirley said to Joyce Sherman. "I'll only be a minute." Shirley guided Joyce to the kitchen.

"Matthew, Joyce is here. Please come in and join us. We're in the kitchen."

"Ah . . . OK," Matthew replied hoping that his wife would hear how inconvenienced he was by her request. "Be right there." He tossed his copy of *The Economist* on the glass-topped table, and walked into the house. Matthew liked Joyce Sherman. He enjoyed having two younger women as neighbors and watching them move about in the summer in their shorts and skimpy tops. For as strident and in-your-face as Monica Clay might be, Joyce was mild as cream—perfect for Sherman, a man accustomed to getting his own way.

Shirley met Matthew in the dining room. "This is terrible," she whispered. "Jamie Sherman's dead. They found his body this morning in his boat out on the lake. The authorities were just there . . . next door . . . and told Tom and Joyce." Shirley grabbed his hand and led him into the kitchen where Joyce seated. Joyce forced a quick smile. He sat down across from her.

"I'm terribly sorry," Matthew directed at Joyce, noticing tears pooling in her eyes. "Shirley just told me what happened. It's must be an awful shock to both of you. How's Tom? How's he taking this news?"

Joyce dropped her head and sobbed. "The way he does everything . . . just like a doctor." She looked up again and Matthew could see the anger in her eyes. "He's over there, and all he wants is to be alone. That's the way he is every time something happens. He withdraws. Doesn't let anyone in. I feel . . . I feel totally useless . . . just . . . worthless."

Shirley reached over and stroked Joyce's shoulder. "Everyone has their own way of dealing with bad news. This is his. He'll come out of it. Wait and see. You need to allow him have his own way."

"Like when don't I?"

Matthew had heard second-hand from his wife about the marital troubles next door—Tom's late hours, the problems with Jamie, the wrangling between attorneys over alimony and the divorce. A barrage of concerns contributed to a withering of the romance between two who were once passionate lovers.

"Who else has been told?" Matthew asked.

"Oh, *of course*, he had to call Karen. He couldn't let the police do that. As if she deserved any consideration. The bitch. She . . . she

hasn't shown Tom anything but ugliness for months and months
. . . turning his kids against him. *Of course,* he'd call her . . . wants
to be alone . . . Won't let me help. But he can call *her*! *Wants* to call
her. What good is trying to make a family . . . have everyone care for
one another if it falls apart when something bad happens. I know
where I stand. That's what this has shown me. Who was I fooling
all of this time?"

"So Andrew and . . . and . . . what's the pretty little girl's name
again?" Matthew asked.

"Ellie," Shirley said.

"They've not been notified. Who's going to do that? They need
to know before hearing it on the news or something else."

"Not me!" Joyce said. "If he's going to leave me out of things,
then he can take care of that himself. I'm his wife . . . not his social
secretary, not his baby-sitter . . . his housekeeper."

"But that's a way to let yourself back in, dear," Shirley said.
"Nobody's themselves at a time like this. He's had a terrible shock.
He won't be himself now for a long time . . . for months. I'm sure
he'd appreciate your taking the initiative and handling these things
for him."

"Oh yeah. Right. Like when I planned a surprise party for Ellie's
twelfth birthday, and he gets home too late for it, and Ellie . . . Ellie
doesn't even show up. She went to her mother's instead. There I
was with a house full of her snotty little country-day friends, and
she doesn't even have the decency to call and tell me where she is. I
was so humiliated."

"But those things happen," Shirley soothed. "Adolescents . . .
we know. We raised four of them. They don't think things through.
You could make yourself more important in their lives now if you
went ahead . . . ."

"Yeah, right. First thing I'd know is that *he* wanted to do it . . . or that *I* didn't do it the way *he* wanted. That's all that would happen."

"Now listen," Matthew said straining to make every allowance for Joyce's behavior, "you were trained as a nurse. You are a nurse! That man over there has received a mortal wound, an emotional wound to be sure, but as severe as any he may ever receive again in his life. He's not as strong as he appears. The divorce weakened him. His children have been coached to be cruel to him. And while he may not acknowledge it right now . . . right today . . . you're one source of strength for him. As a nurse, you need to set your own feelings aside and tend to him. He needs you. He may not act as if he needs help, especially where feelings are involved, but you stand by him. He'll know you're there. Listen to me on this."

"I am listening."

"We're here to help in anyway we can, dear," Shirley said, "but I think Matthew just gave you some good ol' Dutch Uncle advice, and I think he's right. I'm going to stand with you through all of this . . . until we get things taken care of. OK?"

Joyce sat silently for several minutes, sniffing and dobbing her eyes with a wadded handkerchief. She drew several deep breaths. "You must think I am a terrible . . . selfish person. Really . . . I feel so . . ."

"Now, you just wait," Shirley chastised. "What was it we said earlier? 'None of us is at our best in times like this.' This came as a shock to you, too. We're here to do what we can. Nobody's passing judgment."

"You're mothering me."

"Oh, my! How terrible of me!" Shirley said. "Of course! We all reach a point where we shouldn't be mothered any more, don't we? You should hear Matthew play Dutch Uncle to my hurt little

Shirley. I'm supposed to call it 'fathering' and reject whatever he says? I don't think so. Nurturance is hard enough to find, and when is gladly offered, you should soak it up. Besides . . . I'm old enough to be your mother."

"I don't understand," Joyce said looking up at Shirley. "How did you ever learn so much. I feel like I'll never . . . I don't know . . . grow up sometimes."

"We've been around the block a few times," Matthew said. "We hit our share of bumps in the road along the way. Everyone does."

"I'd better go now," Joyce said. She pushed her chair back and stood up. "You guys are so great. I just don't know what I'd do without you . . . especially you, Shirley. It's providential that we moved in next door. God's hand is in it?"

"Buck up now. Call me if you need anything." Shirley walked her young friend to the door. When she returned, Matthew was still sitting at the kitchen table.

"So what did God do again? Withdraw his hand from poor Jamie? I hate that kind of talk. People assume God's behind their good fortune. They need to question why ill fortune finds others from time-to-time."

"Please, Matthew, it's no time for sermons. You were so sweet to that child. I'm proud of you."

"I hate emotional turmoil," Matthew said standing up. "Crying and carrying on makes me uncomfortable. Besides, she's much stronger than she thinks. Tom doesn't value her as he should . . . respect her. If he did, she'd build some self-confidence."

"Mom! Mom!" Michael shouted as he burst through the door from the deck into the Clay home. "Where are you, mom?"

"Here. The kitchen."

"Mom. Jamie . . . Jamie Sherman . . . he's dead. They found him. In his boat." Michael searched his mother's face for a reaction. "The guys say the Lake Patrol towed his boat to the public landing area, and put his body in an ambulance. And it didn't drive away fast or anything. Just turned on the flashing lights and drove away. One of the cops we know from school told us."

"He's dead?"

"Yes. Isn't that terrible. What do you think killed him?" Michael voice cracked.

Monica looked at her son. A boy with the shadow of manhood darkening in his brow, losing the innocent turn to his smile. She wanted to hold him, feel the smooth skin on his back, hold on as long as she could; give him a few more days in the sun—the child of her fulfillment. His earnestness registered poignantly with her. "We may not know for a few days, dear. They'll probably perform an autopsy to determine the cause of his death."

"Like on CSI. Right?"

"Yes. Like that. He wasn't healthy, you know. He had a heart condition."

"He got to be a real cretin. He used to be a nice guy . . . fun, but . . . man . . . the last year or so . . . he changed."

"I know."

"You guys were friendly, though, weren't you, mom?"

"Yes. I suppose. He seemed troubled. I tried to be a friend."

"How troubled? What d'ya mean?"

Monica's dinner preparations could wait. She walked over to Michael, put her hand on his shoulder and turned him around. "Let's go out on the deck," she said. They found chairs in the shade of the house. "How concerned are you about Jamie?" she asked.

"Not very. Just doesn't make sense him dying like that . . . so young. You said he was troubled. Was he crazy? He sure dressed like he was."

"No. Not crazy. 'Troubled' means that a person is up against difficulties that are too much for them. They can't get things on their own terms and feel good about themselves."

"Jees, Mom. Shermans are rich! I mean, they got everything. He drives that old fishing boat, but they've got the really fast *Bayliner*, and a sailboat besides, and four cars. Their house is bigger than ours."

"I know. That's not the problem. His parents divorced. And he's torn between the two of them. His father is . . ."

"His father is cool, mom. Really. I like him, and his stepmother is nice. I just don't figure."

"I'm home." It was Morrie's voice. He had entered the kitchen.

"We're out here," Monica called.

"Hey, Dad."

Morrie smiled at his son as he stepped out onto the deck.

"Dad! Did you hear? About Jamie?" Michael asked.

"Yes. It was on the news on the radio." Morrie looked at Monica. "Kid was playing with fire, wasn't he?"

Monica frowned and nodded toward Michael.

"You mean because he was smoking pot all of the time?" Michael said.

"How did you know about that?" Monica asked.

"Aw, mom, everyone knows that. He even tried to sell Jason some."

"He did not!" Monica snapped.

"Jason said," Michael replied.

"When was this?" Morrie asked.

"A couple of months ago. One day. Down at the dock."

"Why didn't you tell us?" Morrie asked.

"No big deal. Jason didn't buy any. Jason said to be quiet about it because he didn't want Jamie to get into any more trouble than what he was already."

"I'm going to talk to Jason!" Morrie said.

"Oh, God, Dad, don't. Please. I wasn't supposed to tell. Jason'll really be pissed if he knew I told."

"There's no need to talk to Jason, Morrie. Michael, get cleaned up for diner."

"Yeah, right. You guys just want to talk about this when I'm not here."

"That's right. Now, please, excuse yourself," Monica said.

"All right." Michael walked around his father and into the house.

"This is really tragic, but you've got to admit, it takes any concerns you had and blows them all away," Morrie observed.

"Yes. I think it does."

Alan McAllister's children had planned to stay in their father's comfortable lakeside home. His stepchildren, Jennifer and her husband and Rene's son, Nick, elected to book rooms at nearby motels. McAllister knew that there was a message in their choice.

They had come together to bury their mother—his family, not as he once envisioned, but his. He knew about failed dreams. His own disappointments were not life-defeating. He had Denise, although she had not called again, and before Denise, other entertainments. He had friends, and he had money—more money than he would ever spend. Rene was dead. Life lay before him unencumbered. What remained of it, he could fill as he chose. He had time to array his choices.

The viewing at the Scheffield funeral home was scheduled to begin at 7:30. Mark Scheffield was waiting for them at the pillared entrance. "Everyone is here," he said, "please follow me." The rich scent of roses rushed to greet them. McAllister hated the fragrance. He and his three children were led down a long central corridor to a room at the back of the building. There McAllister saw his two step-children together at the end of the room. They turned. Jennifer, the oldest, ran to Nicole, and the two women embraced. The step-brothers were less responsive, neither moving toward each other nor saying anything in greeting. Off to the side, McAllister noticed a teenage girl and a younger boy—his step-grandchildren, Leah and Riley. Both rolled their eyes in disdain watching the reunion.

"May I please," Mark Scheffield said. "This will only take a minute. Only the immediate family members are present." He looked at his watch. "There's time for all of you to file into the reception area and view the deceased without other onlookers present. You may want to go together, or one at a time." He paused. When nobody responded, he turned and opened a door that lead to the reception room. "Whatever you wish. Take as much time as you like. Our policy is not to admit anyone until each of the members of the be-reaved family have had his or her moment with deceased." Nobody stepped forward. He looked at McAllister. "Mr. McAllister, if you would be first, please, and the rest please file in behind your father in whatever order you chose."

McAllister entered the softly lighted reception room alone. A huge bank of flowers towered over the back of the open casket and turned forward on either end to suggest that the deceased was resting in the bosom of a garden. Alive only to his own sensations, he stepped toward the casket without a taking a breath. Rene's head was resting on a gleaming satin pillow, her hair quaffed as she had never bothered in recent years. He hardly recognized her. Stepping closer, he noticed her waxen hands folded across her breast, and he remembered her chest in a flash as it had been when they were younger, when they still made love with the lights on, when they still lusted for each other. He shook off the vision and reached out to the edge of the ebony coffin.

He was grateful that none of the children were watching him. He saw again how Rene had looked when they unzipped the black bag the morning her body was recovered, her face wet and lifeless. Now she was serene, almost ghostly, as if she would sit up in response to an alarm, as if her eyes might suddenly open to look directly at him in a way that she had avoided for so long. He did not like either vision of her. Random memories rushed through him. Their history together was sliding out of him like a roll of film unwinding from a camera. He let it go. He wanted it all to go; them as lovers; as friends, as parents, as they had struggled, as they fought and grew apart. And finally, a frame of them as each knew, in separate ways, that they had gone beyond meaning much to the each other, a frame as each decided never to speak of their alienation, never to do anything to mend it for fear it would be more painful than forging ahead in time indifferent to the other's well-being. He pulled himself up short, took a deep breath, turned and nodded to Scheffield who was standing in the doorway. The children filed in, the two girls first. None spoke.

Chapter 20

The quiet. Raker hated it—especially upon waking. All of his life he had awakened to the sounds of others around him. Rising earlier than he, Susan would slip out from under the covers and glide out of the room closing the door quietly behind her. Coffee took fifteen minutes. The aroma would reach him, and he'd toss the covers back like a cape, roll across her side of the bed, and plant both of his feet on the carpet to begin his day.

This morning nothing stirred. The world had come to a stop, and it fell to him to churn the air into an invitation to begin a new day. It was Wednesday. He was alone.

He shuffled into the kitchen and began his morning ritual. The oatmeal and honey came out of the cabinet above the stove. He retrieved three measuring cups from the drawer to the left of the sink—a full cup for the water, a half-cup for the oatmeal, and one-third cup for the powdered milk. Everything measured and mixed, the oatmeal went into the microwave for five-and-one-half minutes, enough time to put two slices of bread in the toaster, pour a glass of orange juice, and fetch the paper from wherever it had been pitched on the front lawn.

A morning workout at the YMCA had been an inviolate part of his daily regimen. But when Susan needed him at her side during her final weeks at home, he stopped going despite her insistence. "It'll be good for you," she urged. "You know you miss your friends. I'll be fine. You should go." But he would not go—close the door behind him and leave her to fend off the quiet of an empty house on her own.

News of Jamie Sherman's death was in the paper. Most newspaper news articles angered him when he was younger when they reported on crimes that he was investigating and failed to get facts. As time passed, however, he found himself amused with the misquotes and mangled descriptions.

"The body of Jamie Sherman, age 21, was discovered yesterday morning by the Lake Heron Lake Patrol adrift in a fishing boat in the main body of the lake. The cause of death is yet to be determined. Since childhood, Sherman suffered from a weakened valve in his heart that caused it to pump sluggishly. The condition was not considered life-threatening. Authorities do not suspect foul play. Sherman was expected to return to Wake Forest University in the fall to complete a four year course of study leading to a Bachelor of Science degree."

The article gave the background of the deceased's family, but Raker's attention drifted. He folded up the paper and laid it back down on the table. He wondered how Dr. Sherman might be handling his son's death. The doctor maintained angry clinical detachment when Raker and Moran broke the news to him. Perhaps working in life-and-death situations every day shielded men like Sherman from experiencing grief.

His message light was on when he reached his office in Charles City. Gene Phillips had called.

"What is it?" Raker asked as soon as Phillips came on the line.

"Raker. Yeah. Well. Several things. First, the guys finger printed the boat the day of the drowning, the tackle box, the cooler. They printed it again yesterday and found the only fresh prints belong to the victim. No signs of a struggle or anything, but they think the deceased experienced some kind of convulsions. He was wearing flip-flops, and he pretty much kicked them off and his feet were beat up. One toe had a badly torn nail that bled. The blood from it matched the blood in the bottom of the boat. Not a lot of blood, but enough to establish that injury to the foot was recent."

"What about the bag of marijuana?"

"I'm getting to that. The stuff probably came from India or was in an Indian restaurant. I found traces of curry powder in the stuff. I thought it was fluke at first, but I tested several samples, and it turned up in every one. "

"You privy to any other thoughts about this?"

"Not really. Moran's not convinced that the kid's death was an accident but can't account for the death otherwise."

"So he's not pushing any pet theory, or asking you for anything beyond what you have already done?"

"Nope. M.E.'s report's not in yet, but word is that there aren't any surprises in it."

"Well, thanks, Gene. Keep me in the loop."

"Will do."

Raker checked his watch. Nine-twenty. Not too early to call Monica Clay. When he called, she agreed to see him as soon as he could drive out to her home.

"Hey! Raker!" someone shouted as soon as he stepped out of his office. Raker wheeled around. It was Moran. "Where're you going?"

"To see Mrs. Clay. She agreed to see me as soon as I got out there."

"Clay?"

"She's the next door neighbor to the Shermans."

"You're doing this because?" Moran followed Raker back into Raker's office and closed the door behind him.

"I still have questions about the drowning on the Fourth-of-July."

"Jesus. Really? When are you guys going to put that one to bed?" When Moran sat down, Raker realized that the discussion was going to be longer than he wanted. "Look, you remember when we searched the dead kid's room yesterday? We should've found something and didn't. Our guys are absolutely certain the kid was resupplied in Charles City on the fifth. He should have had at least one, maybe two, kilos in his possession. You and I didn't find any trace of them. I thought they'd be on his boat, but again no trace. Only the dime bag which was his personal supply. His stash is somewhere else."

"Unless someone took it from the boat before the body was discovered," Raker said.

"No. Don't think so. No fresh prints. We don't think anyone disturbed the boat before the patrol people picked it up. Wrong time of day, early morning like that, maybe a few fisherman on the lake, but not out in the middle of it. We think the stash is still somewhere he could get at it."

"You're sure he picked it up in the city?"

"Absolutely."

"You were there," Moran said, "at his home, when he returned from Charles City that afternoon."

"I was? The afternoon of the fifth?" Raker walked over to his desk, pulled his notes out and looked them over without sitting down. "Yeah. I was there."

"Did he have anything with him?"

"I wasn't there when he finally showed up. The CSI guys were though. They needed the kid's permission to search the ice chest and the tackle box."

"So they'd have seen him," Moran said.

"They were there when I left. I know they spoke to him because they told us that he denied seeing anyone at the dock the night of the drowning, after his stepmother said that he had. That's what caught my attention, him contradicting himself." Raker sat down at his desk.

"So you don't know that the CSI guys saw him the moment he entered the house," Moran mused.

"No. What was in their report?"

"It didn't say. Sherman could have seen something before he walked in. You guys know that you could've blown our entire case right then and there."

"I don't see how. Fletcher reminded the CSI guys about your interest in Sherman. He told them to make it clear that they were working on the drowning and nothing else. I don't think anyone tripped up."

"We'll never know," Moran said. "We've got to get back and search that house, the kid's car, everything. His stash is somewhere."

"Whatever," Raker said, relieved that the meeting seemed to be drawing to a close. Raker was tempted to say that he thought Jamie visited the Clay house just before speeding away in his boat the evening before he died, but he decided against it.

"You aren't taking this very seriously are you?" Moran observed. "We've got hundreds of hours in this case. We're within a cunt hair of breaking it wide open, and you guys go bungling around. In a stroke of fucking brilliance, the two of you could have screwed up everything."

"We had our case. You had yours. The overlap was unavoidable. I knew very little of what was going on with Jamie Sherman. You guys play your cards so close to the vest that we never know what the story is. We couldn't ignore that a woman died suspiciously in front of the Sherman house the night before. Get real. I'm sorry . . . but I have a job to do also."

"You're making too much out of this woman's drowning. That could have . . . No . . . God damn it . . . that should have taken a back burner in all of this. All I can say now is stay clear the hell out of our way. Fart around with your drowning case until the obvious finally slaps you in the face, and you're forced to close it. But stay out of our way. There's too much riding on what we have going."

"You're convinced the kid's death is gang related, or has something to do with his dealing?"

"Yes. And so's the vandalism of Sherman's car. It all ties together somehow. Even if we lost the Sherman kid, there has to be connection out there somewhere."

"Good luck," Raker said. "Don't get me wrong. I know there's drug trafficking here. I want those assholes off the street as much as anyone. I just think on this particular case, you're barking up the wrong tree. Sherman's death has no connection with his dealing or his activities in the city. He was dealing. He had connections. But none of that has anything to do with his death."

Moran stood up. "You're fuckin' nuts. People in the Sheriff's Department keep making allowances for you because of your wife being sick and dying and you needing time to get over it, but I don't buy it. You're off on a goddamn tangent, some obsession of your own, that makes no sense to anyone, not even your friends."

"Chase your own theories then. I'm convinced I'll be vindicated when this is through."

"*Vindicated!*" What the hell is that? Look . . . what we're working on has years of experience behind it and all our resources. We don't play hunches, cowboy. You stay the hell away from what we're doing. That's all I ask. Ask . . . shit, I'm demanding it."

"I will . . . except where the same people are involved. We need to understand that."

"No. We don't. You need to understand that you stay clear. Got that?"

"I need to talk to more people. If you've got a problem with any of them, we need to work it out. Make a list. Give it to me. Then I'll know. Better yet. Give it to the Sheriff. I can't be responsible for what I don't know. It's your agency's job to keep us informed."

"You'll get your list, and the Sherman family'll be at the top. You don't talk to any one of them at any time. You do not step onto their property. Is that clear?"

"Perfectly. I see no reason why that would interfere with my investigation."

"Your investigation. Shit!"

"Yes, my investigation. And if anything from your department results in interference with my work, I'll protest. I'll go through channels, but I will protest."

"Fine. Play your games."

"We're done here," Raker said.

After the funeral, with his nap out of the way, Matthew walked through the kitchen to the foyer to retrieve the keys to his boat which hung with others on a palette near the back door. The boat key was readily identifiable. Years before, he had fastened a red and white fishing bobber to the chain so that it would float if ever dropped overboard. He smiled retrieving it. The grandkids had great fun chiding him about what kind of a fish he thought he would catch using a key for bait.

Passing back through the kitchen, he was within two steps of the phone when it rang. "Wirth," he snapped into the receiver.

"Matthew. What the hell? Did I call your office number?" It was Mac McAllister.

"No. This is our home."

"Sounded like you were at the office."

"I forgot myself, Mac. Does that ever happen to you?"

"Not recently. Matt, I just picked up the mail and decided to go through Rene's brokerage statements. And . . . Jesus, Matt . . . something's going on in Rene's accounts that doesn't make sense. Have you looked at the June statements?"

"No. I haven't. What's the trouble?"

"She's got fund here that had nearly goddamn three-quarters of a million in it, and it's on its back. The thing's lost almost fifty percent. Brule Mountain. They're hedge fund people, aren't they?"

"That's got to be a mistake. Morrie'd never put Rene in a hedge fund. Give me a chance to look at it and get back to you. You going to be home all day?"

"I guess. People coming and going. But . . . yes . . . get back to me. If you don't get me on the first try, just keep after it. While you're at it, this goddamn account is into margin by more than six-hundred thousand. How the hell can that be?"

"Doesn't sound right. Let me work with it. I'll get back to you as soon as I can."

"Good. I want this straightened out before I take the kids to see the attorney about the estate planning tomorrow."

Matthew walked straight to his den, swung around his desk, and double-clicked on the internet icon before he sat down. Everything McAllister had reported was true. A hedge fund had been purchased the previous December. At the same time, the account had gone into margin to fund most of the purchase. He reached for the phone.

"I need to see you as soon as you can get over here," Matthew demanded as soon as Morrie answered. "Mac McAllister just got off the line asking me about a hedge fund in one of Rene's accounts with a big margin debit . . . saying he didn't understand it. I couldn't tell him anything. You need to explain this, Morrie. I don't like the looks of this . . . not one bit."

"I'll be there in ten minutes." Morrie hung up and walked into the kitchen to Monica. He took two tentative steps toward her. "You OK? I mean . . . after the funeral and everything?"

"I want to get through this. I'm tired of having it ahead of us and not knowing what's going to happen."

"Well, if it is any comfort, the shit's about to hit the fan. McAllister's found the hedge fund and margin problem. Matthew wants me over there as soon as I can make it."

"What are you going to do?"

"I over-reacted once. I'm not going to again. I'll see what they have, play each point as it comes. I've spent myself thinking about. I don't have the energy for any more of that."

"So, that's it? Those two beautiful sons of ours went off this morning like nothing in their world is wrong. Michael's enthusiastic and innocent . . . still so much a boy. You can't fail," Monica said. "You can't, Morrie. I'll never ask another thing of you, so help me God, but you have to get us out of this. I can't look at them. I can't look at this beautiful life we've made for ourselves and know that it could all go away . . . that they'd take it from us."

"It isn't going to come to that."

"It *cannot* come to that. Did you ever think there's a chance they'd blame Matthew?"

"Why would they think that?"

"It's your word against his, isn't it?"

"No. I mean . . . he didn't have anything to do with it . . . nothing at all."

"But nobody knows that except for you."

"Cheryl knows. She's signed for the client."

"She won't want to lose her job. Matthew's retiring. Her future's with you, not him. She could implicate Matthew after he retires. That's doesn't need to be an obstacle."

"I couldn't do that. Matthew's done everything for me. For us!"

"Yeah . . . right . . . as if he wasn't getting anything out of this. You had your own book of business before you went into partnership with him. Don't make out that you're more grateful than you need to be."

"But he's . . . we're friends. Good friends. I couldn't involve him."

"But you could make your wife and your sons face the humiliation of losing our home, our standing in the community . . . the life we have built. You could do that, couldn't you?"

"Jesus . . . Monica . . . that's so calculating. I don't think we're there yet. I don't want to resort to tactics like that. I made a mistake, but it wasn't cold-blooded dishonesty. It was just . . . stupid . . . fucking stupid. But I never intended to hurt anyone."

"We can't be stupid any more, Morrie. We need to make this happen so it turns out the way we want it. It is either Matthew or you, and it isn't hard for me to decide whose side I'm on."

"That's too much for me . . . right now. Too deliberate." Morrie stepped back. "I'm going. I can't stay and talk about this. I'm blaming Rene and playing dumb to any questions that come up. They can chew my ass for letting her do it, but I can handle that."

"What about the signature?"

"What about it? She's not around to say it's not hers."

"What if they prove that it isn't hers? That it's a forgery."

"I'll cross that bridge when I come to it. Just because they prove it's not hers doesn't mean they know who signed it. I gotta go see Matt . . . then maybe into the office . . . to work. I'll see you when I get home this evening." Opening the back door, he turned and said, "You know, this is not what I need. I need support . . . not criticism. Blaming me isn't helping, not in what I have to face." He turned quickly and was out the back door before Monica could reply,.

Morrie's wait-and-see approach worked well for him when he was working for the bank. He never got out in front of anyone when there was a controversy. He never showed anyone his back. But this was different. Monica knew that he was not shrewd enough to get through their trouble. She had to take the lead. She remembered the rock climbing challenges she engaged in right after college. She'd reach a point where turning back was not an option, where backing down was as challenging as moving upward, more so in fact, because she could see more clearly above her to find the handholds and the next tactical step to take; whereas descending, even though it was over the path she had come, her vision was not as good and she could not determine where to find the surest footing. Looking up was easier. Looking up she could focus, exercise control, think clearly, and fear, however close at hand it might have been, was never given an opening. She gave fear no quarter now. Jamie, at least, was out of the way. She had one choice—to move ahead until all of the risk and the danger would be forever behind her.

Morrie refused to consider obvious options. Disaster awaited Morrie's first misstep. She already counted one loss—her respect for Morrie. It drained away and she felt her love for him go with it. For years, she had lived within a breath of recognizing that her affection for him was fading, but as long as their lives kept moving forward, the boys growing, friends all around, the comfort and the fun, she could find the energy to respond to him, even initiate with him. Now she could not imagine rekindling her attraction to him. Intimacy would be a chore. Disappointment knotted inside of her, and for the first time in her life, she sensed defeat at hand.

She agreed to meet with Detective Raker when he called. Perhaps she'd have the chance to thwart any suspicions he harbored regarding Rene's death. When he arrived, she led him back into the family room. Raker was polite, as always, but got quickly to the point.

"There are just a couple of things that we need to clear up," he said. "The Medical Examiner found bruises on Mrs. McAllister . . . on her chest, her sternum and on her arms. We're trying to establish when they might have occurred. Do you recall seeing any bruises at any time during the day before she died or when you spoke to her that night?"

"No. I don't. On her chest . . . did you say? Her sternum?"

"Yes. As if she had been struck there, or run into something." Raker indicated the center of his chest.

"Her dress would have covered it then," Monica replied.

"Well, yes. That's true. Unless she leaned over or something . . . well . . . you understand."

"Yes. Of course. No. I didn't see any bruises on her chest at any time during the day of the party."

"And her arms?"

"Both arms?"

"No. On the inside of her right forearm." Raker held our his arm and demonstrated the approximate area where the contusion were located. "But that hardly matters, does it? You would not have needed to ask if you had seen them."

"Oh, well, I just was wondering how obvious they might have been . . . why I would have missed seeing something."

"And when you tried to speak to her that night?"

"It was dark. They could have been there, but I couldn't see."

"The victim also sustained a blow to the head, just above the hair line over her left eye. Did you happen to see an injury of any kind there?"

"No, detective, I didn't. I'm not being of much help on this am I? I'm sorry."

"You're doing fine, Mrs. Clay. Eye-witness reports vary in matters like these. Have you thought over events since we last talked? Is there anything that you might want to add to what you have already told us?"

"No. Nothing. I haven't been able to get it out of my mind. It was so unexpected. So terrible. It's given me a headache in fact. I have fought migraines all my life. Do you mind if I excuse myself just for a second to get some medication."

"Not at all," Raker responded.

"I'm sorry for the interruption," Monica said upon reentering the room. "I had them since childhood, and I like to nip them in the bud . . . when I first feel them coming on."

"Not at all. I had trouble with cluster headaches for a stretch myself several years ago. Dreaded the onset of them. Do you take anything?"

"*Demerol*. It's very effective. I feel a little groggy afterwards, but it's better than going down completely with a headache."

"I'm sure."

"Was there more you wanted to ask me?"

"I suppose you heard about Jamie Sherman," Raker said.

"Oh . . . of course. I was shocked. Joyce was always so concerned about him."

"I believe you saw him the afternoon before his death. Is that correct?"

"No. Why? What would lead you to think that?"

"He was seen running up to your back door that evening, and someone let him in. Perhaps it was not you?"

"That evening! I thought you said 'afternoon.' Yes. That *evening* I saw him . . . briefly. He came over to the house . . . just for a moment."

"What was that all about?" Raker had played his hunch. Monica had taken the bait.

"He . . . funny . . . I almost forgot. He wanted to talk to my son Jason . . . who was not at home."

"I see. And that was all that transpired between you?"

"Yes. Seems odd Jamie would step into the house only to find out your son was not here." Raker ventured.

"Yes." Monica shifted uncomfortably in on the couch. "I . . . I wasn't sure whether Jason was at home or not, so I asked Jamie to step inside while I went to call him. People upstairs often can't hear you in the back foyer no matter how hard you shout. *Believe me!* I know." Monica forced a laugh.

"You and young Sherman were on friendly terms. Isn't that so also?"

"Well . . . yes . . . I suppose. He . . . ah," Monica drew a breath, "he had a lot of problems. He and his dad didn't get along. He was in therapy, and his stepmother . . . Joyce . . . and he didn't get along well, although I think Jamie was more upset about his troubles with his father."

"In therapy?"

"Yes. At least, that's what he told me. He was supposed to be taking *Paxil* for depression. He just needed someone who'd listen, someone who's not involved. Detached. You know."

"Of course. So he was only here long enough for you to discover that your son was not at home, and then he went on."

"Yes. Just a minute or two."

"How did he strike you?"

"Jamie? I hardly spoke to him. He's always been . . . sort of quietly angry and repressed, but otherwise straightforward with people. A little taciturn, perhaps. Moody."

"Not anxious or agitated?"

"No. I wouldn't say that."

"Any idea where he went after he left you?"

"He went down to the dock. I heard his outboard start up shortly after he left."

"Very good. Thank you, Mrs. Clay. If anything else occurs to you, please give me a call." Raker stood up.

"I will. I feel odd about Jamie and your questions. Is there a concern about his death?"

"A concern?"

"Yes. I heard that he died of cardiac arrest, or something like that. He had a weak heart."

"That's what we've heard in the Sheriff's Department. The case isn't closed yet."

Chapter 21

"There's got to be an explanation for this, Morrie," Matthew said the moment Morrie entered the den. "What's this huge hedge fund position doing in Rene McAllister's account? My God, it shows she bought $749,000 last December. Most of it on margin." Matthew looked up. Their eyes met.

"She wanted it."

"Wanted it? My God, I was hoping you were going to say that it was a mistake . . . transferred in somehow to a wrong account number. A hedge fund! Shit. They're the hyenas of Wall Street. You shouldn't have let her . . . never should have entered the order."

"I was afraid if I turned her down, she'd pressure Mac to move the accounts."

"Bullshit. Mac'd never let her buy this. He'd never move the accounts over something like this. Why didn't you tell me?"

"You weren't around that much in December. Remember? You were getting ready for the holidays. I thought you'd see it on the reports. It put us into the bonus for the year—three percent across our volume . . . nearly eighty-five thousand, and the trade itself was another $16,000. We topped over two-million-eight in volume for the year."

"That's crap. If I was away from the office, how in the name of

Christ was I going to see the reports. They're not available on line. And on margin. Jesus, we never do margin."

"I didn't want it on margin, but I couldn't get her to sell anything to raise the cash. She was afraid Mac'd see the sales in the year-end caapital gains tax report."

"So she knew that Mac'd never approve."

"I guess."

"You guess. My ass. You know goddamn well he wouldn't. You let her con you into it. Margin! Jesus. And this goddamn thing has tanked. It must have lost money from the day one."

"Just the last five months," Morrie said. "We had to stay with it for a year before the managing partner would redeem shares at prevailing market value. It was a lock. There was nothing we could do."

Matthew dropped his head and stared at the top of his desk and then began shaking his head. "Never . . . never would have I have imagined anything like this. We don't do business this way. You and I . . . we . . . we not only don't do business this way, we stand for something entirely different. Mac's not going to stand for it. It's a breach of trust. We need to explain ourselves, or he's going to pull compliance in on this. We should be reporting his complaint ourselves right now."

The two men sat quietly for several minutes. Morrie felt guilt rising within him. He could see Wirth struggling as the implications of what had happened took shape in his thoughts. Morrie wanted to blurt how sorry he was, explain himself, tell the story the same way that he had told Monica so that Matthew would understand. Things were supposed to work out differently. Rene would make a killing in the hedge fund. He would be a hero. McAllister would be pleased and leave the accounts with Morrie when Matthew retired. Morrie couldn't know that the market would fall out from under the fund. That the manager's leveraging strategy, borrowing money against the holdings in the fund, was calculated to amplify gains but had the opposite effect and magnified losses as the market turned down.

"Please," Morrie finally said, "there's so much at stake. We," he cleared his throat, "we need to take one step at a time and arrive at some conclusions ourselves before getting compliance involved, Matt. There's too much at stake. I don't trust them to understand."

Matthew looked up slowly and stared into Morrie's eyes. "Yes. There is too much at stake. I don't know how I can trust our compliance officers to understand something I don't understand myself. My God, I've been so proud of what we have been able to do together. To think . . . Jesus . . . to think that this is . . . the way it draws to a close. You get what I am driving at, don't you, Morrie? You understand?"

"I think so."

"What? What am I driving at?"

"That this probably means the end of our partnership."

"Oh, yes. It certainly means that. I can't trust your judgment. That was at the heart of our working together."

"I know, Matt. I know. I'm sorry. More sorry than you know. But she insisted."

Matthew pushed back in his chair and stood up. "The woman was paranoid. A nut-case. We both knew that. If she wasn't Mac McAllister's wife, nobody'd give her the time of day. A mental flyweight. You *knew* that. We talked about it. Hundreds of times." Matthew looked at the bookcase behind him and rolled his head from side to side. "Why? I can't understand why you didn't come to me about this."

"It was year-end. Everything was rush-rush. People had tax selling to do. Minimum required distributions to process—some needing to be funded by liquidating positions. We had the usual run of last minute in-kind charitable contributions. And the fund itself had a deadline we needed to meet. You've been through it. It gets worse every year."

"That just doesn't fucking wash, Morrie. This was bigger than all that. We've got these goddamn cell phones . . . email . . . we live within five minutes of one another in the city in the winter."

"I know it seems cut-and-dried now. I can't excuse myself. But that's how it happened. I'm as sorry as I can be about it."

"Why didn't you at least sell enough to cover the margin. Even Rene'd know that she couldn't find a way around Mac forever. You had a full year to work on it."

"I . . . I . . . as I say . . . I can't excuse myself. But there's at least . . . at least a partial explanation," Morrie said.

"I don't see it."

"Ever since we split up the McAllister accounts to put the income generating investments in his and the growth positions in hers, Rene was impossible. She kept wanting to withdraw cash. She wanted to sneak money out from under Mac. I reminded her over and over she needed to take it from their joint account. I kept holding the line and she grew more and more abusive with me . . . with Cheryl and Louise. When she wanted to buy the hedge fund, I thought that I could give into her on it. Get back into her favor a little. It was a growth position. I researched it. The manager had done very well in the past, so I agreed." Morrie was fabricating the story. His confidence grew as he noticed that Matthew was being more attentive.

"But three-quarters of a million dollars," Matthew countered. "Why $749,000? My God, if you're a going to bet the ranch, why not a cool $750,000?"

"There was a break-point on the commissions scale at $750,000. It dropped to one-and-three-quarter percent. Anything between $500,000 and $749,999 paid two-and-an-eighth. $749,000 paid almost $16,000 in commissions. $750,000 paid just a little over $13,000. $16,000 put us into the next compensation level and earned a bonus. $13,000 would have left us short."

"God damn it, I've been in this business for almost twenty years, and I never thought like that. If the market drops much more, the collateral positions won't stand the pressure, and a margin call will go out. The company's going to want to be paid back." Matthew tapped at his computer keyboard, alternating screens that produced the current statistics on the McAllister accounts. "Mac probably didn't notice this because the value of the margin debit was almost equal to the value of the fund," he said under his breath. "The growth in the Rene's stocks hid the loss."

"Mac never looks at Rene's accounts," Morrie said. "Her statements go to her in a separate envelope. She didn't know how . . ."

"Look," Matthew said, "I can't deal with the issues between you and me right now. I need to rely on your goodwill a few more days so we can set this straight. We need to find a solution, somehow. An answer."

"She's to blame. That's the answer."

"And we let her get away with it."

"You can make me the fall guy on that, but we need to keep the focus on her," Morrie said.

"Otherwise . . ."

"There is no otherwise. We stone-wall it."

"I can't believe we're having this conversation."

"What other choice do we have? I've had time to think about this, Matt. I saw it coming the day you got the call from Mac telling you he was moving the accounts. I knew then that the hedge fund position wouldn't transfer. That the margin loan'd be discovered. Believe me, this is the only option at this point."

"And you never told me."

"I tried. The night I came over, you were on the deck drinking wine. You were so contented. I couldn't bring myself to tell you. I thought I'd try to get by on my own somehow. But it's beyond me. Then the Fourth party. I didn't want to break in on your fun. I decided to wait until this was forced out in the open. When Rene died, I thought things would turn out better one way or another."

"Some consideration," Matthew snarled. "You see how this plays out. Mac isn't going to sit still for it . . . blame Rene or not. He is too tough a business man. He'll go to compliance. He'll get an attorney. And when the shit hits the fan, you've effectively thrown my reputation into the mix also. You've blown up my plans for retirement along with our plans for our partnership. I'm at a loss . . . a complete loss. . ."

"I know it sounds hopeless," Morrie pleaded, "but maybe Mac won't react as you say. We've one hope and that's to convince him Rene did it, that she's to blame, and it's my fault for letting her get away with it."

"I need time," Matthew said. "I need to think this through. Mac's probably going to want to meet with us . . . perhaps as early as tomorrow. He'll want to clear this up before taking his family to the attorney. So, for now, just get the hell out of here. I'll call if I need to after I talk to Mac."

"I'm going into the office to make sure we have everything we need in case McAllister wants to meet in the morning." Morrie stood up and took a hesitant step toward his partner, "Look, Matthew . . ."

"I don't need to hear it. Just get out."

Raker called Gene Phillips as soon as he reached his car. "Any way you can get the M.E. to check for *Paxil* or an anti-depressant in the Sherman kid?" he asked the CSI technician.

"Yeah. On your word though."

"Of course. And, listen, any test you can run on that ounce bag to see if there is any pain-killer in it . . . *Demerol* for example?"

"Yeah. I guess. Why?"

"Didn't you tell me you had a background in pharmacology?"

"Yes. I wanted to be a pharmacist, but I got interested in this line of work while I was in college and never completed the work to get board certified."

"But you know how drugs can interact with each other . . . produce an undesired side effect in a person."

"Oh, yeah! That was drilled into us."

"Correct me, then, but I seem to remember being warned once about taking *Demerol* if I was on an anti-depressant like *Paxil*. Does that square with your experience."

"Definitely. It's easy to look up, but I remember that because pain-killers were prescribed so often."

"OK. Look it up, just to be on the safe side. I want to find out if the Sherman kid ingested *Demerol* while he was also using *Paxil*."

"I'll get back to you."

Chapter 22

S hirley peered through the dining room and saw the door to her husband's study was ajar. "Everything all right in there?" she called. No answer. She dried her hands and walked to the study door. Matthew was sitting at his desk with his head in his hands.

"You OK?" He did not look up. "Matthew, speak to me." She eased over to the wingback chair that Morrie had vacated and sat down. "Morrie looked awful leaving. You two had a spat, didn't you? I could hear it from the kitchen."

"Worse than that," Matthew said looking up. "He's created the biggest mess. I don't see how we can fix it. I just never . . . never expected anything like this. He got a McAllister account in serious trouble, caved into Rene . . . never told me about it. Bought one of those damnable new hedge funds. Nobody knows how they'll perform. No history to any of them. And the damn thing tanked . . . crashed and burned. Mac's out more than half a million. And I . . . I," Matthew said raising his voice, "I wasn't even aware of it until just a few minutes ago. Damn, damn, damn." He pounded the desk. "I trusted him to use good judgment . . . that he'd come to me if there were problems. He's violated every understanding we had . . . made me look like a fool. A total fool."

Shirley had seen her husband angry many times over their years together. His temper would flare, but within seconds, he would be laughing at himself. The exasperation in his voice now was unfamiliar to her. "Mac's a friend, honey. Can't you explain the situation . . ."

"I can't. Mac may be a friend, but he's a businessman first. I know what I'd do if I were in his position. Any thought Morrie had of holding those accounts after this . . . well . . . no chance. And as for my relationship with Mac . . . it's over . . . once this thing is out of the bag." Matthew stood up and walked to the door to the deck and looked out to the lake. "You see," he said turning back toward Shirley, "we . . . Morrie and I . . . we could survive just about any-thing . . . losing a big account . . . making an honest mistake. That's all part of it. Nobody's right all the time, but you can be honest. You can do your homework. You can be prudent. That's as easy as drawing the next breath. But when trust is gone, that's it. All my plans, my God . . . all my plans have collapsed."

"Honey . . . are you sure you're not overreacting to this?"

"God, I'd be so happy if I were." His eyes flashed his despera-tion. Pain cramped his brow as he tried to a hold back the surge of his shock. "What I'm supposed to do . . . right now . . . is call my manager or the compliance officer. This minute! I've never been put in this position before."

"Come sit down," Shirley soothed. "Everyone knows you. The company. The entire community. Nobody's going to decide you're unforgivably guilty of anything."

Matthew turned reluctantly and walked back to his desk. "I've spent nearly three years building this partnership so that I could turn over my clients to Morrie. I want to retire. I don't want to work another three years, and it'll take three years from the date I sign an agreement to form another partnership. I don't even know of anybody I want for a partner." Matthew tossed his hands in the air. "Nobody in our office certainly."

"Turning your clients over to someone you know was a very nice idea," Shirley replied, "but you didn't need to do it. Everybody retires eventually, Matthew. Your clients will understand."

"I suppose but . . . my God . . . we've been promoting our partnership all this time. If Mac makes a big deal out of this, word's going to get around. Everyone's going to wonder what happened. Why Morrie isn't around any more? Why they were turned over to someone else? I've let everyone down. And . . . God . . . there're some guys in our office I wouldn't want my worst enemy to have as an advisor."

"You're making it sound hopeless. People will understand. It's part of life. If you had a heart attack, God forbid, they'd all pick up and take care of themselves. I love you because you care so much, Matthew, but this sounds like your Catholic upbringing caught up with you."

"You think?"

"You need to give yourself time to think things over a little."

"It's three years work down the drain. Remains to be seen what this does to our good name in the business, and that's the least of it. The company holds me responsible for this too. Partners share responsibility."

"After all those years, surely they'll give you the benefit of the doubt."

"But I trusted him. I did, Shirley."

"I know you did. You've been bitterly disappointed. I feel it too. I don't know what I'll think when I see Morrie again. We'll work through it."

"I really don't want to face Mac. I supposed to call him."

"Well, do it now. Call him so it won't be hanging over your head the rest of the day. Then take the boat for a spin. That's what you set out to do in the first place."

"I know."

"Good. I've got a lot to get ready for the kids on Sunday," Shirley said standing up. She smiled at her husband, scrutinized his expression one more time, and left the room satisfied that he would find his way back to a balanced view of the problem with Morrie and Mac. She heard him greet Mac on the phone as she closed the door to the den behind her.

"Look, Mac, I've talked to Morrie about this situation, and I'm not quite sure I can account for what has been going on in Rene's account. I need more time. I want to check at the office, have the files reviewed, and get the full picture. I can promise a full explanation tomorrow."

"Fine," McAllister responded to Matthew's surprise. "How much time do you need?"

"I'm going in first thing in the morning and go over everything with Morrie. He's on his way in there now and he'll have everything rounded up for me."

"I know you well enough to think there's an explanation for this. I'll see you tomorrow morning . . . get this out of the way before the kids and I meet with the attorney."

"Ah, yes, Mac. That should work. How about the office at 9:30 tomorrow morning."

"Fine."

Many things that the Moran had said over the past two or three days angered Raker, but nothing more than the comment that the local police had been aware of Raker's trouble in handling his wife's prolonged sickness and death. He knew he had trouble staying focused. "Arrogant bastard," Raker muttered. Nothing ran an investigation into the ground quicker than a big ego. As soon as one man thinks he has a case figured, all the energies of the team are bled off either defending a pet theory or attacking it.

His cell phone vibrated on his hip and startled him. It was the Sheriff. "Raker, I got a goddamn list here in front of me that Moran's people sent down. What the hell is this all about?"

"Listen . . . it's kind of complicated. Can I . . ."

"Complicated? It's just a list of names. Makes no sense."

"I know. I was just about to come back into the office. Can I talk to you about it when I get there? I'm only twenty minutes away."

"Twenty minutes? Fine."

"OK, Raker," the Sheriff barked as soon as he saw the detective in the doorway, "what's with this list? You got tangled up with SBI, didn't you? I told you to stay clear of those guys."

"The list," Raker began before taking a seat, "is something I requested from Moran. I'm sorry I didn't let you know in advance. The names on it are people I need clearance from Moran before I can contact them. He kept yelling about how we spooked the Sherman kid and screwed up his case, so I told him to submit a list . . . that I couldn't be responsible for wandering into his case if I didn't know who was off-limits."

"What are you working on that could possibly overlap with those guys?"

Raker looked the Sheriff in the eye, but as usual, his appeal for confidence was blunted by the Sheriff 's steely return stare. "All right. Hear me out. I have until noon today to convince you that the McAllister drowning was not accidental and keep the case open. That was our deal. Right?"

"Ah, for Chrissake. I suppose now you're going to tell me you have a case. We've been over this."

"I know, and I know you don't want the SBI guys upset with you or the department. Just hear me out."

"This'd better be good."

"Our two cases, Moran's and mine, are all tangled up with each other. For one thing, Mrs. McAllister was murdered. There are unexplained bruises on her arms, chest, and head . . . sustained prior to her death, probably while she was drowning. Somebody forced her under water and held her there with the oar we have in custody.

"I think that person was Monica Clay. McAllister's husband was about to move a large account away from Morrison Clay, the suspect's husband. He's a financial guy. The account's worth nearly twenty million.

"Jamie Sherman probably saw the Clay woman at the scene. He reported seeing someone and then later denied it. He saw Monica Clay and was killed because of it. The kid was on anti-depressants, and the dope he was smoking is being checked to see if it was laced with *Demerol*. Traces of curry were found in the dime bag that he had with him when he died. Monica Clay's kitchen smelled of curry when we interviewed her, and she takes *Demerol* for her migraines. Her whereabouts are unknown at the time of the drowning."

"*Demerol*'s not a poison, Raker," the Sheriff countered, "at least not in prescribed dosages . . . certainly nothing that could be inhaled from taking a few hits off a joint. You're grasping at straws."

"*Demerol* in conjunction with a serotonin reuptake inhibitor in a person with a heart condition can cause death . . . a convulsive cardiac arrest. It's called serotonin toxicity. The Sherman kid experienced convulsions. His feet were all torn up from kicking around in the bottom of his boat."

"How'd you find this all out?"

"The M. E.'s report. Some of it's in the CSI analysis. I'm not sure of the *Demerol* yet. The lab is working on it. But it's all beginning to line up."

"You share this with Moran?" the Sheriff asked.

"No. He thinks I'm off the track. He's bent on proving Sherman died because of his drug dealing. Perhaps a gang thing. Sherman was going to be a source for them. They'd just reached an understanding the day before, and then the kid turned up dead. So a gang member found out . . . something. Moran's pissed about it. They've got a lot of time in the case and it's been blown sky high."

"This list, then," the Sheriff asked picking it up and waving it at Raker, "these are the people he doesn't want you to talk to, and you're going to tell me that you need to talk to some of them, aren't you?"

"Maybe. Maybe not. I haven't seen who's on it yet. The one thing that Moran's looking for now . . . probably as we speak . . . is the kilo of marijuana that the Sherman kid picked up in town the day before he died. He needs it to piece together a trail that'll lead back to the suppliers in the city. And he's looking in the wrong place."

"And you know, I suppose, exactly where he should be looking."

"I've got a damn good idea."

"Then tell him, God damn it. What's the hold up?"

"Two reasons. First, he refuses to see that the two cases are related, and he won't give me the time of day. Second, finding the kilo is his case, not mine. I can't prove that Sherman delivered the kilo anywhere, although I think the Clay woman has it. I don't know that I have enough to get us a search warrant on my own case. Moran'd laugh at anything I suggest."

"Why would she have the kilo?" the Sheriff asked.

"A hunch. If Moran doesn't turn it up at the Sherman home anywhere . . . and I don't think that he will . . . by process of elimination, it's at the Clay woman's house."

"Finding it there would prove what?"

"Nothing as far as the drowning in concerned, but it could have implications with regard to Sherman's death and Monica Clay's involvement. If we found the kilo, it'd get Moran back on my side."

"Meanwhile, if Moran doesn't find the stuff, and you go looking for it, you've just tipped off the Clay woman. And maybe Moran'd consider her part of his case and be even more pissed."

"Yes. That's a risk." Raker replied, "but what's she going to do? If it's found on her, she'd be charged with possession with intent to sell. Now that Sherman's dead, she's looking to ditch the stuff as soon as she can. That's what I'd do in her place. We can't allow her too much time."

The Sheriff picked up the list of names and flipped it back on the blotter of his desk. "I think you can wait this out, Raker. Moran could still turn something up at the Sherman home. If he does, you'll be free to do whatever you want. If he doesn't, we'll bring him in on everything. Keep working on the drowning case. You've got enough to keep it open. Just keep making steady progress, as you have been. I'll run interference for you with Moran and his crowd."

"Fine." Raker stood up to leave.

"You think this woman could have killed two people?" the Sheriff asked.

"Yes."

"Any chance she might have another victim in her sights? Any reason to think that?"

"No. I don't think so. I've talked with her. She's a tough lady—athletic, attractive, bright. But not the criminal type. I can't see where she'd have reason. A motive."

"Not unless there's someone out there . . . like this dumb Sherman kid . . . who stumbled on to her with the McAllister woman. What are the chances of that?"

"None and none at all."

"Yeah. Well, what if someone knows something about how she killed Sherman then? This lady likes to cover her tracks."

Raker, pleased that the Sheriff was taking an interest in his case, sat back down. "There was nobody at the scene when the kid died. It was the dark of night out in the middle of the lake. She had everything she needed. The *Demerol*. The marijuana . . ."

"There!" the Sheriff shouted, startling Raker. "How do you know she had the marijuana? What'd you say? Because there was curry in it, and she had curry in her kitchen. Right?"

"Yes."

"There's the reason for your search. You don't go in looking for the kilo of marijuana. You go in looking for the curry . . . and *Demerol*. If the lab finds it in the stuff the kid smoked, you've identified your killer and found the kilo for Moran as a bonus. I like that," the Sheriff said. "I like that a lot." He lunged forward suddenly and snatched up the list of names again. "Clay. Clay's not on the list. Right?"

"I was just out there. Not a problem."

"Great. Stay out of Moran's way. I'll get the search warrant for you, and I want you to go back out there unannounced with a couple of deputies as soon as I get it. Just sit tight. I may need your help with the warrant request. Where will you be? Your office here?"

"Yes. My office. Here. Right."

At the office, Morrie knew that he needed to carry on as if everything was OK. Perhaps there was a way through the trouble now that it was out in open not one big secret between Monica and him. He'd stick to his strategy, capitalize on Rene's death, and hope that McAllister would fall for it. Perhaps, when Matthew cooled off, they could patch things up, and he could stay in the partnership. Rene McAllister was within her legal rights to buy a hedge fund. The account was in her name. Her husband's directions to Matthew and him did not constitute a legal contract. Ignoring his wishes violated an understanding, but it didn't break the law. The phone rang.

"Monica," Cheryl called.

"Well? How'd it go?" Monica asked.

"Give me a minute to close the door." Morrie glanced out at Cheryl, smiled and closed the door. "Matthew was shocked. Stunned. He thought it was a mistake. He never guessed."

"So what'd you tell him?"

"I stayed with my strategy and said Rene McAllister insisted on everything."

"He believed you?"

"Yes. I think he did."

"So?"

"So? So, nothing. He's mad as hell that I let her do it. Demanded to know why I didn't tell him. He knows McAllister will be pissed, and . . . he said he doesn't see how he can trust me again . . . my judgment." Morrie's voice softened to a whisper. "It probably means the end of our partnership. I'll be back with my own accounts . . . just where I was three years ago."

"What's he going to tell McAllister?"

"We didn't decide that. We'll probably set up a meeting with Mac for tomorrow morning sometime . . . early."

"You need to work out a strategy with Matt for that meeting."

"Look, right now, the man doesn't even want to see me, let alone talk to me. I'm just hoping that he doesn't report McAllister's complaint to our compliance department. That'll blow everything straight up."

"Why would he do that?"

"Because Matthew's always been by the book. He's a straight shooter."

"Then you've got to stop him," Monica said.

"No. No. I don't need to do anything right now. He won't listen to me . . . and even if he did hear me out, it'd just make me look more guilty."

"You're can't be the only one with a stake in this. You can't let Matthew report the complaint, say that you did it, and while it looks bad that he didn't know what went on, it's no skin off his nose. He loses a partner. So what?" Monica paused. "You need leverage. Matthew needs to have something to protect too."

"He's been hurt enough. I can't . . . I don't want to add to it. Remember who he is! A friend . . . he was . . ."

"All I'm suggesting is your position would be stronger if Matt was more culpable . . . more guilty . . . than you make him sound. It'd give you some leverage . . . instead of having none at all . . . as it seems now."

"He's hurt enough . . . and disappointed enough now. I'm not adding to his misery. This is humiliating for him. Mac'll have the word out inside of a month, and Matt knows it. The man has some pride you know. He's Mr. Clean in the business. This essentially flushes his reputation and could cost him his job too even though he didn't have anything to do with it."

"So he does have something at stake?"

"Of course. What do you think I've been saying. It means a lot of money for him. Earnings he set aside to be paid during his retirement when his taxes'll be lower . . . deferred compensation. That's at least a million. Bonuses he's earned. Stock options. And he is proud of what he has achieved. That's simple enough, isn't it."

"Then that's the buy in. That's what you've got to use to get him to help convince McAllister that this was all Rene's idea."

"Yeah, well, I don't think that way. I hate that kind of thinking . . . scheming. Besides, he knows! Even if he helps me sell McAllister some cock-and-bull, he knows that I didn't do what a good partner would. McAllister won't overlook that we let Rene get away with it."

"Yeah, right. Mr. J. Alan McAllister lost a half-a-million dollars in the stock market because he wife bought something behind his back, and the broker didn't stop her. I can just hear that making the rounds at the country club. Mac won't want anyone to know about this. How can you be so smart about investing money and so god-damn stupid about people."

"I don't have to listen to this."

"No. Oh, no. Righteous, Mr. J. Morrison Clay doesn't have to listen. He can hang up and watch his only chance of saving his ass get swept away. You wait, God damn it! I've been fighting a migraine all day so you can damn well hear me out. If you won't do this, then I will. Somewhere, sometime between now and that meeting tomorrow, you need to lay it all out for Matthew. You've got to get him to see what's at risk. He's got to fight for his half. You can't take for granted that he knows what's at stake. You owe it to me and your sons. We didn't do this. You did."

"I don't know how to do what you're asking for. I don't operate that way."

"You can . . . and you will."

"Don't hang up!" Morrie shouted.

"Why?"

"I need to know if you got rid of Jamie's package?"

"Yes. God. What'd you think."

"Not in the toilet and not in the lake, I hope."

"Of course not. I drove to a recycle place and buried it a dumpster."

Chapter 23

"Mornin' boss. Good to have you here for a change," Cheryl answered when he buzzed her on the intercom.

"Morrie come in yet?"

"Yes. He's in his office."

"Can you bring me the McAllister files?"

"He's got all of them."

"Well, tell him to come to my office and bring the files with him."

"Yes, sir."

"Cheryl?"

"Yes?"

"I'm sorry. I didn't mean to sound so damned cranky. Can I back up and say 'Good Morning'?"

"Of course. I know your moods."

"You do, eh?"

"Oh yeah. After all these years. Of course."

"Well, let me know the minute Mac McAllister comes in please. Thanks."

"You got it."

Matthew heard a knock at his door. Morrie, not waiting for an answer, opened it and stepped in. He dropped the McAllister file on the conference table. "You want to meet here or in the larger office?" Morrie asked.

"Here. McAllister's more familiar with everything. I hope it makes a difference. Keep it short and to the point. We've got to get this straight with him, then I need to get home and get the boat tuned up for the weekend."

"I think," Morrie said, "we should emphasize the positive things. McAllisters, except for the hedge fund, have had good returns on all their accounts . . . especially with what the market has done so far this year."

"Forget it. Mac called the meeting; we didn't. He wants to know about the hedge fund." Matthew joined Morrie at the conference table. "You got everything?"

"Right here." Morrie slid the file over to Matthew who opened the cover and searched the tabs of the vanilla folders for Rene's trust account.

"On top," Morrie directed.

"OK?" Matthew pulled back and opened the top folder. The copy of the limited partnership agreement, a four page legal contract, was the first in the stack. Matthew shook his head. The government and regulatory agencies kept requiring additional forms to open brokerage accounts and enter into certain investments—limited partnerships, mutual funds, and third-party investment managers— all to make certain that the client knew the particulars regarding the investment, the risks, and the legal rights that presumably protected all parties. Signatures were always required to attest that the client understood. Most rarely had questions. At the close of the sale, clients wanted to demonstrate their confidence in their own decisions and the advisor. Asking anything was a display of distrust.

"The margin agreement?" Matthew asked.

"Ah, that . . . that was just a fluke."

"A fluke?"

"Yeah. When we created the living trust account for Rene, we used a number that had been assigned to Mac earlier. The margin designation didn't get taken off the account when the number was reassigned."

"So who signed the margin agreement?"

"Mac. But that was before we changed the status of the account and assigned it as a single trust account to Rene."

"Didn't it come up on renewal," Matthew asked, realizing that the fluke, as Morrie had described it, would have been caught when the company went through the formality of having the margin agreement renewed with a fresh signature on the second anniversary of the agreement.

"The anniversary was this coming November."

"How did you know it was on margin then?"

Morrie's brows pinched. "I happened to notice it. We had trouble getting a trade to settle. The funds from a sale didn't come into the account to cover a buy we made at the same time, and margin covered it. I was relieved, and I decided just to leave things as they were in case anything happened like that again."

"I thought you told me that Rene insisted on putting the hedge fund purchase on margin?"

"She did."

"How did she know that she had margin on this account? You didn't tell her did you?"

"No. I mean, yes. At . . . at first, I wanted her to sell stock to cover the hedge fund buy. But . . . but I couldn't get her to agree on what to sell, and it . . . it just slipped out. I got tired of her hemming and hawing . . . not making up her mind about anything . . . and I said we could leave it on margin for a little while until she decided.

It was a mistake. I was never able to get her to sell anything. She became afraid Mac's accountant could catch it in the capital gains reporting statement at the end of the year, and she didn't want to explain anything to Mac. She just wanted to show him that she could make money investing on her own."

"You're telling me the truth? Jesus . . . you should've taken the account off margin the minute you noticed it."

"I know. But she was so hard to deal with. If I needed a decision, it could take a week just getting her to return a call. Then she wouldn't decide. It's their job . . .operations . . . to catch that stuff, you know."

"No, God damn it, it's our job to catch that kind of thing. When this meeting is through, I want to know how much of this crap has been going on in other accounts. How many other things have you let slide because it was somehow more convenient."

"Matthew, this is the only situation. I swear. The only one. There was only one Rene McAllister." The phone rang. Matthew jumped up, turned around, and snatched up the handset from his desk. Cheryl was on the line.

"Mr. McAllister is in the reception area. Do you want me to bring him in?" she asked. Matthew turned to Morrie.

"Morrie, you look awful," Matthew said. "You're sweating, for Chrissake. McAllister's here. Go to the men's room and clean up." Then he turned back to the telephone, "Wait until Morrie passes your desk, then go get McAllister."

A minute later, Cheryl swung the door open to Matthew's office, and Mac McAllister stepped in. "Good morning, Mac," Matthew said and extended his hand. McAllister shook hands warmly and moved to take a seat at the table.

"Anyone care for coffee?" Cheryl asked.

"You, Mac?" Matthew asked.

"No. Had my quota for the day."

"Guess not, Cheryl," Matthew said. "Morrie'll be right with us. You've had two or three rough days, Mac. Shirley and I tried to get to you after the service yesterday, but . . . my God . . . they just whisked your family around so fast."

"That's OK. I was getting very tired of all the condolences. People saying what's expected. It's been a long . . . long . . . affair. It's almost over. We've got this meeting and then meet with the kids at the attorney's later today."

The door opened. Morrie entered. The redness was gone from his cheeks. If anything, he looked gray and drawn. Morrie pulled out a chair from the table and turned to McAllister.

"Mac, good to see you. Monica and I wanted to express our condolences. This has all been such a shock."

"Yeah . . . well . . . she's asleep. I just want to put her affairs in order and get all of this behind me. I'm not pleased we had to hold this meeting. I thought you'd know what the hell I was talking about the minute I called, Matt." McAllister said without a hint of either anger or understanding in his voice.

"I apologize. You had every right to expect me to know about Rene's account. I'm sorry that this was necessary also, given all that you've been through."

"What have you come up with?" Mac questioned without registering any acceptance of Matthew's apology.

"Well . . . ah . . . long-story-short," Matthew said, "Rene did actually own the hedge fund . . . as it turns out. There's been no mistake. She bought it when it came out last December. Bought it through Morrie."

"Like hell she did."

"No. No. Mac, she did," Morrie said. "She insisted on it. She'd heard about hedge funds. Her friends were all excited about them. Making money. She wanted to get into one."

"And you let her, for Chrissake. I thought we had an understanding, Matt?"

"We did, Mac. But, please, just hear us out. Morrie worked with Rene on this. He has the full story."

Morrie related, once again, the story of how Rene had insisted on buying the hedge fund. When he concluded, McAllister said, "Well, this is simple . . . just sell the damn thing."

"We can't," Matthew replied.

"What do you mean, you can't?"

"It's a limited partnership. There's an open window once a year when the general partner'll redeem units at market value, but that's not until December. There's no secondary market for it. As things stand now . . ." Morrie started to explain.

"You've got an agreement? Let me see it," McAllister said nodding at the file on the table. "I'll have my attorney go over it, and find a way out of this thing."

Matthew produced the limited partnership agreement and slid it across the table to McAllister. "Jesus, I hate this kind of shit," McAllister said. "Mumbo-jumbo. Only a lawyer could understand it. Is this my copy?"

"Ah . . . no," Matthew replied. "That's the office copy. You should have a client copy in Rene's files."

"She didn't keep records so a person could find anything."

"I'll get this copied for you," Morrie said and reached to take it from McAllister.

"Wait a goddamn minute." McAllister held the paper up in front of him. "This isn't Rene's signature. This is not my wife's signature! What the hell is this?" He looked first at Wirth and then at Clay.

"No. No. It is," Morrie blurted.

"Who witnessed it?" McAllister demanded.

"North Carolina doesn't require a witness on limited partnership agreements."

"Anyone see her sign it?"

"I don't know," Morrie replied.

"If you didn't see it her sign, how do you know. Weren't you there to explain it to her?"

"I explained everything to her. Signing was just a formality. It was the last day of the enrollment period for the fund. I kept trying to get Rene back into the office and finish everything, half hoping she'd change her mind, but on the last day, she said she'd come by during the noon hour. I told I'd only be in until 1:30. When she didn't show, I took the agreement up to the cashier and asked the cashier to have Rene sign it if she came in. I'd tried to do what she wanted. It'd be her fault we couldn't go through with it.

"When I got back from my appointment, the agreement with Rene's signature was in my mailbox. I didn't think another thing of it."

"That's not her signature. I'd know my wife's signature. Who was the cashier on duty when she came in?" McAllister asked.

The question took Morrie by surprise. "Ah . . . Jane. Somebody fills in for her now and then. But . . . yes . . . I remember clearly. It was Jane."

"That the woman I passed on the way in here?" McAllister asked.

"Yes. She's on duty," Morrie responded.

"Have her come in!"

Morrie jumped from his chair. "Ah . . . yes, of course." Morrie called Jane's interoffice extension. "Can you step into Matthew's office . . . just for second, please. . . . No. It will only take a second. Good. Thanks."

All three men fell silent as they awaited Jane's arrival. McAllister looked up at the stout woman who seemed very intent on letting everyone know that she resented being taken away from her work. As she approached, McAllister thrust the agreement toward her. "Did you know my wife? Rene McAllister?"

"No."

"If she walked in here today, you wouldn't know who she was?"

"No. I see dozens of people every day. Some come in maybe as often as once a week. I might recognize one of them. But there's no way that I can remember every client's name on sight."

"This agreement. Do you remember giving it to anyone and asking them to sign it?"

Jane took the agreement and skimmed it. "December 16. Not a chance." She handed the agreement back to McAllister. "So many people come in here to sign documents in December . . . IRA minimum distribution requirements . . . last minute annual IRA contributions . . . transfers to charitable organizations . . . option exercise. There is so much traffic that there's no way I can remember every single request." Jane turned to Matthew and asked, "Do you need me any more?"

"No, Jane. Thank you. I'll explain later."

Matthew waited for Jane to close the door. "Mac, she didn't understand the larger issue here. I'm sure if she did, she would have responded more diplomatically."

"I don't give a damn," McAllister replied. "She's believable. If you guys had talked to her beforehand she'd have known the score. But it doesn't alter the fact that this is not Rene's signature."

"Yes. Yes, sir. It is," Morrie replied, mopping his forehead. "It may not look like hers because of the way she signed it. It's a collated set. It can slip around when it is being signed. The page you're holding is just the imprint of the original . . . the third page under the original. She may have signed in a hurry. Placed it on top of something . . . a book . . . her purse . . . something that could cause the pen to slip. There are reasons why it looks so unfamiliar to you."

"She doesn't make her capital 'A' that way, or the double 'l's' either for that matter."

"I swear that is the truth," Morrie said.

"Of course you do," McAllister responded. "You're in no position to do otherwise. Get me a copy! Where's the original?"

"On file with the general manager," Morrie replied.

"Where . . . in New Jersey somewhere? Get it back here."

"I'd hope that won't be necessary," Matthew said.

"I'm not surprised." McAllister snapped. "Let me see if I got this right. Rene insisted on buying this piece of shit that's now worth almost half of its original value with virtually no prospects of recovering. Right? She threatened to jerk her accounts if you didn't play along. It's on margin because she couldn't decide on what stocks to sell to cover the purchase. You didn't want to sell it to her. You didn't want it on margin. You didn't want to call me. Am I getting all of this correct? Stop me if I've misunderstood, because later this morning, I'm going to be in Brian Doyle's office to let my children and Rene's children know that each of them is getting a quarter-of-a-million from their mother and the rest is going into trust for them until I die.

"The transfer of the accounts is still on. I know that Rene was a handful. I can see her trying to force this into place. But you didn't bring me in on it. I can't overlook that. I never would have approved. The margin should have been closed—slammed shut. I'd never want her to have that kind of leeway, and God damn it, Matt, you knew that. You should've told Morrie here.

"You'll be hearing from me. Tell your girl to get me a photo copy of this. I'll wait in the lobby for it." McAllister stood up abruptly, looked Matthew in the eye, turned to the door, yanked it open, and left.

Morrie picked up the limited partnership agreement and walked out. Moments later he returned and told Matthew that Louise would photocopy and deliver a copy to McAllister. Neither man said anything for several minutes. Matthew finally walked back to his desk and sat down. Dropped his head into his hands. The meeting had been a nightmare. There was no fixing anything now. He and Morrie could be accused of almost anything by McAllister's attorney, and they would be hard pressed to defend themselves.

"That's how she signed those documents, Morrie? That's the truth?" Matthew finally asked

"Yes. I swear it."

"It's the first thing he'll check."

"I know. I know."

"How do you know if you weren't here to see it? If it's a forgery, both of us are through. Me along with you . . . discredited. Fired for cause. It'll cost me a million, maybe two. I can't . . . can't think what all of this means. I go into old age with nothing more than the skimpy savings account I started with nearly twenty years ago?"

"I . . . I just don't think . . . don't think that's the case, Matt. Honestly."

"We won't have a leg to stand on. Couldn't you see when you put Rene into this thing that you didn't have a way out if it didn't work?"

Morrie could not respond. Looking back, no single step seemed to have a detonator imbedded in it, but Matt did not want to listen to him recount the entire chain of events again. The only hope they had was that nothing could be proved about the signature.

"I can't put off calling our compliance people one more minute," Matthew finally said.

"No. No. Matthew, wait. I agree. It's the right thing to do. But . . . but . . . look, there's nothing to be gained if we do. I'm at fault on this, no matter what else happens from here on out, and . . . God . . . I don't want this to splash on you. Just as you said, we may not have a leg to stand on, so how can calling compliance do anything for us."

Matthew looked up. Morrie was right. Neither of them would get any points for reporting the situation. Compliance would take their side initially, argue that McAllister had been receiving statements all along, that he had a chance to catch the purchase, question the margin loan, and that Rene was within her rights insisting on the purchase. It was the usual opening gambit, one that would not cause an adversary like McAllister to blink. If the signature was forged, Morrie could be indicted. No explanations, no excuses. Nothing would mitigate the consequences for either of them.

"Look at this," Matthew finally said, his hand sweeping across his office. "These awards . . . quality awards . . . client retention awards . . . President's Club . . . Circle of Merit . . . pictures of the places Shirley and I have been . . . recognition banquets . . . the art on the wall . . . you and I have pissed all over it. You're right. It doesn't make a damn bit of difference if we report ourselves or not. Simple choice! Firing squad or hanging. Nothing to it."

"But . . . but . . . McAllister isn't going to want the publicity. He doesn't want people to know his wife lost money on a hedge fund. And the signature may prove to be valid. He's angry now. He's had a lot of losses. Look at what an emotional roller-coaster he's been on this week. We should let him cool down. We're just putting the noose around our own necks if we call now, and something may still turn our way if we wait. Face it. It couldn't be much worse."

"What do you mean 'the signature may prove valid'? It is valid, isn't it? You said it was."

"Yes. Oh, yes. A poor choice of words. Of course it's valid."

"I'm going home," Matthew growled. "there's nothing to do here but wait, and I can't stand that. God, this goes beyond anything I . . ." his voice trailed off. He looked up at Morrie. The younger man dropped his head. "I haven't decided about calling compliance just yet. Everything is coming up lose-lose. Don't do one more thing about any of this without checking with me first. You owe me that, God damn it."

"I know. I won't. I'm sorry, Matthew. I am so very, very sorry."

"Save it for compliance. You can go. Close the door behind you."

Chapter 24

Morrie closed the door to his office. Monica asked him to call as soon as the meeting was over.

"So," Monica asked, "how did it go?"

"Awful. Just awful."

"Did you expect anything less?"

"No. I guess not. I hoped . . . but . . . no."

"Did he question the signature?"

"Yes."

"And?"

"He said it couldn't possibly be Rene's."

"How did you handle it? Like we agreed?"

"Yes . . . like we rehearsed. Where Rene came in after lunch and signs it in the reception area."

"So you're not connected with her signing it. You were not there. Right?"

"Yes. I mean . . . no. I'm wasn't. But I'm still not comfortable with the answer. It'll ultimately lead to Cheryl, and I don't think that's fair. She only did what I asked her. She'll get fired. The women are told over and over never to sign for a client no matter who requests it."

"How's it going to lead to her?"

"They'll start asking around whether anyone saw Rene sign it. They're bound to ask our two assistants."

"So we protect a four-thousand-a-month assistant. God, Morrie, you are beyond hope."

"Give me a minute . . . damn it. Just listen for once. It's going to take time . . . maybe a week or two . . . to prove that the signature's not Rene's. Then they'll come back to me, but it would have come back to me anyway. When they do, I need to come up with something that keeps Cheryl out of this. She's got a family too. Her husband just got laid off. I can't let this happen to her. Can't you see that?"

"No. I can't, damn it. It's your word against hers. She'd be expected to lie. And the beauty of it is, she actually did sign it. They could prove that."

"But I told her to . . ."

"No. No. You didn't. She took it upon herself to sign it when Rene didn't show up. It's perfect. I don't know why we didn't think of it sooner. It's absolutely perfect."

"But she's innocent."

"She signed the goddamn form!"

"Well, if it comes to that . . . then we've got to bring her in on it. We've got to do for her what we've done ourselves . . . rehearse with her so she has good answers. Letting her take the blame is vicious, Monica."

"I'm protecting my family and my home. I happen to believe it's more important than any brokerage secretary's job. Why can't I get you there? Why can't you see that?"

"Yeah. Yeah. I see," he said and felt the chill of regret. "This is terrible. I never meant for any of this to happen. I'll never be able to forgive myself . . . "

"It'll be a lot easier to forgive yourself here, in your home with your family, the home that you earned for us, than you would in jail."

"Jesus, Monica, when you talk that way, I don't know who you are."

"When are you coming home?"

"I don't know. Matt's probably already gone. He said something about getting his boat checked out so his grandkids can take it skiing this weekend. I'd better stay. There's a lot to catch up on."

"So? When?"

"Say five."

"Five it is."

Raker was disappointed that the request for the search warrant was denied. Insufficient cause, the Sheriff had explained. Curry wasn't an uncommon spice nor *Demerol* an uncommonly prescribed drug. Finding either wouldn't mean anything. Despite that, try as he might, Raker could not allow that there might be an alternative suspect for the Rene McAllister murder. He felt the same way about Jamie's death. The evidence was tight. Maybe nobody could be placed at the scene of his murder, but too much came together to justify doubling back and reconsidering everything. The clincher would be if the lab found *Demerol* in Sherman's system.

The only troubling piece still in the mix was the Sheriff's speculation that perhaps another victim was being lined up, someone triangulated with the McAllister murder and the Sherman murder. If the motive for the McAllister murder was to keep her husband from moving the accounts to another firm, and the motive for the Sherman murder was eliminate a witness to the McAllister murder, then at least two possible reasons were in play for a third death. Either someone could link Monica Clay to Sherman's death, or someone, in addition to Rene, wanted the accounts moved from the Clay-Wirth partnership and needed to be taken out of the picture. Neither seemed likely.

Anyone with information linking Monica Clay to the McAllister murder would, in all probability, have come forward long before now. There would be no advantage in withholding information. Blackmail was possible but the only person who may have seen her at the scene, Jamie Sherman, was dead now himself. If he was blackmailing Monica Clay, her motive for eliminating him was just that much stronger.

It was possible that Moran could right after all—that Sherman was taken out for gangland reasons. If it was a gang murder, the gang who served as his supplier would have access to Sherman's stash, but they would be taking out their own man. If a rival gang was behind the murder, they would have needed to gain access to Sherman's dime bag to contaminate it. Neither seemed likely.

Everything pointed to Monica Clay as the suspect who deserved the most attention.

Gene Phillips had called while Raker was out of the office. "They found the *Demerol*. I don't know how you knew to look for it, but it was there," Phillips reported on the answering machine. "It's all in the report, buried about two-thirds of the way through it. Way to go." Raker grinned as he erased the message.

With the news, Raker decided to call Tim Moran's office to find out if there were any developments in SBI's pursuit of the case.

"No. Not a thing," Moran said. "We didn't find the kilo the kid picked up. He ditched it somewhere else. This thing is dying while we look at it. We can't find anything to tie Sherman to the gang here in the city. I haven't given up on it. Not yet. But there comes a point . . . why? You been thinking about it?"

"Yes. We know Sherman left the city with the kilo. We know when he arrived at home he did not have it with him. We know when he left in his boat. He hid the stuff somewhere . . . with someone. We need to retrace his steps. Find out who he talked to. Where he stopped."

"Yeah. Yeah. Yeah. We've gone over that. Our guys saw the pick-up in town. They didn't tail the kid back out to the lake because we were about to arrest him anyway. If he spotted the tail, it would tip our hand. We didn't want that."

"So they didn't see him go into his house?"

"No. They dropped the tail as soon as it was obvious that he was headed for home."

"How about the CSI guys who were waiting for Jamie to come home?"

"I talked to them. They were down at the lake when he arrived. They didn't know he was there until his dad called out to them."

"OK. So if Sherman did anything with the kilo, it happened between the point your guys dropped the tail and when he got home."

"Yeah. Right. So?"

"He had a dime bag when his body was found. Somewhere in between the time that your guys dropped the tail and he got away in the boat, two things happened. One, he ditched the kilo. Two, somebody had enough time to lace his personal bag with whatever it took to kill him."

"Laced his what? The only word we have is that he died of cardiac arrest, probably triggered by marijuana. What the hell are you talking about?"

"When the report comes out, you'll see they found *Demerol* in the marijuana. The kid was on anti-depressants. *Demerol* interacts with most anti-depressants to create trouble for someone with a history of a weak heart."

"Where are you getting this, Raker?"

"It's all be in the report when it comes out."

"Who ordered those tests?"

"What difference does it make? The results are there. Let's work with them. I think you searched the wrong house."

"Fuck you."

"No. The only person who had any interaction with Jamie Sherman between the time he left town and the time he arrived at home was Monica Clay, his next door neighbor."

"How'd you get that?"

"Just a hunch at first, and she told me that he was there."

"Fuck. A hunch. God damn it! How do you think that we can . . ."

"Listen, I haven't passed any of this along until now because I couldn't prove it. Now I have her word for it."

"You're forcing your case, Raker. There was no evidence of foul play on Sherman's boat because he wasn't killed there. He was intercepted by another boat out on the lake. He recognized it and climbed aboard and his stash was taken from him. He was drugged and dumped back into his boat to be found when the sun came up. We asked the M. E. to look for any drugs in the kid's system. That's what'll be in the M. E.'s report. It's the only thing that adds up."

"But he did go see the Clay woman before he got into his boat the night he died." Raker said.

"This another hunch?"

"You heard Mrs. Sherman say that she thought Jamie went next door before he headed down to his boat."

"She only said she thought he *might* have gone next door . . . not that he did."

"Right. But I followed up on it. Mrs. Clay admitted that he was at the house for a few minutes. She said he wanted to know if her oldest son was at home. When she reported he wasn't, Sherman went down to the dock and took off."

"What does that prove. They're neighbors, aren't they."

"That's if you want to believe Mrs. Clay. I don't. I think she gave him the bag of marijuana that she had laced it with *Demerol*. That's what killed him."

"You think! What can you prove? No witnesses to the conversation between Mrs. Clay and Sherman. That's my bet. You haven't established that Mrs. Clay had the stuff long enough to do anything with it. You're playing a hunch. You haven't proved that Sherman stopped at his neighbor's on the way home from town and that's critical. That's where your case falls apart. Not where he went the next day. I'll keep everything you said in mind, but I can't do anything with it. We've looked into all these people. They're all solid citizens. Where's the motive for putting the kid away? I just don't see it."

"The Sherman kid saw Mrs. Clay kill the McAllister woman the night of the Fourth-of-July party and . . ."

"Oh my God . . . I don't believe this. You've got that poor woman's death on the brain, don't you. Let it go, for Chrissake, and stop taking up my time with your wild ass notions."

"All right," Raker said. "I think you're barking up the wrong tree. But all right."

"Good. Let it go." Moran hung up. Raker begrudged giving Moran any help on the Sherman case, but now his conscience was clear. He had reported all that he knew and his conclusions. If Moran wanted to ignore them, that was Moran's business. At least

Raker found out that the SBI had a theory for Jamie's murder that sounded good. Moran could pursue it for all he cared. The telephone rang.

"Detective Raker. This is Alan McAllister. You talked to me a couple of days ago about my wife's death."

"Yes. I remember. My condolences, sir. I hope you are doing well under the circumstances."

"Under the circumstances . . . yes. We buried Rene yesterday. These things take time."

"They do, sir. I know."

"I had your card, and I have another matter that doesn't fit with what we discussed related to my wife's death. I'm wondering how one goes about reporting a suspicious signature . . . a possible forgery."

"It should be reported to local authorities. Is it a check?"

"No. A legal agreement. I was going through my wife's papers and came across a document that was part of an investment she made. I don't think it's her signature. It doesn't look like anything I've ever seen by her hand."

"I understand . . ."

"Turning it over to you people for verification purposes doesn't also constitute reporting a crime, does it? There are a lot of implications to consider if it's a forgery. I'd want to think through things before accusing anyone of anything."

"If you turn it over to me, or another law officer, it'll be sent to the state crime lab. If they determine it's a forgery, we'd act and investigate with the intent to make an arrest. It's out of your hands once you turn over the documents."

"Proving the signature is not my wife's does not prove who the forger is, though, does it?" McAllister asked.

"Do you think you know who the forger is?"

"Possibly one of three, maybe four people."

"We'd need examples of your wife's recent signature . . . a series of endorsed checks for example. That'd give us the basis for determining whether the signature on the document was authentic or not. Then we'd ask anyone you identify as a suspect to do the same thing . . . sign their name twenty-five times and write out the signature as it appears on the document twenty-five times."

"How long would it take for the lab to make a determination?"

"Six weeks. Maybe longer. The lab's backlogged. Is a lot of money involved?"

"Almost a three-quarters of a million dollars. I call that a lot of money."

"A forgery involving that amount might move more quickly through the lab, but a suspect . . . or suspects . . . would need to be named. The state would expect the findings to go before a grand jury with other evidence to enable it to make an indictment. What kind of document is it?"

"A purchase agreement in a limited partnership. A hedge fund."

"So a brokerage firm or securities representative is involved?"

"Yes."

"Your best bet is to report it to management of the firm. Is it a national firm like Merrill Lynch or Morgan-Stanley, someone like that?"

"Yes."

"Then call them. Call their home office. Speak to the compliance manager. They'll pounce on something like this. They'd probably produce exactly what you want, proof that the signature is not your wife's. With that established, you could take whatever steps you want in accusing someone."

"Wouldn't they have a vested interest in proving it was my wife's signature?"

"They know that you can take the case through legal channels. They don't want the publicity. They'll act to fend against the accusation, but once it's apparent that one their own may be guilty, they'll fold up like a cheap tent and try to settle with you. The guilty party, whoever it is, will probably be quietly fired for cause."

"Thanks, detective. I'm going to consider it and make a decision in the next couple of days.

"I understand. Actually, it's a coincidence you called. I needed to get back to you regarding your wife's death. The case is still open, and I had a couple of questions for you. Would you have a few minutes if I drove out to your home?"

"My family is still here, all of our children, but I can break away for a few minutes this afternoon."

Raker found McAllister waiting at the door when he arrived. The two men went directly into the study. "You said you had some additional questions," McAllister said.

"Yes, sir. And if any of this is uncomfortable for you, please let me know. We no longer believe that your wife's death was an accident."

"Really?"

"Yes, sir. Remember that I asked you the other day about the bruises she sustained? We believe they were sustained either while she was in the water or while being forced into the lake. We think that she died at the hands of someone else."

"God! Really. Your Sheriff agrees?"

"I reviewed the case with him. He agrees. He's eager to have it resolved."

"My God, I never suspected you'd come up with this. Jesus."

"We're need to find out how she acquired the bruises."

"I know That's bothered me ever since you brought it up. But, never . . . not for a minute . . . did I ever consider she was murdered."

"Sorry. It's got to be a shock. That's why I drove out her. It's not the kind of news anyone wants to report over the phone." McAllister slid back in his chair. "I need to ask if your wife's death will lead to any major life changes for you, either personal or of a business nature?

"You think I gained anything through my wife's death?"

"No. Not at all. The evidence points to the fact that your wife was murdered, but we don't know why anyone would want her dead. Who had motive? Somebody must have thought they'd benefit from your wife's death . . . or some action you'd take with her out of the way. Have you changed any of your personal or business plans now that she is dead?"

"No."

"There's no area in your life that will change? You're not going to move? Go back into business? Or not go back into business? Anything like that?"

"No," McAllister snapped.

"What if both you and your wife were out of the picture?" Raker persisted. "Any reason to think the person who killed your wife could possibly want you out of the way as well?"

"What? Me, a target? God that's something. You don't seriously think that?"

"Would you've thought you wife was in any danger the week before last?" Raker replied.

"No. I never looked at the situation in this light . . . all of this . . . ." McAllister paused and peered through the window that overlooked the lake. "I don't see how anyone benefited from Rene's death. The kids know about what they're getting and what the trusts being set up for, but . . . no . . . I can't see that. They benefit, yes, but they all have their own lives.

"I am," McAllister continued, "moving my accounts from Clay and Wirth. I told them that before Rene died. I am going through with it. They might think that Rene's death would change my mind, but kill anyone . . . never. Not a chance."

"You are moving the accounts?"

"They're the people who sold my wife the limited partnership with the questionable signature. I met with them this morning and went over everything. According to Clay, Rene bought a hedge fund. When I asked to see the documentation, the signature on it didn't look right. They never should have sold it to her. Reason enough to terminate with them. If the papers are forged, maybe I can recoup my losses.

"Clay and Wirth could benefit from my death, awful as that sounds. But I'd need to call off moving the accounts first. I told them this morning that the transfer is going through." McAllister pushed back slowly in his chair and stood up. "I've known Matthew Wirth for twenty years. He's a great guy. Honest. Trustworthy. His junior sidekick might have a slippery side to him, but Matthew's a pussy cat."

"Have you told them that you were going to call their company about the questionable signature?"

"No. I said I was going to take everything to my attorney. They know I'm mad as hell about it."

"So they . . ."

"Yes. Anyone wanting to keep me from reporting the forgery would have a motive to kill me With me out of the way, my kids wouldn't suspect anything was amiss with Rene's stuff, and neither Clay nor Wirth would call any of this to their attention."

"My point."

"Still, I can't see either of them in a criminal light."

"Yet, two people are dead," Raker said.

"Sherman's death assumes a connection between that hippie kid and my wife. There wasn't one."

"Assume nothing. You need to be cautious. If something comes to mind, no matter how trivial, give me a call," Raker said extending his hand. McAllister studied Raker's eyes and gave him a quick hand shake.

Chapter 25

It was almost noon when Matthew pulled into the driveway to his lakeside home.

"How'd it go?" Shirley asked as he entered the house.

"Oh, God, I think I've heard the worst, and fresh hell brews up. Feel like a drowning man."

"That bad?"

"Yes. Mac actually questioned the signature on the limited partnership that's caused all the trouble. Morrie insists that Rene signed it, then turns right around and says that he wasn't there . . . that he left it with the cashier to give to Rene when she came in. I don't know if I can trust Morrie any more. I can't tell if he's being truthful."

"You need to settle back, sweetheart . . . have lunch, relax. Give things a chance. Lunch is ready." Shirley heard Matthew continue to talk as he made his way to the bath. "Wait till you get back in here," she shouted.

When he returned, she studied him. "So, what was it you were saying in the other room?"

"We need to wait to see what Mac's going to do. He's taking everything to his attorney, but there's no telling what'll happen after that."

"So it's out of your hands now?"

"Yes. I'm just waiting for the other shoe to drop. If that signature was forged, someone committed a felony. It wasn't me. But it was on my watch."

"Let's assume it's not forged. Morrie says it's not. He's never lied to you before."

"Everything's happening so fast. A week ago, I was looking at retirement, proud of what I'd earned and set aside. Now, professional disgrace, a potential law suit, disciplinary action from my company, my partnership incinerated, my retirement savings along with it. I thought I could relax and be confident Morrie'd run things the way I did. He's no kid. What'd I do to deserve this?"

"Matthew, you and I always say that what we fear most is the one thing that never happens. You're catastrophizing, sweetheart. You're seeing only the worst possible outcome. Please, slow down. A way through all of this will present it itself. Just see if it doesn't."

"I don't see how."

"Stop trying. Let things rest for a while. You can do that, can't you?" Shirley walked to the refrigerator and pulled out two prepared salads. She looked at Matthew. Nothing she said had consoled him. He could be irascible. It was part of his emotional make-up, of his spontaneous, fun-loving nature.

Matthew picked up his fork and impaled slice of cucumber and held it up as if it were a hunting trophy. "I'll try. But this is tough . . . really tough." Their eyes met. She smiled slightly and shook her head from side-to-side in sympathy with his distress and reached across the table to place her hand on top of his. He looked at their hands, hers on top of his, his no longer youthful but tanned and veined, liver spots more numerous every year; hers, tapered and silken, with a fragility that belied her strength. She had held children and grandchildren, changed them and cooed over them, babysat and scolded them. They had been through so much, long hours, long weeks, sharing hopes and the satisfaction of having them realized. She was right. There was nothing that he could do for the time being. All the decisions that needed to be made up until the moment she placed her soft warm hand on top of his had already been made, and he needed to live with them until circumstances dictated a differently.

"I just hate to say this," Shirley said, "but if there's anything wrong with the boat, we need to find out today so we can get it to the mechanic tomorrow. The kids'll be expecting it to be in top condition for their skiing."

"I won't let them down. Let me grab a nap first. I feel like a man waiting on his execution praying he'll be pardoned at the last minute."

"That's a bit dramatic, don't you think?"

"Yeah, well . . . maybe."

Raker pulled his car off to the side of the road. The possible forgery, the fact the either Clay or Wirth could be responsible for it, was a fresh complication. He considered driving back to his office in Charles City and throwing himself into another whiteboard session but quickly rejected the idea. The board had been overworked. Cluttered. The loneliness that he felt overtake him every afternoon was rounding in the pit of his stomach again today. A dull cold ache would hollow him out—a hole in his gut that sapped his energy until it became a controlling void, like the last thing a man feels before surrendering to grief. He wanted it to stop. To go away. To be filled with something other than wine or beer which he used every night to banish it so he could sleep.

Two questions. Was the limited partnership agreement forged? Was there any connection between the forgery and either Rene McAllister's or Jamie Sherman's murder? If the signature was authentic, he could move ahead with what concerned him the most—head the killer off from striking again, assuming that the killer had tracks to cover as the Sheriff suggested. But McAllister felt the signature was forged. What bearing would it have on the two deaths? On the selection of the next victim?

Why forge the agreement? He saw himself on the witness stand. "Can you say that this document was not signed by a backroom clerk, for example, who may have accidentally destroyed the original and simply replaced it without troubling to secure a fresh signature on a new agreement?" a defense attorney could ask. "Or, a clerk working with either broker who, not wanting to create additional work for her boss, signed it herself? Or," the defense attorney might continue, "perhaps Mrs. McAllister simply forgot to sign the documents and had a friend drop them off for her, and upon discovering her oversight, the receptionist, or the friend, signed her name thinking it a favor?" Any situation was possible. Raker couldn't prove otherwise.

Three possibilities. The killer was the forger. Or the killer knew the papers were forged, but he or she was not the forger. Or, finally, the killer did not know the papers were forged. Raker decided to go with the most likely choice—that the killer and the forger were one and the same. The forger would almost certainly be someone affiliated with Clay and Wirth. McAllister, Clay and Wirth knew the signature was suspicious. If the killer wanted to prevent the forgery from being submitted for analysis, he or she would need to move quickly. McAllister would not postpone taking action indefinitely.

Nobody other than Wirth could be accused if Clay was innocent. On the other hand, if Wirth knew Clay signed the agreement,
Wirth could be the next victim and Clay the likely killer. Clay, however, had been eliminated as a suspect in the McAllister death. His
whereabouts at the time of Rene McAllister's death were known.
Clay also was not implicated in Jamie's death. If the killer was covering his or her tracks, Clay could be eliminated. Unless . . . unless
he was working with his wife. All the evidence in Jamie's death
pointed to her.

Monica! She could know that the signature was forged. Clay
could have told her. Monica could know that Clay was the forger as
well. She'd benefit if its discovery could be prevented. A next victim? Who would it be? Wirth? Certainly if Wirth knew Clay as the
forger. Did Wirth know? Raker needed to find out.

"Yes, detective, he's here. He's taking a nap. You can come to
the house, but I wouldn't hurry," Shirley replied to Raker's opening
question on the phone.

"Who is it?" Matthew called from the front of the house.

"Detective Raker," Shirley called back. "He wants to come by
for a few minutes."

"Tell him it's OK."

"But you won't get your nap," Shirley said.

"I've got too much on my mind anyway. Tell him it's OK."

When Raker arrived, he was astonished to see how much older
Matthew Wirth looked. He remembered the gentleman as vital and
animated. Now tired, face drawn and ashen, Matthew trudged into
the den with Raker following. "What is it this time?" he asked without looking back.

"I don't know if you've been following things very closely,
sir," Raker replied and stepped over to the wingback chair in front

of Matthew's desk, "but we haven't closed the case on the Mrs. McAllister."

"I didn't think it'd take so long. We buried the poor woman yesterday."

"I know. Sometimes it takes while to wrap things up. Can I go back to the last time I was here, sir, and ask you some questions related to that conversation?"

"Certainly. And drop the 'sir' stuff. Makes me feel like I'm in the military. Matthew, or Matt, that's what my friends call me."

"Thanks. Last time, you said that you or your younger partner, could benefit from Mrs. McAllister's death because she had asked her husband to move the accounts away from your firm."

"Yes. But it's no longer true. McAllister told me this morning that he's moving them. We're out of the picture."

"What reason did he give for his decision?" Raker asked.

"Well," Matthew sighed, "I doubt that it has any bearing on your case. It involves how some of Mrs. McAllister's investments were handled. Mr. McAllister wasn't very happy about one item in particular, and he knew I was retiring. He may not have wanted to leave the business with my partner, Morrie Clay."

"I met with Mr. McAllister this morning, and he mentioned he was unhappy about a fund purchase in one of his wife's accounts."

Matthew shifted in his chair. "I know. It's impossible to keep people happy all of the time in my line of work. That's just the reality of it." Matthew began to rearrange items on his desk. "Perhaps it would be better to ask McAllister. He's at greater liberty to discuss his wife's investments than I. I don't know what the implications of anything I say may be. After all, you said it was still an open case."

"As I said earlier, I've already talked to Mr. McAllister."

"Then you don't need to question me, do you? I thought you

were going to be straightforward with me on these interviews . . . or interrogations . . . or whatever you call them. Do I need my attorney to sit in on this?"

"Mr. McAllister said he was not pleased with the way one of his wife's accounts was handled. I thought you might have a different perspective on the issue, so I brought it up with you as well."

"I just don't like these . . . these tactics. Am I a suspect? Or what is the phrase . . . a person-of-interest? I'm sorry. The more I consider this, the more advisable I think it is that I have my attorney present." Matthew pushed his chair away from the desk and stood up.

Raker remained seated in the hope that his host would reconsider. "Please, Mr. Wirth, you're not a person-of-interest. From everything I know of this case, you'd never become one. There's a degree of urgency to my being here . . . to this interview. Please. You owe it to yourself to hear me out. If you want to end our discussion at any time, I'll leave. I've opened our conversation on a sour note, and you have understandably misread my intent. I'm sorry. Please hear me out."

Matthew studied the tired detective sitting in front of him. Matthew knew Raker to be sincere, a man—at least for the moment—he could trust. He eased back into his chair and pulled up to his desk.

"What I've failed to explain, Mr. Wirth, is that we do not believe Mrs. McAllister's death was an accident. She was murdered. Jamie Sherman's death was also not an accident. Evidence indicates one person is responsible for both deaths. I know this is a lot to bring up here, so please, speak up if you have any questions. I don't want any misunderstanding to come out of this."

"I . . . I hesitate because . . .I . . . I'm stunned. Murder isn't something that happens in . . . a neighborhood a like this . . . in circumstances that are so . . . benign. This isn't the inner city. Civilized people live here. People who care for one another."

"I know it's a shock. But it happens. More often than you'd ever guess. But, Mr. Wirth, we're also convinced that the person responsible for those deaths is likely to kill again."

"Incredible! What could possibly be at stake that would make it worth anyone's life? That's . . . astounding."

"Believe me, I'd be happy to be wrong about this, but I can't dismiss that the killer may have yet another person in mind."

"So why tell me? I can't add anything. I don't want to believe anything you've said, but you're the professional. You wouldn't be out here trying to frighten people . . . ."

"No, of course, not. Did you know that the signature on one of the documents in the McAllister accounts has been questioned?" Raker asked.

"Yes. My partner insists that the client signed it. I'm not taking a position on the matter."

Raker noticed that Wirth was growing uncomfortable again. "Speaking hypothetically, what would happen if the signature was found to be a forgery?"

"So you know that's at the bottom of this. Not surprising. You're a very thorough man, Detective." Matthew cleared his throat. "I hope they'll find Rene McAllister signed the agreement."

"What would the consequences be if someone in your office . . . anywhere in your office . . . forged the signature?"

"First of all . . . you'd need to know who did it. Could they prove that? Law enforcement, I mean. Could you find that out?"

"There's no guarantee we would find who did."

"I see."

"But that wouldn't alter the fact that it was forged. Would your company step in?" Raker asked.

"Oh, God, yes. Like a SWAT team. If they decided it was a forgery, it'd cost me my job, my group health insurance when I retire, my retirement funds. It'd cost Morrie Clay his future, and depending on what they wanted to do, it might even have consequences for our two assistants. It would be a terrible, terrible calamity for all of us." Matthew sat straight up in his chair. "There'd be no trial, Detective. We'd all be assumed guilty until proven innocent. We . . . each one of us . . . would be at the mercy of the company . . . Morrie, me, our wonderful assistants. We could spend our life's savings on attorneys, but there are no courts. We serve at the pleasure of the company. Companies are cautious about adverse publicity. I never . . . never dreamed anything like this happening to me or my team."

"I understand, Mr. Wirth. But we need to assume the agreement is forged. Accept it hypothetically, at least, so we know what to anticipate."

"I don't follow."

"OK. Assume someone forged the signature but that it'll be impossible to determine who did it. Assume, further, since the person responsible will not be identified, heads will roll. The company will clean house. Baby out with the bath water. OK?"

"That's exactly how it'd go."

"OK. Nobody wants to lose a job . . . lose face in the community with all the press this will receive . . . lose earning power for years to come . . . that person has a powerful motive for finding someone to blame for the forgery."

"Yes. But . . . what good would it do? Anyone accused of it would deny it. You'd never know who was guilty," Matthew said.

"One person's word against another."

"And how long would the company tolerate that? A complaint from a man like McAllister not being settled, degenerating into an endless round of accusations and denials. "

"Not one minute."

"But if the accused could not defend himself or herself. Dead men can't issue denials."

"That's too cunning . . . too diabolical. . . . I . . . I can't conceive of anyone . . . having that kind of a mind . . . that's perverse . . . psychopathic. I can't accept that."

"This is still a hypothetical. OK? If someone is blamed who can't raise his own defense . . . can't prove that his innocence . . . then the person making the accusation is in the clear, holds onto his or her job. The whole matter can be swept aside. Now, just wait," Raker added quickly detecting that Wirth wanted to interrupt. "Anyone who has been so cunning, as you put it, has probably already put together a circumstantial case that will point to the person they intend to blame."

"Good God, man. That might be logical, as a hypothetical, but it isn't realistic. Anyone with that frame of mind . . . I mean . . . I've studied human nature . . . all my life. I'd stake my life on the morality of the people around me every day. I've been disappointed, yes . . . especially recently. But . . . a lie of omission, the refusal to acknowledge an oversight, that's venial. Serious. Yes. It erodes trust. But it's light years away from the kind of thing you're implying."

"I agree. Two things, however. First, two people are dead. Their deaths are suspicious. Second, there's been a progression in the killer's motives. The next death will be related to the forgery, and the killer's motive will be simple economics. He or she does not want to be identified as the forger, as a felon, and lose a job. The killer wants someone to blame who has been silenced. I could be wrong, but I owe it to you to warn you to be watchful."

Matthew's eyes opened wide. "You . . . you have missed something. Step-by-step, you can construct your scenario. But something's missing. Maybe the signature is authentic. Maybe you'll find that the same person did not kill Rene and poor hapless Jamie. You haven't done that yet. Maybe Rene actually did drown. I'm far more comfortable with those possibilities than I am with the . . . the sinister plot you've concocted here."

"Fine. Everyone I've met in my investigation seems to be a wholesome, law-abiding citizen. But you need to be watchful. It's possible, despite your protest, that one of the people you regard as a friend, a neighbor, or a client, could be a person capable of what I have described."

"Ha, ha, ha . . . one possibility. Right? One in how many possible outcomes? I'm used to dealing with percentages, Mr. Raker. Yours is well thought through, but if it were an investment proposal, it's too much of a stretch for me . . . way too much. Don't get me wrong. I appreciate that you took the time to go over everything, came all the way out here, but as I have said hundreds of times on behalf of clients, your proposition does not fit our situation. Can we end on that?"

"Of course. I just wanted you to know where our thinking is going. . ."

"'Our thinking,' detective, meaning the police force here in the county, or your thinking, meaning just you as an individual officer investigating these matters?"

"My thinking, then, sir . . . if you will."

"Well, you're a man of considerable experience. What you presented may have merit. But I'd have a lot more respect for your theory if you ran it by your colleagues back at the Sheriff's office before you haul it out in front of somebody else." Matthew stood up. "I need to attend to my honey-do list for the day, Mr. Raker. I recoil at thinking your *hypothetical* has the slightest chance of being true, but I will keep an eye out, and I'll call you if I see anything suspicious."

"Thanks. Thanks for your time."

"Not at all."

Chapter 26

"It's a horror too terrible to contemplate," Shirley said as Matthew headed back to the den after seeing Raker to the door.

"What is?

"This house overrun by teenage grandchildren cranky as geese because they couldn't go skiing.

"I know. I need a break anyway." Matthew grumbled and walked to the sliding glass doors and stepped out onto the deck. "Why is the tarp off the boat?" he shouted to Shirley.

"Hi, Mr. Wirth," a voice called out from next door. It was Andrew Sherman.

"Hi, son. How are you?"

"What did you say?" Shirley shouted from inside the house.

"OK. I guess," Andrew replied. "Jamie's funeral's tomorrow. It's a bummer here."

"Just a minute," Matthew said to Andrew and walked back to the sliding doors and repeated his question to Shirley, "Why is the tarp off of the boat?"

"While you were at the office," Shirley replied, "Monica Clay came by and said she'd lost an earring and remembered the last time she wore it was on the Fourth-of-July. She wondered whether it might have fallen off in our boat. She wanted to have a look."

"I didn't know she was in our boat on the Fourth."

"You didn't know where most people were most of the time. I said it was OK and that you'd be taking it out later so she could leave the tarp off. It didn't look like rain."

"Yeah. OK." Matthew walked out to the end of the deck. "I'm sorry, Andrew, about Jamie. It must be pretty tough," he said to the teenager who was alone in the yard next door.

"So sudden. I mean, Jamie and I, well, we weren't that close, him being older, but still I find it, like, hard to believe. I keep thinking he's going to pull up to the dock in his boat and nothing will have changed. You know."

"Yes, son. I do. Are you busy now?"

"Now? Like, right now?"

"Yeah. Now and for, say, the next half-an-hour?"

"No. Nothing's going on. Nobody is doing anything at our house. Just sitting around. Everything's so depressing. Why?"

"I need to take my boat out to test the throttle linkage. I need someone to drive it for me when I open the hatch and see what the trouble is."

"Yeah. That'd be great. I'll tell my folks, and I need to change clothes, but yeah. I'd like that, Mr. Wirth."

"Good. I need to change too. What say I meet you out here in 15 minutes."

"Great." Andrew turned to jog into his house, but Matthew called to him at second time.

"Whoa! Before you go in, could you run down there and turn on the bilge fan. You know what that is? That tub has been sitting for a week after pretty heavy usage, and we need to make sure the fumes are evacuated from the bilge."

"Yeah. I know. Dad's always warning us to turn it on and let it run for, like, ten minutes before we start the engine. No problem, Mr. Wirth." Andrew reversed himself and dashed down to the dock. Matthew watched him as he climbed aboard, stepped up to the helm, looked over the dash for the bilge fan switch, and then flicked the toggle to the *ON* position. Andrew looked back to Matthew. "Got it!" he shouted.

"Can you hear the fan running?" Matthew called.

"Yeah. It's running all right." Andrew looked at Matthew as if expecting some further direction, but upon seeing Matthew turn and go into the house, he jumped back out of the craft and sprinted to his own home.

When Matthew emerged from the house a few minutes later, he found Andrew waiting for him along with Michael Clay. "Is it OK if Mike goes with us? He won't get in the way."

Matthew's anger flared, but seeing the eager look on Michael's face, he was willing to concede. The boy had nothing to do with his father's bad judgment. Michael had always been an enthusiastic, pleasant kid to have around. "Sure. You look like you're already dressed and ready to go."

"I just need to tell my folks, Mr. Wirth. I'll be right back."

"Fine, son." At his word, Michael dashed home, bounded up on to the deck, and opened the backdoor. "I'm going out on the lake with Andrew for a few minutes. I'll be right back. OK?" He did not wait for an answer. He had fulfilled the house rule by reporting in. Whether anyone heard him or not was not a concern. He leaped off the deck and ran back again, meeting Andrew half way to the Wirth dock. "What's the matter?" he asked his friend.

"Ah, my stepmom. Jees. She thinks it's, like, inappropriate for me to be out dressed like this and going boating. Disrespectful of other family members' feelings. I . . . I can't go."

"God, man, that's weird. What does she expect? Everyone should hang around doing nothing until the funeral."

"I guess." Andrew dropped his head and stepped away. "See ya man."

"OK. Sorry. Another time."

"That's cool." Andrew slumped back to the deck to his home.

"Here, Mike," Matthew yelled, "go on down there and warm the old beast up. I forgot a couple of things, my tools, for one. I'll be right down." Matthew tossed the keys on the fishing bobber chain to the youth.

"Cool. Good toss." Michael did not break stride as he snatched the keys out of the air and jogged to the dock.

"The bilge fan's been on for at least fifteen minutes so you don't need to worry about it, Mike. OK?" Matthew shouted, grinning at the youngster's enthusiasm.

As Andrew mounted the steps to the deck to his home, he noticed Mike's mother stepping out onto the deck next door. He waved at her.

"Andrew. I thought you and Mike were going out in the boat together. Where is he?" Monica asked.

"My stepmom won't let me to go," Andrew replied loud enough to be sure that Joyce would hear him.

"So where's Michael?"

"Oh, he's going to go. No problem."

"He's not taking *your* family's boat out by himself?"

"No. We weren't going in our boat."

"I don't understand. Where is he? Whose boat is he going out in?"

"Mr. Wirth's. He wants to take it for a spin to adjust the timing or something. He needs a driver."

"Oh, God! No! No! Michael! Michael!" Monica screamed. "Michael, get back here right now." She jumped off of the deck and sprinted toward the Wirth dock. "Michael! Michael. Stop! Get back here!"

The explosion rocked the neighborhood. The last thing Monica saw was her tanned, thirteen-year-old son, the last child she decided to bear, blown by a blast of white and orange flame through the heavy windshield of the boat. The craft itself disappeared in flame and smoke, vaulting high into the air and then dropping, slamming into the lake.

Michael was thrown into deep water twenty feet out beyond the end of the dock. Face down, his body scudded across the surface when he hit the water.

"Oh, my God! My God! Michael!" Monica was screaming. She dashed the length of the dock and dived out toward her son's motionless body. He was beginning to slip beneath the surface. She powered her way to him through the water and grabbed the back of his tee-shirt. It came off in her hand. She grabbed his shoulder to swing him around to her, but his skin peeled off in her hand and exposed the raw meat of his shoulder muscle. She reached to get a hand under his chin or his arm, any place that she could hold his head out of the water and drag him back to the shore. "Help," she yelled over and over again, until her mouth filled with water and coughing forced to stop.

Matthew witnessed everything from his deck. He shouted to Shirley to call 911. Andrew had turned abruptly at the horrific sound and realized in an instant what had happened and shouted for his father.

"You swim out to help that woman," Sherman shouted to his son as he emerged from the house to investigate. "Keep them afloat until I get there with the boat." Matthew was heading toward the dock which had caught fire. Andrew sped past him just as Sherman called, "Matthew! Matthew! My boat! The outboard. Help me with it." Matthew turned and lumbered toward the Sherman dock. Sherman was pulling on the starter rope when Matthew clambered aboard. "Here! You take it. I will try to pull them in."

Andrew sped past the fire, flew to the end of the dock, and launched himself like a javelin toward Monica and Michael's body. When he reached the pair in the water, he saw that Monica was nearly exhausted in her struggle to keep Michael's head out of the water. He took Michael from her and steadied the boy by rolling him over on his back.

The outboard fired up. Matthew backed away from the dock, then slammed the motor into forward, cutting a sharp turn in the water as the boat leaped to full throttle toward the swimmers and the Michael.

"Swing around to this side and sidle up to them," Sherman ordered. Matthew, an experienced boatman, knew exactly what Sherman wanted and slowed to trolling speed, maneuvering the craft almost within reach of Andrew and Monica, and then killed the engine. Monica appeared close to panic, flushed and breathing heavily. "Are you OK, Monica?" Sherman shouted.

"Yes. Yes."

"Can you hang on? We need to get Michael in the boat."

"I'm fine. Get him aboard, please. Oh, God, please, get him on board."

"Andrew. See if you can swim over here with him. If you can't, I'll jump in and help," Sherman shouted.

"Be careful," Monica cried. "He's terribly burned. Terribly."

"He's going to be heavy," Sherman called to Andrew. "If I can't get him in the boat by myself, I'll need you in here to help lift him aboard."

As soon as his father had a firm hold of Michael, Andrew dived under the boat and came up on the opposite side, grabbed the gunnel and hoisted himself on board. In a few seconds, they had the Michael's burned and bloody body out of the water and lifeless on the floor of the boat.

"Oh my God," Sherman exclaimed at the sight of the boy's burned back. "This is awful. This is as bad as I've ever seen."

"Monica, keep hanging on," Matthew yelled more to remind Sherman that the victim's mother could hear him.

"That's right, Monica," Sherman said, instantly regretting his thoughtlessness.

Hanging on to the side of the boat, Monica pulled herself up and managed a glimpse of her son. His chest was bleeding from where he crashed through the windshield brackets. One leg dangled to the side, obviously broken. One foot was bleeding. Debris from the explosion, bits and pieces, were lodged like shrapnel in his arms and legs and torso. She glanced at Sherman who was staring at her wide-eyed. She released her grip on the side of the boat, slipped back into the water, rolled over, and began stroking her way back the shore.

"Easy, Matthew," Sherman said. "Head for our dock." Matthew pulled the starter cord and as the engine fired back to life, put the outboard into gear and eased the throttle up to a little more than half speed.

Monica saw the boat glide past her when she raised up out of her crawl stroke to catch her breath. Her arms felt heavy, detached from her, mechanically pulling her through the water as if they had a will of their own. Her breath came automatically, as if some part of her had taken charge of her respiration, and she felt enjoined not to interfere. The sight of Michael's charred, blistered back was etched into her mind. Her son's flesh. Her sweet, enthusiastic son. The salty scented skin of the boy had felt like the burnt scrapings from a bar-be-que pan. She could feel it in her hands, hands that were pulling her through the water, the water washing off his hot muscle and skin that stuck to her when she reached out to him, tried to pull him to her, tried to let her strength flow out into him so that he would know she was there, that she loved him, that she could not bear the sight of him in pain, the sight of him hurling through the windshield by the white-hot and yellow flash from the stern of the boat. Her hand scraped the sandy bottom of the lake. She had reached the shallows. She had not noticed the distance between her and the shore narrowing. She could stand up. She wanted to swim on and on because the water hid the horror of what was happening. She pulled her legs up under her and found the water knee deep.

She had come ashore between the docks. The boat with Michael had docked to her right. A fire burned on the Wirth dock to her left. Debris from the explosion had been scattered on the lawn, and bits of wreckage emitted plumes of blue and gray smoke as if they had been placed as signal flares, as if she could follow from one piece of wreckage to the next and eventually arrive at a place where everything would be taken back, where she would discover that nothing had happened. Nothing seemed real—the sounds crashing in on her, the frantic actions of others rolling toward her, intruding and urging her to be excited also, to awake, to be alarmed.

"Monica. My God, we almost forgot about you." It was Matthew Wirth. The EMS attendants had arrived, and Matthew left the boat so that they could work unencumbered. The concern of everyone on shore, even the on-lookers who rushed to the scene, was focused on the EMS attendants as they lifted the unconscious body of the boy from the boat to a stretcher. None watched for Monica to reach the beach. "Over here," Matthew shouted when he finally noticed her. "Over here."

Monica turned and saw her neighbor emerge ghostlike from a cloud of smoky hubbub. Her hand went up in a weak wave. She struggled to grasp what he wanted.

"He's alive, Monica. He's alive. He's badly, badly hurt, but he's alive. They're taking him to the emergency room," Matthew shouted approaching at a trot.

"He?" Monica thought. "He?" Oh, God, yes. Michael. He's alive."

"He's unconscious. He's in shock, but he's alive," Matthew said. Even to his untrained eye, Matthew could see that Monica was in a state of deep emotional shock. Every parent fears the death of a child, dreads it as the worst thing that could ever happen. Children died, nevertheless. On the operating table. In automobile accidents. On the field of sport. But few mothers ever saw their own child die as they looked on, die as perhaps Michael might, blown away like a doll in the bright afternoon. Matthew put his arm around Monica's wet shoulders.

"Where?" Monica uttered. "Where?" She shivered violently.

"At Sherman's dock. He's being cared for. You need to dry off and put on dry clothes. You can't do anything for him. He won't even know you're there."

"Sherman's dock? Why's he at Sherman's dock? Who's caring for him?"

"Is Morrie home?" Matthew demanded hoping to get Monica to focus what was happening.

"Morrie? No. He's at work," Monica said. Matthew looked up and saw Shirley standing at the edge of the deck to their home. "Shirley! Has anyone called Morrie at work?"

Shirley, like the others, had not seen Monica swim to shore. Startled, she turned at her husband's call.

"Yes. I called him. He's on his way."

"How long ago did you call?"

"Right after the explosion."

"About twenty minutes ago," Matthew said and glanced at his watch. Shirley, her attention being drawn to Monica, hurried down to where Matthew and Monica were standing.

"They're going to take Michael in an ambulance any minute now," Matthew said to Shirley as she approached. "She's stunned," he said nodding to Monica. "Can you take her home and get her out of these wet clothes."

Shirley nodded and took Monica by the hand. "Hurry, dear," she said. "Let's get you out of those wet things."

"No. No. Michael! I need to go to Michael," Monica pulled away form Shirley. Matthew hugged her to keep her from breaking away.

"You can't help him now," Matthew said. "You'll see him at the hospital. Monica. Think! You need to get dry and dressed so you can ride in the ambulance with him. They won't let you go this way, wet and shivering."

"Oh. Yes. I need to be with him. I *need* to be with him."

Shirley, nearly overcome herself with Monica's hysteria, tugged Monica's hand. Monica nodded and they trotted to the Clay home where Shirley guided Monica to the master bedroom and began helping her young neighbor get undressed, but Monica pushed her away. Accepting Monica's need to take charge, Shirley hurried to the bath for a towel.

Monica had removed her bra and was stepping out of her panties when Shirley reentered the room. Monica grabbed the towel. "I didn't want him to go. Not him. He wasn't supposed to go," Monica whined.

"We know, dear. We heard you. It wasn't your fault. It's a terrible, terrible accident."

"No. No. Oh God. How did everything come to this?"

"Shish. Shish. Get dressed, sweetheart. If you want to be with Michael, you need to be dressed." Both women heard a siren wail. The ambulance was pulling out of the driveway next door.

"They're leaving," Monica cried. "They're leaving. Oh, God. How could they leave?"

"For his sake, sweetheart. For his sake. Now get dressed. I'll drive you. But you need to get dressed, and we'll get you to the hospital," Shirley said.

Monica, galvanized by the siren, stepped quickly to her bureau, found fresh underwear, bolted to the closet, pulled on a pair of jeans, yanked a blouse off a hanger, pulled it on, and buttoned it as she charged through the house to the garage. Shirley hurried after her.

"Get the keys, but let me drive," Shirley directed, suddenly concerned that she would not be able to control the younger woman.

Chapter 27

Raker met the County EMS Ambulance on Lakeside Drive. Cruisers from the Sheriff's Department followed, sirens knifing through the afternoon. His radio reported their destination—the address of the Sherman home, right next door to Matthew Wirth's. He wheeled about, turned on his pursuit lights, and gave chase.

When he arrived, he jogged down to the lake where a crowd was gathering. He recognized a deputy restraining the crowd.

"It's pretty bad," the deputy said. "Kid's in deep shock, badly burned, some broken bones. They're going to have him out of here in a little bit, just as soon as they have him supported and an intravenous rigged."

"Thanks," Raker said and eased his way through the crowd and down to the beach. The explosion had been spectacular. Debris was everywhere. The hull of the boat, keel up, drifted several yards off shore like a wounded beast. Additional law enforcement milled about. The scene was being taped off. Firemen extinguished the fire that had started on the Wirth dock and the oil slick on the lake. Two men with extinguishers stepped from one piece of wreckage to the next to make certain every threat of fire was extinguished.

When Raker looked up, he spotted two women crossing the

deck to the Clay house. One of them was Monica Clay. He knew that he was standing in her devastation. He had not moved fast enough. "No accident," he said muttered.

"I want," Raker said to the CSI officer in charge, "you to be alert for anything related to the bilge fan, the bilge fan vent, any accelerant or ignition device."

"This your assignment?" the officer asked.

"Let's just say 'yes' for the time-being. OK. All of this," Raker said sweeping across the scene with his arm, "may be part of a case that I've been working on for over a week now."

"Yes, sir. We'd look for everything you mentioned as a matter of routine, that's all."

"Fine." Raker, satisfied that he had been understood, turned again back toward the Clay home and saw the EMS paramedics marching a gurney up to the waiting ambulance. A minute latter, the siren wailed and he heard the truck's diesel growling to gain speed. He wondered whether Monica Clay was aboard. It did not matter. He knew where he could find her.

Sherman followed the gurney through the crowd and watched the attendants hoist Michael into the awaiting ambulance. A firemen started to close the rear door to the vehicle. "Wait," Sherman directed. "Isn't anyone going to go with the boy?"

"Who are you?" the fireman demanded, startled at Sherman's authoritative tone.

"A neighbor. I'm a doctor. I was in the boat that pulled him out of the water. I know him."

Matthew Wirth appeared from around the house. "Tom, are you going with the ambulance?" he asked.

"Yes. Stay here and wait for someone from the family to show up. We can't wait. It's critical."

"I know. I think his mother's in the house with Shirley. We'll bring her. Where're they taking him?" Matthew shouted over the rattling of the diesel.

"County General," the fireman shouted. "Get on board," he ordered Sherman. The fireman swung the door open again so that Sherman could climb in. The door slammed and the siren immediately stirred into a shrill wail. A paramedic glanced at Sherman and then turned back to securing an intravenous tube. "He's breathing," the paramedic said. "Not very deeply, but breathing."

A few minutes later Monica Clay burst through the back door. "They've taken him!" she shouted at Matthew. "They've taken him!"

"I know," Matthew said and noticed that Shirley had followed Monica. "Shirley, they're going to County General. You take Monica in their van. I'll wait for Morrie and follow when he shows." Shirley nodded and walked quickly to the van in the driveway, and she and Monica climbed aboard.

Moments later, Morrie Clay's Mercedes pulled to an abrupt stop when he saw Matthew. "Don't get out!" Matthew shouted running up to the big sedan. Matthew grabbed the door handle but the vehicle was locked. He tried several times to open it as Morrie struggled with the controls to release the lock. Both were mistiming their effort until the door finally popped open. "They're taking Michael to County General!" Matthew said as he fastened his seat belt. Morrie spun the big car out onto Lakeside Drive and barreled off toward Charles City.

"What happened?" Morrie demanded.

"I don't know. I asked Michael to go out in the boat with me. The bilge fan had been running for fully fifteen minutes before I sent him down to start the thing and get it warmed up. He turned the ignition and it blew. Terrible . . . terrible explosion. Threw him through the windshield and out into the lake. Monica dove off our dock to get to him, and Sherman and I went out in a boat and brought him to shore."

"How bad is he hurt?"

"Pretty bad." Matthew looked Morrie to get a measure of his reaction. "He's badly burned. In shock. Unconscious. But he was breathing when they put him in the ambulance, and the paramedics were right there. Tom Sherman is with him. We won't know more until we get to the hospital."

"Monica! Is Monica with him?"

"No. They couldn't wait for her. Shirley's driving her to the hospital in your van. You'll see her there. She's in shock also. Shivering. She didn't seem to grasp what was happening."

The Mercedes sped down Lakeside Drive with the emergency lights flashing. He flew past a Sheriff's Department cruiser which made an abrupt turn about, flashed on its pursuit lights, fired up its siren, and raced to overtake the big car. Morrie pulled over and as soon as he came to a stop, he jammed the vehicle into park and jumped out.

The deputy, alarmed at seeing Morrie out of the car, leaped out is cruiser and shouted, "Get back in your vehicle, sir. Get back in your vehicle now!"

"I need an escort! My son's been in an accident. He's being taken to County General."

The deputy, who had been following the events at on his radio, studied Morrie for an instant and then said, "Follow me." Morrie followed the patrol car the rest of the way into town as it carved a path through traffic. He and Matthew said nothing further until they pulled into the emergency room parking lot at County General Hospital.

Shirley, not having had the advantage of an escort, had just pulled into the lot herself. Morrie was stunned at Monica's appearance. Her hair was wet, matted down on her head and neck, gritty with sand. She gave no sign that she recognized him. "Are you all right?" he asked.

"All right?" Monica echoed. "I . . . yes, I'm . . . I need to find Michael. He shouldn't have gone. I didn't want him to go, Morrie. I tried to stop him."

"It's OK, honey. It's OK."

"No!" Monica screamed. "Why . . . why can't anyone under-stand? He wasn't supposed to go. I yelled and yelled." Monica began to sob uncontrollably.

Shirley put her arm around her. "Let's go and see him. Let's go see Michael. Nothing we say here is doing him any good, now is it?" Monica took Shirley's hand as she had right after the accident.

"You're being too good to me," she said. "I . . . I don't deserve this."

"Come, now. He needs you. Let's go find him."

Raker knew that he had missed his chance. The neighborhood he had come to know so well over the past few days was in chaos. Two people were dead; a third, quite possibly, dying. The residences may have appeared to be the serene and bucolic, but in the deep, cool shadows of the elms and maples, the hypnotic lapping of the waves, pain and terror dropped out of the breeze from the bay. In all his years of police work, he had never grown accustomed to the chill of the murder scene. It rushed to meet him. He could smell it. A smear. A slime. He wanted to get his work done as quickly as possible and move out of the area. He walked back to the CSI of-ficers who had started processing the scene.

"Anything yet?" he asked.

"You're kidding."

"Yeah. I guess. Nothing ever just pops up right away after something like this does it."

"Never. Fumes from the battery and gasoline really are powerful," the officer responded. "If an accelerant was used, we won't find it unless it was something exotic. A half a cup of regular gas dumped in the hatch anytime in the last twenty-four hours would have turned the engine compartment into a bomb. The bilge fan assembly has been recovered, what's left of it, but doesn't tell us anything. The exhaust vent was blown apart. It may have been disconnected or cut. We'll never know. Look," the officer picked up a misshapen, molten piece of urethane. That's the biggest piece we've found."

"An accident then?"

"Carelessness. We'll stay at it, but this doesn't look like it is going to yield much."

"Thanks."

One thing was certain. Nobody would want to kill a thirteen-year-old boy. All along Raker thought the victim would be Matthew Wirth. Something misfired for the killer. He decided to return to Charles City and secure a warrant for the arrest of Monica Clay. He did not want to be too late again.

A nurse rushed up to greet Monica and Morrie as they entered the crowded emergency room waiting area with Matthew and Shirley following them in. "Dr. Sherman has reserved the Chaplin's family room for you. Please follow me." They were led down a corridor. "This is not in use now, so . . . please," she said nodding for them to enter. "Is one of you a parent of the boy who was brought in?" she asked once everyone had filed into a room that was obviously intended to provide privacy for grieving family members.

"I'm his father," Morrie replied.

"You're needed at check in. Follow me, please." the nurse said. Morrie turned toward Monica who had found a seat on a couch opposite the door. She did not look up. He caught Shirley's eye who nodded to indicate that she would look after Monica.

The wild ride to the hospital exhausted Matthew Wirth. The adrenaline in his system spurred him on and kept him alert. He felt distanced from Morrie as he watched his partner leave the waiting room. He did not know Morrie any more. Everything that he had taken for granted about the younger man was gone. What sympathy he felt now was rational, as if he came upon a stranger in distress rather than a good friend of long standing. Matthew's own concerns about retirement, McAllister and the possible forgery, gave way to concern about Michael, the eager youth Matthew had watched grow up. The boy always addressed him as "Mr. Wirth." Had quick smile. The body traits of his mother, athletic and well-proportioned. Moved like gazelle. Matthew enjoyed watching the youngster, whether it was Frisbee, a pick-up game of touch football, or a one-on-one at basketball. Optimistic. Irrepressible. He had been blown away. A promise, on the threshold of being realized, discarded like a candy wrapper into the wind. Why the boat would work well one weekend and then, days later, the fan fail to evacuate the bilge was beyond him. He heard it—a simple fan requiring only the battery to power it. Had someone opened the hatch during the water high-jinks on the Fourth-of-July and inadvertently damaged the flexible urethane vent through which the fumes were discharged?

Matthew caught Shirley's gaze. Her own eyes were red from holding back grief. She sat with her arm around Monica who was slumped forward, her head almost between her knees. A young physician walked into room. Directly behind him walked Dr. Tom Sherman, who had been able to follow Michael through admission and treatment. Sherman was downcast. Matthew feared what might come next. Morrie, released from the inquisitorial at the business office, also appeared behind the pair.

"What is it?" Morrie demanded.

"He's struggling," the young doctor announced spinning around to look at Morrie and then turning to search for the boy's mother. He stepped toward Monica and tried to catch her eye. She did not look up at him. "He has a chance, but only a chance. His internal injuries are very serious . . . very extensive. We're doing everything we can to stop the internal bleeding. One lung is collapsed. His pulse is feint. You may have a long night ahead of you."

"What the hell does that mean?" Morrie snapped.

Young physician frowned. "Young people like your son can put up a terrific fight. They have great resilience. You must never give up on them. But they often exhaust themselves, and the fight ends very precipitously. Very quickly. He is in gravely critical condition." The young doctor would learn with experience that too little information is always better than too much, that ambiguity gives room for hope which delays the onset of panic and grief, but he was a young doctor. He turned on his heel and left the room.

Monica jumped to her feet. "He has to live!" she shouted after the doctor. "He has to. I never meant it. I never . . . never . . . that he would . . . Oh my God . . . I'll do anything if only he can live. I don't care about anything else."

"There, there," Shirley said rising to her feet to calm Monica.

"You . . . don't understand. . . I'm so, so sorry. You don't understand? You! You're the one who should be grieving. Your life's behind you. Ours . . . my children . . . my husband . . . is still in front of us . . . still to be lived. Don't you understand? I have . . . I can't live with this . . . my sweet . . . dear son. You've seen him! I have . . . oh my God . . . I can never . . . never forgive myself . . . for all that I've wanted . . . for the love of him . . . my sweet . . . sweet Michael," she sobbed. She turned to Matthew on the other side of the room, "I'd never have traded him. Not for everything we have. . . never . . . but I've done this."

"You've been through too much, sweetheart," Shirley soothed. "Please, sit down."

"She needs a sedative," Morrie said. "Can't they help people in a time like this?" He turned to Matthew. The two men looked at one another momentarily and Morrie dropped his gaze. "I'll get someone for her," Morrie said and walked out of the room.

A few minutes later, a second physician entered the waiting room. "Mrs. Clay?" he asked.

"Me?" Monica looked up.

"Can I see you for a minute?"

"Is he . . . is he . . . Michael . . . all right? When can I see him?"

"He is doing as well as anyone can expect. Dressing his wounds . . . his burns . . . it's a slow process. You'll be able to see him when we're finished. I need to see you now. I want to know if you're all right. You've experienced a terrible shock."

"No. No . . . I'm fine."

"Come with me anyway, please. Just for a minute. Just to be on the safe side."

Monica turned to Shirley who nodded at her, urging her to go with the doctor. Taking Shirley's smile for reassurance, Monica walked over to the doctor. He took her by the upper arm and guided her out of the room.

Raker met the two uniformed officers he requested by radio at the hospital when he arrived. "They are in the Chaplin's parlor," the admitting clerk replied, "the grieving room. Through that door down the corridor on the right."

"Is the kid OK?" Raker asked.

"I don't know. We don't always hear at this station."

He found the Chaplin's Parlor and pushed his way into the room. The two officers followed. Everyone looked up as they entered. Raker looked for Monica who had left minutes earlier with the physician who was attending to her.

"Detective Raker," Matthew greeted.

"Mr. Wirth. What's the status on the boy?"

"No change. We've been hearing the same thing for about half-an-hour. He's in very serious shape." The two men shook hands.

"Where's Mrs. Clay?" Raker asked.

"She's taking it very badly. She's with another doctor, just across the hall there. She's . . . well . . . almost delirious. He must be evaluating her for a sedative or something."

"What do you want with her?" Morrie growled. "Whatever it is, it can wait." Raker wheeled about and studied Morrie.

"Routine, Mr. Clay. Please do not concern yourself."

"If it's routine, then it can damn well wait until this is over . . . until my son is out of danger."

"You may be right, sir," Raker said but gave no hint that he would be leaving. Then turning to Matthew, he said, "Can you step outside with me, just for a minute. There's no point in disturbing the others here."

"Of course," Matthew said and followed the detective out into the corridor.

"Did you see what that happened?" Raker asked once the door to the parlor closed behind them. The two men began to stroll down the corridor.

"Yes. Terrible. Just terrible. I told one boy, the Sherman boy, to go down and turn on the bilge fan fully fifteen minutes before anyone tried to start the engine. Young Michael, who was an afterthought really, ran down to the boat ahead of me. I saw him clear as day. He found the key, stuck it into the ignition, turned it, and the whole thing blew. I've always heard about that kind of thing but never imagined it would happen to me . . . or anyone I knew."

"Was the boat not operating properly."

"That's all I've thought about. Yes! It ran well a week ago. Several people operated it. Starting, stopping, and starting it again."

"And nobody had it out in the meantime?"

"No."

"Anybody work on it, service it, anything like that?"

"No. In fact, that was why I was taking it out. To see if anything was wrong. It was behaving a little balky when you gave it full throttle. That's why I asked for Michael to come along for a short ride. He could run the boat while I checked things out."

"Did anyone else have access to the boat today or earlier in the week?"

Matthew paused. "Probably doesn't mean anything but Monica Clay was on the boat briefly today. She said she lost an ear ring and that it might have come off when she was in the boat. She went down and looked around for a little, but that was it."

The two turned to go back to the parlor when a door opened and Monica Clay emerged. She looked up the corridor at the two men but did not acknowledge them and walked back into the Chaplin's parlor. Raker picked up the pace. Before he reached the door to the parlor, a nurse appeared in the hallway from the larger waiting room at the entrance to the emergency department. She and Raker arrived at the parlor door at the same moment.

"Wait a minute, Detective," Matthew said quietly. "This may be bad news." Raker stepped back.

"The doctor said it would be OK for you to take these Mrs. Clay," the nurse said holding out two tablets and a paper cup full of water to Monica.

"What is it?" Monica asked looking up.

"Just something to help you feel a better. It will calm you."

"I don't want to sleep."

"It won't make you sleep. It'll just calm you," the nurse said.

"Go ahead, dear. I won't let you sleep through anything," Shirley reassured her. Monica accepted the paper cup in one hand and the two tablets in the other.

"Both?" she asked.

"For now," the nurse replied. Monica raised the two tablets to her mouth and followed with the cup of water, swallowing fiercely. The nurse smiled. "If you need any later, just tell one of the nurses at the emergency station. OK?"

"Fine," Shirley said on Monica's behalf. The nurse turned and walked out of the room. Morrie followed her with his eyes and became aware that Raker was back in the room.

"This is no time for any questions, Detective. Not now," Morrie said.

"I can see that," Raker replied. "I'm not here to ask any more questions." Raker walked over to Monica. "Mrs. Clay, you are under arrest for the murders of Rene McAllister and Jamie Sherman. You have the right to remain silent. Anything you say from this point forward may be used in a court of law against you. You have the right to an attorney to represent you in the matter of these charges. If you cannot afford an attorney, the court will appoint one for you. Do you understand your rights as I have just recited them to you?"

"What the hell is this?" Morrie roared, jumping to his feet. "Jesus Christ! Our son's fighting for his life. We have a right . . . what the hell?" An officer stepped forward to block Morrie from moving any closer to Raker. "This is outrageous! My God! How can you! You . . . you preposterous son-of-a-bitch . . . don't you know anything . . . why . . . why in the name of God . . . what's going on here?"

Raker looked at the second officer who, taking his clue from the Detective, took Monica Clay by the arm and gently urged her off the couch.

"There's never a good time for this, Mr. Clay. I'd like to be considerate of your circumstances, but two people are dead who did not get any consideration whatsoever. The intended victim of the explosion is still alive and deserves protection. We're taking your wife into custody. You need to call an attorney so that she has representation. She will be arraigned either later today or tomorrow morning, and her attorney should represent her at that time. Since she'll be accused of capital crimes, no bail will be set. She may be in custodial company to keep watch with you . . . for your son's sake . . . over his recovery. But I have no justification for postponing her arrest."

"I didn't want any of this," Monica said looking at Morrie. "I just wanted what we had. What we had together . . . with the boys. I've lived all my life outside . . . seeing what others had . . . what they could do. I was so glad . . . finally . . . we were there. I couldn't see that ending. Couldn't. Now all I want . . . the only thing is Michael . . . for him to be back with me."

"Mrs. Clay," Raker said, "anything you say can and will be held against you in a court of law."

"This is barbaric!" Morrie shouted. "You heartless bastard. Your superiors . . . our . . . our representatives are going to hear about your sadistic handling of this. She's in shock." Morrie tried to step around the officer who was restraining him. "She's had nothing to do with anything. Nothing! You hear me!" Confronted with the quiet determination of Detective Raker, Morrie's anger ebbed. He turned to Monica and said, "I believe you, sweetheart. Someone's made a very . . . very serious mistake, but you . . . you please . . . do as the officer says . . . just keep quiet. . . say nothing . . . you understand. Say nothing at all. I'll get an attorney down to see you wherever they are taking you."

Monica nodded and walked with the uniformed policeman to the door which swung open before they reached it. The young doctor who had spoken to them earlier walked into the room. "What's all this?" he asked seeing the uninformed policemen with Monica.

"Mrs. Clay is being placed under arrest," Raker replied.

"Ah . . . well . . . ah . . . I need . . . to . . . say that your son, Mrs. Clay . . . Mrs. Clay . . . we thought . . . he rallied for a while . . . but like I said . . . young people . . . their condition can fail so precipitously . . . and . . . and we lost him. He slipped away on us. We tried everything, but he did not respond. I'm sorry, very sorry. We did everything we could." The doctor looked at Monica and then to Morrie and then turned abruptly and left the room.

Monica doubled over, pulled her hands to her face and dropped to her knees. Anguish charged through her, ramming its way up her throat and out into the room, her mouth straining to expel her pain. She uttered no sound. Light rushed from the room. She saw only her emptied self, darkened with grief. Cramped with remorse. She saw her young son, so perfectly formed, whom she bore knowing the mileposts of pregnancy and its discomforts because she wanted him. In giving him birth, in the awe of holding him for the first time, she felt capable, enriched and at peace. She saw the knife slitting the bilge fan vent, saw her son blasted out of the bright sudden flame and refused to search for anything, word or thought, that would bring her relief.

Chapter 28

As the Labor Day weekend approached, Matthew decided that the skiing season was over and called the boat storage people to pick up his new ski boat and put it into dry dock for the winter. He had been reluctant to buy another boat. The scars on his lawn from the debris of the explosion faded slowly over the weeks that measured out the grief and regrets of the summer. He vowed that he would replace the charred timbers on his dock, otherwise the only other remaining evidence of the tragedy, in the spring when whatever abuse the structure suffered due to winter weather could also be repaired.

His grandchildren prevailed in his decision. They enjoyed skiing. They loved the lake and weekends there, and Matthew realized that the losses suffered over the summer should not rightfully be extended to include them by denying them their fun. He was through forever, though, with inboard powered boats. The craft at this dock now was powered by twin seventy-five horsepower Honda outboard engines. He would never again need to remind the boys to make certain that the bilge fan ran at least ten minutes before starting the engine.

He remained troubled for weeks about the explosion. Always careful with his boats, maintaining them well, he was disciplined about safety precautions. Had he, in fact, heard the bilge fan running the afternoon when happiness vanished from the shore for the rest of the summer? He was finally convinced. The unmistakable whirring sound was there. Slowly, his obsessive review of the events leading up to the explosion gave way to simple, deep grief for Michael, for Tom and Joyce Sherman, for Jamie, and for everyone who survived the terrible first week-and-a-half of July.

Independence Day would never be what it had been. Another party, even a small one, would profane the memory of the victims. Monica and Morrie were yet another loss. He missed them. His grief could not crouch forever behind his anger and disappointment. He had loved them and their two sons as extended family, as a younger brother and his wife. His affection may have been spent on phantoms, projections of his own yearnings for how he wanted his life's work to conclude and his desire for continuity which having them as neighbors provided. He struggled to convince himself that he had seen both of them for who they truly were. His affection and respect had not been misplaced. They had changed, slowly over time so that he hardly noticed, until each had become a different person.

He was pleased when Mac McAllister called and asked to meet with him to work things out with Rene's account.

"I've had a summer of losses," McAllister said over the phone. "I can't absorb another one. We haven't been the best of pals, but I have always thought highly of you . . . respected you. Any man who can start over at the age of fifty-one and accomplish what you have . . . I admire that. I don't want to have any part in your undoing . . . seeing you denied the success your hard work has earned. Can we talk a few things over? I've got to believe we can find a way out of this mess without hurting anyone else."

"Of course," Matthew replied.

"The club?"

"The club. When?"

"An hour from now?"

"See you there. In the bar?"

"Yes. My usual table."

McAllister was there when Matthew walked into the dim room. Matthew walked toward him and extended his hand. "Well, Matt, what gives?" McAllister asked.

"I don't know. This has been very depleting. Clay and I broke up our partnership, as you know. That goddamn hedge fund is still in the one account. You never acted on your suspicions about the validity of that signature?"

"No. For the longest time, it just seemed I was adding misery to the lives of a couple of people who had already suffered enough. After a while, I didn't care any more. What would it prove? That they were not Rene's? So what? Every time I thought about calling your company, I found myself thinking everyone has been through so much hell, why add to it?"

"I appreciate that on Clay's behalf . . . on my own as well."

"Besides, anything I did without thinking it through would cost you far more than it would me. It seemed better to wait until everyone found their heads again."

"I must have thought about calling you a hundred times," Matthew said. "I'd see you here at the club, but I just couldn't bring myself to do much more than nod in your direction. It's been very uncomfortable."

"I know. I saw that. If you wanted to call, why didn't you?"

"Didn't know your frame of mind. You were pretty hot the day you left the office. Not that I blame you. Then all hell broke loose with the boy getting killed. That was so sad. Such a great kid."

"What would you have said had you known I was open to your call?"

"I wanted to settle everything. It didn't really occur to me until Monica was indicted. I'd lost respect for Morrie. He didn't turn out to be the man I thought he was, but, Jesus, his wife being indicted. I was there when she was arrested and before they left the hospital, the young doc walks in tells them that their boy is dead. I haven't the heart for some things."

"You haven't answered my question."

"All right. Morrie still has his older son to get through school. Monica is accused of capital crimes. Held without bail. Morrie tried to visit her, but she refused to see him. She proposed the divorce; not him. He had attorney fees to settle for her, for the divorce, and she hadn't even gone to trial yet. He needed his job, even if we weren't going to work together any more. People left him in droves over the publicity. Both of us dreaded what might be next. Either you'd call the company or turn in the signature to the police. We weren't any good to one another either . . . just plugging away, each on his own, hoping for the best, keeping the income coming in as long we could. Upshot of it all, though, Morrie needed money . . . badly. So I sucked it up and walked over to his lakeside place one weekend and asked him if he was going to sell—either his Heron Lake place or the house in town."

"What'd he say?"

"He didn't know. He was astonished to see me and still overwhelmed by everything . . . lost his son, his wife, and his partnership. I finally suggested he could get a a-million-and-a-half, maybe a million-eight, for his lake place. He only owed a couple hundred thousand on it, and if he sold it, he could repay you for the losses on the hedge fund, pay off the attorneys, get around the legal trouble that was looming for both of us and he'd keep his license."

"Sounds like a decent proposition. What was his reaction?"

"True to his nature, he couldn't decide. He was more comfortable . . . let me rephrase that . . . he was the least uncomfortable letting things ride to see if Monica might be acquitted . . . to see if you were going to call the company. He didn't want to move too quickly, probably believing that he could pick his way through things once someone else took the lead."

"So what did you do?"

"Morrie attributed Monica's confession to Michael's death and the explosion to simple hysteria. The forensic people never did prove anything about the explosion. Hard proof, if there was any, was blown to smithereens. He refused to believe that she had anything to do with your wife's death. Kept saying that Monica expected too much of herself . . . whatever that means. Well, reality struck. he finally posted a For Sale sign in the yard. It's the wrong time of year and the market's weakening, but desperation must have taken over."

"Great! Why don't I buy it from him?" McAllister said. "How can we put this together? First, we forget about the signature thing so your company's oversight people don't get involved."

"I don't follow," Matthew replied.

"I didn't say how much I was willing to pay for the house, did I?"

"No."

"Say $750,000, pending comps to verify market values."

"My God, it could work if you are willing to do it and he goes along."

"Why wouldn't it work?"

"You realize what this overcomes? Morrie can put value in your hands without any cash moving between the two of you, something that would be questioned in an audit."

"Let's go see him and make the offer."

"Just one thing, Mac."

"What?"

"Why do you want to do this?"

"Long story. Not the kind I'm good at." McAllister drew a deep breath. "I thought I could walk through Rene's death like a man with an umbrella on a rainy day. Not going to get wet. But I did. I did in ways I never thought. She was a troublesome to live with, and there wasn't any affection . . . and damn little respect . . . between us at the end. When our children came to town to bury her, and hers showed up too, I watched them walk behind her coffin through the cemetery and realized one day they'd be walking behind mine, and when they did, things being as they are, they'd do it for the sake of appearances only. My kids don't like me, Matt. Her kids hate me. I haven't given them much reason to feel otherwise.

"I don't believe in a heaven or a hell. Once we go to sleep, it's for keeps. The only real miracle about humankind is that we are here at all, surviving on a speck of a planet spinning through an infinite universe." McAllister shifted uncomfortably in his chair. "If we find meaning in our lives, it needs to come from how we live with one another. You can find all the hell you want right here any day you want a piece of it. I'm no moralist, but I want to make some changes in my life. It's time for me to lower the temperature for a few folks, people whose lives my decisions impact.

"I could see what Morrie had done to you. I knew you too well. I don't owe Clay anything, but I didn't want to catch you in the cross fire. The money's mine, and I intend to get it back, but with the least amount of damage to all parties concerned. If I can do that, my own life means more to me. Make sense?"

The McAllister's offer astonished Morrie's realtor—all the more when Morrie accepted it. Matthew, as soon as the transaction was concluded, reported to the office manager that he would be retiring at the end of the year and that his accounts would be turned in for distribution to others at the firm according to company policy.

On the first morning of his retirement, Matthew Wirth spoke of his relief at finding everything was going to work out well for Shirley and him and their family. "Life is a little like crossing a big body of water in a boat," he said at the breakfast table. "You really don't notice that you're going anywhere when you're out in the middle of it. The only time you can see that you're moving is when you are close to one shore or the other . . . as you begin your journey and as you see it drawing to an end."

"Is your destination in sight?"

"No, not yet, but it seems to be taking shape on the far horizon."

The End

Epilogue

Monica Clay was indicted for second degree manslaughter in the death of Rene McAllister and first degree murder in the death of Jamie Sherman. The evidence against her, especially in the case of Jamie Sherman, upheld the charge of murder in the first degree as the *Demerol* and the curry powder Jamie inhaled matched exactly with the compounds a search of the Clay home produced. Only the absence of premeditation mitigated the sentence of second degree manslaughter in the case of Rene McAllister. The forensic work of technician Gene Phillips played a dramatic role in convincing Monica's attorneys that their best course was to bargain for a lighter charge. Not wanting to subject her surviving son to more publicity, Monica pleaded guilty to both counts. In return, she received a twenty year sentence for the manslaughter charge and a life sentence for murder, the sentences to be served concurrently. She would be eligible for parole after serving twenty years.

Monica filed for divorce following the entry of her pleas and found she was required to wait twelve months in the State of North Carolina before presenting her case to the court. Morrie grew to accept that Monica was guilty of Rene McAllister's and Jamie Sherman's deaths, a realization that her guilty plea helped bring about. His remorse over the loss of Michael physically changed his appearance so that he looked a much older than his actual age. He never accepted that Monica had anything to do with their son's violent death.

Monica became depressed and was transferred to a psychiatric prison hospital.

Detective James Raker testified extensively at Monica's trial. He realized upon concluding his work on the case that the position as liaison officer for the Melville County with the community of Heron Lake was not turning out as he had hoped. In his investigation of the boat explosion, he and Matthew Wirth became better acquainted and eventually good friends. Matthew happened to mention Raker's resignation to Mac McAllister one day during a round of golf, and McAllister, in turn, introduced Raker to Denise Becker who offered him a position as head of security in her division at Southern World Textiles.

Mac McAllister began traveling more extensively, often with his own children and stepchildren, and they became frequent guests at his Pelican Bay home.

Matthew and Shirley Wirth decided one night over a glass of wine in front of the fire in the Charles City home that they would never again stay at the lake for the Fourth-of-July holiday but would travel to visit friends instead.

LaVergne, TN USA
07 December 2010
207735LV00005B/67/P

F
HOH

7/5/11